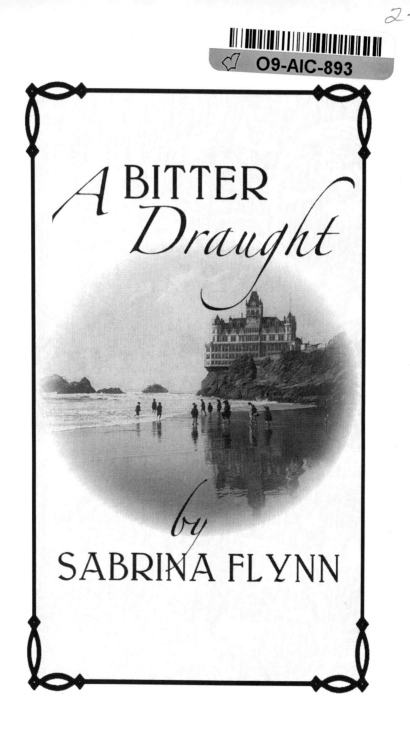

A BITTER
Draught

by
SABRINA FLYNN

For Grandma Letty,
who lived her life with zest
1920-2014

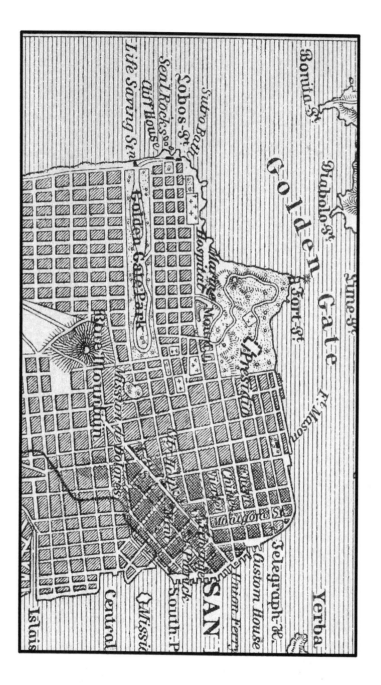

"For all evils there are two remedies - time and silence."
—*The Count of Monte Cristo*

1

Land's End

Wednesday, February 14th, 1900

HIS LINE WENT TO the edge of the world, then it dropped right off into freedom. J.P. Humphrey glanced towards the looming rise as his streetcar began its final climb. In the two years that Humphrey had operated the Park and Ocean line, the expectation of what waited over the hill never dwindled. There were never two sunsets alike, never the same two clouds in the morning, and the taste of fog over a calm sheen of grey was a constant comfort to the aging conductor. In San Francisco, fences did not hem people in; the city was one step away from the world.

The streetcar reached the hill's peak, the fog parted over the moonlit sea, and for the first time in two years, Humphrey didn't notice. There was a young woman on his line. She sat on an outer bench, on the edge of the runner, and had not so much as uttered one word, or even looked at the conductor. She had a neat little hat, and her hair was done up, but a few tendrils had escaped. It reminded Humphrey of the sunset—all fiery and bright, even in the dark.

The streetcar tilted, beginning its smooth descent. Humphrey glanced at his operator Simon who was no help at all with women. The large man was good with turntables and rough passengers.

Humphrey cleared his throat, summoning courage. "This is the last line, ma'am," he said to the woman's back. "There's no other cars that run til morning."

On the weekends, he expected a few late night beach goers to be waiting at the station, but on a Wednesday night, it was uncommon. So was a young woman traveling to the ocean at night.

"I know," the woman said. Her voice was faint, she might have said more, but even those two words made his ears strain.

"Are you meeting someone, then?" Humphrey ventured, hopefully.

She tilted her head, as if bending her ear towards his words. "The sound of the surf is soothing, don't you think, sir?"

"That it is, ma'am." This close to the shore, he could hear the rhythmic wash of waves. He looked at the water, surprised that he'd missed that first sight. But the woman was right, Humphrey could sit and listen to the tides all night.

That was what the woman needed, he decided. Fresh air and space, as every San Franciscan craved—to be left alone to live their own lives. Humphrey decided to keep his own to himself instead of bumble his way where he wasn't wanted. So the conductor said nothing more.

At the station, the streetcar stopped, and Simon stepped down to walk his customary circuit of the trolley.

"End of the line, ma'am," Humphrey said, stepping down to offer his hand. The redhead accepted, keeping her eyes on the street. When she stood on solid ground, she looked at Humphrey for the first time. The conductor blinked. The young woman's hair might look like the sun falling into the sea, but her eyes looked as if the light would never rise again.

It took Humphrey a moment to realize that she had a little envelope in her gloved hand. "Would you mail this for me, sir? It's important."

"No trouble at all." He accepted the envelope, and the task. "Can I help you with anything else, ma'am?" he blurted past his mustache, breaking his silent promise to mind his own business.

"Just that," she replied, smiling. Rather than reassuring, her smile put him on edge—it looked like a pair of fishhooks had twitched the corners up. Before the conductor could think of anything else to say, the woman turned, and walked towards the end of the road, to the long stretch of lonely shore.

There was no one waiting on the platform, just as Humphrey had suspected. He blew a breath past his lips, and consulted his pocket watch as Simon stepped into the car. Both hands pointed to twelve, on the dot. Another perfectly timed shift.

Humphrey squinted at the envelope, tilting it towards the light of the streetcar. The address was bold, addressed to—the city of San Francisco. He frowned. No name, no number, or even a street. The postmaster wouldn't do a thing with the letter. The young lady must have forgotten to address it, but when Humphrey looked up, searching the darkness for the lone passenger, she was gone. The street was empty.

Humphrey glanced at the envelope again. Muttering under his breath about redheads and their strange temperaments, he opened the envelope, hoping he wasn't going to get arrested. It held a neatly folded slip of paper. When he unfolded the slip, a single line of elegant words ran its width. A cold prickle pierced Humphrey's neck and crawled down his spine, producing a shiver that no San Franciscan wind had yet managed.

Two Queens

Thursday, February 15th, 1900

TWO QUEENS STARED at the gambler from his hand. The women were blonde, pale, and buxom. It wasn't his preferred deck. These two cards had a vapid expression that made him ache for a sharper set of eyes.

"You're bluffing," a voice said.

Atticus Riot looked from the irksome women in his hand to the young man sitting across the table. Bart Martins was a confident fellow, slim and dapper, with an easy smile that had charmed his way into the expensive suit he wore. His tongue was smoother, and he had made ample use of it throughout the night, goading and boasting with every hand. Five players had begun the night. One had dropped out, two had gone bust, and Riot and Martins remained.

In reply, Riot carefully set down his cards, removed his wire-rimmed spectacles, and polished the glass with a silk handkerchief. As Riot did so, he nodded towards the impressive pot: bills, large and small, and a cufflink. The latter was Martins' contribution to the pot, a gaudy decoration with a gold spade in the polished center. No proper gentleman would wear such a thing.

Martins smiled. "I know you're bluffing, and just to prove it, I'll raise." The swell pushed the remainder of his money into the pool.

Riot put on his spectacles and looked at his opponent. "I'm afraid that won't do."

"Six hours without a word, and now he speaks," the swell announced to the room. But his admirers were slumped on a bench in the corner, snoring.

The gambler said nothing more.

Martins would not be intimidated. He unclipped his pocket watch, dangled it in front of Riot's eyes, and set it on the table with a smirk. The gold chain curled around the mound of cash.

Riot leaned forward, his hand pausing over the gold. "May I?" When the swell nodded, he picked up the pocket watch, checking its make and worth. The latch gave smoothly, and Riot read the inscription on the inside of the cover:

To my beloved —Your Rose forever

Riot clicked the watch shut and replaced it with care. "There's an art to bluffing, Martins." The taciturn man's voice was deep and unhurried, and it roused the dozing audience. The women stirred from where they slumped and the men looked up from their whiskey. "The key is to be sure, and now I am. You see, when you bluff, you can't care whether you win or lose, and you, my young sharp, have a lot to lose, as did the man you stole that from."

"That's *my* Rose," Martins said.

"You're the one whose bluffing." Riot backed his words with his own pocket watch, sliding it towards the pool. "I call."

Martins laid down his hand triumphantly. A row of spades challenged—a Flush.

Riot frowned at his vapid queens. "*Your* Rose belonged to another man—a worthy man who never harmed a hair on her head." He slowly rearranged his cards. "I know three things for certain: the first being that Mrs. Cottrill was taking her husband's time piece to a watchmaker's shop to repair on the day that she was brutally murdered."

"Fine," the swell smiled pure charm. "You caught me. I won the watch in a poker game—as I'm about to win yours. I am sorely grieved for the woman."

Riot ignored the swell's claim, reaching into his pocket. "Second, that I am an honest man, and that watch is worth more than my contribution; therefore, let me add something more to the pool." He withdrew a cufflink from his waistcoat pocket, a gaudily decorated one with a gold spade in the center of black that matched the one in the pot. Martins' right eye twitched. "You lost one of your cufflinks. I found it in a grate, in the very alley where you assaulted and strangled Mrs. Cottrill."

In a flash, Martins pushed back his chair, gripped the table, and shoved. But Riot was already on his feet, stick in hand. He sidestepped the toppling table, and lunged, stretching leg and arm, reaching towards the swell's chest. The silver tip struck, catching Martins square in the solar plexus. The swell staggered back, gasping for air, and Riot stepped forward, twirling his walking stick with one smooth sweep. The silver knob connected with the man's head.

Cash and jewelry littered the floor. And so did Martins. The women and men moved forward. Riot thumped the point of his stick onto the floor, and they froze. "The police will be here shortly," he said, calmly.

The room cleared.

Atticus Riot brought his right hand up, fanning out the cards beneath his eyes. "Thirdly," he said to his unconscious opponent. "I never bluff." He laid the cards on Martins: two queens and three aces—a Full House.

✛

The proprietor rushed into the room. "I'll have no fighting at my tables," he said brandishing a shotgun.

"There's no quarrel over your table, sir," Riot explained. "This is a police matter." The proprietor tensed, and Riot didn't much care for that twitch in his finger, considering the double-barrel so readily at hand. "The quarrel doesn't involve you either. I'm a detective; not a lawman. If you don't want police attention, I suggest helping me drag this murderer outside."

"Murderer?"

"Of a woman—a man's wife."

The proprietor set his shotgun aside, and bent his shoulders to the task. As the big man dragged the dead weight out, Riot bent to retrieve the pocket watch and cuff links.

"Took you long enough, A.J.," a short, wizened old man yawned from the corner. Tim tugged on a bushy white beard and climbed to his feet, throwing his arms up to stretch. A crack echoed in the hollow room. "Gawd, I'm gettin' old."

Riot looked at his gnomish friend. "You've been old for as long as I've known you."

"As the oldest and most decrepit here, I'll just start with the cleaning, then." Tim chortled, rubbed his hands together, and began his chore, picking up the scattered cash.

In short order, Martins was cuffed and loaded into a waiting wagon. Riot pulled the brim of his bowler low, squinting at the brightness of the morning.

"A fine night's work, A.J.," Tim said at his shoulder.

Riot looked over, and down at the balding pate of his friend. "Doesn't bring her back, now does it?"

An eye for an eye, my boy, a whispery voice rasped in his memory. Riot dislodged his spectacles to rub the bridge of his nose. Zephaniah Ravenwood was as fond of quotes in death as he'd been in life.

"But not for you," Riot murmured to the memory.

Tim frowned at the detective, rocked forward on his feet and back on his heels with a low whistling breath. "Smith and me will take Martins down to the jail. You could use the rest."

"And you don't?" Riot inquired.

"I'll sleep when I'm dead." Tim spat, and hopped into the wagon. "You want a lift to Kearney?"

"I'll take this watch by Mr. Cottrill's."

"You sure you don't want to wait, A.J.?"

"If you were the husband, would you want to wait for news?"

Tim clapped a floppy cap on top his head. "While you're at it—you can write up the report."

"I'll retire from this business," Riot threatened.

Tim snorted, and nudged the horse forward with a click of his tongue.

"Watch him, Smith," Riot said to the young man guarding their prisoner. The large, ex-patrolman nodded in affirmative, and Riot watched the wagon roll into the waking city.

✛

Every evening the Barbary Coast lured hungry men with its glitter and lights, but in the morning, in the grey light of day, the streets and alleyways crisscrossing the nine blocks of vice looked as drab and worn as the women who sold their bodies there.

A lonely bread wagon trundled past, and Riot turned east, towards the docks. Whereas the Barbary Coast baited men with lust, the harbors lured Atticus with hope. Every day for the past month, he had walked the harbors, looking for a single cutter. It was a dim sort of hope, the kind that inflated his heart with the piercing of a needle.

Ever the romantic, his dead partner huffed from the shadows. Riot shoved the voice away, and just to prove he wasn't the romantic, he defied the voice and cut straight for Market.

Thunder washed over Riot, a cacophony of rattling cable cars, bells, and the frenetic pace of morning commuters. With a smooth gait and the click of his stick, he maneuvered the morning rush, weaving his way through a stream of cable cars and cabriolets, to a side street where a small tobacco shop vied for space between a tailor and a barber.

Riot had no taste for cigar, cigarette, or pipe, but he had business with the proprietor of the *Fragrant Rose*. The bell chimed above the door and a wave of spice and wood washed pleasantly over him. A curving counter guarded a wall of treasures: hand-carved pipes waiting for a loving touch.

Silas Cottrill walked from the back room. The tobacconist was as tidy as his shop. Everything about him gleamed, from his bald head to his dark skin, pristine apron, and polished shoes.

"Mr. Riot," Silas greeted. His customary smile had been absent for two weeks, but there was hope in his eyes. Hope that would not bring the dead back. Justice, however, mattered. It didn't remove the pain of loss, but it eased it enough for a man to step over, and get on with his life.

Riot removed his bowler. "I've tracked down your wife's murderer. A swell and swindler by the name of Bart Martins. He has a fair knot on his head, but he's alive and in police custody." Riot reached into his coat pocket, and brought out a pristine handkerchief. He set it ceremonially on the counter, and unwrapped the silk, revealing a timepiece.

Silas touched the gold, and closed his eyes. A weight left his shoulders and he breathed a little easier. After a moment, and maybe a soft prayer, he picked up the watch and tucked it carefully away.

"I'll see he hangs," Riot said.

"For murdering a Negro woman? The police all but accused my wife of harlotry."

"There's good and bad everywhere, and a whole lot of grey, Mr. Cottrill. It just so happens that I know where to find all the colors. As I said, I'll see that he hangs for his crimes."

Silas closed his eyes, and nodded. "Thank you, Mr. Riot. There's no price fit to repay you for what you've done. Make sure your agency sends me a bill. If there is anything I can ever do for you, just ask."

Riot ran a hand over his trim beard. "There is something. A fair trade of services."

Mr Cottrill glanced over his shoulder, at the wall of pipes. "I didn't know you were a smoking man. You can have your pick. No trade necessary."

Riot shook his head. "I'm not a smoking man, but I am a man who has his ear to the ground. During my investigation, I discovered that your wife had a cousin by the name of Mabel."

"I know her well. She's right grieved over Rose's murder."

"Mabel works for a Mr. Alex Kingston."

Silas' face turned grim. "That she does."

"Is she mistreated in his employ?"

"Not to my knowledge."

"But you dislike him."

"I don't much trust any man with that much money."

Riot nodded in understanding. "If any word of him should reach your ears, Mr. Cottrill, I'd be obliged if you passed it on."

"Are you investigating Kingston for a crime?"

"Let's just say that I like to see justice done."

"A fair trade, is it?"

"It is, Mr. Cottrill."

Silas nodded, and extended his hand. Riot shook it, firmly.

At the door, Silas stopped Riot with a word. "It helps, you know. My Rose is at peace now."

Caught in the act of donning his hat, Riot turned to regard the tobacconist. "I imagine so." Riot set his bowler on his head and touched the brim.

The sun was bright, bringing a promise of another warm, San Franciscan winter day. Riot's right temple throbbed. He resisted the urge to rub the stripe of white hair that hid a bullet scar. He'd find no rest in sleep—not with old memories that reminded him of business left undone.

In no mood to tempt his luck, Riot hopped aboard a cable car heading west on Market, away from the Ferry Building. The car was full. He stood on the runner, fingers resting lightly on a pole as the car rattled through chaos. The clock tower was the gateway to San Francisco, a heart of travel, and if the building was the heart than Market was an artery. Wagons cut in front of the cable cars, motorcars weaved in and out, and pedestrians ran for their lives.

Riot felt the personal touch of eyes. He swept a casual gaze over the passengers, trying to pinpoint the source, but it was near to impossible in the crush; the cable car was packed as tightly as a sardine tin. Worse, he had a number of enemies.

Despite the masses traveling through the city, one began to recognize the regulars: conductors and gripmen, flower vendors, newspaper men, shoe shiners, and a stream of commuters who rode the ropes every morning like clockwork. San Francisco was a sea of familiarity masked in the obscurity of the masses.

The cable car stopped in the heart of Market, at Lotta's fountain, a cast iron monument holding its own in the shadow of towering buildings. Over half the passengers disembarked, hitting the sidewalk and hurrying away.

Riot stepped down, and recognized a woman with umbrella in hand preparing to navigate the runner. She wore a broad-brimmed hat atop a full head of brown hair, vibrant lip rouge, trim jacket and matching green skirt that hugged an hourglass shape. Twice this week, he had ridden the cable car with her, and each time had offered his hand. He did so now. Gloved fingers touched his own.

"Thank you, sir." Her voice was deep and sultry and something in her manner pricked his senses. Instead of heading directly towards the Ravenwood offices, he escorted her across four lines of cable cars to the sidewalk.

"Ma'am," he made to touch the brim of his hat, but as he pulled away, the fingers tightened over his own.

"Oh, dear," the woman said faintly. She wobbled, her fingers loosened, and she fell.

3

The Art of Swooning

ATTICUS RIOT CAUGHT THE fainting woman in his arms. Her hat tumbled off and the umbrella thudded to the ground. Little cries of concern rippled from the masses, but most walked on; some slowed, and only two stopped. With the woman's hat off, Riot got his first clear look at her face.

"Hello, Miss Bel," he whispered to the limp woman in his arms.

An eye cracked open. Today, the color was amber, reflecting the sun and her lush brown hair. "At least do me the courtesy of feigning surprise," she said out of the corner of her mouth.

"Nothing surprises me where you are concerned."

"I didn't want to faint in some strange man's arms," she explained, as if that clarified everything.

"Most women don't get to choose."

"Most gentlemen would look worried," she retorted. "I require an ambulance."

"Do you?"

"Some panic would do, Mr. Riot."

Riot looked to one of the two gentlemen who had stopped. "This woman requires an ambulance," he said calmly. "The office there will likely have a telephone." The helpful stranger hastened inside the steamship office. "Anything else?"

Isobel's gaze flickered to the *Chronicle* building clock tower, and back to her savior. "What ever you generally do when a woman faints in your arms."

"This is a first."

"Improvise, then."

"You there, sir," Riot said to the lingering man, an older gentleman with a trustworthy air. "Could you gather her things?"

The man bent to comply, and Riot lifted Isobel in his arms, carrying her towards the steamship office. A flustered looking clerk opened the door, and Riot deposited her onto a lobby couch.

The first gentleman appeared. "They've telephoned for an ambulance."

Riot nodded, kneeling beside the couch to unbutton the first three buttons of her high-collared blouse. Too many men were breathing down his neck.

Riot turned. "Not to worry, I'm a doctor," he announced. "I think she's overheated. Give her room to breathe and go on about your business." Whether it was the authority in his tone or the mention of work, he could not say, but all the clerks returned to their desks.

"She'll be all right, then?" the older gentleman asked.

Riot accepted her hat, handbag, and umbrella. "I believe so, with proper care. I'll attend to her until the ambulance arrives." The two gentlemen tipped their hats and exited. Riot removed his bowler and dutifully began fanning his patient.

"Now what if I were too heavy for you to carry?" Isobel murmured when they were relatively alone.

"I'd drag the couch out to you," he replied.

She was studying him under her lashes. Despite the face powder, eye-liner, wig, and lip rouge, she could not disguise her bone structure. He tried not think about the undergarments she had used to achieve her current hourglass shape. All in all, it was a masterful disguise.

"There have been stranger sights," she mused. A ripple of movement caught his eye at the back, and she fell silent as the manager came to check on the commotion.

Riot fended off the gruff manager with assurances that the woman was not going to die in his lobby, and stood his ground when the man suggested that they wait outside for the ambulance.

"I'm sure you have work to do, Mr. Brown," Riot said sharply. The manager took his point and stomped off to shut himself in his office.

When Riot turned back to his patient, she asked, "Aren't you the least bit curious what I'm doing?"

"Fainting, obviously," he replied. Riot perched on the side of the couch, blocking the clerks' view from Isobel. She opened her eyes to his.

Those eyes beckoned, and her red lips distracted. Riot had the sudden urge to wipe off the gaudy paint and touch the lips beneath. He tore his gaze away, searching for a less alluring distraction. "Nice umbrella."

"There's a sword inside," her eyes flashed.

"Can you use it?"

She arched a brow. "Mr. Riot, I lived with a fencer in Venice. What else would a young lady be doing in a man's residence?"

Riot opened his mouth, shut it, and tilted his head.

"Nothing is more tantalizing than a sword and its sheathe," she whispered with vigor.

Riot adjusted his spectacles. "I've missed you."

"You hardly know me."

"I investigated your murder. I'd say I know you well," he argued.

"I hope I never have cause to investigate yours."

"There are better ways to get to know a gentleman," Riot agreed. "But if that unfortunate event should ever occur, I have every confidence that you'd bring my murderer to justice."

"And God won't find mercy in my soul."

"I'm touched." And he meant it. "How have you been, Miss Bel, aside from your current vaporous condition?"

"Settling. You?"

"Resettling," replied Riot.

"You've been frequenting your offices," she said.

"And I see you've taken up with the enemy," he noted.

A flicker of surprise flashed in her eyes. "How could you possibly know what I'm about? You've only just recognized me."

"Have I?" Amusement danced in his eyes.

"You're lying."

"I wouldn't lie to you."

"How dull." But Riot had pricked her ego, and she snagged his bait. "You've offered your hand to me, without a hint of recognition, twice in the past week."

"So I have."

Her brows drew together. "How long have you known?"

Riot placed his bowler over her glare and consulted the hands of his pocket watch. "Fifteen minutes."

"Deplorable," she snorted.

"It's a good disguise," he admitted, retrieving his hat. "But, considering your history, I'm not entirely sure it's wise."

"Not you." There was immense satisfaction in her voice. "The ambulance service."

"For my own sake, I hope they take another hour."

"For the sake of fainting women everywhere, I hope not. How did you know what I'm up to?"

"You glanced at the *Chronicle* clock when the gentleman said he had summoned an ambulance," he explained. "That, and your preoccupation with the ambulance."

Grey eyes narrowed. "If not lying, then at the very least, you're guessing."

The faintest of smiles played on his lips. "Am I?"

"Yes, you are," she stated with certainty. "You're buying time, in hopes I'll slip up and confirm your suspicion— whatever that might be."

"In that case, I don't have much time left. Emergency services have improved since Annie Laurie pulled this same stunt."

"It's been done before?" Dismay, mingled with admiration, filled her voice.

"I'm afraid so."

"Damn," she swore. Making a sudden, miraculous recovery, Isobel sat up and grabbed her hat. An office of startled eyes looked up from their desks. Isobel waved away their surprise. "Coffee," she stated. "I just need a stout cup of coffee."

But it was too late. The ambulance interns rushed inside the office, firmly told her that she was *not* all right, and worse, Riot whole-heartedly agreed. Between the three men, they bullied her onto a stretcher.

"One moment," Riot said, gathering her things. The interns paused, and when Isobel snatched her umbrella and hat from his hand, Riot bent close. "Dinner, Miss Bel?" he murmured.

She answered his invitation with a glare.

4

She Wrote Her Will in Sand

ISOBEL SAAVEDRA AMSEL (FORMERLY Kingston) swayed with the ambulance wagon. The shaking was inevitable on San Francisco's cobbled-streets, but she had hoped for squeaky springs, ached for a grimy cot, an ill-kept wagon bed, or even blood on the planks; unfortunately, everything was spotless.

The taciturn physician measured her pulse, listened to her heart, and stared into the depths of her throat with nothing but chasteness. Not one inappropriate grope, or even so much as a leer from the broad-shouldered intern.

Isobel blew out a breath of frustration. The physician stuck a thermometer between her lips. She nearly spat it out, but subsided, determining to salvage whatever she could from her botched ruse.

When the mercury stopped on a boringly common

line, the physician removed the glass, read it, and shook it out. "It will only be a few minutes, ma'am." The physician offered her an avuncular smile of reassurance, and nodded to his intern, who carefully laid a blanket over her body.

Isobel closed her eyes, cursing her incompetence. When she was fifteen, she had been sent to a young ladies school in Dresden, returned to a whole mess of trouble when she was nineteen, married a blackmailer when she was twenty and faked her own death two months later. And before that, she had roamed San Francisco and its bay like a wild thing. Hardly any time to keep up with the daily news.

Still, it was no excuse. Isobel vowed to read every sensational newspaper story that had been published in Riot's lifetime. Thoughts of Riot surfaced, and she cursed herself again, trying to block out his warm eyes, the ease with which he had lifted her, and his mere proximity—the smell of his hat, of sandalwood and myrrh; felt and polish. How had he guessed what she was up to? An innocent glance at a clock and mention of an ambulance was hardly telling. But the man could read her like an open book. It was vexing.

A buzz pricked her ears, and she seized the distraction, turning her mind to the two gentlemen in the wagon.

"…life-saving crew fished the poor woman out. Pretty thing, too," the broad-shouldered intern was saying.

"Suicide?" asked the physician.

"Thomas said it looked that way. There was a message written in the sand, right on shore. Can you believe that?"

"A bit risky if you ask me. I'm surprised the tides didn't wipe it clean."

"I'd imagine a girl who's about to do herself in isn't exactly concerned about that sort of thing."

The physician grunted with agreement. "It's always a shame, that."

Isobel had had enough of her charade. She sat up. The men protested, and she cut them short with an edge in her tone. "I didn't faint, gentlemen. I work for the *Call*." Before the indignation in their eyes had a chance to surface, she shook both their hands, firmly. "Charlotte Bonnie, pleased to meet you. I'm doing a follow up story to—" What had Riot said her name was? "Annie Laurie. To test San Francisco's emergency response services." From the looks on both their faces, she wagered that the original story had not been favorable. "I must say," she assured, "the improvements are extraordinary. And you, gentlemen, are *exceptional*."

Isobel graced the men with her most charming smile, and whipped out her fountain pen and notepad. "Your names, if you please?"

"William T. Cook," the broad-shouldered intern supplied. However, the physician looked wary.

"This article will reassure the ladies of San Francisco that their bodies are in good hands with you gentlemen," Isobel explained, innocently.

The intern coughed, and the physician cleared his throat but her words loosened his tongue. "Dr. Francis Davies."

Isobel dutifully wrote down their names and dotted her I's. She frowned at the uneven scrawl. The rattling wagon certainly didn't help her impatient hand. "Now look here, if you take me to the receiving hospital, then I'll miss my deadline for this story. And you won't see your names in the *Morning Call*."

"You think it'll make front page?" Cook asked.

"I don't honestly know," she sighed. "I hope it will. A

woman's got to make an honest living. But say—if I had *two* stories to submit, like the suicide you mentioned, I could add your names to that one too and it'd double your chances."

"There's a morgue full of suicides, ma'am," Davies pointed out.

"But it's not everyday that a suicide writes her note in the sand, now is it?"

The physician pondered her question, and before he could make up his mind, Isobel made it for him. "Where was the body discovered?" she asked the intern with pen poised.

"Ocean Beach, by the Olympic pier. She was floating in the water."

"Do you know what she wrote in the sand?"

"It was odd," Cook said.

Isobel waited patiently for the broad-shouldered man to dredge up the words.

"*Violet loves kindness, and she does not always get it in this country.*"

"That doesn't sound like a note from a desperate woman to me," Isobel frowned.

"That's what Thomas told me," Cook shrugged.

"You said she was a redhead, didn't you?" Davies asked. His partner nodded. "In my experience, they are of a certain temperament."

Isobel waited, hoping that this would at least elicit a lewd comment, or even a glance from Cook, but both men kept their thoughts to themselves.

When the ambulance wagon rolled to a stop, Isobel gathered her things, thanked the two men, and headed to the closest cable car terminus. Her luck had turned.

A woman, redheaded or no, did not write her last

words in sand.

✛

The sea greeted Isobel like an old friend. Its salt kissed her lips, the waves washed against her ears with gentleness, and the horizon beckoned her home. With the sea a step away, Isobel was never caged.

Standing on the dunes, she tore her gaze from the ocean blue, and focused on the long stretch of shoreline. A group of morning walkers and eager tourists mingled on the sand. But instead of gazing at the sea, the crowd had their collective eyes on a spot of sand. In the middle of the crowd stood two surfmen in their blues. And farther down, by the pier, another two lingered, dressed in their white duck-cloth and rubber-soled slippers. The police, it appeared, had come and gone. And the reporting vultures had not yet arrived. Isobel was the first such vulture. There were a dozen suicides a week in San Francisco. Most were hardly news worthy, but this might attract attention for different reasons than Isobel had.

A line of gawkers stood at the top of the road leading to the Cliff House—a six-story chateau that risked the cliffs to bring civilization to the sea. To the majority, it was a marvel; but for Isobel, it was an eyesore. She blocked the clumsy hotel from view and focused on navigating the sand dunes. Not an easy feat in her current guise. Heels were impractical for walking, but supremely practical for attracting attention, which was exactly what she currently needed.

As she sunk into the sand with every aggravating step, the lightness in the air turned heavy with the touch of death. The sun seemed dimmer, the air colder, and those gathered wore solemn masks that couldn't quench the excitement rippling through the crowd.

Death was a curious fellow. He brushed the shoulders of some, settled on others, and for the truly unlucky, he hounded their every footstep; either way, everyone felt his passing. Except Isobel. She much preferred to chase the phantom. And when she neared, she sensed his presence. That heavy footprint that he left in his wake.

The crowd kept a respectable distance from the writing in the sand. No one wanted to erase the last message of a troubled woman. The tide would do the job soon enough, and nothing would be left of the woman named Violet. The message was exactly as Cook had recited: *Violet loves kindness, and she does not always get it in this country.*

A peculiar sort of message for a woman contemplating suicide. Had the woman always referred to herself in the third person? When teetering on the edge, had Violet stopped being her, and looked down on her body with a detached sort of eye? The message sounded more like a threat, or mockery.

Isobel walked the message's length, thirty feet in all, written in a large slanting hand. It had been carved into firmer sand that had been smoothed by the tide. Footprints churned the area around the message. Boots and surfmans' slippers walking the length as she did now, only much closer. The onlookers had trampled over the writer's footprints.

Ever conscious of the tides, Isobel consulted her internal table. High tide was at half past midnight, and low was an hour before sunrise: six o'clock. High tide would come again at noon. She looked at the beach, estimating that the message could have been written any time after three o'clock in the morning. A wide window of time.

Satisfied, Isobel stepped towards the message (in between the *not* and *always*), planted her umbrella in the ground and bent her knees. Corsets were not conducive to bending; however, she fancied that she made for a pretty picture of feminine delicacy.

A blue-uniformed surfman hopped forward. "Hold on there, Miss. You're to keep away from there."

"I have no intention of disturbing the words," Isobel replied, never taking her eyes off the message.

The man moved to her side. "Still, this is police business."

Isobel had seen what she wanted. A sharp, careful point had carved the message into the sand. She straightened, taking in with one upward sweep the surfman's shoes, the uneven crease of his trousers, his bowed-legs, paunchy belly, red nose, and finally his eyes. "Police business—surely this is a child's scrawl?" She tilted her head towards the man, looking at him from beneath her broad-brimmed hat.

"No, Miss," he answered, puffing up his chest. "There's been a death. A woman was dragged out of the water not long ago."

"Murdered?" Isobel gasped.

Disappointment entered his eyes. "The Deputy Coroner declared it a suicide, and carted the poor girl away."

"How dreadful," she whispered. And she meant it, if not for the reasons the surfman assumed. It was a truly dreadful thought that the police had dismissed the death so quickly. "Did you discover the unfortunate woman?"

"No, Miss. That gentleman over there spotted her in the water," he said pointing.

'That gentleman over there' was a large middle-aged gentleman wearing a homburg and monocle. He held a small dog and he stroked its fur rhythmically.

That was another thing about Death. People liked to linger in his cool footprint, breathing the air that he touched, reminding them of their own living state.

Isobel touched her fingertips to her lips, careful not to smudge the rouge. "Do you know, I have a friend named Violet. Did the police happen to mention her last name?"

"I'm not sure that they know that yet." His features sagged in sympathy.

"She has red hair—" Isobel began, and the man's face grew alarmed.

"Perhaps you best speak with my crew. Jasper and Gower fished her out—I mean, er, recovered the body." He offered his arm, and she accepted it, along with his name, Willie Saxby.

"Charlotte Bonnie," she returned.

Saxby left orders with the other guard, and escorted her through the growing crowd. The monocled gentleman and two surfmen in white stood by the Lurline Pier. It was known as the Olympic Pier by most. Both names were incorrect in Isobel's none-too-humble opinion. The Lurline Pipeline would have been more apt. It was an intake pipe with a filter that pumped saltwater into two downtown baths: the Olympic Club and the more public Lurline bath.

There was a wire rail on either side of the pipe line and a big free standing gate to keep trespassers off its length. But the only thing the gate served to do was to tempt boys (and the occasional girl). Children circumvent-ed the gate with ease to sit on its pump, or balance along its rounded length and fish off the end. Once upon a time, Isobel had ventured down to jump, intending to swim back. The surfmen and their longboat had fished her out of the water. The tides could be dangerous, but it all depended on the ocean's mood. Isobel, being on familiar terms with the tides, had been infuriated by their 'rescue'.

When Isobel and Saxby neared, the small dog began to growl at her. She planted her umbrella and glared at the little beast.

Introductions were made. The younger of the two surfmen looked about her own age: twenty. He had the lean, broad-shouldered build of a swimmer, straw-haired and tan and smooth as a wet seal. His name was Tobin Gower. The second surfman, Mr. Jasper, was older, a veritable walrus with a musculature that spoke of long days of rowing. And lastly, the monocled gentleman who had spotted the girl, Nigel Harrison. The Englishman held himself stiffly and looked as though she should recognize his name. Isobel did not.

"It seems Miss Bonnie may be acquainted with the deceased," Saxby explained. "Maybe you can put her mind at ease either way by describing the girl."

Tobin Gower's sun touched features paled. He mumbled apologies and avoided her eyes, focusing on the dog instead. Isobel kept his reaction in the forefront of her mind as the others tipped apologetic hats.

"I'm not sure," she hastened. "Violet and I weren't especially close, but if I can assist, then I'm willing. Perhaps you best tell me what you told the police."

Harrison swept a gold monocle over her, and began a recitation that hinted at many dry retellings. "I walk Brutus every morning at sunrise. When we reached the top of the Cliff House road, I turned, as I always do, to appreciate the view. That's when I noticed the peculiar message. We went down to investigate, and as I was standing there, where the surfman currently is, I looked at the empty beach. A bit of white caught my eye, tossing in the water by the pier. I can't say why, but something worried me enough to skirt the gate, and walk out onto the pier to get a closer look. It was a young woman. Quite dead."

"Did you drag her out?" Isobel asked.

"I can't swim," he explained, looking away in shame. "I hurried straightaway to the life-saving station."

Isobel made appropriate noises of understanding, and looked to the two members of the life-saving crew, who had likely pulled more dead bodies out of the unforgiving sea than breathing ones (as well as protesting little girls who had only wanted to swim to shore).

The Walrus picked up the narrative. "As Mr. Harrison was saying, she was quite dead. But the er—" he hesitated, looking to the other men for help.

Isobel read his unease. "I was trained as a nurse, Mr. Jasper. I'm not the squeamish sort." This, of course, was an utter lie, she was not a nurse unless one counted the poking, examining, and dissections of dead animals.

Satisfied, the Walrus went on. "The fish and gulls hadn't yet gotten to her, so she was as serene as the dead can be. She had red hair, longish, about mid-back, I'd wager. Blue eyes, perhaps, but it's always difficult to tell with the dead. A pretty thing."

This statement prompted another question. "Clothes?"

"Wearin' nought but her undergarments," he admitted. "Course the rest was bundled up and filled with sand to weigh her down."

"How was her clothing weighing her down if she wasn't wearing it?"

"It was tied around her legs."

"The rest of her clothing being?" Isobel prodded.

"Skirt, blouse, and a matching coat."

Isobel swallowed an impatient growl. "The color?"

"Grey, I think," the Walrus scratched at his drooping mustache. "There were some little flowers on the hem."

"Violets?" she gasped.

"Why yes, Miss, I think you're right. Little purple ones." His features fell as realization struck. The dead woman might be her friend after all. To Isobel, it was simple—what other stitching would decorate a grey skirt worn by a woman named Violet? While some might claim it was a lucky guess, Isobel called her conclusion common sense.

"Any birthmarks, freckles?"

The Walrus cleared his throat. "I didn't look any closer than was proper."

Isobel studied the other three men. They were, to a man, apparently perfect gentlemen. What she wouldn't give for just one proper scoundrel today. She aimed her eye at the swimmer who had not uttered more than a murmur.

"Did *you* notice anything?"

"No, Miss Bonnie," he mumbled, avoiding her gaze.

Isobel could tell a lot about a person by looking them in the eye. It was a knack she had always had. From as far back as she could recall, she had puzzled over the effect that a charming smile and a flattering word had on the masses. Adults were easily swayed by, what to her, was clear deception. Salesmen and politicians, especially, oozed slime. It was a gift that had never steered her wrong, like her unerring sense of direction. Isobel never got lost—not at sea, not underneath, not on land, and not with people.

And now, she thought of Violet's red hair and her supposed message—'not of this country'. "Was she wearing a rosary?"

"She was," said the Walrus. Another startled look, and

he corrected himself. "Maybe not. It was a little lamb with a cross."

Isobel frowned, and added a faint tremble to her voice, "Violet's Agnus Dei." A Catholic symbol denoting sacrifice.

Eager to prove that the woman was not Isobel's friend, the Walrus continued, "She had another necklace on too. A little black square of cloth, but I didn't get a good look at it."

It sounded like a devotional scapular, but Isobel could not remember the color's significance. Although Isobel's mother was Portuguese, and therefore Catholic, her German father was not, and the only time Isobel set foot in church was for baptisms and weddings.

"Violet did have a scapular, but so many do—I don't know if she's my friend or not," Isobel said with a flutter of distress.

"You can view the body, you know," Saxby offered.

"One can do that?" she asked.

"Tell the coroner that you might know the woman, and give him my name. I'm sure he's eager to identify her."

"I'll go straightaway," Isobel said. Before Saxby could offer his arm again, she latched onto to the lean swimmer. "Would you escort me to the terminus, Mr. Gower?"

Given the vice lock she had on the swimmer's arm, he had little choice in the matter.

"You can end your shift, Tobin, and call it a day," Saxby said.

"Gentlemen," Isobel lowered her lashes, and they tipped their hats as her quiet suspect led her over the sand. She leaned in close to the athlete. He was strong and wiry, and his strength was apparent beneath the thin duck cloth, but there was more. Tobin Gower was wound tight as a spring about to break.

"You look ill, Mr. Gower," she noted.

"Tired, I suspect," he mumbled.

"Mr. Saxby said that you could end your shift. Does that mean you work all through the night?"

Tobin did not say a word. He didn't need to. Isobel knew the answer.

"Do you patrol all night?" she pressed. "Or just sleep?" The accusation proved a suitable enough prod to loosen his tongue.

"Depends on the night," he said. "Some nights there are troublemakers on the beach. When the storms start and the waves crack, then there are wrecks to watch for, and warn the public away."

"What about last night? Was there anyone on the beach?"

The arm felt like iron beneath her hand. "It was quiet," he said.

Isobel tipped her head to look up at the tall fellow. The wind caught her hat, and it flew off, tumbling into the sand. Tobin hastened after, bent to retrieve it, and straightened. When he returned her hat, Isobel looked him square in the eyes.

The man looked more than tired; he looked guilty.

"The dead *are* quiet, Mr. Gower," she said.

"What?" This time, he did not avert his gaze, but his eyes widened.

"The dead are quiet," Isobel repeated, putting steel in her voice to drive through him like a sword point. "But they don't always go quietly, and they certainly don't stay that way."

"What are you getting at, Miss Bonnie?"

Isobel took her time resettling her hat. When she was

satisfied with its placement, she tilted her head up to look at the man. "You've the look of a man with blood on his hands."

Tobin stepped back as if he had been struck. "A woman is dead. On my shift. Course I feel responsible. But there's lost souls who come from downtown nearly every day to throw themselves in the sea. They don't give a wit about anyone but themselves—most especially the men who have to fish them out."

"Then why are you acting as if you shoved her in yourself?"

Tobin ran a hand over his face, turned, and walked towards the life-saving station. Isobel flung helplessness aside, and stalked after her prey, or tried to at any rate. Damn her heels and his long stride. He outdistanced her in no time.

"How do you know Violet was from downtown?" she called after him.

"The terminus is that way, Miss Bonnie." Tobin Gower practically ran from Isobel's diminutive five-foot presence. The corner of her lips lifted with satisfaction. Something, as the saying went, was definitely afoot.

5

The Silence

THE DEAD *WERE* QUIET. And pale. Not a breath, not a stir, or a flutter of unease. Isobel could stare at the corpse until her own lips turned blue, and no one would notice. There was more life in a chair, because the absence of everything the woman once was howled into the silence.

Isobel studied the greyish-white slab of flesh, wondering what Violet's laugh had sounded like, what her fears looked like, and what those eyes had seen before ending in the sea.

Isobel had seen her own death more times than she could count: a speeding wagon, a wild horse with fury in its eyes, an aggravated bull, blades and guns, fierce winds, the cold glint of a man's eyes, and always, the welcoming deep. But she had taken that final step in name only. Isobel had made Alex Kingston a widow. Her name was dead, but she still breathed.

Isobel touched the lifeless hand on the table. It was not much larger than her own. She picked up Violet's hand and, turning it this way and that, studied the palm, the knuckles, and finally the fingernails.

Whatever Violet's occupation, it did not involve hard work. Unlike Isobel's own roughened hands (it was fortunate that gloves were a part of a lady's ensemble), Violet did not possess a single callus. And her nails reinforced that observation.

She reached for the left hand, and a throat cleared behind her. "I can't imagine why you'd need to examine the deceased's hands to determine whether she is your friend, Miss Bonnie."

Isobel turned slightly, eyes flickering to Deputy Coroner Duncan August. The fit doctor was in his mid-thirties. With chestnut hair and a fine profile, he looked more suited for a Society soirée than a morgue. Intelligence shone from his green eyes.

Isobel weighed her options, and decided on a direct approach. "Is there really no reason you can think of?"

"There's reason, but not the ones for which you entered my morgue."

"I'm here for the reason I stated, Dr. August. To identify the body."

"You don't know her."

"I do not," Isobel admitted. "But I'd like to find out her name as much as you."

"Why does it matter to you?" he asked.

"What did you conclude?"

"I can have you removed, Miss Bonnie."

"Then you'll never know why," she said, straightening.

August crossed his arms. "I could have you arrested."

"On what grounds?" She arched a brow. "Failing to identify a body? You strike me as a more reasonable man than that, Dr. August."

August rubbed his smooth chin. "She drowned. It's a clear suicide."

"And that is precisely why I want to know her name."

Confusion flickered over his eyes. "I don't understand."

"I don't think this was a suicide," she announced.

"On what grounds?" August parroted, stepping forward to look down on the corpse.

"The message in the sand," Isobel replied. Without asking permission, she launched into a closer inspection, starting with the woman's head.

"Most suicides generally leave a final note," August pointed out.

"But how many refer to themselves in the third person?"

An impatient breath swept past August's lips. "Anyone who commits such a rash act is clearly insane, Miss Bonnie."

"Did you notice these bruises on her arm?"

"Caused after death. When the surfman pulled her from the water."

"And the scar on her head?"

"I noticed," he said testily.

Isobel swallowed her disappointment. She preferred to be the one who noticed things first. "It looks as though it was quite severe."

"Which might explain her suicide. No doubt, the woman suffered from headaches, and who knows what other delusions. Are you with the newspapers?"

Isobel did not answer, or perhaps she did not hear, as something had caught her attention. She frowned at the woman's red hair, and spread a bit on her palm, turning it towards light. It appeared to be dyed. Just to be sure, she reached for the sheet.

"Miss Bonnie!" the Coroner protested. His hands were strong, and he tugged the sheet back in place.

Isobel glared. August stood his ground. "Yes, I'm with the *Call*, but I'm not looking for a story—I'm a detective of sorts."

"A detective?" August sounded dubious.

"Give me ten minutes, that's all."

"It's against procedure, I'm sorry."

"At least look into her death further."

"There's a morgue full of unidentified bodies," he stated firmly. "I intend to place an inquiry with the newspapers. If she's spent any time at all in San Francisco, then someone is bound to respond."

Isobel smirked at the coroner. "You're afraid I'll find something that skipped your notice. I understand. Men don't tolerate being outwitted by a woman."

August frowned at her. "I don't miss things."

"How do you know for a certain if you don't let anyone else examine the bodies?"

"Because I attended University."

"So did I." Isobel did not add that it had only been for two months.

"What did you study?" His interest was genuine.

"Law."

Duncan August laughed. It was a single, full-throated sound that echoed off the cold walls. He quickly stifled his amusement, glanced at the empty room, and finally the body, with an apologetic look. Isobel noted that look, and quickly switched strategies.

"Dr. August," she said softly. "You've given me enough

of your time. I'm likely mistaken. It's only—my sister was murdered in much the same manner, and I need to put my own mind at ease, or this death will haunt me."

August looked at her square. "You're a good actress."

"I'm a better detective," she challenged.

"Ten minutes," he said. "I hope that I won't regret this."

"A man, or woman, should never regret anything. There's no going back," she murmured, folding back the sheet.

A triangle of black at the juncture of thighs confirmed that the woman was not a natural redhead, which also explained the lack of freckles. Satisfied, Isobel turned her attention to the rest of the body, making a thorough examination. There were no telling marks on the skin, nothing under her fingernails, and no other unusual scars. But then, Isobel had not expected to find anything. The sea had a way of scrubbing one clean. A tattoo, however, would have been convenient.

Isobel straightened with a sigh to find August watching her in a superior manner. "I have two minutes left. Where are her things?"

He walked over to a wall of drawers, retrieved a sack, and placed it on an unoccupied table. One by one, Isobel examined each item, and placed it to the side: a matching grey walking skirt and jacket with little purple violets, blouse (no tears or missing buttons), shift, a cameo brooch, and two necklaces: the Agnus Dei and scapular.

Isobel looked at the round disc of silver, and turned it over. There were no engravings. She set it aside, and picked up the scapular, spreading the black square of cloth on the table. As with most scapulars, there was a holy image on the front. A woman, presumably Mary, stood with her usual glow, while two men kneeled at her feet. Instead of a traditional promise on the back, a red cross decorated the other side. The red cross knocked her memory. *The Help of the Sick* scapular. Nurses often wore them.

A number of conspicuous items were missing: corset (who wanted to die in such a thing?), shoes, hat, gloves, and handbag. She questioned the coroner about the missing items.

"They were not found," he confirmed. "Likely swept away."

Isobel narrowed her eyes at the man as if he were a particularly dense child. "Swept away? So the woman stripped down to her under things, filled her skirt, blouse and jacket with sand, then carried all that unnecessary clothing into the sea with her?"

"Perhaps she didn't want anyone to profit from her death."

"Or perhaps her murderer carried the items away," Isobel suggested.

"You've exceeded your allotted time by four minutes, Miss Bonnie."

"So I have," she extended her hand. Startled, he shook it. "Thank you, Doctor. I'll share anything I find with you. I don't expect you to do the same, but just in case, you can contact me at the *Call*." Isobel hoped at any rate.

"I will share," he said, surprising her. "I was going to contact the newspapers with the details. A kettle of reporters will dig up any story."

"Whether or not a story is there. Give me one day," she bargained. "If I don't get results, then you can throw it to the vultures."

"One day," August nodded.

Isobel gathered her things, and left Duncan August to

his room of quiet dead.

✛

Isobel passed from the shadow of San Francisco's sky-scraper, through its arches on Market, and into the *Call* building's gilded bosom. Her heels clicked on the marble as she walked through the crowded lobby of suits, reporters, and morning diners headed to the top floor. The flow took her towards the elevator and she let herself be caught in its grip.

Voices droned in the cramped confines: women chatted, newspapermen talked business, and Isobel shifted facts like pieces on a chess board. It was early in the game yet. The opening moves gathering for something greater—all centered around Violet.

On the thirteenth floor, the doors opened, and Isobel stepped into a fog of cigar smoke. A dozen clacking typewriters beat on her ears, and in between the steady clicks, the shuffle of papers, harried voices, and half-smoldering tempers assaulted her senses. A clang of telephones were cymbals to the discordant orchestra.

She steeled herself, fighting down an urge to find the nearest stairwell and flee. Determined, she gritted her teeth and wound her way through desks until she found one suitable for her designs: empty, neat, and painfully clean. The occupant, a Mr. Abrams according to the name plate, was either a rare breed of meticulous newsman with no deadline, or absent.

Isobel hoped for the latter as she set down her umbrella, handbag, and finally her backside. She tore off the typewriter cover, located paper, and carefully fed it into the Underwood. Her own single-finger tapping joined the drone.

"What's all this, Miss?" a voice pierced her focus and burst it like a bubble. She glanced up in irritation, leaving her project only half done. The owner of the voice had sparse red hair, the jowls of a mastiff, and a mess of a nose that resembled a lopsided mushroom.

Isobel erased the irritation from her face and summoned a smile. "I'm terribly sorry, my typewriter sputtered out on me, and the editor wants this article by noon."

"We haven't met," the Mastiff changed his tone to molasses mixed with oil. "I know all the pretty faces."

Isobel thrust out her ink smudged fingers. How, and when she had acquired ink, she could not say. "Charlotte Bonnie. I was hired on Monday."

The man took her hand and kissed it with all the suavity of a pimp. Finally, she thought, a scoundrel—in the wrong place. "Mack McCormick."

"Charmed." Isobel retrieved her hand. She doubted Mack had spent a day of his life in Scotland, not with the affected accent (she was surprised he wasn't wearing a kilt) but his knuckles had the scarring of a pugilist, and his nose spoke for itself.

"How are the matches this week, Mr. McCormick?"

Surprise flashed across his eyes, and his chest swelled until the buttons looked about to burst. He placed a chewed cigar between his lips. "You're a sporting woman, then?"

"Not that kind."

He chuckled. "Never been to a match, then?" Mack answered his own question. "Women tend to shy away from the brutality."

"Probably reminds them of home and their husbands."

Mack did not know how to reply to her observation, so

he fell back on charm. "And what of Mr. Bonnie? Is he a sporting man—or the squeamish type?" He had, at least, noticed the ring on her finger.

"Mr. Bonnie died under suspicious circumstances. Poison." Isobel smiled. "Let me know when the next match is. I do love watching men beat themselves senseless. The bloodier the better."

The large man took a step back. "Right," he murmured. "I'll leave you to your work."

"Have a pleasant day," she said cheerfully, returning to typewriter.

A paragraph in and the flare of a match interrupted her furious key poking. Isobel tore her eyes from the page, and looked up to the face of a heavyset woman with the look of an imp in fine clothes.

"You don't work here," the intruder said.

"I aim to by noon," Isobel admitted.

The woman laughed, full-throated and free. Isobel liked the older woman immediately. "Cara Sharpe," the woman said, thrusting out a hand, one that showed wear.

Isobel stood and shook hands, supplying her own *nom de plume*. There was strength in the newswoman's grip.

"Watch yourself around Mack, but I wager you already know that. I've never seen a woman get rid of him so quickly."

"I believe I left him with the impression that I'm a murderess, but I thank you for the warning."

Cara's rouged lips curled like a tabby cat, one that was sitting in a glow of confidence. "The newspaper is a tough business, even for the men. They're fiercely competitive, and as a woman—"

"One must be smarter."

"And quicker," Cara agreed. "We also stick together. If

you last, the Sob Sisters keep their desks in a quieter room."

"The Sob Sisters?"

"A nasty nickname given to us by our male counterparts," Cara explained. "Women reporters tend to write more personal pieces. But what most these fellows don't like to admit is that those articles usually make the front page."

Cara winked, and sauntered off, leaving a trail of wispy smoke. Isobel watched her leave, noting that everyone got out of the woman's way, and even nodded in greeting as they did so. Whoever Cara Sharpe was, she had seniority, or the editor's ear. Isobel sat back down at her pirated desk, and frowned at the nearly finished article sitting on the ribbon. Coming to a decision, she removed the paper, tore it into neat strips and let them flutter into the trash bin.

If Isobel were going to secure a job at the *San Francisco Call*, she'd need something that would make every woman stop and read.

✢

Isobel marched up to a horseshoe-shaped desk and handed her article to the harried desk editor. "I'll be at Abram's desk. Let me know if it makes the cut. Cara Sharpe is waiting for me."

The squinty man blinked at her like a light-blinded mouse. Before he could open his mouth and formulate a question, she made herself scarce, following the sound of clanging telephones to three booths. As soon as the occupant left, she dashed in, shutting herself in a cocoon of tobacco smoke and muffled noise. Ten more minutes in the newsroom, and she would go mad. Pushing a mounting headache to the side, Isobel picked up the earpiece, inserted her nickel, and requested the Park and Ocean Railroad offices.

Long minutes passed as the pleasant voice at the switchboard made the necessary connections. "Hello there, I hoped you might help me. I left my handbag on the Ocean Street line yesterday morning. The conductor might have passed it onto the next shift. Are they on the telephone? Oh, I see. You would? It'd put my heart at ease. Thank you."

Isobel scribbled down names and address, and clicked off to summon the switchboard operator. This time, she requested the Cliff House Railroad. Her inquiries were a shot in the dark, but it was a shot nonetheless. Violet could very well have been living in the Ocean Beach area, or been staying at one of the holiday hotels, but given the quality of her clothing and dyed-hair, Isobel would wager that she was from downtown, or out of it entirely. She recorded the name and address of the conductors for the Cliff House line and asked the operator to connect her with Mary's Help Center, a home and hospital for women and children.

No one remembered treating a Violet, or any woman with so severe a head wound. Isobel thanked the Daughter of Charity, and bothered the operator again. There were a hundred different possibilities: that Violet received the head wound as a child, in another country, that her name was not Violet at the time (or ever), or that she was treated at a hospital with no Catholic connections. But Isobel did not like to wait, not for the morning edition of the newspapers and the off chance that in this hectic, self-centered city someone would claim the dead woman—especially if she had been a prostitute.

That was the beauty and tragedy of San Francisco. Any one could sail into port and reinvent himself a dozen times over. No one asked questions, or gave a wit about a person's past. In the city by the bay, one was who he (or she) claimed to be.

"St. Mary's Hospital," a brisk voice crackled on the other end.

"Charlotte Bonnie here," Isobel greeted, stretching a finger to plug one ear while pressing the earpiece firmly against the other. "I've a friend named Violet who, some years ago, received a nasty head wound on the back of her head. The old wound is currently giving her issues, but she'll only see the physician who treated her. The funny thing is, she can't remember the name of the hospital, but she wears a Agnus Dei and a black devotional scapular."

"What was the physician's name?"

"I'm afraid she can't remember," Isobel said in despair as she had to the other nurse, and repeated the description.

"Red you say?"

"Dyed, yes," Isobel answered. The sister asked her to wait, and Isobel held her breath.

Five minutes later, the line crackled. "There was a Violet Clowes whom we treated last year. She had a nasty head wound. The nurse remembers her well. Violet converted during her convalescence."

"Splendid," Isobel exclaimed. "Will the nurse be there for a few more hours? Wonderful. I'll bring her in. What is the nurse's name? Sister Mary Riley. Thank you, that ought to reassure Violet."

Isobel hung the earpiece on its hook, and returned to Abram's island of order. Her thoughts picked over the information: Violet Clowes, who was not born Catholic, or with red hair. Clowes wasn't exactly an immigrant's surname, but then it was so easy to change one's name. Isobel did it every day.

"Miss," a voice that reminded her of a yipping lap dog snapped her to the present. Isobel looked up to find the desk editor with her article in hand. "I don't recognize you."

"Just hired on space and detail," she said, supplying her name, and stealing his hand for a shake before he could refuse.

"And who gave you this detail?"

"It's an exclusive."

"Is the story true?"

Isobel began gathering her things. "The things that count," she said with a small smile. "You can confirm it with Brown's steamship office on Market. Does it pass?"

"It'll make the morning edition." He handed her a five dollar bill. "For the column."

Isobel tried not to scowl at the bill as she walked out of the torturous office. With that pay, she'd need to make up a whole heap of stories.

6

A Twisting Trail

SISTER MARY RILEY WAS not the stern, no nonsense, knuckle-thumping nurse Isobel expected. Her eyes shone with joy, and when Isobel offered a hand, the nurse encompassed it with both of hers. Warmth and comfort radiated from the woman like a stove, and her kindness burned. Something pricked Isobel's eye, and she blinked to rid herself of it, swallowing down a sudden swell of emotion.

"I'm sorry to hear about Violet's troubles, but not surprised. Where is the dear girl?" Mary asked. The nurse's eyes flickered over Isobel's shoulder as if Violet was hiding in the sunlit room. Isobel could affect apologetic meekness with the best of them, but one look at the nurse decided her course.

"I lied," Isobel stated, bluntly. "I'm afraid she's not with me, or anyone in this world, Sister."

The joy turned dark—not with anger but acceptance. "Violet finally committed suicide, then?"

With that single sentence, all of Isobel's theories and murderess hopes were dashed. "She tried to kill herself before?"

Mary turned a critical eye on her. "Did you know Violet at all?"

"I did not," Isobel replied. "I'm working with the coroner as his investigator." It was nearly the truth.

The Sister of Mercy touched her own devotionals hanging around her neck: the black scapular and Lamb of God. "Violet did attempt suicide—the year before last, in late 1898, with morphine and chloroform. Violet Clowes is her stage name. Her real name, as far as I know, is Elizabeth Foster. She was comatose when she was admitted to the hospital. After her discharge, she complained of constant headaches."

Isobel frowned. "Even with her past, I'm not entirely convinced it was suicide, but the coroner is ready to write it off as one. Either way, I'd like to find the truth of the matter."

"You sound as if it's personal."

The comment struck Isobel, and sent her off kilter. This would be, or was supposed to be, her very first murder investigation. She wanted to catch a killer—perhaps it *was* personal. She recovered quickly. "Shouldn't it be?"

"There's murder everywhere, Miss Bonnie. God will put things right," Sister Mary said with the reverence of the devout.

"Well, until he does so, one less murderer roaming free will put my mind at ease," Isobel retorted. "Did Violet have a habit of referring to herself in the third person?"

"How do you mean?"

"Violet was found floating in the ocean, her clothes filled with sand, and a message written on shore." Isobel recited the odd message.

"Curious."

"You see why I'm suspicious?"

"I do," the nurse agreed. "But then nothing about Violet made much sense. Did you know she was trained as a nurse?"

"Where?"

"A nursing school on the East Coast. After her parents died in a carriage accident, she moved out here."

"Was she working as a nurse when she took the morphine and chloroform?"

"A governess, I think. I don't really remember," the Sister admitted. "Violet's first stay was short. She was back on her feet within a matter of days. Friends came to fetch her. It wasn't until after her head injury that we became better acquainted. She mostly talked about the stage."

"The stage?"

"Theatre," Mary Riley confirmed. "A light fixture fell on her head."

Isobel considered this. From nurse, to governess, to the stage. After the first suicide attempt, it was doubtful that she'd be able to find employment as a nurse or governess. Violet's character would be called into question. No one wanted a suicidal nurse caring for their children.

"Do you remember where the accident took place?"

"I don't know, but at the time she was rooming at the Y.M.C.A. for ladies. Miss Wheeler has been the superintendent for years. If you like, I can write a note of introduction."

The Sister paused before she left. "Miss Bonnie, as strange as the message was, serious injuries can change a person. I'm not sure the woman who came to the hospital was the same woman who left."

⁂

Her feet ached. Isobel wanted to rip off her impractical heels and toss them at the next man who turned his head to admire her silhouette: bosom pushed out, curving spine, tapered waistline, and sumptuous hips—all affected by undergarments.

Surely a gentleman noticed the inconsistencies between a garbed female and an unclothed one? Although, in Isobel's experience, thought appeared to be elusive to the male species when the latter was involved. At the very least, undergarments aided and abetted her deception. It would not do for anyone to recognize her in San Francisco. So she endured her disguise as Charlotte Bonnie, whose purpose was to attract attention, not walk. And certainly not to fall into Atticus Riot's arms. She clenched her teeth and mentally kicked herself for her impulsive whimsy.

Isobel readjusted her gloves as she walked towards the Y.M.C.A. It was an orderly brick building, well maintained, and quite rectangular. As much as Isobel loved her clipper ship, the *Pagan Lady*, it wasn't always ideal for her purposes, not only because of its inconvenient location and security issues, but also for the attention her constant coming and going might attract. She required a less conspicuous place, where she could come and go in secret. Unfortunately, the Y.M.C.A, with its strict curfew and rules, would not do.

A young Chinese woman with a cross around her neck and a plain blouse and skirt on her slight body opened the door.

Isobel resisted the urge to bow. Childhood habits died hard. Hop, her family's butler, had been more beloved uncle than servant.

"I'm here to speak with Miss Wheeler. If you could show her this note."

The girl gestured Isobel into a sitting room, and abandoned her with the words, wait and please.

Thoughts of Hop brought an ache to her heart—for her father, for Hop, for her twin, and surprisingly, her mother. Had Isobel unconsciously sought out Riot, or was it simply chance and spontaneity that had possessed her to involve him in her stunt? Perhaps it was a craving, to brush against someone who knew she lived—a bridge to her past.

Further thoughts on the conundrum were cut short when Miss Wheeler marched in like a brigadier general. The bosom beneath a lacy blouse was thrust out like a pigeon's, and her hair was pulled in the opposite direction by a severe chignon. Here was a woman who took the virtue of her tenants personally.

Isobel shook the hand that was offered. "I remember Elizabeth well, but there's little I can say on the matter. Only that the news is not surprising. The girl was not right in the head."

Isobel appreciated bluntness, and returned the favor. "When did Violet —I mean Elizabeth board with you?"

Miss Wheeler had brought a leather bound book with her, and now, she adjusted her pince-nez, opened the accounts and consulted her records. "She arrived November 2nd 1898, under the name Elizabeth Foster."

"The month she tried to kill herself."

"Three days after she arrived," the woman confirmed. "I nearly gave her notice, but afterwards, she found employment as a companion to an elderly woman and moved out herself. Shortly after, the woman died, and Elizabeth returned at the end of January. Not two days passed, and she fell ill. She had me summon a physician."

"Another suicide attempt?"

"I feared so," Miss Wheeler confided. "But the physician said it was a gastric ailment and thought she would recover. When Elizabeth did recover, she started acting peculiar."

"In what way?"

"Elizabeth changed her name to Violet and dyed her hair—*red*." Miss Wheeler paused, arching a confiding brow as if such a change was the ultimate sin. "She began leaving early in the morning, before it was light, and did not return until just before curfew. She stopped dining with the other boarders, and kept to herself. A week later, she informed me that she was studying for the stage. As you can imagine, I tried to dissuade her."

Isobel nodded in sympathy, not for Miss Wheeler, but for her own twin brother, who had defied their parents in every way possible to pursue the stage. "Did she find employment?"

"She was studying music with a Mr. Emilio Bolden. I do not know the particulars, but shortly after that, in February, the stage light fell on her."

"Do you recall the theatre name?"

Miss Wheeler shook her head. "The injury left Elizabeth—Violet by this time, queerer than before. As soon as she recovered, she left for Los Angeles with the Kiralfy Theatre Company, and I did not see her again."

Isobel filed away every detail, sorted the pertinent ones, and concluded that Violet Clowes was either impulsive (unlikely for a nurse) or fleeing—someone or something. "Before Violet's first suicide attempt, did she have many visitors?"

"I'm not a hotel guestbook, Miss. Bonnie."

Isobel thanked the woman, and paused at the door. "If you should remember anything more, leave a message with —" She nearly said the *Call*, but remembered that she was supposed to be a city-sanctioned investigator. "The coroner's office, with a Mr. Duncan August."

7

The Other Half

VOICES WASHED OVER ISOBEL as she walked into the *Liaison*, a cafe where swirling lines and gold gilt collided with pond fronds and soft paintings. A group of assorted men crowded around a table for four. As with every diner in the restaurant, the men's garb varied, from stiff collars and creased trousers to flamboyant velvet suits and ruffled shirt fronts.

The whirlwind of male enthusiasm centered around a slight man with golden hair that caressed his shoulders. The man was striking: grey eyes, high cheekbones, delicate lips, and a voice that drawled over his crowd of admirers.

Isobel seated herself at a table in the corner. The waiter appeared. She ordered tea to calm her mind and sat sipping as conversations flowed over her ears.

She drank her first cup, and ordered a second. Unfortunately, when she reached the dregs, the group of men, having nothing better to do than occupy themselves with idle talk, showed no signs of uprooting themselves. But then the focal point of the gathering had that affect on people. Laziness was catching.

Isobel fished the depths of her handbag, retrieved pen and paper, and scribbled a note, folding it and pressing into the waiter's hand with instructions to pass it to the 'handsome blond gentleman'.

The waiter did not so much as blink. In a cafe called *Liaison* it was hardly his first delivered note.

Beneath the rim of her broad hat, Isobel watched the waiter deliver her message to the gentleman. Without breaking his narrative of a Parisian *faux pas*, the man casually unfolded the note and glanced down.

All conversation stopped. Grey eyes flickered to the lone woman sitting in the corner. Isobel tilted her chin, catching his gaze with a flash. She tossed a dime on the table, and stood. But the man rose as she did. Defying her instructions, he walked right up to her. Their grey eyes were level, their noses identical, and whereas one was pale with fright, the other burned with fury.

"I said outside," Isobel growled under her breath. In reply, the man slapped her, hard. Every voice in the cafe fell silent at the strike.

Shock reigned.

With the sting of his flesh radiating on her skin, Isobel calmly collected her things, and left.

⁜

The sting followed her to a little garden square. Isobel sat on a bench beneath a shaded tree, and waited in the relative quiet. She did not know if he would come. But he did. She stood, steeling herself for what was to come.

Brother and sister faced each other, one a mirror of the other. Grey met grey. "I had hoped to avoid a scene," Isobel said calmly.

"You bastard!" Lotario hissed. He slapped her again, on the other cheek, but the tears in his eyes hurt far worse than the pathetic blow. Isobel stepped towards her twin brother, and he went into her arms, burying his face in the crook of her neck.

"If I'm a bastard, then so are you," she mocked, stroking the nape of his neck. A sound, half-sob, half-snort, exploded against her collar. "I'm sorry, Ari. I thought you would piece everything together."

Lotario squeezed her once, sniffled, and stepped back, dabbing his eyes with a lacy handkerchief. Kohl stained the white.

"Of course I knew," he sniffed. "The moment that detective showed up asking to buy the *Pagan Lady*. He didn't strike me as a sailing sort. But that was after your funeral, Bel. You let your twin brother believe that you were murdered for a *full* week. And it was just that—a suspicion. The detective wouldn't say a word, even after I interrogated and tried all my tricks on the fellow. I could only hope. I might have flung myself into the sea," he announced.

"You love yourself far too much for that. All your beauty would go to waste. Besides," Isobel said dryly, "you can swim." She reached into her handbag for a mirror, thumbed the latch, and turned it towards Lotario so he might arrange himself. When he was satisfied, she clicked it shut, and found her twin studying her in a thoughtful, calculating way.

That look heartened her greatly.

"You owe me," he said slowly. "All that business with Kingston—you never would tell me what you were up to."

"Because you would have done something foolish, just as you did in the cafe. If I'm found out, I'll be in a heap of trouble, and that goes for anyone who knows I'm still alive. Trust me, Ari, I'm better off dead."

"I can keep secrets," he protested.

Over the years, it was a sentence she had heard countless times—generally followed by a lengthy pout. Lotario was the opposite of discreet.

"You've never trusted me." And the pout began.

"I don't trust anyone," she quipped. A flash of pain contorted his features, and she sighed, pulling him down onto the bench. They sat in silence for a time, watching lives pass in and out of a moment.

"I didn't want you involved," she admitted. "It was dangerous, still is, and you could have been hurt—I can't bear the thought of anyone, especially Kingston and his ilk, ever finding out about you."

"God forbid a scandal should ever touch me," Lotario snorted, and waved a languid hand. "Please, in the future, don't go to such drastic measures in my name. I'll simply move to France. I don't see why you had to fake your own death to protect me. That doesn't make a wit of sense."

She hesitated, only for a moment. "I needed to get away from Kingston."

"Your pig of a husband," Lotario stated, glancing at his nails. "There are less dramatic ways of ending a relationship, you know. It's called divorce."

"Not when blackmail is involved. Kingston was ruining Father and the family business."

Lotario blinked. "What could he possibly have been

blackmailing Father about—his book collection? And why put yourself at risk? Mother and Father sent you away to Europe. The two of us are stains on our family name."

Isobel sighed. An old argument, an old pain, still raw. Isobel steered the conversation away from those treacherous familial waters by confiding in her twin the full story: the accidents, the lost contracts, her investigation, and subsequent confrontation with Kingston (an extremely foolish one), his offer of blackmail-laced marriage, her ongoing investigation into his affairs, and finally, their older brother's true involvement—and Curtis' death.

"You *shot* Curtis?" Lotario whispered. Rather than accusation, there was sympathy—a sympathy that she would have traded for anger any day. Lotario's hand tightened on her own, and she withdrew to adjust her hat.

"I need your help," she said.

Lotario's eyes narrowed to slits.

"You can't breathe a word to anyone."

"*You* need *my* help?" he repeated. There was a low, dangerous edge beneath his lilting voice. "You came back from the dead, not because the brother with whom you shared a womb for nine months might be comforted to know his twin is alive, but because you needed my help?"

"If you'd like to think of it that way—then yes."

"You *are* as cold-hearted as I told that detective you were."

"You told Riot that I was cold-hearted?" she demanded, and instantly regretted her slip of control.

"Riot," he tasted the name, and leaned forward. "The prim looking bookish fellow with a deliciously dangerous way about him? Is that where you've been? I wager he knows his way around a boudoir."

"He's all yours," she replied indifferently.

Lotario pursed his soft lips. "I doubt that. My charms appeared lost on him."

"Keep your doubts." But the touch of Riot's hands lingered in memory. She looked down at her umbrella, and casually rubbed a gloved finger along its handle. "Since you neglected the *Lady*, I sailed her to Alameda to have her refitted, and then took a train to Los Angeles," she confided. Even she wasn't foolhardy enough to sail down the California coast in winter.

"Kingston?"

"I see your brain is working for its daily hour."

"It only turns on for you, dear sister."

"You should use it more often."

"I prefer the other one I was given."

"Still living at the *Narcissus*?"

Lotario smiled like a cat in the cream. "It suits me. As does singing and dancing at various venues. What do you need from your sprightly brother?"

"Two things: I need you to keep your ears to the ground for any morsel of information involving Kingston —and to keep your tongue still," she warned.

"My tongue is usually occupied while my ears remain open."

"Multi-tasking," she mused. "We have something in common after all."

Lotario winked, and settled back on the bench, draping an arm around her. "Tell me about this Riot fellow." He scooted closer.

"Most people would ask after the second favor."

"I'm not most people."

"There's nothing to tell, Ari," she said primly. "Will you help me, or not?"

"Don't keep me in the dark," he warned.

"I won't," she promised. Lotario held her gaze a moment, searching for deception; satisfied, he sat back, crossing his legs. Her twin smelt like rosewater and spring, and she leant into the lithe body that mirrored her own in so many ways save their gender. Flesh and bone were reunited after a long separation.

"And your second request?"

Isobel told him of her current investigation, of Violet Clowes and her strange message written in the sand.

"You don't know Emilio Bolden?"

"The theatre is a whole different world," she replied. "That's why I came to you. You know everyone."

Lotario basked in her compliment for a full a thirty seconds before he replied. "I happen to know Emilio, or Leo as he's called by friends, but this Violet sounds like stage decoration. Actors come and go all the time. I don't bother learning the names of bit actors unless they're tall, dark and handsome—like your fellow Riot."

Isobel clenched her jaw, and nearly hit her brother over the head with the umbrella in hand. "Riot's not tall, and he's not my fellow."

"Pining for Kingston?"

The jab pushed her too far. Isobel brought her hand up. The slap jolted his head to the side.

"That will leave a mark," Lotario drawled, unconcerned.

Isobel stood, breathing hard.

"Remember, sister dear," he said. "You do feel after all."

Isobel glared down at him. "Always pushing, always prodding."

"You must have bullied me in Mother's womb," he said, pulling on a pair of thin gloves.

"Is it possible to question Leo today?" she asked impatiently.

"We may not *question* Leo, but we can certainly make a social call and see what emerges," Lotario corrected. "We'll have to visit one of my dressing rooms and change first. Leo knows me as Madame de Winter." Lotario's favorite book was the Three Musketeers (and every thing mother and father had not wanted him to read). "I think," he corrected, tapping his chin in thought. "Perhaps not," he sighed.

Isobel waited.

"What's more shocking: discovering a man dressed as a woman or a woman dressed as a man?"

"I think it would depend on the situation."

"Hmm," Lotario agreed. "Do you know, I was once taken to the station by an overzealous patrolman who thought I was a woman disguised as a man. You should have seen the look on the matron's face when she had me disrobe for proof." Isobel laughed, and Lotario's eyes danced. "Admit it, you've missed me," he said.

"Was that ever in question, my dear brother?"

8

Masquerade

THE HACK ROLLED TO a stop in front of a slim, two-story house with a cheerful conical roof on its tower. Isobel stepped down, and turned to help her companion, Madame Lucie de Winter. The lady alighted with prim grace and a silky voice. "Wait for us," she said. Her voice was heavenly, and she could afford the luxury of a waiting hack. Whenever Lotario donned a costume, he preferred to be addressed by his chosen name, and in truth, Isobel could not think of Lotario as a man, but then she never did—he was simply her twin who changed faces like the wind.

Lucie paused to open her parasol, and Isobel jabbed a pointed elbow into her side, but there was no rushing the fashionably dressed opera diva.

"Try to behave," Lucie said, frowning at Isobel's choice

of clothing: flat straw hat, tie, blouse, and dark skirt, with blissfully comfortable boots. A pair of costume spectacles completed her scholarly disguise.

Lucie stopped to admire the roses, commented on the lovely lattice-work, and turned to exclaim over the view as if they had all the time in the world.

Rather than drag her twin along, Isobel climbed the steps, and waited. Light piano music and a dreadful wailing beat on the bay windows. When Lucie and her swishing skirts deigned to join her on the porch, Isobel stabbed the bell button with the tip of her umbrella.

A harried, grey housekeeper opened the door. The moment she caught sight of the elegant caller, her face softened to polite formality. "I'm afraid Mr. Bolden is with a student."

Lucie supplied her calling card. "I'll wait."

The housekeeper showed them into the entrance hall, but instead of following the woman into the front parlor, Lucie swished down the hallway.

"Madame," the housekeeper's scots accent came through, and she hurried after, but before she could reach the rude guest, Lucie opened the sliding doors to the center parlor. The music cut off and the braying donkey raised her voice to compensate. Mr. Bolden gathered himself up from the piano to be outraged, but one look at the intruder transformed him into a jovial bear. The music teacher's height rivaled his girth and his sideburns connected with his jowls, curling into a waxed mustache.

Mr. Bolden slashed a hand across his throat. The student fell silent, but the echo of her screeching lingered. She was a willowy young woman, with hair piled atop her head and frills cascading down her long body.

"Madame de Winter," Mr. Bolden swept forward.

"What an honor."

Lucie offered a bored hand, and the tutor kissed it with noisy lips. When he straightened, Lucie stepped forward, kissing the air over the man's cheeks. "You are looking well, Leo."

"Life is good," Mr. Bolden agreed. "And even better now. I don't suppose you've graced me with your presence to show my student the difference between an angelic voice and hell on earth?"

The student blushed, not in shame, but in fury. Isobel half expected the butcheress of the arts to stomp her foot and leave in a huff. When she did not, Mr. Bolden looked disappointed.

"I'm afraid not," Lucie replied, barely glancing at the student. "I wish a moment of your time."

"In the middle of the day?" Mr. Bolden raised his bushy brows twice.

The housekeeper scowled, and when the full weight of her gaze fell on the man, he cleared his throat and guided Lucie into the front parlor. Largely ignored, Isobel followed, blending into the wall paper.

Before the housekeeper slammed the sliding doors shut, Mr. Bolden ordered the butcheress to practice her scales. The wailing commenced.

According to Lotario (currently Lucie), Emilio Bolden was the premier music tutor in San Francisco. Isobel wondered how much the student's parents were paying him to tutor their ungifted daughter.

Sunlight bathed the front parlor, pouring through the ceiling to floor bay window. The African marble hearth, redwood paneling, and velvet chairs were a testament to Mr. Bolden's tutoring, if not his manners. He slid open the hallway doors, stuck his head out, and hollered for tea.

When he shut the door again, he noticed Isobel.

"Pardon me, Mademoiselle!" His eyes flickered over her with an assessing gleam. "A protege of yours?"

Lucie laughed softly. "Charlotte sings like a donkey. And dresses the part," she added distastefully. "But she can act, Leo."

Mr. Bolden studied Isobel with renewed interest, circling her like a purveyor of horses.

"I'm pleased to meet you, Mr. Bolden," Isobel said, taking a seat on the settee near the hearth. "Lucie says that you are the best tutor in California."

"The lady never exaggerates," the tutor boasted.

"Was that ever in question?" Lucie asked, settling on a chair by the window. The sun made her glow, demanding attention. Isobel admired her twin's ability. When Lotario wished it, he could captivate a room.

"If you ladies continue, I will burst from praise," Mr. Bolden preened.

"Or sweet cakes," Lucie quipped.

Mr. Bolden guffawed like a canon boom, momentarily silencing the donkey in the adjoining room. No doubt, he was an impressive baritone.

"I have missed singing with you," Mr. Bolden said, earnestly, perching his bulk on the chair opposite. "We make such beautiful music together."

"As have I, Leo, but you are training the next generation. There's a lot to be desired."

"Few have ever come close to you," Mr. Bolden confided, reaching for Lucie's hand. She summoned an artful blush.

"Charlotte has a friend who studied with you."

"Oh?"

"What is her name, dear?"

"Violet Clowes," Isobel supplied.

Mr. Bolden repeated the name, staring at the inside of his head. "Oh yes, Violet," he murmured. "A fair soprano and a talented soubrette."

"Did she find employment after your tutoring?" Isobel ventured. "I lost contact with her."

The tutor looked down his wide nose at her. "All of *my* students find employment."

"Even the donkey braying in the your music room?" Lucie deflected the slight with an undeniable one.

Mr. Bolden raised his eyes heavenward. "Perhaps not all," he admitted, leaning back in his chair.

The door slid open and the housekeeper rattled in with tea. As the woman arranged the tray, Mr. Bolden turned his gaze on Isobel, studying her with far more intelligence in his eyes than she would have credited him. Isobel tilted her eyes down, and reached for a cake. An observant person would not miss the resemblance between the two women.

Lucie took a dainty sip of her tea. "I would like to meet this promising student of yours, Leo. Not everyone earns your praise." Isobel marveled at Lucie's ability to keep the china free of rouge.

"I hadn't seen her for some time, not since an unfortunate accident, but she recently called last month. She came for a reference."

"Oh? And did you give her one?"

"Of course," he huffed. "She's singing at the *Tivoli*."

"How convenient," Lucie said. "I have two evening performances there a week. A lovely venue, but you know I don't mingle back stage. Do you have an address?"

"Mrs. Cook will have it," he said.

Isobel stood. "I'll fetch it." She slipped into the hallway

as the two friends dove into the latest theatre gossip. All of Isobel's instincts were prickling. A woman of talent and employment hardly sounded desperate.

Upon request, Mrs. Cook consulted Mr. Bolden's appointment book, located Violet's name and gave her an address—no telephone number. As Isobel wrote it down, she took note of an older address. The listing was in the Pacific Heights area. Violet, it seemed, had begun singing lessons while she was working as a caretaker. The tutor's fees were extravagant. How on earth did Violet afford such lessons? Did Leo make an exception for the truly gifted, or did he make other arrangements with his pretty young students?

Isobel flipped to the current day, memorizing the braying singer's name. If the woman should ever buy her way into a role, she'd be sure to skip that opera. Before Mrs. Cook could snatch the book out of her hands, Isobel closed it with a thump.

"Are you on the telephone?"

Mrs. Cook scowled.

"Madame de Winter has an appointment," Isobel explained. "I can certainly interrupt her visit with Mr. Bolden, or I can ring her next appointment and move it to a more convenient time."

The Scots woman cocked an ear towards the parlor. Good-humored laughter bellowed from the room. Since an employer in a good mood was better than a grumpy one, Mrs. Cook showed Isobel to the telephone nook in the hallway.

When the housekeeper left, Isobel rang the Cliff House Railway. Her messages had reached the evening shift conductor, but no one had reported finding a handbag and the conductor did not remember a woman with red hair wearing a grey dress.

She thanked the office, and requested the cable car building. "Hello there, I called this morning about my missing handbag. The evening conductor left a message?"

A thrill zipped through her like an electrical charge. It was the same feeling she had whenever an opponent was cornered and the King was within reach. She swallowed down her excitement, and concentrated on the voice in the earpiece.

The conductor remembered Violet; however, there was no handbag, and he was sorry to say that he did not deliver her note, but was glad to hear that she was well.

"Note?" Isobel asked in surprise. "Did the conductor, Humphrey, say what it was about?"

"Well you handed it to him, didn't you?" the man asked.

"Oh," Isobel cleared her throat. "Yes, of course." Absentmindedly, she hung the earpiece on its hook, and considered the wallpaper in silence.

Violet's last known residence was on Jones Street, the Sapphire House. It wasn't far from here. On the other hand, The Park and Ocean line was a good ways, and she would have to transfer at Golden Gate Park.

Decided, Isobel plucked up the line and asked to be connected with the morgue building. After long minutes, an inquiring voice crackled over the line. "Can you deliver a message to Deputy Coroner Duncan August? Yes, tell him Charlotte Bonnie called. The woman's name is Elizabeth Foster, her stage name is Violet Clowes. She resided at 415 Jones Street, the Sapphire House. Thank you."

With a thrill of triumph, Isobel stood and consulted the watch that hung from a chain around her neck. Four o'clock. She had tracked down an unknown woman's name in a matter of hours. Truly, a far better detective than actress.

Humming tunelessly, she went to extract Lucie from her social call.

✤

"Why would Violet leave a note with a conductor?" Lucie asked as they bumped and rattled towards Jones street.

"Perhaps it was her intended suicide note," Isobel mused. "But it doesn't explain the message carved into the sand."

"Makes it even stranger."

The thought considerably cheered her.

"Will you ask around the theatre with your usual discretion?"

Lucie laughed, a note of music in their rattling world. "Am I ever discreet?" she asked, leaning into Isobel.

"You're utterly indiscreet. I'm hoping that it will mask your *careful* inquiries."

"I swear I won't let anyone coerce me into walking onto a pier and jumping into the water. Besides," Lucie waved a languid hand, "I can swim."

Isobel was uneasy. The theatre world was a small one. Infiltrating the theatre and asking after Violet would attract attention; fortunately, it was also her twin's domain. "When is your next performance?"

"I'm dancing at a hall tonight at ten. I sing at the *Tivoli* tomorrow."

"Be careful, regardless. I can bear Curtis' blood on my hands, but not yours."

Grey eyes turned on Isobel in surprise. The eyes shimmered for a moment, but thankfully, Lucie recovered before she burst with sentiment. "Where are you lodging and what have you done with my *Lady?*"

"I'm sleeping on her," Isobel answered.

"She does have a soothing affect on the body," Lucie mused. "Where are you berthed?"

"Folsom Street Pier."

Lucie wrinkled her nose. "Definitely no place for my Ladies. I worry about you."

Isobel straightened, turning away to watch the passing houses. "You shouldn't. I've always been better off alone. You know how I loathe looking after others. It only distracts."

"I could have helped with Kingston," Lucie returned.

"You would have been a liability." Isobel looked at her twin, leaving no room for argument. "It was better to convince Kingston that we were estranged; that the last I saw of you was in Europe. He's a blackmailer and murderer. I don't want you anywhere near the man."

"And the thought of you married to a blackmailer and a murderer is supposed to comfort me?"

"You live in a brothel," she pointed out.

"It's a bathhouse, and I like it," Lucie preened.

Isobel had never understood her twin's living arrangements, but she left it alone, pressing her point. "It was a game; simple maneuvering, that's all. I played my part like you play yours in the theatre. And now I have the advantage. Kingston doesn't know I'm alive, he's left off our family, and I discovered Curtis' true colors. I won."

"Then why are you still after Kingston?"

"Before I—killed Curtis," her voice shook, and she cleared the grit from it, "he said that Kingston moved in the same circles. That there were powerful men in the shadows, and that he was an *Engineer*, like Kingston, but not so clumsy. I think that Kingston is more blunt tool than Engineer."

"So you're swimming into deeper waters?"

"Don't I always?"

"You do, that's the problem. And you leave me behind to worry."

"I don't want to see you hurt."

"Bel, do you imagine that I want to see you hurt?" Lucie asked, softly.

Isobel was quickly regretting her choice to confide in her twin. "You shouldn't come with me to Violet's residence."

"But I'm intrigued."

"You're too noticeable."

"I could be Violet's friend from the theatre."

"True," Isobel admitted.

"I might as well bask in your presence until you sail off to China."

Isobel sighed. "It's always tempting."

"How will I reach you if I discover something?"

Isobel considered her options. She may, or may not have a desk at the *Call*, and there was always a chance that a message would be intercepted by her competition. Unfortunately, the Deputy Coroner wouldn't do for Lotario and his many faces.

"Send whatever information you uncover to Ravenwood Agency—until I can find a more permanent address." The delay was entirely due to her lack of funds. Isobel had spent the last of her money on dock fees, but she wasn't about to tell Lucie; twin, or no. Isobel did not like for others to pay her way, unless she was shamelessly spending the funds of a criminal husband.

"Ravenwood Agency? Isn't that the name of the

agency where Riot is employed?"

"It is," confirmed Isobel. "You can trust him." The words slipped past her lips without thought—as sure as she knew she was breathing. The realization startled her.

"Trust?" Lucie asked, surprised. "I didn't think you trusted anyone but yourself."

"I'm talking with you, aren't I?"

"My dear sister," her twin drawled in a masculine voice, "I don't even trust myself. Madame de Winter is a shameless flirt and gossip."

"Madame de Winter will find her balls kicked if she so much as breathes a word about this business to anyone."

"Your diplomacy has always been intolerable."

9

Sapphire House

A STURDY WOMAN WITH a mop of old-fashioned curls and small beady eyes opened the door. She squinted at the two women on her step. The woman's gaze settled on Lucie, who smiled pleasantly in return.

"Charlotte Bonnie," Isobel introduced, catching the woman's attention. "I'm with the coroner's office." In one sweep, Isobel took in the woman's expensive earrings, out of date clothes, and rough hands. She spoke her conclusion out loud. "You're the landlady of Sapphire House."

"That I am. Mrs. Kathy Beeton, and a fine clean house I run. No trouble here."

"I'm afraid one of your residents found trouble elsewhere. Does a Violet Clowes rent a room from you?"

The landlady sighed, turned and walked away.

Isobel looked at Lucie, who lifted a shoulder. She had

expected some suspicion over her investigating claim.

Mrs. Beeton walked passed the parlor and led them upstairs. The floorboards creaked under her weight. The railing was polished, the rails dusty, and the runners worn. The same could be said of the rest of the hallway. The door knobs gleamed, but the small table holding a vase had not been dusted for sometime.

"Do you employ a housekeeper?" Isobel asked.

Mrs. Beeton stopped in front of a door, and drew herself up. "I do all the cleaning myself. Always have." She fiddled with her key ring, trying each key twice before coming back to the first and inserting it into the lock again. "What's the girl done, then?"

Isobel raised her voice in case the woman was hard of hearing. "We're with the coroner's office, Mrs. Beeton."

"Coroner? She's dead then?"

"If it's the same woman, yes. You may be called upon to identify the body."

"Well, the Violet here didn't come home last night. Boarded a month and five days. Paid twenty dollars for the month." Mrs. Beeton opened the door.

Isobel stepped inside the sun drenched bedroom. Flowers greeted her with a pleasant scent, and a generous mirror displayed her severe reflection. The room might be cheery, but it was empty, save for the furniture and a single travel trunk on the floor. Violet had packed.

Lucie strolled into the small room, running a gloved hand over the crisp bedclothes. She turned to the mirror, and adjusted her lacy hat.

"When did you last see Violet?" Isobel asked as she gazed down at the trunk.

"Was she murdered, then?"

Isobel turned. "We're trying to determine that."

The landlady squinted from Isobel to Lucie. "You say you're with the coroner's office?" It was more reminder than question, and Isobel smiled.

"Yes, ma'am."

The woman looked relieved. And then turned her gaze on the wallpaper. Isobel waited as the landlady dredged up a memory. A great clicking ring moaned once from the foyer as the grandfather clock chimed half past four. The sound knocked the elusive thought from Mrs. Beeton's rattled mind. "Yesterday morning. Ten o'clock sharp, on the third ring."

"Did Violet seem despondent?"

"Why no, not at all. Pleasant girl. Always in good spirits. As I said, she paid her rent in advance. Twenty dollars for the month."

"Was she intending to find other lodgings?"

The landlady smiled, seemingly unaware of the conspicuous trunk sitting in the center of the room. "I don't see why. I didn't bother her about the lateness of the second month. That's how pleasant she was. She brought me violets once, just like those." The landlady pointed to the three vases in the room.

"Has her trunk always been packed?" Isobel tapped the luggage.

"It was there yesterday."

"Why did you enter Violet's room yesterday?"

Mrs. Beeton stiffened at her tone. "To polish the doorknob, of course."

"And a fine polishing you gave it," Lucie enthused.

"Why didn't you report her missing?"

"It's none of my business," the landlady huffed.

Isobel ignored the batty woman, and knelt beside the trunk, testing the latch. It was not locked. As she riffled through the dead woman's worldly belongings, Lucie took up the conversation.

"Do you remember what Violet was wearing when she left?"

"A grey skirt?" Mrs. Beeton did not sound sure. "With her red hair done up like your own. Very pretty, that. And a hat with flowers. It made her look tall, but then she was, wasn't she? Oh, what a lovely diamond!"

Lucie preened shamelessly as the landlady admired her necklace.

Splendid, the landlady was a magpie. "Was Violet wearing jewelry?" Isobel asked abruptly.

Without hesitation, the landlady answered. "She wore a lovely silver brooch with an ivory profile of a woman." The brooch that Isobel had discovered pinned to Violet's blouse.

Violet's clothing was mostly of the cheap pre-made variety, but there was a single dark blue dress that was tailored. The kind that a governess or school teacher might wear. There were books, too: on spiritualism, vapid romances, theatre, nursing, and one tattered pamphlet on family planning that Comstock had declared illegal.

"Did Violet have any gentlemen callers?" Isobel asked, as she began a careful search of the undergarments.

"I don't recall any visitors."

The slim case wrapped in her undergarments said otherwise. The 'hygienic device' was fairly new. Both the pamphlet and the rubber cap were illegal (and entirely sensible as far as Isobel was concerned). Isobel clicked the box shut, and replaced it.

"Did you know she was in the theatre?"

Mrs. Beeton shook her head. "No, you're mistaken. Violet is a nurse." She fell silent for a second. "Dead, you say?"

"Unless we are mistaken," Lucie soothed.

"We are not," Isobel stated.

Mrs. Beeton wobbled, and Lucie stepped forward, taking her arm. "Why don't you show me your parlor. The sun must be lovely this time of day."

The two left Isobel to the trunk's contents. Free of prying eyes, Isobel scrutinized each item, one by one, before setting it on the floor. By her estimate, the clothes would fit the tall woman she had viewed on the morgue slab. She picked up the book on spiritualism, and it fell open to a chapter entitled 'The Restless Dead'. Underlined words leapt off the page: anger, fury, atonement, and release. There were no notes in the margins.

Isobel set the book aside, and picked up the one on nursing. A looping hand filled the margins, but since there was no title of ownership, and it appeared as if the book could have been secondhand, there was no way to know if the handwriting belonged to Violet. This hand was nothing like the severe slant on the beach.

Isobel plumbed the depths of the trunk, but found nothing else of interest. No weapons, plenty of makeup, hair dye, and one vial of lavender perfume. She turned to the trunk's lining, searching for irregularities. Her fingers caught on a slight, square impression.

Carefully, Isobel parted the seam, and pulled out a photograph. Violet Clowes, or as she was likely known then, Elizabeth smiled from the photograph. She wore a nursing uniform and stood between two others: a woman of her own age and a handsome man in stiff collar. There was an air of familiarity between the three.

Isobel flipped over the photograph. A faint lead mark dated the picture: *1896—Hal, Liz, Elma*, written in the same, looping handwriting as the nursing notes.

"That's the property of the coroner," a deep voice said from the door way.

Isobel did not miss a beat. Without turning, she thrust the photograph towards the Deputy Coroner. "Is your investigator still busy?"

"The morgue is still full," Duncan August replied. "If only he were as industrious as you. I barely recognized you, Miss Bonnie."

"It's amazing what a change of clothes can do. A sturdy pair of shoes can increase one's productivity. Perhaps your investigator should give it a try."

"I'll pass the message along."

"The handwriting doesn't match the writing on shore."

"The message was written in sand, likely with a stick, hardly suitable for handwriting analysis."

"I suppose not," Isobel admitted, standing.

The physician examined the photograph, then looked at the empty room. "Not much here."

"So it appears," she said, turning her attention to the wardrobe. As she began a methodical search of the room, she related the details of her investigation. August didn't appear to know what to do with himself, so he poked around inside the trunk.

"The landlady didn't report her missing?"

"Mrs. Beeton is more concerned with polishing doorknobs than her boarders' whereabouts. She's senile and has poor eyesight. Spectacles might help," she said absently.

"But her scones are delectable," Lucie moaned, obscenely.

Duncan August turned on his heel, taking in the elegant, silk-scarfed woman framed in the doorway.

Lucie extended a gloved hand. "I saw you pass in the hall. I had to meet you."

"Madame de Winter," August said when he rediscovered his voice.

Isobel nearly threw a pillow at her twin. It appeared the Deputy Coroner was also a theatre enthusiast. "I saw you sing at the *Tivoli* last month."

"I hope you heard as well."

"A divine performance." August looked from the singer to the dowdy would-be investigator, trying to connect the pieces. For a man who identified corpses all day, the similarities in bone structure was hard to miss.

"We're cousins," Isobel supplied before he could ask.

"I find Annie's activities amusing."

"Annie?"

"Charlotte," Isobel nearly growled, and then put on a smile. "An old joke between us."

"She's like a dime novel character, don't you think?" Lucie batted her eyelashes, distracting August from her name slip. "It's so entertaining to watch her little adventures unfold."

"I must admit, I had not expected results, especially so soon."

"She's gifted."

"Like you," August smiled.

Lucie fluttered her lashes, and stepped forward, running a gloved hand down his arm. "Such a lovely cut on you—and those fine hands."

Resigned to her distracting twin, Isobel focused on the trunk, ignoring the exchange of flirting words. Satisfied that there were no hidden nooks or loose papers, she opened the window and thrust half her body out the third-story window. An iron fire escape climbed the back of the building. A ledge, just under the window, ran five feet to the first railing.

Gripping the windowsill, she adjusted her center of gravity, and bent at the waist, hanging from her hips to stretch towards the ledge. A cry of alarm filled the room where her legs remained. Footsteps neared, but before a hand could grab her coat and haul her back, Isobel placed a hand on her wig, righted it, and slipped back inside. She had seen what she hoped would be there: scuff marks on the ledge.

"Miss Bonnie!"

"Entertaining, isn't it?" Lucie gushed. "Do show me that photograph."

With Isobel safe, August obeyed the charming woman. Isobel glanced in the mirror, and nudged her wig a fraction.

"I'm going to take these books, Dr. August. They may help shed light on Violet's death."

The physician left the photograph in Lucie's hands, who casually tucked it in her handbag.

August smirked at the spiritualism book. "Are you going to consult the otherworld, Miss Bonnie?"

"The possibility appeared to be on Violet's mind."

"Surely you don't believe in ghosts?"

"It doesn't matter what I believe; what matters is what Violet believed. I'll return it when I get this sorted out— unless you'd like to wait on your investigator?"

"As Deputy Coroner, I can hire whomever I like," he admitted. "As long as you keep me updated."

"I am, aren't I? Do you have an official looking card that I can present to people during my inquiries?"

August hesitated, and then brought out his billfold. He handed her a card with his name, but more importantly, his title at the coroner's office. Pleased, Isobel tucked it away. And Lucie brought out her own elaborately embossed card, displaying it under August's nose. He looked at it like a donkey being led with a carrot.

"Give this to the doorman whenever I'm singing and you'll have a box seat."

"I can't, Madame——" August protested. "That would be bribery."

"That's why I waited until after you accepted my cousin's help. Now, it's simply an invitation. I hope we meet again, Dr. August." Lucie placed her card in his hand, and swept out with a rustle of silk.

Isobel left a very perplexed coroner in the room, and when she joined her twin, Lucie confided, "I collected the names of the other boarders from the landlady in case you needed them."

Isobel scanned the slip of paper. No Elma or Hal, or any other name she recognized—not surprising. "I'll question them later."

"Who knew a man who handles dead flesh all day could be so charming," Lucie said after they climbed into the waiting hack.

Isobel's eyes slid over to her twin. "Careful, Ari. August is a city official."

"One who you've told a string of lies to. What if he, or anyone for that matter, recognizes you as the late Mrs. Kingston?"

Isobel did not reply. Both sister and brother played a dangerous game. But then the two had always walked a dagger's edge.

Amid the rattling and uneven streets, Isobel opened her carpet bag, pulling out the clothes she had pilfered from Lotario's dressing room. Dressing was as practiced and swift as any costume exchange. As in the theatre, she wore what she could of the next costume. Ladies coat and skirt were stripped, revealing a shirt and trousers. With deft fingers, she buttoned up a waistcoat, attached a stiff collar and tie, shrugged into a coat, and ripped off her wig and hat, smoothing her short hair.

"What on earth did you do to your hair?"

"I cut it," she said, slapping a flat wool cap over the offending desecration.

Lucie patted her own hair for reassurance. "It's dreadful. And black. The color may never be the same. You know that, don't you?

Isobel looked at her twin. "I don't care."

Lucie sniffed, but let the subject lie. Instead, she removed her gloves and brought out a slim case. The seasoned actor dabbed her fingertip in the dark powder and spread it artfully over Isobel's face. When she was satisfied with shading that gave the impression of stubble, Lucie made a few, quick adjustments to her stiff collar and tie.

"Where are you off to?" Lucie finally asked.

"Ocean Beach to question the conductor."

"Too deep."

Isobel cleared the faulty male voice from her throat and tried again. "If Violet left at ten in the morning," Lucie's approving look told her she was pitch-perfect, "then that leaves a whole heap of time before the message was carved into the sand. Can you find an excuse to stop by the *Tivoli* sooner?"

Lucie laughed softly. "I have a number of excuses— and one very handsome one. What do you want me to do with your clothes?"

"In the Ferry Building cloakroom, there's a bored Southerner by the name of Richardson who doesn't ask questions when cash is involved. Leave the carpet bag with him."

A block from Market, Isobel thumped her umbrella on the roof, signaling the hackman to stop.

"It's a good thing I stopped worrying about you," Lucie said.

"Because you know I'm never careful."

"All the same, I could come with you."

"You're like a peacock in a mire," Isobel replied. "Whether it's as Paris, Lotario, or Madame de Winter, you attract attention wherever you go."

"I can't help it, you know."

Isobel smiled. "I know." Surprising both herself and her twin, she leant over and kissed her cheek.

Before Lucie could say a thing, Isobel hopped from the hack, hit the pavement and was already shrugging into a peacoat as the fog embraced her shadow.

10

Ocean Beach

THE STREETCAR ROLLED THROUGH a silver world. Fog brushed her cheek, concealing the sand dunes to the south and the lush park to the north. For the third time in the same day, Isobel rode the Ocean and Park line. This time as Mr. Henry Morgan, a runner for the Deputy Coroner. Isobel stood on the rear platform, talking with the conductor. J.P. Humphrey remembered Violet well.

"Boarded at Golden Gate Park last night—on the last run." There was a drawl to the conductor's voice, a long and low sound that complimented his bowed legs. Replace his flat conductor's hat for a Stetson, and all would be right with the man. Isobel wondered if wrangling streetcar passengers was much different than cattle.

"Did the woman say anything to you?"

Humphrey sucked on his teeth, searching for his customary tobacco. Long habit caused him to spit on the cobblestones. "Not until the end. Reached into her handbag, and pulled out a letter. Asked me to mail it for her. Funny thing was, it was addressed to the City of San Francisco."

"Did she take the handbag with her?"

"'Course."

"Was anyone else on the line?"

Humphrey shook his head. "And no one was waiting at the station."

"What did you do with the letter?"

Color rose in the unforgivable complexion of a man who spent his days under a canopy in the dark. "I was worried about the young woman, you see. Women don't generally ride the last line alone. When I saw how the letter was addressed, I opened it."

"What did it say?"

Humphrey cleared his throat. "The note said, 'I am innocent. Think well of me'.

Isobel arched a brow, noting the use of 'I' and not Violet. "Was it signed?"

"No, nothing else. It was that odd, it was. So I went straight away to the life-saving station at the end of the park. Handed it over to the first surfman I found. I was worried the girl might do something foolish."

Isobel frowned. "Was the surfman tall, blond, clean-shaven, and fit?"

"Why yes, yes he was," Humphrey replied. The streetcar stopped at the terminus. A knot of beach goers waited in the fog, weary and joyful from a sunny day in the sea. Isobel thanked the conductor and stepped down. A strong hand grabbed her shoulder, and she looked up into the worried eyes of J.P. Humphrey. "Was the girl all right, then?"

"The woman is dead." There was no accusation, no sympathy, just plain blunt fact in her voice. The conductor's throat caught with dismay, but Isobel did not notice. Her feet were already moving, and her thoughts sped to the guilty looking surfman she had spoken to this morning.

✣

With ornate scrollwork and a neat little fence, the life-saving station resembled a giant-sized gingerbread cottage rather than a boat house. Its wide, double doors were open, and Isobel walked from the mist into the garage, where a thirty-six foot longboat sat on a wagon. Its wheels were a foot over her head, and the grips pointed towards the ramp, poised to spit crew and boat out to sea.

She smelled oil and grease, and noted movement under the wagon, towards the rear axle. A surfman in his blues was oiling the wheels. Unruly blond hair snuck from beneath his cap. She recognized the fit swimmer immediately.

"Tobin Gower," she said.

The man jerked and knocked his head on the hull. Rubbing the knot on his head, he stared at the unannounced guest, taking in the flat cap, smooth face, peacoat, and trousers. His gaze fell on the umbrella in her hand, but to the unobservant, it was unremarkable.

"What do you want?" Tobin asked, ducking from beneath the hull. He drew himself up to his full height.

Keeping to the shadows, Isobel reached into her coat pocket, and withdrew Duncan August's card. "I'm with the coroner's office."

Tobin narrowed his eyes. And for a moment, Isobel feared recognition, but it was only wariness. "You here about the woman who was found this morning?"

"I'm here to get your statement."

"I gave my statement."

"A version of it," she corrected.

"I have work to do." Tobin ducked under the hull, and she moved with him, keeping to the mouth of the boathouse in case he decided to bolt.

"I'd talk if I were you, Gower. As it stands right now, you're looking more and more like a murderer."

The whites of Tobin's eyes shone in the dim light. He was pale as moonlight. "You're not the police." Tobin tightened his grip around his oil can, tensing as if to throw it at his accuser.

"You're right, I'm not," she said. "I'm one of the Deputy Coroner's investigators, and I'm going to give you the chance to come clean. The police won't be so lenient." She spoke quickly. Men backed into corners were dangerous men. "I interviewed the streetcar conductor. He handed you a letter. Why didn't you inform the police?"

Tobin's broad shoulders sagged. "It'll cost me my job. I bungled things badly."

"Now's the time to fix it," Isobel urged. "Not when the police get wind of the conductor's story. What happened?"

"It seems as if you already know." It was the words of a defeated man, not one who was preparing to run.

"I'll keep what I know to myself, and see if your version matches with mine. So don't lie to me, Gower."

"I wasn't about to," he frowned. "After the conductor caught me on my patrol and gave me the letter, I found the woman and followed her from a safe distance. I just watched her to see what'd she do, to keep her out of danger. When she sat on the beach, I stayed back, hiding in the sand dunes. All she did was sit there for two hours with her knees tucked up to her chin—that's it."

"Why didn't you approach her?"

A heavy sigh swept past his lips, he looked down, scuffing the floor with his boot. "It was a lonely spot—I was afraid she'd think I meant to assault her, and it'd give her a fright. You know how hysterical women are. I didn't want a fainting woman on my hands, or a screaming one. What would I have done, then?"

"So you *lurked*, instead."

"The woman never saw me," Tobin defended.

Isobel bit back a retort, but she recalled how the man could barely meet her eye this morning. Was it guilt, shyness, or a bit of both? She sincerely doubted that most women would have more than a moment's unease in the chiseled swimmer's presence. He looked like a giant puppy.

"How did she get from the beach to the water?"

"It got cold, so I went back to the station for my coat," Tobin faltered. He must have sensed her disapproval because he hastened to say, "Just real quick. I went back straight away, and then she was gone."

"Did you see anyone else on the beach, or nearby, at any time?"

Tobin shook his head. "Like I said, it was cold."

"It was also a full moon and a clear night. Did you see the message in the sand?"

"Not that I noticed. I thought she decided to leave."

"What time did you return from retrieving your coat?"

Tobin shrugged. "Half past three—four o'clock maybe."

"Think," she urged.

"Probably more towards four. When I returned to the station it was about a quarter past."

"Did you keep the note?"

Tobin nodded, and walked towards the back of the garage. Isobel followed cautiously, keeping both eyes on the surfman and the shadows. There was a shelf of large pigeon holes, and he reached into one, all the way to the back. When he returned, he surrendered a tattered letter over to the waiting investigator.

The letter said just what Humphrey had recited: *I am innocent. Think well of me.* Unlike the handwriting on the beach, this was done in the same loopy, if hasty, hand as the notations in the nursing handbook.

A thought struck Isobel, and she voiced her suspicion. "Who did you report this to?"

"Jasper."

The Walrus, as she had dubbed him. She could hardly forget the breadth of his shoulders.

"I ran into Jasper when I got my coat, and then spoke again when I returned. When the fellow with the dog found the woman, Jasper told me to keep it under my hat. That it'd look bad, and I'd be made a fool."

"It *was* foolish," she confirmed. "But then so was his advice. As one man to another, you had best tell the police, or you could be facing the noose."

The large Adam's apple on Tobin's neck dipped, and he nodded, sketching a hasty cross over his chest.

Isobel reached into her coat pocket and brought out a notepad and pencil. "Write your name, and the same words that were on the beach this morning."

"Why?"

"Do it," she ordered.

The tall man rolled his eyes, and put lead to paper. As he was writing, Isobel thought about the large rower. "Did Jasper leave after you told him the woman had left?"

"Yes, he was headed out for his patrol."

Tobin handed her the notepad. She glanced at it, satisfied. "Where is Jasper now?"

"It's his night off."

Isobel repeated the question.

"Raleigh's Tavern."

✛

Noise pushed at the walls of the tavern, not the posh Cliff House or the amusement park tents, but a sprawling wooden building with a haphazard plan. With umbrella in hand and her Colt Shopkeeper nestled against the small of her back, Isobel walked into the stifling smoke.

A piano man tapped at the keys to the hum of conversation. Top hats and bowlers bent over a Faro table, and two serving girls with drinks wove their way through tables occupied by gentlemen and a few ladies. Thankfully, this was no Barbary Coast dive.

Isobel relaxed with the atmosphere and scanned the crowd for the Walrus. She exchanged a nickel for a beer, and took a long drink. Belatedly, she realized that she had not eaten since early this morning. The thick brew went straight to her head and her stomach demanded more.

Cheers erupted from a back room. She followed the raucous sound to a knot of men who crowded around a table. Unfortunately, her five feet of altitude was not conducive to peering over hats. She slipped through the crowd to the center.

The Walrus sat in a chair facing another burly man. The combatants' faces were a picture of strain; elbows planted on the table, hands locked in a game of strength. A number of tumblers, some upright, others overturned, sat on the edge.

It was not yet nine o'clock and the Walrus looked near to soused.

With a surge of strength, the Walrus slammed his opponent's hand on the table. The crowd held its breath as he reached for a tumbler, brought it to his lips, and jerked his head back, downing the whiskey. The crowd cheered, money exchanged hands, and the Walrus scooped up two quarters from the table.

Isobel was not known for her patience. At this rate, she'd be shivering in the cold all night, waiting for a drunk to sober up. She took a breath, and then she took a risk. As soon as the defeated opponent stood, she stepped forward and slid into the vacated chair.

The Walrus narrowed his eyes at his small challenger. She answered with a cheeky grin, slapping a quarter on the table. The crowd bellowed. No bets were placed. A pity, Isobel thought.

"Scared?" she asked.

The Walrus snorted. "It's your money, boy."

Isobel planted her right elbow on the table top and leant forward. The Walrus gripped her hand. It felt like being held by a rock, and the fleeting sound of crushing bones filled her ears. She shook the imagined fear away and focused on her opponent, on the fact that there had been no marks on Violet's body, no sign of abuse.

Isobel leant forward, and whispered, "I'd like to talk with you about a handbag."

The Walrus' finger's twitched, betraying him as sure as a shout.

"I don't know what you're going on about, boy." The arm flexed, and the back of her hand slammed on the coarse wood. It stung.

The Walrus tossed back another whiskey, and reached

for his quarters. Isobel put a hand over his, stopping the movement. She placed another coin on the table, and gripped his hand.

"You told Gower to keep his mouth shut. I want to know what you did with her things."

The hand over her own tightened. His eyes smoldered. Isobel did not flinch. Wood smacked the back of her hand for a second time.

"You best go, boy." His grip was like iron.

"Drink your whiskey, Mr. Jasper," she urged amid the crowd's laughter. Never taking his eyes off her, he let go of her hand, and reached for another tumbler, tossing back the burning liquid. Isobel placed another quarter on the table. The Walrus hesitated, clearly struggling through the haze of alcohol, considering his options. But leaving the table while facing a smoothed-faced young man was hardly becoming of a local champion.

This time, when the Walrus gripped her hand, she whispered, "It will likely be your last." Muscles flexed. And Isobel brought her left hand up beneath the table—the hand that gripped her umbrella. Amid the cheery hum of conversation, Isobel jammed the handle between her opponent's legs.

The Walrus coughed in pain, his hand went all wobbly, and she slammed it on the table top. Clumsy with drink, he tipped back, trying to get away from the source of pain. She hooked the handle around his ankle and yanked. With a bellow, he crashed to the floor, scattering the crowd.

Isobel grabbed a tumbler and tipped back her head. Whiskey burned down her throat, and the crowd cheered when she set the glass down. She scooped up her winnings, and hurried over to the flailing Walrus. As he struggled to rise, she bent over him making to help, and smacked her elbow against his forehead. The back of his head hit the floor like a fish. To her pleasant surprise, he did not move.

"Had one too many, I'd wager," she announced. "Could someone help me drag Mr. Jasper out back to the pump? Some cool air will help set him right."

✛

The second bucket of water roused the Walrus from the grips of whiskey and a fierce elbow. Isobel set the bucket beside the hand pump, and stood over the man like a hunter over a trophy kill.

Jasper squinted up at her. His attacker was a slip of shadow in the cool fog, but the voice that reached his muddled ears was pure threat.

"You best tell me what happened when you went back to search for the woman on the beach."

The Walrus started to roll over. Isobel speared his jacket to the ground with the tip of her umbrella. "I prefer you stay there, Mr. Jasper."

"Who are you?" he coughed.

"Coroner's investigator," she supplied, liking the sound of it more and more. "As it stands right now, you're my prime suspect."

"The girl wasn't anywhere about when I went back!" he protested.

"What about her things?"

Jasper's head clonked on the mud with a squelch. He took two deep breaths, body tensing, but Isobel wasn't one to wait. She goaded his thigh with her umbrella. "If you think the handle hurt, wait until you feel the tip."

The threat loosened his tongue. "There was a handbag and shoes on the shore, right by the pipeline gate, but I didn't see her there in the water. I swear it. I figured the tide had already took her, like it does with most."

"No wonder you wanted Gower to keep quiet," she glared down at her captive. "Where is the handbag and shoes?"

"I gave the handbag to a tart I fancy."

"After you took all the valuables," Isobel concluded.

"There was a few dollars, that's all."

"I'm not concerned with the money. What was in there?"

"Feminine type things. I don't know. Some papers, coins, a few dollars. I needed the money." He shrugged, as best as a man could laying on his back in the mud.

"What did the papers say?"

"I don't know." The big man turned red. "I can't read."

Isobel narrowed her eyes. She produced her notepad, and ordered him to write his name. Jasper sat up. His brow furrowed with concentration, and his hand shook like a sailor's without rum. When he had produced his mark, she glanced at the paper. The *J* was barely legible, let alone the rest.

Isobel studied the man carefully, searching for deception, for ill intent, but the facts coincided with his story so far. "You best hope this tart of yours still has the handbag and its contents. If you turn in Violet's things, I might just put in my report that you found it near the dunes this evening. Do we have an agreement?"

"We do," he sighed.

"Good."

11

The Pagan Lady

COOL, SILVER AIR SWIRLED around Isobel's ears as she walked towards the Folsom Street Pier. This time of night, the docks had settled, leaving mist and shadows and creaking hulls. There were lights burning on a few small craft, casting pools of dark rather than light; other water gypsies like herself, roving from port to harbor, sailing wherever the winds took her. Not all were as law-abiding as she.

The Harbormaster's watchtower was tangled in the masts, but then, he was deep in his cups and near-sighted to boot (precisely why she had chosen this dock). Safety was secondary to obscurity. The revolver resting against her back and the umbrella in hand possessed a reassuring weight that made up for the Harbormaster's work ethic. It helped, too, that he was a forgetful sort. Not the type to notice a woman leaving and a young man arriving, or for that matter, a stranger on her cutter.

Isobel stopped beside a piling, frowning at the light seeping through a shuttered porthole on the *Pagan Lady*. A lantern was burning in the saloon—her saloon. The thought prompted her to reach for her Colt, but she stopped. She'd be exposed if she climbed down the companionway. Instead, she reached down and untied her laces, leaving her umbrella and boots on the dock.

Isobel slipped off the pier. Her bare toes touched the fore rail, and she crouched, bobbing with the tide while she listened. The lap of water and shift of rigging greeted her ears.

Moving quietly, she touched her foot on deck and lowered herself, keeping to the cover of the brief bulwark. A shadow leapt over the coaming and landed silently on deck. It trotted towards her, and she cursed silently.

A large orange and white Tom greeted her with an inquiring meow.

"Quiet," she hissed, softly in his ear. He smelt like fish, and she decided he was a dreadful guard cat. Ignoring the purring feline threading himself through her legs, she withdrew her key, slipping it into the forward hatch lock. It clicked. Using the shifting rigging to conceal her movements, she carefully opened the padlock and cracked the hatch.

Light seeped into the forward cabin from the saloon, showing two berth bunks and a neat tangle of ropes, block and tackle, and spare sails. In one silent move, Isobel opened the hatch, gripped the sides and lowered herself down, closing it as her foot found the ladder rung. She stepped down onto a coil of rope, and reached for her revolver.

With a breath, she steeled herself, cocked the hammer,

stepped into the cabin door, and aimed.

A bespectacled man sat in her saloon, reading. His raven hair, streaked with a wing of white, gleamed in the lantern light. Calm brown eyes looked up from the page, ignored her armament, and found her eyes.

"Ahoy there."

"Damn you, Riot." Isobel scowled. Heart in her throat, she uncocked her revolver and slid it into its holster. "I might have shot you."

"You might have," he agreed, shifting his left hand. His own No. 3, hidden by the book, was cocked and ready in his hand. He released the hammer, and slid it beneath his coat, uncrossing his legs and standing. "You're late."

She was tired and hungry and the long day had slowed her mind. His words made no sense. Riot pushed his spectacles higher on his nose, and reached into his coat pocket, producing a telegram slip.

The message was brief: *Folsom Street Pier -B*

Isobel decided right there and then that she was going to murder her meddling twin. "I had to see a whore about a handbag," she said instead, not giving Riot the satisfaction of answers.

"You're excused," he said with a quirk of his lips. "You have a half-starved look about you, Bel."

"And you look as though that's your third glass of brandy."

"I was waiting a bit," he admitted.

"Not worried, I hope?"

"Now why would I be worried about you?"

"You have that look about you."

"Puzzled, more like."

She surrendered. "Lotario's doing."

Realization lit his eyes. "I see." The two words held

disappointment, and he cleared it from his throat. "You came clean with your twin."

"I did."

"Your brother was stricken by your death. Although I think Lotario had his doubts when I bought the *Pagan Lady* off his hands. A well-played revenge."

Isobel wagered that there was a lot Riot was not saying. Her twin was a theatre diva, and Lotario had likely been dreadful to the detective.

Riot turned to gather his hat and silver-knobbed walking stick. "It's twice now that I've boarded your cutter uninvited. I apologize, Miss Bel. I'll take my leave." He slipped on his hat and touched fingers to brim.

"Stay—" she blurted out, immediately grimacing at her own demand.

Riot paused. Those eyes of his swept over her, and the intelligence behind the glass made her shiver. "Perhaps another time. It's late."

His insistence on departing nettled her, and she dug in her heels. "Are you taking back your invitation for dinner?"

For a long moment, Riot considered the question. "I would not dream of such a thing," he finally replied, removing his hat and replacing it on the hook.

A swell of relief filled her heart. "Good, because I'm tired of talking with Watson." And truth be told, if she were to admit it to herself, Riot's words were like honey, deep and reverberating, and she found that she had missed the sound of his voice.

"Watson?" he asked, looking around the saloon.

Isobel jutted her chin towards the cat who was sitting on the top of the companionway. "He doesn't add much to a conversation, but he's a wonderful listener."

Amusement danced in Riot's eyes. "I'm sure his human

counterpart would be honored."

"If only he could manage a revolver," she sighed.

"I'll stay on one condition."

Isobel arched a brow. "Are all your invitations to dinner conditional?"

"Bel, you look dead on your feet."

"I am dead, remember?"

"I'll cook; you sit."

"I think I'm too tired to eat," Isobel admitted.

"I'll give your meal to Watson if that's the case," Riot said, shrugging off his coat. She noted the shoulder holster and gun under his right arm. Not many would be expecting a man to pull a gun with his left hand. He unbuckled his holster, and hung that up, too. It had that worn look, the kind of leather that molded and moved with a body like an old friend.

"How did you make good with Watson?" The last intruder who had boarded her boat was greeted by a hissing and spitting flurry of fang and claw.

"I have my methods."

She snorted, and it knocked loose a thought. Nearly kicking herself, she darted up the companionway. Cold air slapped against her bare feet. She had nearly forgotten about her boots and umbrella. Both were where she had placed them. She snatched her belongings from the pier, and scanned the night. The fog roiled past her eyes, and somewhere off in the distance, a bell rang. All was peaceful.

Isobel climbed back to her floating island. Riot was moving confidently around the small galley. His sleeves were rolled up to his elbows, and a paper package of shrimp sat on the counter. She looked down at Watson, who twined around the detective's legs.

"Traitor," she said.

Riot glanced over his shoulder in surprise.

"Not you; the cat."

"To be fair, I cheated."

"I won't hold it against him." The shrimp was making her own mouth water.

As Riot struck a match and lit the burner, she noted a twining dragon, much faded from time, on his forearm. Isobel filed the detail away for another time. She had other things on her mind. Leaving him to poke around the galley for food stores, she deposited her belongings, rummaged through a drawer, and took a fresh set of clothes to the forward cabin.

While she washed her skin with frigid water, a tune drifted into the compartment. Riot was humming. *Vivaldi*, she recognized, and his voice was far from disagreeable.

Freshly scrubbed, Isobel emerged to the smell of sautéing shrimp and cooking rice. She pulled a warm sweater over her head and sat on the settee, reaching for her treasure trove of evidence: a spiritualist's book, a mysterious note, and more importantly, the contents of Violet's handbag.

A steaming cup of tea distracted her. Isobel accepted Riot's offering, and leaned back on the cushion. It felt so good that she propped her wool-stockinged feet on the berth. "I finally have a murder, Riot," she said to his back. "At least I think I do."

The man in her galley checked on the rice, and added more seasoning to the shrimp. She knew he was listening from the set of his shoulders and the tilt of his ear, so she went on.

"The woman looks to have killed herself. No marks, no signs of struggle, but there's this message…" And she told him all that she had discovered.

The recitation cleared her thoughts and the food that he placed in front of her gave her a second wind. While she ate, Riot sat across, picking at his own bowl of rice, looking through the evidence.

When her belly was full and silence settled on the cozy cabin, Isobel sat back with a sigh. "Even if Violet killed herself, and I don't think she did; suicide is a murder of a sort. There's always the why of it, and that starts somewhere, doesn't it?"

Riot did not reply. He set down his bowl and his gaze grew distant. Isobel wagered he was looking at time, memory, and regret. She wondered what sadness he saw in the glass.

"I wager," he murmured at last. Riot shook himself out of the thought, and reached for the letter she had discovered in Violet's stolen handbag. He crossed his legs, and began to read aloud.

"We often write for you to right your wrong. How many times your lives are burdened by an unwillingness to acknowledge mistakes on your part and ask forgiveness.

"As long as life lasts on earth in your weak, erring human nature will make mistakes and give offense. Faith and dependance on the good spirits will lessen the number of these mistakes and offenses, but this is not all that is necessary.

"There should go hand with this willingness to acknowledge mistakes and ask forgiveness. Perhaps there is no other duty to your lives that come so hard to the majority of you as to say, I was in the wrong, you were in the right. Please forgive me, and yet many heartaches would be spared, how many friendships would stand the test of time. How many family quarrels and home separators would never occur if you would acknowledge mistakes and show your sorrow for them.

"So many times you believe you are not in the least to blame when others think you are, and consequently do not feel called upon to ask forgiveness, inasmuch as you think there is nothing prejudiced in favor of yourselves and your actions, and cannot clearly judge in such matters, but if you take the matter to your spirit guides and ask our guidance as to what you should do and abide by our answer we will guide you in the right way and you will many times be surprised at the different outlook that comes to you after you ask our help.

"And whenever there is the slightest chance that you may be in the wrong—right it by asking forgiveness," Riot finished.

The other letter was much the same. Despite the cheerful Shipmate stove, she shivered, drawing up her legs and crossing them Indian style.

"It's written in the same hand as the message on the beach. And in the third person."

"Apparently from the spirit world," he noted. "In twenty years, I've never had a suspect from the otherworld. You lucky soul."

"I certainly wouldn't want a dull murder. Do you believe in ghosts?"

The edge of Riot's lip twisted in a rueful smile. "I have plenty of my own, but they don't generally write me letters."

"There's a theme in both letters: forgiveness and error."

Riot rubbed a hand over his trim beard. The gesture drew her eyes, and she began to count the strands of grey interspersed in the black.

The sound of his voice brought her back. "Do you think this 'spirit guide' persuaded Violet to jump into the water?"

"That's my working theory," Isobel said. "Violet strikes me as a woman who was on the run, but it could very well be my suspicious mind putting a mirror to my own circumstance."

"All a detective has is his, or her, instincts. Most San Franciscans lead a fairly transient life, but this strikes me as odd, too. Violet's accidents coincided with her moves and her sickness along with a sudden aversion to dining with the others at the Y.M.C.A."

Isobel took a thoughtful sip of tea. "The falling stage light is suspicious, but accidents do happen—especially in poorly managed theaters. But why not just brain her over the head in a dark alley?"

"Indeed," Riot agreed. "Mundane murders are near to impossible to solve."

"I'd wager they're usually spur of the moment impulses."

"Or a hired gun." This wasn't a man who was speaking of the hypothetical, but from experience.

Isobel took another sip of tea, studying the man across the table. A hundred questions churned inside her head, all wanting to come out in a snap-fire rush. A distraction, indeed.

Isobel roped in her thoughts. "I think we can rule out hired killer in Violet's case," she said wryly. "If one was involved, then I'd suggest he find another line of work."

"Hired guns aren't noted for their intelligence, but I agree. It could very well have been her own mind," he observed. "As Miss Wheeler said, Violet's accident changed her, and the landlady wasn't sure if the same woman who left was the same who came home. People who kill themselves aren't in their right mind."

"Aren't they?" she countered. "Perhaps some, but I think most are perfectly sound in mind. They're backed into a corner with no escape. It's a final spit in the face of society."

Riot did not reply. His eyes searched her own. There was sadness and understanding and a whole world of hurt. She looked away, focusing on the evidence. "If she wasn't right in the head after her first suicide and subsequent accident, maybe she was hearing voices. Could her head injury have caused her to develop an entirely different way of writing?"

"I wouldn't discount the possibility. Stranger things have occurred."

"Then maybe she was running from herself—her own madness."

"In that case, you may have a short investigation on your hands."

"Either way, I'll follow the trail to its end."

"If you should require anything, Ravenwood Agency is at your disposal—and me for that matter," Riot added, quietly.

Isobel looked at the remains of her dinner, recalling her last words to Riot before she sailed south, standing on a pier, right after he handed over the proof of ownership to the *Pagan Lady.*

'I've been cooped up too long. I need to feel the wind for a bit and get my bearings.'

'Where will you go?' he had asked.

'Wherever the winds take me.'

And that had been that. Except she had only been gone a month. Strange, freedom beckoned, and yet she had returned. Isobel still had misgivings about returning, but there was unfinished business, and she had never liked leaving a game half-played.

And here they were again; sitting in the saloon as if no time at all had passed. The man made her soft.

"Thank you for your offer, but I can handle this myself," she said, firmly, standing up to clear away the tin plates.

"The offer stands, regardless," he said easily.

Isobel didn't trust herself to speak; instead, she occupied herself with filling the washbasin.

"I called on your family."

This brought her up short. And she reckoned that was the intent.

"Oh? How are they?"

"As well as can be expected. I suppose you'd like to hear that life goes on."

"I like to hear the truth."

"Your parents are grieving," he said. "Kingston, at least, seems to be leaving your family's affairs alone."

"And my mother?"

"She still has a sharp tongue."

Isobel snorted. "Then she'll live." She rolled up her sleeves to scrub the pots and tins. "You likely think me cold-hearted, but my parents shipped me off to Europe when I was fifteen. When I returned, four years later, they were like strangers to me."

"Not cold-hearted, but human, yes."

She glanced sideways at him. "Don't you mean resentful?"

"I don't know about that. You seemed to have occupied yourself well enough in Europe." There was a twinkle of mischief in his eyes that made her smile.

"Fair enough," she said.

"May I ask where the winds took you?"

Isobel clucked her tongue. "Not as patient as you like to think."

"It *is* late," he said.

"Tired, Mr. Riot?"

"Not especially. I've been keeping to a nocturnal schedule of late."

She arched a brow. "A case?"

"I asked first," he replied, reaching for the medicinal brandy. He poured two cups; one for himself and one for her.

"When Tim let slip that you were aiming to retire, I didn't believe it for a moment. I was right, I see."

"Just biding my time, more like."

"For what?" she asked.

"Why do you think?"

His eyes seemed to smolder in the swaying light, and she returned her gaze on the pot. "I think you've drunk a fair amount of brandy."

Riot chuckled, a near soundless laugh. "Maybe so."

When the dishes were done, Isobel hung up the towel, and sat on the opposite settee, reaching for her brandy. The amber liquid soothed her senses, and Watson settled himself on her lap. As she sipped and thought, she idly ran her fingers through his soft fur.

Riot spoke first. "That day in the cemetery, you helped me realize that I have unfinished business here. I don't much care for men, or women, who get away with murder and blackmail. I've always been one to poke the rattlesnake's hole."

A laugh escaped her throat. "You? I don't believe it. You're as cautious as they come, Riot."

"Am I?" He tilted his head.

"I don't really know," she admitted. "I haven't yet investigated you."

He smirked. "One day, I'm sure to trip up, and you'll know."

"I hope not."

"So do I."

"I'll have your back, then," she said softly.

"Of that, I have no doubt," he raised his glass, and they both drank.

When she emptied her cup, she said, "I traveled to Los Angeles, to see what I could discover about Kingston's activities. When I was—courting and married," Isobel cleared the sudden dryness from her throat, leaning forward to pour another glass. When she had taken a long swallow, she continued with strength. "Kingston took two trips to Los Angeles. Fairly short ones. I hoped to discover what business he had down there."

"What did you discover?"

"Not a whisper of him."

Riot frowned. "Do you think he misled you about traveling south?"

"I don't know what he did, or where he went," she sighed. "At the very least, it must have been something secretive. He hid his tracks well. Unfortunately, it could have been something as mindless as an affair with another man's wife. Regardless, the dates might lead me down another trail." She frowned in consideration. "I was hoping to discover what Curtis had hinted at—these men in the shadows." Her trip had been a blow. Her one hope, her one lead in trying to find solid proof of her ex-husband's criminal activities—all blown to the winds. It was a defeat that did not set well with her, and admitting it left a sour taste in the back of her throat.

Riot removed his spectacles to clean the glass. His dark lashes brushed the skin beneath his eyes when he blinked, and she wondered if they brushed the glass of his spectacles, too.

"There is a number of powerful men lurking in shadows," he said, rubbing the lens with a pristine handkerchief. "And they're good at staying there, but eventually, one of them will make a mistake."

"I suppose it's just a matter of hoping I'm not the first."

"Patience is a virtue."

"Never been my strong point," she admitted. "That's why I intend to occupy myself with murder and madness."

"Not needlework?"

She glared, and a smile lit his eyes; not the quirk of rueful lips, but a rare curve that showed his white teeth. Two of his teeth were chipped, one upper canine and one lower incisor. "You're a rare soul, Bel," he said with warmth.

The words surprised her, but only for a moment. She recovered and smiled like a cat over the table at her guest. "You might not think so well of me in the morning."

12

A Detective's Lot

Friday, February 16th, 1900

"DO YOU RECOGNIZE ANYONE in this photograph, Miss Taylor?" Isobel asked for the eighth time in the hour. She slid Violet's photo across the table, stopping under the cheery woman's nose.

Miss Taylor smiled at the three people stuck in time. "Why yes, she lives here, doesn't she?" She poked a finger at Violet—or Elizabeth as she was known before. Five of the eight tenants had pegged Violet with their fingers; unfortunately, lodging house life was not the most sociable. Everyone was too busy trying to make his wages.

"I was hoping you could tell me for a certain."

Miss Taylor considered the face again. "I'm not sure," she said slowly, "but she does *look* familiar."

"Do you know her name?"

"I'm afraid not," the woman admitted. "Mornings are so chaotic, what with everyone coming and going. Although I always make a point to share a smile with my neighbors."

"Were you at the house on Wednesday?"

Miss Taylor shook her head. "I work at the phone company as a switchboard operator, from six to six. My off days are Thursdays and Fridays, and I usually spend them reading."

Isobel frowned at the lodger. "Thank you, that will be all."

But Miss Taylor was not about to be dismissed. The woman leant forward, her eyes bright. "Are you a real investigator?"

"Yes." Isobel bit out the word. At the moment she was closer to a criminal on the verge of battering a list of lodgers who knew absolutely nothing.

"The things I hear on the lines. It has always given me a taste for putting my nose where I shouldn't," Miss Taylor confided. Her cheeks were flushed, but Isobel suspected excitement rather than embarrassment. "I've never met a lady detective, or a gentleman, for that matter." Miss Taylor continued to rattle on, apparently listening to conversations all day left her parched for her own.

Isobel mentally crossed this woman's name off her list of interviews, and then stopped. She studied the woman for a moment, came to a decision, and interrupted the current narrative about a lovestruck contortionist. "You know, Miss Taylor, all good detectives require ears in the right places."

Miss Taylor's eyes lit up, and Isobel felt like a pie sitting on the windowsill. The woman snagged on her words and ran.

"I'm that excited, I am," Miss Taylor grabbed her hand and pumped it with vigor. Isobel didn't quite know what to say, feeling as if she had been the one recruited, not the reverse. Was there a rule against that in the detective business? Surely Sherlock Holmes had never been recruited by one of his Irregulars?

An Irregular. Isobel did not know what to do with one. She had never considered establishing a network of informants—she preferred to work alone. What did one do with an Irregular? Isobel tilted her head, studying the switchboard operator. What was an Irregular, but a pawn? She knew what to do with pawns. Having a piece in play, on guard and alert, was better than none at all. Hopefully sacrifice would not be needed.

Isobel deftly extricated her hand from the enthused woman. "I'm afraid I've given out all my calling cards for the day," she lied through her teeth. "Would you happen to —"

"Of course I do," Miss Taylor unbuttoned her handbag, and thrust a paisley calling card decorated with cats under the detective's eyes. Isobel carefully accepted the card, trying not to look at it any longer than necessary. "I am that thrilled, I am. Was one of the people in the photograph murdered? The woman who I thought lives here? I was right, wasn't I?"

"I can't discuss the matter at this time," she replied smoothly. "I require ears and eyes, Miss Taylor, not tongues. I'll be in touch." Isobel gave a slight nod that was returned with an equally cryptic wink. No doubt, the woman's shelves would be filled with all sorts of fanciful material.

Isobel gathered up her things, and walked out of the

dining room. Out of the ten lodgers, she had caught eight. Two recognized Violet, four weren't sure, and two didn't know her at all. And no one had heard strange noises in the night, or so they claimed. All in all, it was a wasted morning.

Isobel found Mrs. Beeton polishing doorknobs on the third floor. She reintroduced herself for the fourth time, explained that she was with the coroner's office (again), and finally coaxed the landlady to open Violet's door.

The room was empty, except for furniture and flowers. Duncan August had taken Violet's earthly belongings into custody. Not that there had been much.

Isobel made a slow revolution as she recited the words in sand. "Violet loves kindness. And she does not always get it in this country." Sorrow, or the last prod of a cruel mind?

Having grown up with nine brothers, Isobel knew that tongues could be wickedly sharp. Whether large, or small, a family could be a battle ground of cruelty and spite. Siblings knew precisely how to cause pain. And Isobel had generally answered taunts with a fist and a kick and a hasty retreat. She'd been a furious scrapper who'd made up for her diminutive age and size with dirty tricks.

As her mind spun in all directions, grasping for thoughts to untangle this knotted puzzle, her eyes landed on the flower vases. Three bouquets burst with violets. She was glad that the wall paper didn't contain more of the purple flowers.

Isobel bent over the freshest bouquet and sniffed. Sweet and calm. Relaxing for a girl who had been plagued with headaches.

She sniffed at the next arrangement of violets. Nothing. Isobel returned to the first, and sniffed again.

The sweetness was gone. She stepped back, looking from one to the next. The petals were in varying stages of decay. Most women discarded the wilting bouquet and replaced it with a fresh one. Why keep all three?

During her two years at a finishing school, Isobel had noticed the puzzling preoccupation her fellow prisoners had had with pressing flowers between pages of books, saving little notes, or treasuring a ribbon that was won at a fair where a young man had spoke to them once.

Foolishness, in her opinion. If Isobel wanted to remember something, she remembered it. Sentimentality was a nuisance. She rubbed a dry, brittle petal, and watched it crumble. Suspicious, she plucked the bouquet out of its nest and tossed the flowers on the desk. The water in the vase was clean, a bit murky, but nothing alarming. She picked up the vase and swirled it around, looking for any hint of something hidden at the bottom. Nothing. For the sake of thoroughness, she slowly emptied the water into a washbasin, and checked again—still nothing. She repeated the process on the remaining two vases but her efforts were unrewarded.

Isobel considered her options. This was not the end of the line. Lotario would indelicately be asking questions at the *Tivoli*. She had yet to call upon the home where Violet worked as a caretaker. There was the Kiralfy Theatre Company and unknown nursing school, but both were likely out of the city. As for tracking down the spiritualist with whom Violet may have consulted—that would be like looking for a cork dropped into the bay.

A dash of pink called to Isobel. She eyed the bit of ribbon wrapped around the stems. All pink. She untied each, and laid them side by side. The fabric was identical. Given the degrees of decay in the violets, all three ribbons had been cut from the same cloth over a two week period.

Isobel smirked, snatched the ribbons, and marched out of the room.

⊹

A yawn cracked Isobel's jaw. As she walked through the early morning fog, she reflected on how soothing Riot's visit had been. They had talked for hours; comfortable in silence, in the lap of waves, and unhurried to fill the gaps between.

This morning, when she had awoken to Watson's plaintive demand for food, she realized that she had drifted off to sleep, probably while talking or listening, and was still dressed in her male garb with the added addition of a blanket.

Despite her dreamy fatigue, the thrill of an investigation had propelled her out of bed. She had needed to catch the lodgers before they left for the day. Coffee, she decided, was the thing for her at the moment.

The city was wide awake, and the newsboys were already hoarse. She exchanged nickel for newspaper, and found an empty chair in a crowded cafe. With coffee ordered, she turned to the morning edition of the *Call*.

A satisfied curve lifted her lips. The words *Mysterious Savior Foils Attack* was on the front page, a small paragraph that continued on page three. A much exaggerated event, but not entirely untrue—simply pieces reassembled from another time. What mattered, were the bits that could be confirmed.

There were plenty of witnesses who saw a woman faint on Market, and as for the ambulance men, Isobel had praised them to heaven, claiming the woman had fled the ambulance out of concern for her reputation. Isobel wagered that Davies and Cook would keep their lips sealed.

Neat and Tidy. Not bad for a first day.

Isobel turned the pages, raised an eyebrow at an advertisement for *Doctor Sanden's Electric Belt and Suspensory for Weak Men*, and scanned the rest of the paper.

Finding no mention of Violet's suicide, Isobel looked to the other tables. When she spotted her prey, she stood, and walked over to the gentleman reading the *Chronicle*. "Excuse me," she smiled, shyly. "I'm so sorry, but might we trade?"

Before the startled man could reply, she wrenched his paper from his hands and replaced it with the *Call*.

The gentleman's mouth worked. Before words emerged, she retreated to the corner with her prize. The *Chronicle* did not mention a woman who wrote her will in the sand either. Apparently, suicides were not news. Such deaths were common place; everyday occurrences of desperate people who were at their wit's end in a city that did not care (unless one managed to kill oneself in an inventive way).

Isobel counted out pennies for her coffee, frowned at her scant remaining funds, and decided a trip to her other job was called for. Streetcars, telegrams, and telephone calls added up—to say nothing of her dock fees.

When the man with whom she had exchanged papers abandoned his table, she tucked the *Chronicle* under her arm and appropriated a biscuit and bacon from his left over plate. Gathering pride around her like a mantle, she raised her chin, and strode out with her breakfast.

✢

The operator pulled back the elevator doors and voices assaulted her senses. Bracing herself, Isobel walked into the newsroom, spotting a feminine form disappearing down an adjoining hallway.

Isobel nearly ran after the glimpse of swishing fabric. It was too early, and she was too tired to cope with the bang and drone of the desks. She hoped Cara Sharpe had not forgotten her.

The Sob Sisters inhabited a room at the end of the hall. When Isobel entered, three women looked up, their gazes shrewd and assessing. Cara was not present.

There were five desks in all, a window that let in sunlight and fresh air, and only three typewriters clacked—a less chaotic beat than the cavernous newsroom. It was bliss.

"I hired on yesterday," Isobel said by way of introduction. "Charlotte Bonnie."

"You're the one who shot down McCormick in five minutes," said a straight-laced woman with a severe chignon.

"Charming fellow," Isobel replied.

The other two women laughed. One, an older woman who looked as though she had seen it all, and the younger, a woman who looked as though she wished she hadn't seen a thing.

The severe woman introduced herself as Sara Rogers. The older woman went by the name of Rose, and the younger by the name of Jo Kelly.

"We don't assign desks since it's rare for all of us to be in the office at once," explained Sara. "If the desks are full, you'll have to wait, or find an empty one in the corral."

"Not a problem." A breeze ruffled the papers on the desk closest to the window. It was empty, so she took it, not minding the disturbance one bit.

"Who hired you?" asked Rose.

"I hired myself."

Kelly snorted. "Have you published already?"

"The Mysterious Savior," Isobel replied.

"So you're H.B. Finn." The older woman made a sound, somewhere between a chuckle and a cackle that had a tinge of madness in it. "Cock and Bull story," she wheezed.

"Got her front page," Kelly pointed out.

"All front page articles are rubbish," Sara said, primly.

The three women grinned, and turned back to their machines.

Isobel searched through the drawers, discovered a supply of paper, and fed a piece into her typewriter, preparing to spin a yarn about the girl who wrote her will in the sand. But the sight of the typists working brought her up short. She watched Sara's fingers fly over the keys for a minute, and then tried to mimic the finger placement. Finishing school had not included any practical lessons that involved earning a wage—unless she counted snagging a wealthy husband. Every tutor and student in attendance would have frowned with disdain at Isobel for abandoning her breathing gold mine.

The keys felt odd beneath her fingers, spread out as they were, but it seemed a more efficient way than her two fingered jabbing technique. Determined, Isobel applied herself to the task.

Sometime later, she surfaced, realizing that two of the women had left. Jo Kelly remained, reading over a manuscript. Isobel frowned down at her watch, and hastened over to the mousy desk editor.

Mr. Griful looked as though he had been trapped in

the curve of his horseshoe-shaped desk all night. The comparison was fitting. The editor represented the luck everyone beseeched to get their story into the papers. Isobel resisted the urge to rub his balding head; instead, she said, "You published my article about the mysterious savior yesterday, under my *nom de plume* H.B. Finn."

"No guarantee for today," he said gruffly, taking her latest story.

"It's an exclusive story. No other newspaper will have it."

With interest, the man squinted at the words, and Isobel left him to it with her breath held. She sunk into the chair at her non-desk, and stared out the window, thoughts flying.

After a time, she became aware of the touch of eyes. Isobel glanced to the only other occupied desk.

Kelly smiled. "You look familiar."

Her heart lurched.

With effort, Isobel kept her voice casual. "Most people do. I was thinking the same about you. Berkeley?"

Kelly shook her head. "Saint Mary's."

One hook detached itself from Isobel's heart. "Maybe at a cathedral, then?"

"I don't think so." Kelly looked thoughtful. "Are you Catholic?"

"Only when I have to be."

Kelly smirked.

"How long have you been with the *Call*?" asked Isobel.

"Six months now. I cover the society news. Who's who and all that fuss."

And there was the hook that remained. Isobel *did* re-member the woman from the dizzying number of social engagements she had attended while investigating

Kingston. Isobel's marriage to Kingston had made a grand appearance in the newspapers, followed by her disappearance and death, but thankfully, the photograph of her was obscure. Still, Kelly was fashionably dressed, and pretty— just the type to mingle at social functions.

Not liking this line of conversation, Isobel deftly knocked it far away. "Say," she leaned in conspiratorially. "Who's Cara Sharpe?"

Kelly's eyes widened a fraction. "You don't know? She's a long time reporter and has the editor's ear. If there is a story, Cara will sniff it out, or drag it out kicking and screaming; better than most out there."

"And you?"

"I do well enough," Kelly shrugged, and reached for a cigarette. "It's a cutthroat business."

"So I'm told," Isobel replied, and changed tack. "Is there an archive in this building?"

"Down in the basement." Kelly's hand shook as she opened a silver match safe. "They keep all the old newspapers, there. It's cold and dark."

Despite the sun and flare of match, Kelly shivered, taking a shaky drag. Whether the blonde, fair-skinned Irish woman disliked the archives in particular, or dark places in general, Isobel could not say, but the fear was there.

"I'll look for it. Thank you." Isobel stood, said her goodbyes, and went to harass the editor.

Mr. Griful handed her five dollars.

"For an exclusive?" she asked, sharply.

"Unsolved, unknown—it's a start, but not an exclusive," he argued, avoiding her gaze.

Isobel wagered she was being short changed. She narrowed her eyes at the mousy man, snatched back her paper, and slapped down her five dollar bill. "I'll take my story to the *Chronicle*, then."

Mr. Griful shuffled papers around his desk. "I'm busy here. I doubt they will want it," he said by way of dismissal.

Isobel marched towards the elevator. Half-way there, Mr. Griful abandoned his bluff, hurrying through the desks to intercept her.

"Miss Bonnie, wait, please." He motioned her to the side, and she arched a brow, waiting. "I'll be generous. How about six dollars?"

"Here is how it's going to play out, Mr. Griful. I will demand fourteen, and you'll offer eight, and so on. But what I really want is ten, so unless you're prepared to pay me what my article is worth, then I'll take my story elsewhere."

"Fine."

"And ten for each additional article." The editor's mouth worked, but one look at her face sealed the deal.

"Ten it is."

13

Madmen and Violets

AN IRON FENCE SURROUNDED the overgrown property. The fence climbed with the hill, until it towered over her head. Beyond its iron, the house where Elizabeth 'Violet' Foster had worked hid in a forest of pine and eucalyptus. But whether the fence was guarding the street or the house, Isobel could not say.

She stopped at the gate. It was locked. Curtains covered the house's grimy windows, and hedges spilled onto the front walkway. Perhaps the old woman who Violet had cared for was a spinster without kin? Still, it seemed strange that no one would step forward to claim, or even sell, a house in San Francisco.

With skirts, jumping the fence during the day would attract attention, so Isobel walked on, circling the block until she found a promising lane that dove down the hill behind homes.

There was a locked gate at the back, too. But the fence was wood instead of iron. Isobel scanned the ground, noticed a scuff mark in the dirt, and tested the nearby board. It was loose.

Removing her hat, she squeezed through the opening. A button caught and popped off her coat, and she cursed under her breath as she fought through the tangle on the other side. Detaching herself from the last bramble, she stepped onto a narrow track.

Birds chirped and leaves rustled. The backyard might have been peaceful if the whole of the place didn't feel as if it were holding its breath—waiting. The windows were like eyes, and their watchfulness pricked her senses.

Cautiously, Isobel approached. Shotguns were an acceptable way to greet trespassers, and despite the neglected appearance, there were scuff marks on the path that led to the grocer's door.

Sparing a glance at the windows, Isobel crouched, studying the marks in the dirt. Unfortunately, the ground was hard and she was no tracker—not like in the stories at any rate, and while she had been on the look out for an authentic Indian Scout her entire life, she had not found any willing to teach her. Of the marks she could make out: one was a large boot with a long stride; the other a smaller foot, possibly a child's; and the third, was most definitely the square impression of a woman's heel.

Isobel stood, dusting off her walking skirt as she scanned the back of the house. With a mental shrug, she marched up to the porch, and pounded her umbrella against the door.

A faint noise, like scurrying rats, sounded beneath her feet. She squinted through a crack between boards, into the shadows underneath. But all was quiet in the echo of her demand. She knocked a second time, and then, on a whim, tried the door knob. It was locked. A newer mechanism by the look of it.

Isobel stepped off the porch and squinted at the upper-story windows. "So is the house deserted or have the owners gone on holiday?" she asked the lurker under the porch.

No answer.

"A dare, was it? Were you the only one with the courage to enter, or do you always play here? I won't tell anyone."

Her query was answered by a shushing noise. There was fear in that sound, and it was no child's voice. She gripped her umbrella and took a cautious step back.

"Best not to wake the dead," a masculine voice whispered.

"Show yourself," she demanded sharply.

"You're trespassing."

Isobel took a calculated guess. "And you're not?"

The caution in the voice put her on edge. She glanced up at the windows. Threat hung in the air. She expected to see the wrong end of a revolver. But nothing moved in the windows. Isobel shook off the sensation, and took a step closer.

"Do you have claim on this house?" asked the voice.

"I have questions is all. Looking to purchase it."

The man snorted. "Some places are best left alone— better burned than bought."

"You're living here," she pointed out.

"Of like form, we are. Better burned most say."

"Who are you?" Isobel asked, peering into darkness.

Shadows moved under the porch. A vague impression

of rags formed in Isobel's mind. When no name was given, she tried again, "Does anyone live here?"

"Live." A raspy chuckle grated across her eardrums. "Live is a curious word. You can go your whole life without living. Breathing—yes. On and off." The voice changed positions with every answer.

"How often do people come and go?"

More shuffling, but no reply. The man either did not know, or he did not want to say.

"Did you know the old woman who used to live here?"

"She was murdered. Done in."

"What happened?"

"I don't know."

"How do you know she was murdered, then?"

"Creaks and groans—the house talks."

Isobel tried not to appear dubious. "Does the house say anything about the older woman's caretaker—a young woman named Elizabeth?"

"Dead."

A chill zipped up Isobel's spine. She had a strange sensation of talking to the house itself. "Who are you?" she pressed.

"Trouble and misery."

"Trouble *and* misery—are there two porch dwellers under there?"

The voice chortled. "There are many porch dwellers, as you say."

"And have any of them seen someone coming and going?"

Again, silence. Isobel bit her tongue, resisting the urge to fire off another question. She remembered Riot's use of silence, of waiting, seeming as if he could wait until the end of time.

A full minute passed before she was rewarded for her grudging patience. "A man and woman comes and goes. The house whispers."

"Recently?"

"Time flies under the porch," the voice murmured. "Players in a play, ghosts in the night, trouble and misery."

The words were distant, fading. Whatever window of sanity the porch dweller possessed had closed.

"Best leave now. Quick, the house has ears," the voice urged. The shadow scurried away.

Isobel considered chasing the vagrant out of his hole, but dragging a deranged porch-dweller into the light of day was likely to warrant screams instead of useful information. Aside from that minor sticking point, something in his voice had worked its way beneath her skin.

With a backward glance at the watching house, she squeezed through the fence slat, replaced the board, and shook the unease from her mind. Walking briskly, she made for the city offices to make inquires about the forlorn house.

✢

Sunlight streamed through leaves, touching the ground with a gentleness that caressed the earth. Isobel stopped on the pathway and inhaled, savoring the sharp pine and soothing eucalyptus. This ground was alive. So unlike the tangle of vegetation trying to bring down the abandoned house. Isobel could think of it in no other way. Her fictional hero, Sherlock Holmes would have scoffed and called her fanciful, but she could not shake the wrongness of the place.

The park helped. Thousands strolled through Golden

Gate Park everyday. It was spacious and the pathways twisted through miles of cultivated wildness. Unhurried couples walked arm in arm, and mothers let their children run free. Laughter tickled her ears. She watched a group of children, garbed in white dresses and dapper knee breeches, playing Blind Man's Bluff, and wondered if she had ever played so civilly. Unlikely.

Isobel's feet took her to the music concourse. The crowds were denser here, and a forest had replaced the metal tower in the center of the oval. It was a far cry from the electric lights and dazzle of the International Exposition six years ago. One of the last times Isobel had ventured into San Francisco before being shipped off to Europe in disgrace. A quiet cover up for her uncivilized ways.

She stopped at each flower vendor along the paths, and finally, in front of the great stone amphitheater, a cloud of purple caught her eye, luring her closer like a fish on a hook. The flower seller smiled at her from beneath a broad straw hat. She wore spectacles that sat on a red nose. A sure sign of a horticulturist: sensitive to the flowers she loved.

"Sniff that one first, and you'll smell no other," the woman said, blowing her nose. "Violets are thieves. A flirty flower that come and go as they please, taking your nose with them."

Isobel remembered her experience with the violets in the lodging house room. As a child, no matter how many times her mother had told her not to touch a hot stove, she tried again—just to be sure. She put her nose to the bouquet and inhaled anyway. For a moment, she was transported to some dreamy glade. But on the next, the smell was gone. She tried another flower, but the violets were swift thieves.

"Told you," the woman smiled. "That's the wrong flower for you, Miss. Violets are a delicate love."

"What flower suits me best?"

The flower seller surveyed her domain, walking back and forth, inspecting her dainties like a general and her troops.

"These," she pointed to an ivory flower with a center that progressed from blue, nearly purple, to black. Its petals were delicate, multi-layered, and complex. "Anemones."

"And what is their meaning?"

"Fragility."

"I am certainly *not* fragile," Isobel snapped, and then bit her tongue. Berating a potential witness hardly smoothed the way for an interrogation.

The woman's smile never faltered. "It's a windflower, Miss. Sometimes called the Daughter of the Winds."

"Oh," was all Isobel managed. She suddenly felt an overwhelming fondness for the flower.

"Some say they are easily crushed by the wind, but I've noticed that they only bloom where the wind is strongest. They have remarkable staying power, they do. A strong storm will crush them, but not destroy, and the next year, they'll bloom with more beauty. Won't find a rose or a violet blooming in the wind."

Isobel touched the petal, and then the ribbon that bound the stems. She did not know what to say, so she focused on her investigation. "Do you always wrap your flowers with pink ribbon?"

"Lately," the woman confirmed. "I've a bit of curtain that I found at a rummage sell, so I cut it up for spare fabric."

Isobel started to weave a tale, but thought better of it,

sensing that the flower seller was too keen to deceive. "I recognize this ribbon," she said plainly. "From a woman who recently died. She was fond of violets. There were three bouquets in her room; all in various stages of decay, and all three were wrapped with this very same ribbon."

"A young woman, older than yourself, with reddish hair?"

"Yes." Isobel showed the vendor August's card. "I'm with the coroner's office. I'm trying to discover what she did before she died."

"Violet was her name," the woman said.

"Yes, Violet Clowes."

"A shame. Murder, was it?"

"I think so—others don't."

A couple approached, and Isobel stepped aside as the flower seller accepted coins and a greeting, replying with flowers and well wishes.

"What do others say?" the woman asked when the couple was out of ear shot.

"Suicide."

The woman frowned, and shook her head. "Violet was in love, that was for a certain, with a hundred-leaved rose."

"Pardon me?"

"Sincere love," the seller supplied. "But violets and roses aren't suited for each other."

"Does the rose have a name?"

"Mr. Hal. Always as polite as could be."

Isobel produced the photograph from Violet's trunk. The woman nodded at the smiling man. "There they both are." Sadness colored her cheer. "He'll be crushed, you know."

"Do you know where I might find Mr. Hal?"

As the woman considered the question, she fussed over

an arrangement of daisies. Satisfied, she dusted off her apron, and said, "You know, Mr. Hal said something once —about how my flowers were finer than any at the Palace Hotel. I told him that couldn't be true, and he swore, saying his shop didn't have any so fine. He told me he'd put a word in with the shopkeeper. I thanked him, but I said that my flowers love this park, and we get by just fine." Gnarled, twisted fingers stroked a petal with fondness.

"That is a grand place to start," Isobel nodded. "Did you happen to see Violet and Hal on Wednesday?"

The flower seller nodded. "I saw Violet, only she wasn't with Mr. Hal as she usually was in the evening."

"Who was she with?"

"I saw Violet waiting, like she sometimes does for Mr. Hal. Right over there, on the steps. But he never showed. As I was packing up my things for the evening, she walked off down that path, there. I should have talked to her."

"You had no way of knowing. Do you remember the time?"

"It was getting dark. Maybe around six o'clock? I never check the time." She tapped her spectacles. "My eyesight isn't what it used to be, but I've still got the greenest thumb in the park."

"Thank you. You've been very helpful." Isobel gave the woman a dollar.

"That's far too much."

"Worth the information you've given me."

Color rose on the woman's cheeks, and she thrust a bouquet of windflowers in Isobel's hands. She started to refuse, but there was a proud tilt to the woman's shoulders.

Isobel accepted the flowers, and buried her nose in the bouquet. Fragile and wild. She smiled, and started to leave, but stopped at a sudden thought. "Why isn't a hundred-leaved rose a proper match for a violet?"

"The thorns," the woman replied without hesitation. "They can tear a delicate flower apart."

14

The Mysterious Savior

SUNLIGHT STREAMED THROUGH THE window, bathing a boy's body in warmth. He lay on the floor, his head wedged between two posts, as he kicked his feet lazily in the air.

Atticus Riot closed his door softly and stepped over to the railing. Far below, prisms cast by the stained-glass window danced on the foyer floor.

"Are you stuck again, Tobias?"

The boy jerked in surprised, catching his ears on the rails. He twisted around and looked up. A wide grin split the young face.

"No, sir. This slat is a bit wider than the rest." This time, Tobias moved with care, easing his head from between the rails.

"It appears so," agreed Riot "Remember that you're

still growing." Next month, Tobias would be stuck again. He rested a light hand on the head of tight curls before moving towards the stairs.

Footsteps hurried after the detective.

"It's nearly noon, sir."

"Indeed."

"You gonna need me and Grimm today?"

"I do not know," he said truthfully.

"Did you catch the murderer?"

Riot glanced down at the boy. "How do you know I was after a murderer and not a thief?"

"Because Ma says that you run yourself ragged when it's important, and I figure," the last word was punctuated by a hop from stair to stair, "that you don't seem all that concerned with money, so it must be a scoundrel."

"You must get your eyes from your mother."

"Don't remember my father. Can't say," said the boy. "How do you know?"

"You're as perceptive as she."

"What does that mean?"

"It means," said a woman who stepped from kitchen to hallway, "that you are too nosey for your own good, Tobias White. Leave that poor man alone and get to your chores." She gave her son a swat to urge him on his way.

"Morning, Miss Lily."

"You look well rested, sir," she returned. "I've kept your breakfast warm. Would you like to dine on the patio or in the servant's dining room?"

Riot shared an amused glance with the woman. Miss Lily was more landlady than servant; yet, she insisted on calling the cheery round table by its proper name.

It had been over a month since Riot returned to San Francisco, and he still couldn't bring himself to enter the formal dining room where the other lodgers generally ate. Miss Lily, to her credit, had never asked why he avoided the room, but always welcomed him at her family's table. The arrangement suited Riot. He might legally own the house, but Miss Lily ran it, and ran it well.

Today, he indicated his preference for the terrace. Sun baked the bricks, and he took a seat in a cool breeze, appreciating the garden, the blue sky, and the song of birds. The chair across, however, was empty, and his thoughts drifted in the direction of his heart.

The clink of silver brought him back. Miss Lily set down the tray and poured his customary tea. There was enough food on that tray for four large men. "There is no need to go to all that trouble for me, Miss Lily."

"So you've said." She added his customary drop of milk, and laid out three newspapers: the *Bulletin*, *Call* and *Chronicle*. "News travels quickly in my community," Miss Lily explained.

"You've heard already?" he asked, surprised.

"For something like that, how couldn't I?" She said it with pride. "I've watched you these past two weeks: barely eating, out all night, coming back worn as could be. Not many would go to such lengths for a Negro."

Riot looked at his landlady. Her skin was as rich as coffee and her eyes were all kindness. "I've seen a lot of blood in my day, enough to know it's all red."

Kindness turned to sympathy. "Maybe you've seen too much."

"Probably so," he murmured.

"Can I get you anything else?"

"A word, if you please."

Miss Lily waited, expectedly. Riot turned his cup on the saucer, gathering his thoughts. "I once heard a rumor

—more of a whisper—that there was a network of servants in the Negro community who reported to a collector of sorts. I never was able to pin the rumor down, but I saw the consequences of misplaced information first hand."

"Some rumors are true; others aren't," Miss Lily replied, cryptically. "If any whispers are passed on from this house, they'll say it's a fine, upstanding lodging house with quiet folk."

Riot inclined his head. "You have my gratitude."

Miss Lily shook her head. "None needed. My family lives here."

"And a better home it is for it, but—" Riot hesitated. "I think you should know that my profession is a dangerous one. Trouble has come to this house before."

"Mr. Tim told me the history of this house when I first cleaned the dining room." The woman was not one to beat around a bush.

The words—dragged into the open—stung. It roused another voice, one of memory and pain.

'*You're a sentimental fool,*' rasped Ravenwood. '*I have always said as much.*'

A flash of memory seared the back of his eyeballs, of blood and death and staring eyes. The sun turned cold and his throat went dry, making it difficult to swallow. Riot could not reply. His fingers twitched, wanting to reach for a gun.

"I'm sorry, Mr. Riot. I shouldn't have said anything," she said hastily. "I know your business. And I know trouble. You're not the only one with it. My own may find this house one day."

"In what form?" he managed.

"You'll know him when he comes." Miss Lily left Riot to his breakfast and his thoughts.

Riot did not know where Tim had found Miss Lily, but the old goat was as color-blind and money-blind as they came, and he had a soft spot for people who were down on their luck. Riot had experienced the man's generosity on more than one occasion. Although, at times, Tim's wing was a dubious one.

He edged away from the dark past, and focused on the day's tragedies. The words *Mysterious Savior Foils Attack* caught his eye.

'As scores of busy travelers walked obliviously past, a harried, panicked scream was thrown from a narrow lane. Fate found the ears of an attentive listener. Without hesitation, a gallant, unknown gentleman dashed down the alleyway. At the end of the lane, a woman, having lost her way, was cornered by three villainous scoundrels. Dark-haired and well-dressed as he was, the hoodlums thought the gentleman easy prey. The three men met the would-be-rescuer with cudgels and sharp blades. With nary a concern for his own skin, the stranger rushed into the fray, distracting the men long enough for the woman to flee. Near to fainting, she ran, breathless and dizzy with the sounds of a scuffle thundering in her ears.

What happened in that alley, she could not say. But soon, she related, footsteps became apparent, and when, in a fright, she glanced behind, the dashing stranger was there. 'He was,' the woman said with a blush, 'possessed of raven hair, strong jaw, and a straight nose that would inspire artists.'

Eye-witnesses claim that the young woman swooned on the sidewalk of Market. The gentleman easily scooped her up in strong arms and carried her into Brown's Steamship Company where he laid her gently upon the lobby couch, proclaiming himself a physician. With fair and deft hands, her rescuer unbuttoned her high collar. The young woman's bosom heaved with shaky fear…'

Atticus Riot tilted his head at the preceding, and in-creasingly engaging, paragraphs. But soon the outlandish narrative was interrupted by a feeling of watchfulness. He tore his eyes from the page, and lowered the paper a fraction.

A full-figured woman in a white tea gown sat across the table. Her hat was tilted at a stylish angle and the sun caught her auburn hair. Riot hastily folded his paper and made to rise.

"No need to get up, Mr. Riot," she said. "You were absorbed."

"Apparently so," he said, offering a half-bow before sitting. "My apologies, Miss Dupree."

"It's a lovely day. I hope you don't mind if I join you for breakfast."

"Not at all," he said easily.

Miss Dupree kept nocturnal hours. She was a late riser, and, in the month since his return, they had shared more than one breakfast together. Her eyes flickered to the article on page three. Sumptuous lips curved. "Captivating read," she said.

"Indeed," Riot agreed. Hers were not the only set of eyes. Riot was aware of a rustle in the hedge: Tobias, footpad in training. Unfortunately, the boy's ears were already keen.

"You wouldn't happen to be the dark-haired stranger with 'fair and deft hands'?" There was subtle suggestion and smooth flirtation underlying her words.

"It says here that he is a physician," Riot pointed out.

"True," she said, stirring cream and sugar into her coffee. She did not sound convinced. And neither was he. The article had Bel's mischievousness all over it.

"Still," Miss Dupree continued, "You came to mind when I read it."

"Now why would you think this article involved me?"

"You have a certain tilt to your shoulders. And," she added suggestively, "you appear well rested." Miss Dupree knew men. Gauging a man's mood, temperament, and eagerness was a matter of life and death in her line of work.

"A solved case," he replied.

"My congratulations."

Riot regarded the woman. She was attractive, poised, confident, and experienced. Not for the first time, he wondered why she lodged in Ravenwood house. A woman such as she could wrap a wealthy man around her finger twice over. As a mistress, she could have a house of her own; instead, she sufficed with a single room—the largest to be sure, but still a room. Did she lodge here for protection, loneliness, or something more?

"Thank you," he inclined his head. "I very nearly feel like celebrating. Are you free tonight, Miss Dupree?"

"For a man who *very nearly* wants to celebrate? Never. But for a man who would like to celebrate, I would be delighted to join you." Her voice was a deep slow purr.

"Dinner and the theatre?"

"That would be lovely. I enjoyed our last evening out. You make for a most agreeable escort."

"As do you."

"Shall I keep the entire evening free?"

"The performance is only two hours."

"And the night is long," she smiled.

"Indeed it is." Riot folded his napkin, stood, and slipped on his fedora. As he reached for his stick, she eyed the long length of it. He smoothly touched the brim of his hat, tucked the *Call* under an arm, and strolled away, feeling a lingering gaze on his back.

At the end of the driveway, Tobias made a mad dash,

running to catch up. Riot stopped, and turned, frowning at the boy.

"Don't you want Grimm to get the hack, sir?"

"Tobias, your brother is not my personal hackman."

"But he likes it."

"Does he?"

"Yes, sir."

"Well I *like* to walk."

Tobias' shoulders slumped.

"And," Riot added, "your mother has plenty of other chores that need doing."

The boy kicked the dirt and Riot took pity on him. "I'll need the hack tonight."

"Yes, sir, I'll let Grimm know."

"Until then," Riot said, firmly, "get back to the house before your mother catches you out here."

Tobias blew out a breath, turned, and dragged his feet up the long drive.

15

Another Unlucky Soul

AS RIOT WALKED INTO Ravenwood offices, he gave a slight shake of his head at the raven-shaped plaque on the door. Tim, it appeared, had already polished it for the day. It was a small office. Desks in the main room, a consultation room off to the side, and on the other, Riot's own office.

Montgomery Johnson leaned in his chair, boots propped on the desk. He had a long mustache and mutton chops and a cigar stuck between his lips. "Afternoon, Riot," the detective drawled with a puff of smoke. "Did you have a nice beauty rest?"

"I slept well, thank you," he replied. "How is the Pacific Street case progressing?"

Johnson shrugged his broad shoulders. "I've been up working since the crack of dawn, unlike you. Tim's been waiting. You've a client."

Riot glanced at the consultation room, and went in the opposite direction. Tim could never say no to anyone. But then Riot wasn't much better.

He hung up his hat, slipped his stick into the stand, and paused, glancing towards the massive desk. For a moment, he saw Zephaniah Ravenwood sitting in his customary place. It was the man's desk, brought from the house after his death. The man was tall and solid, as expressionless as a crag with a crown of snowy hair and eyebrows that rivaled an owl's. In life, Ravenwood was legendary, and in death he lingered. Riot could not shake his presence.

The memory frowned across the expanse of wood. *'Don't look so dull, Riot.'*

"I'm not one for paperwork," he murmured. Whether it was to himself or the shade, he did not care to answer.

'Paperwork is a detective's reward.'

Riot chuckled. "Is that why you always shoved it onto me?"

'Whether with lawyers, judges, or women, you have a way with words.'

"Curse my smooth tongue," he smirked and sat down in the opposite chair, reaching over to turn a stack of papers around: the evidence and testimony for the Cottrill case.

'If you like,' Ravenwood steepled his fingers. *'However, I always found you useful. I freely admit, my one failing was tact.'*

"Only one?"

A bushy white eyebrow arched. *'Name a second,'* the memory challenged.

"Impossible to only name one."

Ravenwood harrumphed. His dark eyes flashed.

"I have one knack, and you have one fault. It was a fair

trade."

'*The true mark of a partnership.*'

Riot rubbed the scar beneath his hair. "You know I can't remember," he whispered. "Not all of what happened that day."

'*I'm a patient man.*'

At this, he snorted. "Then you're also delusional. You were never patient."

'*When it mattered, I was.*'

"And when was that?"

'*With you, my dear boy.*'

A worried voice interrupted Riot's conversation. "A.J., are you alright?"

Riot blinked, and the shade vanished. He realized he had been talking to air. He swiveled around in his chair to find Tim standing absolutely still. The only time Tim stood still was when there was murder in the air, and apparently, when he was questioning his young friend's mental state.

"Tired, I suppose." Riot smoothed his hair, and gestured towards the vacant chair. "I've always thought this desk was pretentious."

"Would you like a dainty tea table instead?"

"Only if you embroider me a lace tablecloth."

"Done," said Tim.

Riot didn't bother asking whether his wizened friend could knit lace tablecloths. Tim was an old miner who took self-sufficiency personal.

"What unlucky soul do you have for me today?" asked Riot.

Tim removed his short cob pipe and poked at the bowl. "A man in his late twenties. I thought it best if you handled this one."

"That bad?"

"Curious, more like." Which translated to difficult, hysterical, or dangerous. In the general run of things, all three.

✛

Bert Dunham stood by the window looking down on a moving world. Two days ago, his world had stopped. Time was caught in a mire, and the weight of the earth pressed on his broad shoulders—the man could barely find air.

The dazed man was in his late-twenties, trimmed hair, a drooping mustache with two days of unshaven beard. He held a stetson in his large hands, turning it, feeling the rim, and ultimately ruining the lay of the hat. Straight-backed and rigid, Bert looked like a scared animal about to bolt, but Riot could not say where his client-to-be planned to go —only away.

"Mr. Dunham," the detective said. "Atticus Riot."

Bert turned towards the detectives, his gaze slow to focus, and slower to react to Riot's outstretched hand. When Bert moved, Riot shook his hand firmly, and tightened his grip for a moment, offering the man an anchor to the present.

The gesture helped. Some life entered the handshake.

"Sit if you like, Mr. Dunham." Riot indicated a chair and pulled out one for himself. Tim edged towards the wall. "How can I help you?"

"My wife—" Bert's throat caught, like there were words that just didn't want coming out. It took the younger man a bit to work his way past the lump. "My wife is dead. She killed herself—so the police say."

Most would have asked, 'But you don't think she did?' Riot, however, was not most. He sat and waited, and let the silence stretch, hoping the man would find his own way. And as Riot patiently waited, he studied his client: tanned skin, broad shoulders, a faint smell of copper on his rough clothes, sure fingers, and nicks and cuts that slashed over callouses on his hands. Riot fancied he could see the touch of death upon the man, like a stain on his skin, as sure as the sun had colored his neck red.

"I came home from work—" Bert's voice trembled, and Riot intervened, offering a distraction.

"You work with electrical wiring," he noted.

Bert blinked. "Yes, an apprentice." His eyes flickered to Tim who slouched in the corner trying to blend into the paneling. "I don't think I mentioned that to your associate."

"You didn't," Riot confirmed.

Despite his grief, Bert had a head on his shoulders. A good sign, that. The detective did not explain how he knew: the callouses and cuts and coppery smell, all indicative and common to electricians. Strength was needed, too, and a fair amount of intelligence.

In another life, Atticus Riot had been a cunning gambler and a swift shot. During his gambling days, he looked for an opponent's tell and counted cards, all in a flash that lacked conscious thought. Those same talents made him a fair detective.

"That would put your wife's death on the fourteenth, on Wednesday. What happened that day?"

Knocked from his grief, and reminded of his trade, Bert found his voice. "I came home from my work in the evening. It'd been a short day. The house smelled wrong, acrid and sweet all at once. I found my wife in the bathroom. It was like she'd been sick all over, but her mouth was—" Bert choked, as if he would be sick, and the next word came out as a thready whisper. "Burnt."

Riot was on the verge of pouring a fortifying drink, but the young man pulled out his own flask and took a desperate swig. Bert did not describe the next futile moments of trying, and failing, to revive his wife, or mention the anguish. It was like falling. And Riot knew that sensation well.

Instead, Bert skipped to the facts: steady, reliable, controllable.

"There was a bottle of carbolic acid on the kitchen floor. Elma was always so worried about the nicks I got that she kept a bottle on hand. She was a trained nurse, you see. Knew how to dilute it and such..." Bert trailed off, staring at his hands like a pair of murder weapons.

Before guilt drowned the young man, Riot caught his attention. "Did your Elma leave a note?"

The young man reached into his pocket and retrieved a much handled piece of paper. It had been ripped from a notebook. Riot unfolded it with reverence. The words were startlingly familiar, one he had glimpsed the night before.

'Dear Bert, I am not guilty. God knows it. Goodbye. -Elma'

This note, however, was written in a staggered, clearly shaking hand.

When Riot looked up, the young man broke down, and words rushed from his lips, each one chipping away at his composure. "It don't make no sense. Elma and me got up early, to go shopping before my shift. She was in high spirits. We were expecting our first child—the police said it was hysterics. Women issues. They won't look further into her death." The last thread of his control broke, and the man's grief filled the room.

Riot hastened over to a sideboard and poured a cool glass of water from the pitcher. When he returned, Bert drank gratefully.

"I'm sorry," Bert said, wiping his nose with a handkerchief. The initials B.D. had been carefully stitched into the fabric with a little border of flowers.

"Is this your wife's handwriting, Mr. Dunham?" asked Riot.

"It's shaky, but it appears so."

"Do you know where the paper was taken from?"

"Ripped out of her journal," the man replied. "There's a page missing."

"You read her journal?"

Bert nodded, looking abash. "I thought maybe it'd say more—explain what she thought she'd done, but it didn't. Elma was excited, she was happy with me."

"Does she have family?"

"A brother, Henry Erving, he lives here in the city."

"Does he have any idea what this note might mean? Something from Elma's past maybe?"

"Truth be told, I forgot all about him." Bert rubbed his head. It was hard to think behind a veil of grief and a medicinal flask. "I've only met him once. Elma and me married three months ago. We met at the County Hospital where she was working. She treated me for a gash. It was like getting hit by an electrical jolt. There's no ignoring that. We were married a week a later," Bert admitted with a blush.

"Did she have friends, or visitors?"

"Maybe at the hospital? I don't really know. She quit nursing without a second thought. Like I said, we were— getting to know each other. But my landlady, Mrs. Fleet, said that just before noon, a woman by the name of Violet called."

The detail pricked at the scar on Riot's scalp. His fingers twitched, wanting his walking stick, or more aptly, his pistol. Danger took him that way, but he had long ago schooled his reactions. To all outward appearances, however, he was as cool as the glass in the young man's hand.

"What did this woman look like?"

"Mrs. Fleet said she was very pretty, tallish and pale, with reddish hair."

"Was she wearing a grey dress?" Riot asked carefully.

Bert met his gaze, looking puzzled and surprised. "Yes, Mrs. Fleet said she wore a grey dress with purplish trim."

Tim stirred in the corner, and Riot could feel the questions wanting to boil over from the old man's tongue. But Tim was too professional to grill him in front of a client.

"Mr. Riot," Bert steeled himself. "I'd like you to find out why my wife drank that poison."

"I'll accept your case, but I must warn you, Mr. Dunham, you may not like the answer."

"I *have* to know."

✢

"Where do you want to start on this?" Tim tossed the addresses and pertinent information they had gleaned on the desk.

Riot glanced at the list of names. "I'll search the house and locate the absent brother. See if you can interview the neighbors, or get Smith to do it if you like. And ring the city morgue. I'd like a postmortem done. Request a Mr. Duncan August."

"I'm going to need more than that, or a whole lot of graft; the morgue won't do a postmortem on a clear suicide."

"Inform the coroner that it's related to Violet Clowes."

"To who?"

"How's Johnson really coming along with the Pacific Street case?"

"Vague as can be, but by his smirk this morning, I reckon he's at least making progress."

Riot nodded, but Tim wasn't about to be thrown off track.

"Does this mysterious Violet have anything to do with why you were gone all night?"

Riot came clean. "Bel's returned."

Tim's white brows shot up, and his beard nearly twitched with excitement. "Did you hire the girl, then?"

"Bel's hardly a girl," he said dryly. "And I don't intend to hire her."

Tim looked up at Riot. "She's a damn fine investigator."

"I don't think she'd accept my offer."

"Why the devil not?"

"It's complicated," Riot replied calmly.

"You're yella'."

"Maybe so," Riot admitted, "but I won't be the one to ask."

"As a full partner, I will. The agency needs fresh blood to replace the old cranky man who's threatening to retire at the drop of a hat."

Riot glanced at his reflection in a wall mirror. He grimaced at the grey in his beard and the white stripe in his hair. He thought of Isobel—vibrant, full of life and possibility, and he felt his full forty some years. Then his eyes found his gnomish friend whose white hair had migrated to his chin long ago. It cheered him greatly.

"I suspect Bel prefers to find her own way."

"This isn't some charity case, A.J." Tim plopped down

in the chair behind the desk. It leant him an official, if comical air, considering the small man was nearly lost behind the expanse of wood. "That Miss Bel of yours is a natural investigator. She would have solved Johnson's case days ago."

Riot looked at the man, hard. "She's not *my* Bel."

Tim slapped a hand on the desk. "You just said it all," the old man cackled. "All spitfire and will; I'd tread carefully, too. How'd last night go?"

"None of your business," he replied, primly.

"I noticed a definite spring in your step, but I couldn't account for it, until now." Never mind that Riot had been sitting down when Tim first walked in. A point he nearly voiced, but stilled his tongue—it would likely steer the conversation into uncomfortable waters.

Tim removed a small tool from his pocket and began scraping out his pipe into the wastebasket. "And it *is* my business," the old man murmured, sullenly. "I won't be around forever."

The quiet words seemed louder than a shout. Riot eyed the top of his friend's wrinkled pate with concern, but Tim appeared ornery as ever. "What does your age have to do with Bel and me?"

"Because every detective needs a partner." There was an emphasis on the last word.

"Maybe I'll get a cat," Riot quipped. "Besides, you have plenty of years left in you."

"By whose count?" huffed Tim.

"Your own. You never did learn how to add properly."

"That tongue of yours will get you into trouble, boy."

"Far too late for that."

16

A Woman's Mind

ATTICUS RIOT STOOD IN the upper-story rooms where a hopeful couple had once lived. He was surrounded with touches of life: a framed flower, hand-stitched details on the tablecloth, a souvenir from Sutro Baths—all gone cold. Death lurked under the pleasant facade, and today, Riot's old friend smelt acrid. Sharp bile mingled with blood and an overpowering attempt to scour the smell with lye.

"What time did the woman call on Elma?" Riot asked the landlady.

Mrs. Fleet was a kindly woman, a widow of his own age, with plump cheeks and a sturdy disposition.

"A bit before noon," Mrs. Fleet answered.

"How long did this caller remain?"

Mrs. Fleet sighed. "I'm afraid I don't know. I left, you see. Three times a week, I meet with my knitting circle."

"Were visitors rare?"

"Very," the woman said. "Hardly any at all, aside from the occasional client who hired her for stitch work. She was a lovely girl."

"Were you close?" he asked, gently.

"I wouldn't say close, but we got along amiably. I think it's important to give boarders privacy, especially the newly-wedded, so I let them be as much as possible. Elma was a nurse, that much I know. Used to talk about some of her patients. She worked at Cooper Hospital here in the city."

"Do you know why she quit working as a nurse?"

"It's not proper for a woman to work when she's married," Mrs. Fleet lectured. "Elma may have attended nursing school, but I'm sure it was only until she could secure a husband."

This naturally led into his next line of questioning. "Did Elma seem happy with Mr. Dunham?"

Mrs. Fleet smiled. "Mr. Bert has boarded with me for many years. He's a dear, and she seemed happy with him. I never heard raised voices. Young love, you know."

Riot did not precisely know, but he nodded anyway. And waited. There was an introspective look in the woman's eye. He dared not disturb the forming thought.

"You know, there *was* something—it might not mean anything."

"No detail is inconsequential," Riot reassured.

"Elma was always keen on meeting the postman. Said it was to save me the trip. She'd sit in the bay window and wait. The slightest noises would startle her."

"Did she ever receive letters?"

"I assume so."

"Did you ever see one of the letters?"

"She was quite persistent."

"About Elma's visitor, the woman, what did she say precisely?"

"She asked if Elma was at home, and if she might speak with her. I asked after her name, and she simply said she was an old friend who wanted to surprise her, so I went and called Elma down."

"And was Elma surprised?"

"She seemed puzzled, a bit wary, as if she didn't recognize the visitor. The woman said, 'Don't you remember me? It's Violet.' I showed them into the parlor and offered to fetch tea, but the woman said she wouldn't be long."

"And Elma said nothing?"

"No, nothing at all, so I left them to their business."

What Riot would not give for a nosey landlady. "Can you describe this woman?"

The questions continued, answers returned, until Riot had emptied the poor woman's head of minutiae. The mysterious visitor began to take shape, matching Violet's description: near to six feet tall, fine bones, reddish hair, pale green eyes, a high, stiff collar on a starched blouse, a short grey jacket and a matching walking skirt that brushed the ground. And a beaded handbag.

"And there was her brooch. It had a little flower on it."

"A flower?"

"Yes, carved from the ivory."

✥

Footsteps approached, and then stopped. Riot did not look up. The familiar heel to toe rock and scent of tobacco told him all he needed to know.

"Anything?" asked Tim.

"An eye full," Riot drawled. "Elma's journal details every progressive day and symptom of a woman with child. It's a wonder women let us men anywhere near."

"Don't question divine providence."

"All Elma wrote about, save for the last page, which was ripped out to pen her suicide note, was of her delicate condition." Riot looked up from the page, casting his eye around the bedroom. "She seems a dedicated journalist, but this only starts when she discovered she was with child —a month after Bert and she were married, mind you." Riot gently closed the leather bound book, and set it on the writing desk. "I found two other notable items." He produced a slip of paper. It was a list of banks in the city. All crossed out. "Then there are these, likely left over from her nursing days." Riot flipped open a nursing book and tapped a margin.

Tim peered at the neat notations. "*C.T. 3:00 pm*," he read aloud. His face screwed up in confusion. "A lover?"

"Could be any number of things."

Tim blew out a breath. "Yet another reason to recruit Miss Bel. She could help us decipher the mind of a woman."

"I'm not so sure about that," Riot stated.

"It's about time we hired a lady detective," Tim persisted. "Pinkerton's been employing women since the War. If it weren't for Ravenwood and his damn prejudices, I'd have hired a few over the years."

"Then ask her, Tim. I'm not going to stop you. I just won't be the one to do it," Riot said firmly. He turned to the room. "The clothes in the wardrobe and jewelry aren't what I would expect of a woman who made a nurse's wage. Her husband said she had those things when he married her."

Tim scratched his head, squinting at the list of banks. "I can see a nurse nicking medicine for profit, but why have a list of crossed out banks?"

"That's an excellent question." Riot opened the next booklet, on the treatment and diagnosis of insanity. Symptoms were circled: staring, vacant eyes, headaches, hearing voices, hallucinations, hysterics, absence of menstruation, and the list went on. The words stung. According to the paragraph, Riot should have been locked up years ago.

"The rest of the book is neatly underlined, while these are circled."

Tim squinted at the page. "Maybe Elma was worried about her friend Violet? From what you told me, she was already half-way to the mad house."

"Aren't we all?"

Tim rocked on his heels and looked around the room with the innocence of a child. "Not me, no sir."

"Says here that denial is a main indicator."

"Damned if you do, and damned if you don't."

"Did the neighbors see anything?" asked Riot.

"There's a charming gossip-monger across the way who saw the visitor. Claimed the woman had a limp, and came by a hack."

Riot arched a brow. "I don't suppose this neighborhood spy had a description of the hack?"

Blue eyes narrowed dangerously. "As if I'd tell you. You'll have me scouring every single hack in the city."

Riot waited.

"Yes, the old woman did," Tim sighed. "Enough of a description to maybe find it. There aren't many corpulent hackmen who wear a straw hat."

"Excellent."

"I'll telegram my person in the Union," Tim said,

scratching his beard in thought. "Might take awhile."

"I have a few to send off myself." Riot fished out his silver pocket watch, and consulted the hands. He closed it with a click. "You might find something in here that I missed. See if you can find anything out about that list of banks. I'll stop by the brother's residence today."

"And the county hospital?"

"Tomorrow. I've an engagement tonight."

"With Miss Bel?"

"Leave it, Tim."

The old man gave a low whistle, and changed the subject. "It strikes me as odd that the husband knows so little about his wife. Even with a quick wedding, seems as though three months would be plenty of time to acquaint themselves."

"Young love?"

Tim pinned him with an eye. "I'd wager a burning urge in the loins and the natural consequences."

Riot glanced at the diary. "Two months of vomiting, constant urination, and mad cravings for salted beef, sardines, and licorice—mixed together."

Tim displayed his gold teeth. "I was once holed up with a lady who had a constant craving for wood shavings."

"No wonder the police were so quick to blame Elma's suicide on hysteria," Riot mused.

"But a woman with child doesn't usually crave poison."

"What happened to your lady friend?"

"Tired of me, packed her things, and moved to Oregon. Her son became a lumberjack."

✤

"Fled you say?" Atticus Riot asked the landlady.

Mrs. Irish was as proper as they came, with grey-streaked hair, a high collar, and a cameo brooch at her throat.

"Mr. Hal—that's what I call him—flew out the door, just like that. He's not been back since. It's not like him. I reported him missing on Thursday, but the police said that young men will do that. They've not sent anyone to investigate."

"I hope, in the absence and carelessness of the police, that you will allow me to assist."

Mrs. Irish eyed the black raven on ivory paper. The letters shone, giving the card an official appearance. Ravenwood Agency was known in San Francisco. The woman switched her gaze to the detective's attire, from the top of his hat, to the cut of his suit, and finally, she met his eyes. There was worry in those eyes. "I would be most grateful, but what has brought you here? It says you're a detective."

"I'm afraid I have some ill news for Mr. Erving. His sister is dead."

The woman closed her eyes, briefly. And gave a slight shake. "That's ill news indeed."

"Were you acquainted?"

"I met her twice. A respectable lady."

"So I'm told. Were her visits amiable?"

"Of course, Mr. Hal was happy to see her."

At the landlady's invitation, Riot stepped inside, removing his hat. True, it wasn't uncommon for a man to pick up and leave, not in a transient city like San Francisco, but Mrs. Irish did not strike him as a woman who tolerated a negligent lodger. Riot's instincts were prickling, the same feeling he had whenever a game was about to turn sour.

"Is Mr. Erving your only lodger?"

"He is," she sighed.

"What happened the day he disappeared?"

"Mr. Hal came home from work on Tuesday. He was in a splendid mood. He went upstairs, still whistling, then returned with two theatre tickets—to the *Tivoli* no less. He went back upstairs, the whistling died, and next thing I know, he shot right out the front door."

The landlady showed Riot to a second-story room, a spacious one, with its own private bathroom. The first thing Riot noted was a pair of spectacles sitting on the side table. "Did he wear these for reading?"

"No, not for reading, but for far away things. He never left the house without his spectacles. You can see why I'm worried."

Riot did indeed. He was near to blind without his own. Under the watchful gaze of the landlady, Riot conducted a thorough search of Henry's belongings. The man was tidy, near to meticulous. The bookshelves were full of medical manuals. He questioned the landlady.

"Henry is studying to become a physician, but he ran into hard times, and had to put aside his studies," she replied.

"Where did he attend college?"

"Here in the city, at Cooper Medical College."

"Do you know if he was courting anyone?"

The landlady smiled. "I think so, but I never met her. When he first came to live with me, about a year ago, he was very despondent, but his mood gradually brightened. He seemed to be getting back on his feet."

Judging by the notations in the books, Henry Erving was close to attaining his medical degree. The desk held a journal, leather bound and much abused, but not near as detailed and insightful as Elma's. It was typical of a busy man. Dates, with cryptic references to the day's activities: *V —G.G.* was written at least three times a week, starting a month and a week ago. Precisely the time that Violet Clowes had returned to San Francisco.

Riot flipped further back, until he found what he was looking for: '*V —Y.M.C.A.*' approximately when Violet returned from her job as a caretaker and fell ill.

"No accusation intended, Mrs. Irish, but why did you wait until Thursday to report his absence? Did he make a habit of staying away from his rooms?"

"Only for a night, once or twice a week. I never asked where he went, and he never said." Color rose on her cheeks. Even a proper lady such as herself was not naive to a young man's habits. "When he didn't return Wednesday evening, I began to worry."

November 2nd 1898 caught Riot's eye, the same month Violet had first tried to kill herself. The initial *V* was penned in the journal. Riot stood and walked to the shelves, scanning the books until he spotted a familiar manual on insanity. Tucked in the pages of madness, Riot discovered a photograph. The gentleman was chiseled and handsome and possessed a professional air.

There was no notation on the back.

"Did Mr. Hal ever have any visitors?"

"No, he was a quiet lodger. We got along well. Although," she said, "there was a gentleman who called on Tuesday. He said his name was Garrett, and that he was a friend from work wanting to repay a loan. However, his story didn't add up, because if he was a friend from work, he would have known Mr. Hal wasn't at home. I didn't invite the caller inside."

The landlady had a right to be suspicious, and he

appreciated her cunning mind.

"Did you inform, Mr. Hal?"

"No, I didn't get the chance."

"Do you recognize this man?"

Mrs. Irish looked at the photograph and quickly shook her head, but then she paused, and took the photograph from his hand, studying it carefully. "This man looks very similar to the man who visited, only the fellow Garrett was of a rougher sort. He was a large, broad-shouldered young man with a crooked nose."

Riot tucked the photograph back into the book. "Do you mind if I take Mr. Hal's journal and this book?"

"If you think it will help."

"I do," Riot reassured. "And I'll give the police a firm nudge."

17

The Absent Lodger

ELABORATE PHAETONS ROLLED UNDER twin arches into a grand courtyard. As Isobel walked past, she dusted off her coat, feeling ill at ease in the grandeur of the Palace Hotel. She was loathe to enter the place. The wealth, the finery, the opulence, brought back uncomfortable memories of the long, drawn out role she had assumed to foil Kingston —that of an impulsive socialite. Sharing his bed was of secondary concern. Kingston was not a kind man, he was not a gentle man, but then neither was she; Isobel was a hunter, and the man had never penetrated her mind.

Still, losing grated on her, and failing had been a blow. For all her strength and determination, she had abandoned the game, staged her own death, and ran without an ounce of proof against her blackguard of a husband. All she had to her name was a list of his clients, his associates, a stack of coincidence, and not a single crack at his safe.

Patience, Riot had told her. She needed it in spades. Advice that would have served her well before confronting Kingston with her suspicions. But that was an ongoing catastrophe for another time.

Isobel reined in her thoughts as she walked into the Palace grocer. Parisian labels, cheeses and elaborate breads, Belgian chocolates, and a dizzying array of goods filled the pristine shop. She swept her eye over the crowd, searching for anyone who might have known the late Isobel Kingston. Fortunately, her peers wouldn't spare a first glance in her current guise: a scholarly working girl, come to gawk at the wares.

She located the shopkeeper, a crisp, white-aproned man in his fifties. He promptly greeted her with a perpetual smile. Isobel remembered the man from when she had shopped with Kingston. Small chance that he'd recognize her as the stylish young wife who once hung on the attorney's arm.

"How can I help you, madame?" the shopkeeper asked. He did not blink at her attire, or show her a wit less attentiveness than he had to the woman who threatened the displays with the width of her hat.

"I won't keep you—" she glanced at his name tag, "Mr. Perkins. Do you have an employee by the name of Hal?"

The man considered her question. She nearly marked this lead off; however, when she produced her photograph, recognition lit the shopkeeper's eyes. "That is Mr. Henry Erving. Yes, he works here. Perhaps I can assist if Mr. Erving was helping you with a matter?"

"I need to speak with him."

The man arched a dubious brow.

"I'm with the coroner's office. He may be able to identify a corpse."

The shopkeeper looked startled, and then scanned his shop to make sure her words had not disturbed the primness of his domain.

"I'm afraid he's not in today. I received a telegram on Wednesday saying that he was ill. It's not like him at all. He's been nothing but reliable."

"I see. Do you have his address?"

"I'll check my books."

"And may I see that telegram?"

"I'm afraid I discarded it."

✛

The landlady stood on her doorstep with arms crossed. She did not reach for Isobel's offered card. Instead, she leaned closer, inspecting it like a legal letter. What Isobel wouldn't have given for another Mrs. Beeton.

"This card claims that you're Duncan August," the landlady of Hal's residence stated. "A detective came by earlier."

"A detective?"

"He's looking into the matter."

"What matter is that?"

"It's a matter for the police—not a young woman without a calling card. You should find yourself a good man and start a family." The landlady stepped back, preparing to close her door.

Isobel jammed her umbrella against the wood. "I'm widowed." She did not mention that she was the dead partner.

The landlady was unconvinced. "Unlikely. You're probably with the press. And I'll not have a scandal in my house. Find yourself a respectable profession."

Isobel's hand tightened around her umbrella. Before anger got the better of her, she withdrew the wedge, and the door slammed shut. The resulting squeak of surprise cooled her temper.

A brisk walk doused it completely. She wondered if Riot had ever experienced such obstacles, and contented herself with imagining the landlady's face when she returned in the morning with Duncan August's authority. Still, her errand had not been without benefit.

Henry Erving was missing. Was there some connection with Violet's death? A lover's spat gone wrong? Had he thrown Violet over for another woman, and, in a moment of insanity—what? Violet calmly sat on the beach until the wee hours of the morning, written an obscure message in the sand, and then thrown herself into the sea?

Suicide was either an impulsive act or a carefully planned one. Passion or determination, there was no between. Violet did not strike her as the kind of woman who planned things. A heartbroken woman wouldn't wait for hours on end.

In the fading light, Isobel turned the corner, and strolled around the back of Henry's residence, eyeing the windows. This was not a building like Sapphire House, but a private residence. A well-kept stick-style home, tall and narrow with a square bay window. Like most houses in San Francisco, rooms were let, and boarders often became part of the family—whether they liked it or not. Unfortunately, the windows were as closed-lipped as their owner.

There were any number of ways into the house; however, Isobel was loathe to risk police involvement when she could simply wait until she spoke with Duncan August. Still, patience was not her forte, and what little she possessed was running thin.

Frustrated, she consulted her watch, and stretched her legs, forcing her tired feet to move.

⁜

Isobel knocked on the Sapphire House for the second time in a day. Mrs. Beeton answered the door. The landlady looked at Isobel with suspicion, and no recognition. Without hesitation, she supplied her card.

"Charlotte Bonnie with the coroner's office."

The landlady squinted at the card, scrutinizing it as she had earlier in the day.

"Has Mr. Crouch or Mr. Leeland returned?" Isobel carefully extracted her now tattered looking card from the landlady's hand.

"Mr. Crouch arrived on the first ring of the sixth chime," the landlady replied, shuffling away from the open door.

Isobel took this as an invitation. She stepped inside, and found the magpie polishing a grandfather clock in the hallway. Isobel consulted her own watch, noting that Mrs. Beeton's clock was ten minutes fast, or hers was slow. She frowned, and clicked the little watch shut. Isobel was not the most diligent of clock minders. Mrs. Beeton, however, was winding the grandfather clock with the reverence of a saint and his holy symbol.

"Is Mr. Crouch in his—never mind, I'll find my way."

The house smelled of polish, and doorknobs gleamed in the gaslit hallway. When Isobel reached the room beside Violet's, footsteps strode briskly to meet her. The door jerked open, revealing a gaunt man in his sixties with wild silver hair and thick scowling eyebrows. "How many times have I—" The man stopped mid-growl when he saw his visitor.

Isobel introduced herself with much repeated words, but he ignored her and thrust his head into the hallway, looking right and left. The scent of pipe tobacco clung to his dark suit.

"Is something a matter, Mr. Crouch?" she asked.

"Mrs. Beeton is 'the matter'. She's been in my rooms again." There was a tinge of Scotland left over in the man's voice, and from the way he dropped the end of his words, she placed his birth country in Glasgow.

"That appears to be an irritating habit of hers."

The man looked at Isobel for the first time. He grunted, and stepped back, thrusting a long finger at the inside of his door. The brass knob gleamed.

Isobel tried not to smile.

"It's not amusing, young lady."

"No, I suppose not." Isobel glanced into his room and her breath caught. Books, and more books lined one side of the room. A bushy brow arched, and his grey eyes softened.

"What can I do for you, Miss Bonnie?"

With reluctance, Isobel tore her gaze from his treasure, and produced Violet's photograph. "Do you recognize any of these people?"

Mr. Crouch fumbled with his pocket button, withdrew a monocle, and twisted it into his right eye. He bent over the photograph.

"No," he declared.

"No?"

"No," he repeated.

"This woman," Isobel thrust a finger at Violet, "lived in the room next to yours."

"May she rest in peace, then." He stepped back and started to shut the door.

Isobel stopped its momentum with her foot. "How do you know she's dead if you didn't recognize her?"

"*Lived*," he pronounced pompously. "You said lived, not live—past tense. Grammar, Miss Bonnie, it matters."

"So it does," she said, thoughts flying towards the strange letter. The words brought to mind Riot as he had read its contents. His voice was deep and steady, and she wondered how a whisper in the dark would sound. Mr. Crouch tried to push her foot out of the way, and she quickly slapped her thoughts back on trail.

Isobel smiled pleasantly, undeterred. "Was the woman who shared that wall with you a quiet lodger?"

"My books muffle the noise. There were no screams, no late night gasps, or hysterical sobbing fits if that's what you would like to know." He intended to shock, but his comments only managed to endear.

"No thumping bedposts against the wall?" she added cheekily.

Not even a tinge of red on his sunken cheeks.

"If you will excuse me," he huffed. "My books are more interesting company."

"Reading a Christmas Carol?" Isobel very nearly called him Scrooge, but managed to catch herself before giving in to impulse.

"Dickens was a self-satisfied butcher of prose who treated words like the insufferable lace on a woman's frock."

"And what of people who refer to themselves in the third person?"

This caught the man's attention. "Context," he demanded.

"Your impression, first."

Crouch scowled, but curiosity burned in his eyes. "Separatism from one's self," he snapped out each word. "Either to draw attention to a good trait or distance one from a bad. Diminishing importance, the individual versus a group. Sarcasm, grandeur—since there is no context, choose one." He waved an irritated hand.

Crouch was tall and thin, but his shoulders were hunched with age. Despite his proximity to Violet's room, Isobel could not imagine the aging scholar climbing out a second-story window onto a narrow ledge. Since he was an unlikely suspect, she told him of Violet's message in the sand.

"A woman who thought the world owed her all, no doubt, much like yourself." Crouch was unimpressed.

"And what of this?" Isobel produced the strange letter.

"Do you make a habit of bothering old men in their castles?"

"Only ones who appear to possess half a brain," Isobel returned sharply. "It remains to be seen whether yours is functioning in its entirety." She started to tuck the letter away, but he snatched it from her hand, motioning her impatiently inside his domain.

The room smelled of pipe tobacco and books, and Isobel was reminded of her father. The memory made her heart ache.

Crouch took the paper over to his orderly desk while Isobel swallowed down emotion and focused on his shelves.

"The tightness, narrow spacing, severe slant," he talked quickly, in a disjointed, sporadic manner. "Withdrawn, or meticulous—most definitely intrusive." Crouch pinned her with a glare. "As your hand would likely be."

"You can analyze mine after if you like. My partner

and I deduced as much already." The words left her lips without thought, as words often did.

Before Isobel could mull over her slip, Crouch continued, "The tension bleeds off this paper, doesn't it?" he whispered. "Not one to be talking about forgiveness *at all.* It's as if the writer were holding a knife to the reader's throat, demanding an apology. And here, do you see?"

Isobel peered over his shoulder.

"The slant in the letters lessen, every few sentences, as if the hand forgets who he is."

"Nearly every two sentences," she nodded. Riot had pointed out the same thing.

"If the mention of spirit guides did not clue you in—a madman wrote this."

"A man?" she asked in surprise. Riot had thought it a woman's hand, but she had disagreed. Isobel did not think it was possible to determine gender by a handwriting sample. They had argued the point for a stimulating hour.

Isobel frowned at the words. Every time she looked at the letter from the otherworld, it made her queasy.

"Do you make a study of graphology?" she asked.

"I make a study of words," Crouch grunted. Isobel found herself being corralled towards the doorway. She thanked him for his perceptive opinion, to which Crouch answered with a slammed door on her heels.

When she became a woman of a certain age, Isobel sincerely hoped that she was as ill-tempered as Crouch.

With one final interview remaining on her list of names, she climbed the stairs to the third floor and knocked on the elusive Mr. Leeland's door. No answer. Not even a whisper of noise from within.

Isobel was not keen on returning to Sapphire House. With a determined air, she located Mrs. Beeton, who was fiddling with a flower arrangement.

"Do you happen to know when Mr. Leeland is expected?"

"Why he's home, dear," Mrs. Beeton said.

"Yes, you told me that this morning, but there's no answer at his door. When did Mr. Leeland return?"

Mrs. Beeton repeated his name, searching her flickering brain for recognition. A light brightened in her squinty eyes. "Just before the third chime on Wednesday, at five o'clock in the evening."

"Have you seen him since Wednesday?"

"Wednesday," the landlady repeated. "That's when he arrived. I change the flowers on Monday, polish the silverware on Tuesdays, the brass on Wednesdays, the railings on Thursdays, the knobs on—"

Isobel cut her off. "Mr. Leeland left some papers of mine in his room. Might I fetch them?"

"Of course," the landlady beamed, patting her hand. Isobel followed the woman, hurrying her past the shiny knobs to the desired door.

"Hallo, Miss Bonnie," Miss Taylor greeted in the hallway. The cheerful woman stood in front of her own door, right beside Mr. Leeland's. She winked, and buttoned up her lips with a gesture.

As Mrs. Beeton fumbled with her keyring, Isobel returned the greeting, minus the gestures.

"I don't think Mr. Leeland is home," Miss Taylor said. "Although, he's a very quiet neighbor, it's hard to tell. And Oh, Miss Bonnie, I have a friend who works with me at the phone company. She would be delighted to *meet* you." Another wink.

"Would she?" Isobel asked uneasily.

"Quite," Miss Taylor confirmed. "When you call, ask

for either of us by name. There'll be silence for a bit, but we'll take better care of you than the others. Mrs. Wright is my friend's name."

Isobel barely heard the woman as the landlady tried one key after another. None worked. "May I?" Without waiting for permission, she plucked the keys out of the landlady's hand, and tried herself. None of the keys turned the lock.

"Mrs. Beeton, how many keys do you have on your ring?"

The landlady listed each key and their function in tedious detail. The final total was fifteen keys. There were only fourteen on the keyring.

"You've one missing," Isobel pointed out.

The old woman's eyes widened in outrage. She snatched the keyring from Isobel's hand and began to count; on confirmation, she began to wobble.

"I'll find the thief. I'll evict him. I've done it before. It's a cursed room—I've had nothing but trouble with every tenant who rents this room."

"The last one died," Miss Taylor explained excitedly as she ushered the shaky landlady into her own room.

Isobel frowned at the lock, wishing not for the first time that she knew how to pick one. It was surprisingly difficult to find a willing teacher whom she trusted at her back. Burglars were generally an unsavory sort and trying to get a foot in one of the Locksmith Unions was near to impossible—especially for a woman. As with all trades, they kept their trade secrets close.

Miss Taylor was busy pushing a glass of gin into the pale landlady's hands. The room was a haven of quilted cats, doilies, and porcelain figurines. Isobel shuddered, focusing on the books. As she suspected, every manner of

sensational literature inhabited Miss Taylor's shelf, including a few French novels that raised a brow.

Isobel went straight for the window. A cushy armchair
sat in the light with a stack of books on the little table. She
leaned over the armchair and unlatched the window. To
the right was the fire escape, and to the left, Mr. Leeland's
room. She unpinned her hat, set down handbag and umbrella, and without a thought, climbed out the widow.
Stone reassured her feet. The beauty of long skirts was the
ability to wear whatever footwear she desired. Her rubber-
soled canvas deck shoes were perfect for the stone. She
reached towards a sturdy iron drain pipe. Screeches followed as she edged along the ledge towards the next window. Calloused fingers, from years at sea and climbing,
gripped the uneven brick with ease. A head poked out,
paled, looked down, gasped, and disappeared.

Isobel reached the next window in the time it took for
the two ladies to work up the courage to look out again.
She planted one hand on the sill, and turned herself sideways, balancing on the ledge. She nudged the window
open. It slid easily, soundlessly, a recently oiled mechanism.

Isobel looked inside, and then hopped down, landing
on the soft rug. The room was empty—not just of inhabi-
tants, but of everything save furniture. Before the women
decided to follow, or worse, faint, Isobel hurried across the
room. But the lock turned, and the door opened.

Miss Taylor stood in the doorway looking triumphant.
"We found the keys. They were right out here on this table
behind the flowers."

Isobel frowned, irritated that she had not noticed the
missing keys.

"Not that your window entrance was not impressive,"
Miss Taylor hastened. "Well there's not a thing in here!"

"Are you sure Mr. Leeland didn't give his notice and move out?" Isobel asked.

"No, he did not," the landlady replied, snatching the keys.

"Are you *sure?*" Miss Taylor prodded slowly. "You have misplaced a key once, or twice."

"I've never misplaced a thing." The words possessed the finality of a stomping foot. Miss Taylor daintily cleared her throat, shared a look with Isobel, and shook her head.

Isobel opened the wardrobe, the dresser, searched the neatly made bed, looked under it and rifled through the desk. The mysterious Mr. Leeland had left nothing behind, not even a speck of dust. The room was spotless.

She looked to Miss Taylor. "Did you ever meet Mr. Leeland?"

"Once, briefly. A young man, perhaps thirty-five—very striking. He had the most beautiful pale green eyes. Quiet and well-mannered. He asked after my work."

"Did you ask after his employment?"

Miss Taylor blushed. "He was so attentive and charming that I quite forgot to ask. I took him for a maitre'd or an actor. When I told him where I worked, he was concerned over the long hours, but it's not really as bad as all that. Remember, I have Thursdays and Fridays off, so if you call on one of those days, ask for Alice."

"Did you tell that to Mr. Leeland?"

"Yes, I believe I did."

"I see. And you usually read most of the day—in that armchair?"

Miss Taylor nodded in confirmation, and Isobel produced. the photograph of Elma, Hal, and Violet again. "Did he look anything like this fellow in the photograph?"

"No, no Mr. Leeland was much more striking. Fine-boned. The fellow here is more squarish, don't you think?"

Isobel took one last look at the empty room. "Who cleaned the room after the last tenant?"

"I clean all the rooms," the landlady said proudly.

Miss Taylor leaned in close. "This room is a little *too* clean, if you ask me," she whispered.

Isobel grunted in agreement, catching her meaning. There were any number of explanations for a man skipping town. Most men, however, did not steal a key to assure that his landlady did not enter, and then clean the room before leaving—whenever that might have been. And more importantly, if that had been the case at all. Mrs. Beeton was not the most reliable of witnesses.

18

An Operatic Affair

EVENING DINERS FLOCKED INTO the lobby of the *Call* building, while businessmen fled for safety. The newsroom had not changed. Isobel sought quieter space in the back room.

Jo Kelly sat at one of the desks, studying a stack of photographs and prints, while Cara Sharpe perched on another. The older woman scrutinized Isobel through a haze of smoke. "Productive day," Cara noted.

"I do my best."

"Nice article. Smoke?"

Isobel shed her hat and coat, and gratefully accepted a cigarette. With a flare of sulfur, she touched the spark to the end and sucked on the gasper like a fine wine.

"You have two messages." Kelly held out the telegram missives.

Isobel had a lot of experience with reading letters that

weren't addressed to her, and she knew how a resealed envelope felt. As a child, she had made it a point to open every single piece of delivered mail. Curiosity was an addiction.

As she casually opened the first telegram with a blade, she wondered which of the Sob Sisters had stole a peek. The first was an answer to her inquiry about the talking house. The current owner hailed from New York, a Mansfield Randall. It was a dreadful name, but not familiar. Feeling as though she had discovered a brick wall, she flicked the second open.

NEED TO TALK -R

The telegram said two o'clock. She blew out a breath, jammed her cigarette into the ash tray, and hurried to the telephone, closing herself into the confined space. On a whim, she asked for Mrs. Wright. The connection was short, and within a minute, a taciturn voice crackled over the line.

"Number please."

"This is Miss Bonnie."

Professional curtness blossomed into whispered excitement. "I see Merrily passed on my message."

"Yes."

"There have been three reported murders today, a fire, an opera singer threw a fit at the *Tivoli*, and a French gentleman rang you at the *Call*."

"A French gentleman?"

"So he sounded."

"I don't think the person on the other end took a message," Mrs. Wright confided with disapproval.

"Oh, I see."

"Miss Taylor said you were a detective." Shrewd accusation sounded from the other end.

Isobel quickly diffused it. "I'm working undercover at the *Call*."

"I thought as much," Mrs. Wright sounded impressed.

"Er—the opera singer. Did she have a name?"

"Madame de Winter."

"Can you keep your ears out for any news surrounding the singer?"

"Of course," the woman whispered, and then in a normal tone, "How may I help you?"

"Ravenwood Detective Agency."

There was a long minute of silence. "I'm afraid there is no answer."

Of course not. It was late, and the offices were small, not enough to warrant a night operator. She glanced at the telegram and narrowed her eyes. Lotario could be toying with Riot and her again. "Thank you, Mrs. Wright, I look forward to meeting you." And she did. Her pawns could prove useful—but first, they had to prove trustworthy. Isobel set that thought aside for another time. Right now, what mattered is that they were willing, and far more trustworthy than her fellow Sob Sisters. Despite Isobel's overactive imagination and suspicious nature, she could not, for the life of her, imagine Miss Taylor driving a woman to suicide.

She hung the earpiece on its hook, and looked at Riot's (likely Lotario's) telegram. The message could mean anything: an expression of gratitude, another invitation to dinner, or worse, he had stuck his finely-shaped Roman nose into her investigation. Surely Riot wouldn't—would he? The thought made her seethe.

When Isobel returned, Cara's dark gaze flitted over her. The two women were discussing the layout of a society piece, but from that single glance, the hairs on Isobel's arm raised. She, too, had plenty of practice at switching subjects mid-sentence.

"Any leads on your will in the sand story?" asked Cara.

"It's shaping up. Does the whole newsroom know about it?"

"I saw the proofs for the morning edition. By tomorrow, everyone in the city will know."

Isobel certainly hoped so. When an opponent knew he was being maneuvered into a corner, he usually started making mistakes. Perhaps it would drive a bit of information out into the light of day. That, along with a swarm of reporters.

"A word of advice, Bonnie." Cara took a long drag from her cigarette, and casually crushed the stub. "Even if you uncover the full story, string it along as much as possible. The reading public loves a good story, especially when a pretty young woman is involved."

Isobel looked sharply at the older woman. There had been a minuscule emphasis on her last words. "I'll keep that in mind."

"Some stories will make your career."

"I'm just trying to pay the rent."

Feeling ill at ease with the two reporters, Isobel gathered her things, and fled. She felt exposed, as if Cara Sharpe had already deduced her secrets.

Hunger did not help her shakiness. She walked down to the street, bought a sad looking sandwich from a vendor who was closing, and retreated back inside the *Call* building, riding its lift to the basement level.

The archives felt like an old attic: cold, dark, and musty. The quiet calmed her senses. But there was another presence in the dim light. A tall, solid man with broad shoulders and a cocky black mustache. He was searching through the newspapers. She took him for the archivist.

"Excuse me, where might I find newspapers for January 1899?"

The man appeared surprised, but only for a moment. He hopped to it, showing her the proper drawer. It rattled opened, displaying a row of newspapers hanging on horizontal poles.

"New to the paper?"

"Started this week," she replied, rifling through the dates.

"Typesetting?"

"Reporting."

"A rough business."

"So is the city."

"It is," the man agreed. There was a faint sigh. "Let me know if I can help you with anything else, Miss."

She barely heard the man. He faded back into the archives and she set her eyes to the task, starting with the thirty-first of January. Time stretched and pages of tiny print blurred. She reached up to rub an ache in her neck, when an obituary notice snagged her attention. A notice for Victoria Foster, residing at the very same address where Isobel had slipped through the fence and talked to a man under the porch. Victoria Foster, at the time of her death, was survived by a brother and a granddaughter: Mansfield Randall and Elizabeth Foster.

The house was Violet's, or her Great Uncle's at any rate. Why the devil was Violet jumping from one boarding house to the next?

Isobel walked straight to the lift, and headed for the nearest Western Union.

✛

The voice of an angel flowed past deaf statues, through the door, and finally settled on Isobel's ears. The *Tivoli's* lobby was empty save for attendants ready to rush her to a seat. She passed pond fronds and gilt and showed Madame de Winter's personal calling card to the staircase guard. Surprise flickered over the man's face. She was hardly dressed for a reserved box.

Pulled by Vivaldi's Aria, Isobel followed the man upstairs, and was shown into Madame de Winter's reserved balcony. There were only two guests tonight, one of whom she recognized. She sat in the shadows, and looked to the gas lit stage.

Madame de Winter's voice haunted the air, and the singer's presence demanded the eye. Dressed in a baroque wig and finery, the slim opera diva swayed with her song.

Isobel closed her eyes, appreciating her twin's high, clear, contralto—castrato if anyone had known what lay beneath the satin and lace. But not a true castrato in the physical sense. Lotario could reach heights both vocal and physical.

The voice wrapped around her mind, lifting her heart, and sinking into her breast. Isobel floated, somewhere far away from the mesmerized audience. It was like the wind and the sea, and for a moment, her mind stilled.

Applause shattered the peace, a battering against her eardrums that reminded her to breathe. Isobel snapped open her eyes, recalling why she had come. A two-fold errand. Duncan August was an added sweet on the pile.

Belatedly, she stood with the audience that had surged to its feet, and leant forward, tapping the coroner on the arm. He turned, eyes widening with surprise. And then, quite charmingly, blushed, as if she had caught him with graft or in bed with Madame de Winter. Instead of shouting over the roar of the crowd, she pressed a note into his palm and slipped through the curtains.

The hallway was empty. The applauding audience was aiming for an encore. Lucie would likely give them two; she could never resist the spotlight.

Farther down the hallway, voices pierced the drone. Two men stood on the grand staircase. Isobel's heart stopped, and her feet faltered. Alex Kingston dominated the deserted lobby, conversing with a small, blondish man with upswept mustaches. Her ex-husband was as solid and severe as ever. She steeled herself against his presence, swallowed down her twinge of fear, and strode down the carpeted stairway without missing a step. Both men were walking up the stairs, deep in quiet conversation.

She kept her hat tilted towards the two, and her ear.

"This isn't Honolulu..." the smaller man said, but before she could hear the next words, the doors erupted, spilling the audience into the corridors. Isobel cursed her twin for denying the crowd an encore.

Isobel felt the large man turn, mid-step on the stair. Eyes touched the back of her neck, and a cold chill trickled down her spine. Fingers twitched for a weapon, but before she could surrender to impulse, her heel touched the flat carpet. She swallowed down an urge to bolt, to race into the safety of the theatre crowd, but she kept an even pace. And then stopped. Her thoughts spun, her legs disappeared, and she was vaguely aware of staring like a simpleton.

Atticus Riot escorted a woman through the crowd. Silk left the woman's shoulders bare, clinging to an ample bosom. A diamond was nestled tenderly in its valley. His lady was shapely and lush and she hung on his arm so closely that her breast brushed his elbow. Riot whispered in the woman's ear, and she laughed.

Slyly, his keen brown eyes took in the stunned young woman. A flash of surprise, a moment of relief, a twinge of worry, and then his gaze traveled over her shoulder. Without misstep, Riot maneuvered his stunning companion around the frumpily dressed statue, and greeted the man on Isobel's heels.

"Kingston, it's good to see you again."

There was familiarity in the words, more than a business transaction. A small, curious part of Isobel nearly stayed to listen, but the largest part, now angry and berating herself, urged her to flee. She listened wholeheartedly to the latter, and seized the opportunity to melt into the mingling crowd.

She wove her way towards the backstage access, but a large imperious bouncer in jet held the gate against a tide of reporters. Jo Kelly was in the knot.

Isobel switched directions, letting the crowd sweep her towards the exit. Before she plunged into the night, she stole one last look at Riot and the woman on his arm.

✛

The fog slapped sense into her, and its tendrils soothed her burning skin. Isobel's ears rang. She slipped down a dark side lane, picked her way past the refuse, and rounded the corner to the back of the *Tivoli*. A single gas lamp lit a lone door. She knocked.

A slat in the door slid to the side. She produced Madame de Winter's elaborate card. The eyes behind the door looked right, and then left. The door opened. A large man who was as black as his suit ushered her backstage.

He looked her over with a dubious sweep, but kept his thoughts to himself as he led her through the chaos.

Isobel made no introductions. She didn't have to. Madame de Winter was shrouded in mystery, and the theatre was well used to her varied tastes.

The bouncer knocked on the opera singer's dressing room door.

A chiseled, smooth-faced gentleman answered. He was tall and handsome in a pretty sort of way, with a faint line of kohl tracing his light eyes. Isobel leaned to the left, peering past the man to where her twin sat at a dressing table. Lucie wagged her sculpted eyebrows in the mirror.

"I have a visitor, Walter. Make yourself scarce." Lucie blew him a kiss in the mirror.

A look of longing passed over the man's face. He turned annoyance on Isobel, and brushed past without a word.

Isobel stepped inside, and shut the door, collapsing onto a fainting couch. She tried not to think of what the couch had seen, a simple matter as the lush woman with Riot dominated her thoughts.

She refused to glance at her own reflection, targeting her twin instead. "Did you send a telegram to the *Call* today?" she interrogated.

Lucie pulled off her wig, set it carefully on its stand, and began wiping off the white powdered makeup. With a few practiced swipes, Lotario emerged. He studied Isobel in the mirror.

Instead of answering her question, he asked one of his own, "Have you eaten?"

The question caught her off guard. "A sandwich," she replied distractedly. Never mind that she had taken a single bite. Her sandwich must still be in the archives. Swallowing her sudden hunger, she pressed the issue. "Answer me, Lotario."

"I didn't."

"But you sent one to Riot, yesterday."

Lotario fluttered his long lashes innocently.

"I'm going to kill you, Ari."

Lotario stood. "Until then, help me get out of this lovely thing." Anything to distract her mind. "Did Riot find you?"

"He's here at the theatre," she answered through her teeth. "With a lady. They appeared to be on intimate terms, so would you give up your fanciful romanticism."

"It's not fanciful," he sniffed. "You just need to assert yourself and crush the competition."

"I don't want to," she growled.

"*Clearly.*"

The subject needed to be changed. Isobel snatched at another; one Lotario never tired of discussing—himself. "Who is Walter? Your current lover?" Isobel asked as she worked at the buttons.

"Hopeful, more like. I met him last night." Lotario sighed. "It's agonizing—the not knowing. The guessing."

"And danger," she added.

"Hmm." He shrugged a slim shoulder. "At least the *Narcissus* is safe. There's no guessing there. You do remember how to enter unseen?"

"Of course." She lifted the dress over his head. As she carefully draped it over a chair, Lotario let the bulky undergarments fall, until he stood in bodice, lacy drawers, stockings, and delicate boots. He reached for a silk robe, picked up a basket, and joined her on the divan. The basket was brimming with shiny fruits, decadent chocolates, cheese and crackers, and a bottle of champagne. Lotario knew her well enough not to suggest she eat; instead, he tempted her by popping a chocolate between his painted lips.

Isobel reached for an apple. "Did you discover anything about Violet?"

"After you abandoned me for more thrilling waters, I paid an unannounced visit to the theatre, feigning a sudden foreboding. I had a dream."

"Convenient."

"Naturally," he agreed. "A premonition that tonight's performance would be a disaster. I demanded that the entire theatre rehearse. During the rehearsal, I told them a story I once heard about an unfortunate accident that befell a promising actress, and demanded that they check all of the stage lights." Lotario frowned. "I doubt any of the stagehands slept. But people started talking, of course. One actress remembered the girl, and the accident, and then of course, everyone did. Eager to be noticed, as is the curse of actors everywhere, a friend of Violet's—Lola, came forward, happy to share the tale."

"Nicely managed."

"Of course it was," Lotario waved a hand.

"Did you actually learn anything useful?" Isobel asked around a mouthful of fruit.

Lotario's gaze slid sideways. "Leo wasn't exaggerating. Violet had a promising future. Apparently, the accident occurred at the *Columbia.* I can attempt to insert myself there, but a year in the theatre is a long time; I doubt I'd turn up anything."

"All leads should be explored."

Lotario sighed. Work was not his forte. "Lola said that Violet left rehearsal on Wednesday to meet her gentleman friend at Golden Gate Park. She suspected marriage was in the air, and being a romantic, thinks Violet ran off to elope."

"Without a word?" she asked. "Did Lola say whether Violet enjoyed being an actress?"

"For a woman, it's more lurid to join a theatre than for a man to appear on stage in a corset and garters."

Lotario had a point. Lola might see marriage as a chance to restore a fallen reputation, or secure a rich husband. It took a rare man (usually a fellow actor) to allow his wife on stage.

"At times, I would give anything to switch places with you," Lotario confided. He untied his robe, and stood, studying his profile in the mirror. In corset, drawers, and stockings, he looked, save for his luscious hair, as Isobel would wearing the same: fine cheekbones, sleek muscle, and a lithe physique. Utterly the opposite of the shapely woman on Riot's arm. "But then I think of all the limitations you face in a society that frowns upon a slit instead of a prick."

Isobel took a bite of her apple.

"In the end, when clothes are removed, even with my preferences, I have more freedom than you."

"And that, dear brother," she said, walking over to the costume rack, "is precisely why I've come to raid your dressing room."

"You know," he said sullenly. "You took my favorite trousers yesterday, and I only have so many."

"This is my only wig," she retorted.

"I'll drop off your clothes at the Ferry Building again, but only if you leave the clothes you've taken. Someone is going to start noticing my missing male garments."

"Deal."

"And I'll see what else I have lying around."

Lotario knew she would not accept money from him, but clothing and supplies were another matter. She appreciated the offer.

Isobel began shedding clothes. "What else did you learn?"

"Violet was friendly enough, but she kept to herself—no enemies that I could discover. It's not as if her fellow actors were fighting for her roles. She had a small part in the current production of *Carmen*, but who can say with actors; everyone is trying to claw his way to the top. The incident at the *Columbia* was deemed an unfortunate accident by the police."

"What about the Kiralfy Theatre Company?"

"There is no such company," Lotario stated.

Isobel paused. "None?"

Lotario shook his head. "I checked—thoroughly."

"Where was she for a full year, then?"

"I couldn't think of a discreet way to ask," he admitted.

"Her story will be in the newspapers tomorrow. That might give you an opening."

"I suppose I could think of an excuse to speak with Lola again," he sighed. "The newspapers have their uses." It was said with distaste. The elusive Madame de Winter was a popular target.

"So they do. I wrote the article," she very nearly preened. Instead, she transferred needed items from her handbag to pilfered coat, and stuffed the rest of her feminine clothing into a sack.

"Vulture." His eyes glittered.

"A girl's got to make a living."

Lotario snatched the sack from her. "You're going about it the wrong way. Whoring pays far better."

"I played the whore for two months as a married woman," she said dryly. "I didn't much care for it."

Sympathy flashed in Lotario's eyes, and she turned away, slapping a battered bowler on her short hair. He eyed the tattered suit she had selected. "What viper's pit are you venturing into now?"

"You'll only worry if I tell you."

"Bel," he hissed. "What if you don't return?"

"Then I'll be dead twice over."

He tried to growl, but it was more huff.

"Don't worry," she said, patting her coat pocket, "I'm armed." She picked up her ambiguous umbrella, and paused, turning to her flustered twin. There was worry in his eyes.

"For the love of God, can't you tell me—just in case?"

Lotario did not like nighttime adventures, or daylight ones for that matter—or much of any excitement that took place outside of a luxurious hotel.

Isobel took pity on her twin brother. She told him. But from the look in his eyes, he was not reassured. Before he could protest, she stepped into the hall, nearly running into a group of tipsy socialites.

"Pardon me, ladies." Isobel tipped her hat, and quickened her pace, seeking the cool, concealing mist of the night.

19

The House

THE PROBLEM WITH BREAKING into an abandoned house was the creeping worry that it was not empty. Isobel shifted on her feet. She stood beside a hedge wall, across the street, watching the silent house where Violet's grandmother had died. Light from its neighbors' homes poured through cracks in the curtains, but the warmth didn't reach the overgrown yard.

When the fog thickened, and the lights in the surrounding homes began to flicker, Isobel detached herself from the hedge and walked down the street. The young person with bowler and umbrella turned the corner, circled the block, and strode down the deserted access lane.

Moving stealthily on rubber-soled shoes, she nudged the loose fence board aside, and slipped into the yard. Isobel crouched in the foliage, listening to the night. A fog horn bellowed, and the leaves rustled with the tell-tale whisper of a passing possum. She relaxed, stowed her bowler and umbrella beside the fence, and moved swiftly to the back porch.

All was quiet. She peered into the deeper shadows, searching for the porch-dweller. If the vagrant hid during the day, then he would likely roam the nights. Just to be sure, she gave a hushed hiss, listening for movement.

There was no answering noise.

Isobel slunk around the side, gripped a window ledge, and pulled herself up, squinting through a break in the curtain. No light; no movement. As her eyes adjusted to the dark, blobs of paleness became apparent—the indistinct outline of covered furniture.

Isobel lowered herself, walked a few feet back, and reached for the cast iron drain pipe. She began to climb. An easy ascent for a girl who had spent her childhood climbing the mast in a heaving sea. In seconds, she reached the second story, and stretched her fingers towards a window sill. The ornate siding gave her toes purchase, and she edged along, until she came to her chosen window.

An unnerving stillness lay beyond the glass. Clinging to the side of the house, Isobel waited, listening to the creaking wood and rustle of leaves far below. She shifted, maintaining balance, and fished out her Tickler, unclasping it with a single hand.

The flat, thin blade slid easily beneath the gap at the bottom of the sash window. With the tip of her blade, she caught the crescent-shaped lock, and nudged it out of the hook. Isobel pocketed the blade, eyeing the disrepair. Wood shrunk in cold weather, which caused windows to rattle in their tracks. Putty fixed the issue, but she doubted anyone had serviced this window in some time.

The low, mournful call of a fog horn sounded in the distance. She opened the window. The rattle shook her nerves. But before the horn's echo died, she slipped inside, and shut the glass.

The room was dismally dark. Blood roared in her ears. Still as a statue, she waited, her mind conjuring lurking enemies. Monstrous shapes emerged from the black. She swallowed fear, and turned the beastly spider back into the table that it was, the floating face into its porcelain mask, and righted the reaching hands to lamps on the wall.

A musty smell crept down her throat. She tasted abandonment; a dry emptiness where nothing was left to rot.

Isobel walked lightly across the room, and pressed her ear to the wood. The house groaned; a soft release, like a breath from pained lungs. Unease chilled her bones.

Despite all her cold logic, Isobel could not deny the feeling. Call it womanly intuition, or a primal sense; this house held secrets.

Isobel brushed the door with her fingers and grasped the handle. The door cracked open. She peered into the hollowness. It smelt of dust. No whispers, or sleeping breaths. Ducking back inside, she unfolded her pocket lantern, and put match to candle.

Dim, reflected light deepened the shadows beyond her little orb of sight. Ready to snuff the candle at a whisper, she stepped into the hallway, and crept towards the back. The house creaked, but not from her footsteps.

A large, canopied bed sat in the master bedroom. Its curtains were drawn. She tried to swallow down her fear, but her throat was filled with dust. She waited, listening to the room. When nothing stirred, she moved forward, nudging the curtains aside. The bedclothes were flat. No sleepers, or decomposing bodies. A fine, even layer of dust covered the quilt.

No one had disturbed this bed in quite some time. Gaining confidence, she moved through the other rooms, conducting a cursory search. All were empty.

Keeping to the side of the stairs, where the wooden slats sat closest to the wall, Isobel snuck down to the first floor. The wood fussed anyway, but its groaning was constant; not enough to alarm any lurkers.

Dusty sheets covered the furniture in both parlors and dining room. She moved into the kitchen. The faint aroma of burnt wood lingered in the air, the counter gleamed, and the water basin was near to glowing in the wick's flame. An overzealous cleaner had been here. Her mind skipped to Mr. Leeland's room.

Isobel shone the lantern over the grocer's door. There was no key. On a whim, she tried the door, but found it locked. With her lantern close to the floor, she retraced her steps to the dining room. She crouched, studying the carpet. The dust was disturbed near a large window. She shone her light over the window. It looked out of place.

Isobel had seen its like before. Running her finger along the base of the wall, she felt for a small groove, and was rewarded with a latch. A jib door, used for moving large objects in and out of the house, specifically coffins.

With a quiet heave, the heavy door slid upwards with ease. Unlocked. She let it slide down, and moved towards another stairwell. Most Queen Anne style homes had a ballroom. Not the fancy, ornate ones of a palace, but a simple wooden room where family and friends might gather and dance.

She descended the steps. A faint smell pricked her senses. Coldness, cleanliness, a lack of dust, and a whisper like a biting day. She hugged the paneled walls to the hollow ballroom, moving along their border like a tense wraith.

In front of a large hearth lounged a spacious divan with a clean pillow and folded blanket. Ashes swirled in the hearth grate. At night, especially in the fog, smoke from a chimney was unlikely to be noticed, and the windows that ran the length of the room were high, but low to the ground outside.

Was this where the porch-dweller spent his nights, or was it, as Isobel suspected, a rendezvous for two lovers: Violet Clowes and Henry Erving?

Isobel tore her gaze from the only signs of life, and walked across the floor on light feet towards an adjoining hallway. The first room was a small cloakroom, the next was storage. Both had keys protruding from their locks.

The hallway curved with the house. She peered into a launder's room with a barren sleeping cot, and then turned the key to the next room. The first thing she registered was the smell: a cool sharpness like a fish on ice. She passed from a small, empty bedroom into the adjoining bath. Sight came next. The lantern's light illuminated a head, neck, and shoulders in a claw-foot tub.

The breath in her lungs fled. And for a moment, she waited, willing the man in the tub to move, to spot her and give a cry of indignation, but there was a wrongness in the air—the head bent too far back. She stepped over the threshold.

All her hopeful imaginings of finding a corpse had not prepared her for the reality. Throwing all the rules of investigation to the winds, she moved forward, her own mind chastising her action as laughable, and placed her fingers on the man's neck, searching for a pulse.

She held up her lantern and looked at the face. There

was no life left in Henry 'Hal' Erving. He wore the mask of death.

A click penetrated her shock. She backtracked, moving into the hallway. The air stirred. Someone was here, in the house. Isobel smothered her light. Moving quickly, she withdrew a key from its lock, palmed it, and darted into the storage room.

She turned the key from the inside, and dropped it into her coat. Air returned to her lungs. Isobel crouched, peeking through the keyhole. Footsteps worked their way around the ballroom. Two pairs, she decided. The hallway lightened, and she moved to the back of the little room, drawing her pistol.

The footsteps clicked past her door.

She crept closer, waiting, straining to hear a whisper of a voice, an exclaim of surprise over the dead man in the tub, some reassuring sound that didn't scream that a murderer had returned to gloat over his victim.

Light erupted in the keyhole, blinding her. Isobel leapt back. The door flew open with a crash. She fired off a shot. The tang of metal and hot air filled her throat. A light blazed, a shotgun cocked, and a man's voice pierced the echo of gunpowder.

"Shoot first and ask later, Bel?"

"That's one way to get the police here," another voice grunted.

Isobel stood in the center of the storage room, blinking away spots.

"Are you going to lower that pistol, or are you planning on shooting at me again?" A tentative head, now hatless, poked around the corner.

She scowled at Riot. "Don't you *ever* announce yourself beforehand?"

"I thought you were in trouble."

"In a storage room?" she snapped, tensing her arm. The head disappeared. "How the devil did you know I was in here?"

Isobel realized she was still pointing a revolver at the open door. She took a breath, eased the hammer down, and lowered her arm. The sound brought Riot into full view.

"It's the only door without a key."

"So you kicked it down?"

"It seemed infinitely logical at the time." He sounded flustered.

"Logic would have shouted a warning."

Riot picked up a handheld box light and directed the beam on the floor. The dark, moist outline of her deck shoes led right to the door. Heat filled her cheeks, and Riot ducked back behind the wall.

Isobel followed him into the hallway. "If I was in trouble there would have been *two* prints, and a whole mess of a fight." She nodded to Tim, who held his shortened shotgun like he still had need of it. A top hat lay on the floor.

"Who the blazes kicks down a door wearing a top hat?"

Given that Riot was still dressed in his formal attire, it was obvious. He did not answer. Isobel started to walk down the hall, realized her lantern was dark, and silently cursed the man and his fancy electric box. She struck a match. "This is my murder investigation, Riot."

"This isn't a game," he said, firmly.

"Life is a game." She closed the reflective case with a snap.

"You keep telling yourself that and one day you'll

believe your own lie."

Isobel stopped at the doorway. "That's my plan."

"It's a piss poor one, Bel."

"Then I'll be left with the piss."

"And a dead man in a bath. I'll leave you to deal with the police." Riot bent to retrieve his hat.

"Is your lady friend here, too?" she asked of the man in evening wear. "I wouldn't want to accidentally shoot her."

Tim edged along the wall like a slow moving statue.

"No, she's not," Riot replied primly. "I dropped the lady off at my harem." He settled his hat at a jaunty angle.

The words gave her pause. Her lip twitched, but the stirrings of humor turned cold when she noticed a hole in his coat. A pit opened in her belly.

"Did I shoot you?" she breathed.

Riot glanced down, surprised. He stuck a finger through the hole. "Only thread deep."

Heat drained from her cheeks. She felt cold as a corpse, and Tim rushed forward, arm out. She batted him away. "I'm not about to faint." The old man hopped back and she took a deep breath. "I apologize, Mr. Tim," she said civilly. "It's been a long day."

"Looks that way," the old man cleared his throat.

"Are you going to ask her, Tim?" Riot inquired.

"Ask me what?"

"Never mind," Tim's gaze bounced between the two. "I'll just be going outside to wait for the police." When neither answered, he bolted.

Isobel looked at Riot, felt a whole jumble of confusion, and decided that the corpse would be easier to deal with. Shoving all the unwanted emotions into a nice tidy box and sealing it with more locks than were decent, she marched into the bathroom.

20

Convergence

A THROAT CLEARED. A warning, before Riot drifted near. The man was not taking chances.

"It's my first corpse," Isobel said by way of apology. She stood at the threshold of the bathroom.

"I tend to trip over them."

Isobel looked at the detective, searching for any sign of humor. There was none. She crouched, lowering her lantern to study the tiles. "Lotario told you I was here," she stated.

"I threatened him on pain of death." And here a hint of humor crept into his deep voice.

"I'm sure my brother suffered greatly."

"I twisted his arm and everything." Riot shone his box light at the gas lamp. "The mantle is intact."

"And the floor is wet as if someone recently scrubbed

it."

"Did you notice any marks when you first entered?"

The flare of a match and scent of gas produced light. The bathroom glowed with the lamp as Riot shook out his flame.

Isobel closed her eyes, dredging up memory. "I don't remember," she admitted. Fear had given her a tunnel-like vision and the corpse had been at its end. "I shouldn't have walked in without checking."

"I checked the man, too." Riot crouched beside her, studying the tiles. "I don't see any other marks."

"I suppose you are a tracker, too?"

"No where near as gifted as the scout who taught me."

Isobel clenched her jaw. The wind was determined to throw Riot on her course. She had not imagined that her Indian scout would be dressed in top hat and tail coat.

"I apologize for treading on your crime scene," he said, softly. "If you'd like me to leave, I will, but I've been wanting to speak with you all day."

Isobel arched a brow in question.

"Bert Dunham hired Ravenwood Agency to discover why his wife Elma killed herself. She drank carbolic acid on Wednesday, right after a woman named Violet visited."

She blinked, mind reeling at the implications. "What are the odds?"

"Given Ravenwood Agency's reputation and lower fees, I'd wager on those odds," he said matter of fact.

"Tell me all—later."

"If you'll return the favor," he bargained.

Isobel offered a hand, and he shook it with an amused glint in his eye. Both detectives turned to the latest unfortunate. As she moved forward, Riot stood, watchful. She took her cue, and began a cursory inspection.

There were no obvious marks from the shoulders up. No bruises, cuts, or contusions. The head arched backwards, as if to rest on the edge of the tub, only the rim was too low, and the neck arched severely back. Isobel carefully parted the cadaver's brown hair, searching his scalp for any signs of trauma. She bent close, sniffing near the lips. Nothing abnormal aside from the sickly stench of death. She peeled back his lips. The jaw was clenched tight and his arms were stiff with rigor mortis. Her gaze traveled down, into the murky water.

"Riot," she said slowly. "I don't suppose we could drain the water?"

"The police will be here soon enough." He adjusted his spectacles, and bent close, peering into the murky bath. "He's wearing a belt of some sort."

Never one to wait, Isobel shrugged out of her coat, thrust it at Riot, and rolled up her sleeve. A protest was on his lips, but before he could vocalize, she plunged her arm beneath the water. It was frigid. Belatedly, she hoped the water was not poisoned. "It's some sort of apparatus, or device," she said, exploring. "Oh."

"What?"

"I think it's one of those electric belts."

Riot stared without comprehension.

"*Doctor Sanden's Electric Belt and Suspensory for Weak Men,*" she explained. "It's suppose to restore lost manhood and potency. There's an electric loop around his—"

"Yes," Riot held up a hand. "I recall the advertisements." He turned a shade lighter.

Aware of her arm submersed in water with an electrical device, she quickly withdrew it. "Not a pleasant way to die," she mused. "Would a belt like that kill a man in water?" Her knowledge of electricity was sketchy.

"Tim may know. He likes to tinker with electrical devices."

"Tinker as 'strap one on and climb in the tub'?"

"Wouldn't be the first time," Riot acknowledged. "He's been pushing me to purchase an electric car, and I've been holding out for that very reason."

Isobel grinned and tried the cold water tap. The pipes knocked and moaned, and water flowed. She washed her arm in the frigid rush.

Riot handed over her coat and walked out of the bathroom.

As she rolled down her sleeve, a rough patch on the enamel caught her eye. Isobel ran a finger over the spot, and then bent close. There were four marks, two on each side, faint scratches on the curled rim of the tub. She dropped down to hands and knees.

"There's burnt coal in—" Riot paused, found her missing, and then looked down, "the boiler. It's cold."

"Takes at least a day to cool down."

"So it does. Did you find something?"

"Scratches on the enamel."

Riot's shiny shoes clicked on the tile. He joined her on the floor and she pointed out the marks. "It's an old tub, but the marks appear uniform," she explained.

Riot reached beneath his coat. He brought out a small, leather case with a clasp, opened it and unfolded a magnifying lens. "Scratched in the same direction," he noted, handing her the glass.

Isobel examined the marks, and nodded. As he tucked the case away and stood, something caught her eye in a groove between tiles. "I may need that again." She stretched her arm underneath and plucked a strand from the grout.

It was a small, coarse, hair like thread. She examined it under Riot's glass. "Too thick for hair," she wondered aloud. "It looks like thread from a rope, or canvas."

Riot reached beneath his coat again, and she exchanged glass for envelope.

"You certainly are useful to have around."

"I aim to please."

The adjoining room appeared to be a small servant's room, likely inhabited by the gardener or maid of all work. The bedclothes on the narrow bed were tucked to perfection, and a tidy pile of clothes sat on the chair.

"How did you discover this house?"

As they made a thorough search of the room, she filled him in on the pertinent details.

"A flower ribbon," Riot mused.

"What?"

"You saved yourself days of footwork."

"My feet were tired."

The edge of his lip quirked.

Isobel paused, her hand under the mattress. "Hello," she said. Riot stepped over as she withdrew a thin box. She opened it, and arched a brow.

It contained a neat pile of pornographic photographs: all male figures. The faces had been carefully left out so as not to incriminate. Isobel shuffled through the men captured in time. There were no names on the back.

"The wonders of science," she sighed. "Every new development is turned towards the basest instincts. These could belong to Violet just as easily as Henry. Although I don't find men in corsets and garters appealing."

Riot cleared his throat. "There's no way to tell if those belong to either of them. It could have been left by a former occupant."

"True, but these could be why Henry killed himself—if he did at all."

"There's no note," Riot pointed out as he searched Henry's billfold. Isobel leant near, looking at the contents. It contained a few dollars and his calling cards.

Finding nothing more aside from cleanliness, they moved into the laundry room, where Isobel related the name of the previous owner, her connection with Violet, and the theatre friend's suspicion that Violet had gone off to elope.

"That hardly fits with the photographs."

"Perhaps it was a ruse," she argued. "Henry was courting Violet to throw off suspicion. It wouldn't be the first of such arrangements."

"Henry's journal had regular notations of V and G.G."

Isobel narrowed her eyes. "*You* were the detective who beat me to Henry's residence," she accused.

"I suppose so."

"The landlady wouldn't budge. Told me to go find a husband and have children."

"Is Mrs. Irish still conscious?"

Isobel snorted. "I can't say that I wasn't tempted to try out my umbrella." She shone the box light down the washbasin drain. Finding nothing, she turned to the cupboard while Riot kept up his end of the bargain and began with Bert Dunham's visit to the agency.

"Elma kept a journal, detailing every single day of her pregnancy. A sure deterrent if you should ever heed Mrs. Irish's advice."

"I've been married once; I'll not repeat that mistake." A small box, shoved to the back of the top shelf caught her eye. She handed it to Riot.

"*Dr. Mackenzie's Improved Harmless Arsenic Complexion*

Wafers," he read. "Two wafers left."

"It's well and good that it says harmless," she said dryly.

"The lies people will believe," he sighed.

"And what risks women will take in the name of beauty. On account of my athleticism, a few of the finishing school girls used to beg me to lace their corsets so tightly that I feared I'd puncture a rib."

"Did you?"

"No," she said. "I found it amusing to watch their meager tightening efforts."

Riot turned the box over, searching for a date, or identification number; unfortunately every druggist in the country sold the wafers. He sniffed at the inside of the box, and frowned. "Did any of your tight-lacing friends take these?"

"Why?"

He held out the box, and she sniffed. Garlic. A very strong odor. She flinched back. "That's powerful."

Riot nodded. "I think we best ask a chemist to analyze these." He set the box next to the photographs in the servant's room, and as they moved through the rest of the house, he continued his report.

It was as succinct and thorough as his side of the search. They moved through the rooms together, never stepping over the other's toes, always seeming to know where the other would begin.

"Henry left his spectacles?" she asked with surprise in the master bedroom. "Would you ever forget your spectacles?"

Riot was currently on hands and knees, inspecting the underside of the bed. He looked up and removed his spectacles. "Bel, everything is a blur."

"What about now?" She moved closer.

"No."

Isobel edged forward until she stood three feet away.

"Now," he admitted with a grimace. "I doubt Henry's eyesight is as bad as mine. He wouldn't have gotten very far."

"Still, it sounded as if he wore the spectacles regularly. What could have spooked a man so badly?"

Riot considered her question as he resettled the wire behind his ears. After a moment, he stood and dusted off his trousers. "Perhaps Henry thought Violet was in trouble."

"Love," she mused. "That's enough to make a man kick down a door." Her words were flippant, but all her cleverness fled when he looked at her.

"More than enough."

His gaze was unwavering, and she could not decide if she wanted to take a step back or take a step forward. Caught with indecision, she tore her eyes from his, and nodded towards the door. "Trouble or no, worry doesn't explain the dead man in the bath, or the photographs."

"No," he agreed. "Still, I can't imagine any scenario that would entice a man to strap on an electric belt and climb into a bath."

"Not even guilt?" she asked. "Lotario, as flippant as he is, still keenly feels society's scorn."

"Maybe so, but I'd expect a note."

"Aren't the photographs enough?"

"I'm not convinced."

"I'll be sure to write you a dissertation when my own moral insanity gets the better of me."

"Too late. You're already dead, Bel."

She smiled. "There is that."

✢

Inspector Geary resembled a gargoyle. Everything about him sloped forward as he frowned at the corpse. Thick brows, heavy jowls, and a neck that rested on his expansive chest. All of it was held up by an impressive gut that had likely taken a lifelong supply of ale to develop. Geary's hands were in his pockets. He looked bored.

"This house is empty. How'd you get in here, Riot?" the inspector grumbled.

"As I said, our investigation led us here. The jib door was unlocked." Riot only knew about the jib door because Isobel had told him. She suspected that he had lockpicks on his person. However, as much as she'd like to, now was not the time to inquire.

Isobel stood in a corner beside Tim, trying not to draw the inspector's attention. She felt exposed without her hat. It was still outside in the overgrown yard. Remaining had been a risk, but she had never witnessed a police investigation. Still, if her gender were discovered, Riot would be pulled into a mire of trouble. The thought made her uneasy.

Geary grunted. "Isn't that always the case with you and your lot?"

"I've the luck of a gambler, Inspector."

"You and your fine clothes can drain this water." The chain on the plug was broken, and Geary was not about to reach into that water.

"Bastard," Tim muttered. When Geary turned sharply, the old man smiled amiably, and rocked back on his heels, whistling under his breath. Mischievous eyes slid over to Isobel; she nearly laughed. The old man reminded her of a leprechaun.

"This man is involved with an ongoing investigation. The coroner will want us to wait," Riot stated.

"The coroner is sleeping. I've a mind to secure the house and take this up at a reasonable hour. It's not as if the stiff is going anywhere."

Even now, the clomping boots of two uniformed policemen thudded on the floorboards above. From the sounds of it, the two were conducting a half-hearted search.

Tim cleared his throat, rocked back, and then settled on his toes. "I took the liberty of sending a hack for Deputy Coroner August."

"Isn't that liberating of you." Geary hooked his thumbs in his waistcoat. "You're not in charge here. I am. Drain the water, or leave."

Isobel wondered at the open hostility. There was clearly history between the men, and from Riot's clipped tones, she had a distinct feeling that it wasn't a good one.

As Riot shrugged out of his coat and unbuttoned his cufflink, a thought occurred to her. Isobel selected a glass jar from the cabinet, removed the loose bits of cotton, wiped it out with a cloth, and stepped forward to fill the jar with a sample of water. She closed the lid.

"Good thinking, Mr. Morgan." Riot slipped his arm into the tub. Water edged up his sleeve, marring the snowy shirt as he reached for the broken plug. A pop signaled the open drain and a faint whirlpool accompanied the water's demise.

Four sets of eyes watched the bathtub empty. When the belt was revealed, Inspector Geary chuckled. "What a sodding pervert," he leaned out into the hallway and shouted, "O'Hare, come have a look at this. He must've been trying to get his prick to work for the ladies."

Riot stiffened. Before he could take offense for her sake, Isobel drove her elbow into his ribs. As the gentleman detective coughed, she took the opportunity to check the cadaver's wrists and ankles.

Despite Isobel's earlier arguments, she shared Riot's doubts about suicide. Rope marks would have cleared up the question, but there were none.

As the three policemen crowded in to snicker at the humiliating belt, Isobel appropriated Riot's light box, and slipped out through the jib door. After discovering Henry, and the subsequent search, she had forgotten all about the mad vagrant.

She circled around back to the porch, and crouched, flipping the switch. Light illuminated the darkness. The ground was cracked and dry, far too hard for any footprints. She played the light around, expecting a mattress, a blanket, some sign of life, but there was nothing.

Isobel hunkered down, creeping beneath the planks, pointing the beam at the foundation. A grate caught the light.

"Interesting place for a vent," Riot's voice drifted from the hollowness.

"Oh, God," she breathed.

The outline of his face appeared. "What?" he demanded.

"I held a conversation with—I thought he was a vagrant living under the porch. He was mad as a hatter, Riot. What room are you in?"

"The storage room." His soft reply sent a chill down her spine.

"Does that grate open?"

She heard sounds of fiddling, and an oiled creak. "It

does, but no man could fit through this." When silence stretched, he nudged her with a worried word. "Bel?"

"I think the man I spoke with—he must have been inside."

"Did you see him?"

"Only shadows. It sounded and looked as if he was moving, but I suppose it could have been a trick of the light. I should have dragged him out, or ventured inside."

"Would you be upset if I told you that I am relieved you listened to your instincts?"

"Yes."

"I had best not say it, then," he whispered.

"You had best not," she agreed. "I'd hate to shoot you again."

"My tailor would be furious."

"I'll be sure to send a polite note absolving you of responsibility."

"How thoughtful of you," she heard a smile on his lips. "Have you ever salvaged burnt documents?"

"Let me get my hat and umbrella first."

✢

The curled papers did not look promising, but even a single legible fragment could prove insightful. The brittle remains, she knew from her own experiments, could disintegrate with a breath. She eased a flat pie tin under the ash on the hearth and carefully lifted. Riot held a salvaged box at the ready. It was lined with wool padding. Careful not to disturb the ashes, she placed the tin in the box, and picked up a pair of tweezers. With the utmost care, she plucked the first of many remains from the grate and added the fragment to the padded container.

Voices and footsteps interrupted the tedious work. Riot excused himself with a soft word, and interrupted the inspector's grumbling introductions.

"Atticus Riot," he offered a hand to the coroner. "Sorry to disturb you at this hour, but I thank you for coming, Dr. August."

"It's an honor to meet you," August replied, shifting his heavy doctor's bag and leather case to shake hands. "I've studied all of Ravenwood's cases. To think you worked with the man himself."

Isobel glanced over her shoulder in surprise. The younger man towered over the seasoned detective, but there was deference in his manner. In stark contrast to Inspector Geary's attitude, August was all business and professionalism.

"I'm told that this case is tied to the death of Violet Clowes."

"It is," Riot confirmed.

"How did you become involved?"

"My agency was hired to look into another suicide: Elma Dunham. My investigation crossed paths with Charlotte Bonnie."

"Ah, yes, a—determined woman." August said politely.

"Indeed."

Their voices faded down the hallway.

Isobel deposited the final charred fragment into the makeshift container. She switched on the box light, and shone it into the hearth. When she was assured of nothing missed, she sealed the box, donned her bowler, and walked into the bathroom. The little room was crowded with men and bags. She contented herself with standing in the lamp's shadow.

Duncan August pulled a folding pocket camera out of

his case. As he assembled the tripod, she leaned forward, peering at the jumble of equipment: measuring sticks, collection boxes, slides—everything a coroner might need for collecting forensic evidence. From the look of his equipment, she suspected that August was a student of Lacassagne's methods. It reassured her greatly.

"Was the bathtub filled?" August inquired.

"It was," Riot replied.

"I see."

"The inspector here ordered it drained," Isobel offered from the doorway. "We saved a sample in that jar." Ignoring the scowling gargoyle, she reached inside her coat and produced the envelope. "And we found this under the bathtub."

August accepted the envelope with a question in his eye.

"This is my assistant Mr. Morgan," Riot introduced. "Can you test Violet Clowes for arsenic?"

The coroner nodded without recognition. "I'll be sure to look at this."

"I have a box of tablets I'd like you to look at, too." The arsenic wafers went into August's collection bag. Riot pointed out the rough patches on the enamel, and politely asked permission to analyze the collected ashes.

"Of course," August said. "The police are overworked as it is. I'll telephone your office when I have my findings."

"We'll take our leave, then," Riot offered his card.

"Will you be speaking with Miss Bonnie soon?"

"In the morning."

Isobel was pleased to see that August intended to share.

Riot tipped his hat to both men, and Isobel followed him out the door.

"August seems a diligent coroner," she noted.

"It appears so."

Tim stood waiting in the ballroom with the box of ashes. The bounce in his heels was gone. He looked old and tired, and Isobel wagered that she didn't look much better.

"There's a spare room at the house," Tim offered. She hesitated a split second, and he dove right into the gap, adding, "Otherwise we'll have to drive you clear down to the piers."

She nearly announced that she'd walk, but it seemed foolish. And truth be told, the thought of scrubbing the day's grime away with cold water was wearisome. "Do you have hot water pipes?"

Tim flashed his gold teeth. "Enough to fill a bath." He blushed at his own words, recalling, no doubt, that she was a woman.

"Ravenwood house it is," said Riot.

A hack waited outside with the police wagon. A dark-skinned young man sat solidly in the seat, waiting like a graveyard statue. She remembered him from her last visit to Ravenwood house.

Grimm sized her up with a glance. The young man's gaze seemed to pierce marrow and bone.

Riot opened the hack door.

"I'm in male garb," she muttered.

"Habits die hard."

"Habits will give me away," she whispered, climbing inside. Isobel fell into the seat and received a startled yelp. She stood, bumping her head on the carriage top. A pair of puzzled, sleepy eyes stared from the darkness. The eye widened with alarm.

"Tobias," Riot said, gravely. "One of these days your mother is going to discover you hitching a ride on the hack."

"She hasn't noticed so far, sir."

"I'll tell her," Tim grumbled, "if you don't get your hide out of there."

The boy scrambled out and clung to the back. Isobel settled on the seat and accepted the box of ashes. The carriage sagged as Riot slid in beside her.

Tim shut the door on Riot's heels.

"Brothers?" she asked.

Riot nodded. "Grimm doesn't talk." The hack lurched forward.

"I don't blame him," she said, resting her head against the padded seat. "Eyes like that have seen too much."

"I have yet to discover what his eyes have seen."

"Always the protector, Riot?"

The arm touching her own tensed. He did not look at her, but stared at the knob of his walking stick. His fingers traced the filigree. "Only returning a favor."

There was a quietness to the detective. As tired as she was, it could have been her own imaginings, but the longer the silence stretched, the louder it got. Isobel cracked an eye at the man, studying his profile. The hack drifted from shadow to lamplight. In the near dark, he looked chiseled from stone, like a cliff on the shore—unreachable.

"Just say it."

He glanced at her. "What do you imagine I would like to say?"

"I haven't a clue," she admitted. "But you look as though there's some quiet like words wanting to come out and you are trying to find the proper order."

"I haven't found the order yet."

Isobel narrowed her eyes. "Before you tell me that I shouldn't have gone into an abandoned house alone, you should reconsider. Whenever there's a squall, I reef my sails and head straight for the storm. I don't like relying on others. People inevitably let me down. At best I part ways; at worse I get a blade in my back."

Riot slowly spun the stick on its tip in a thoughtful manner. The hack leaned, rolling around a corner, pressing her shoulder against his. Warmth radiated from the man, and she quickly edged back, preparing for a verbal fight.

"That's not what I was going to say, but since you are preoccupied with the subject, I'll bite."

Isobel started to deny his claim, but the argument rang hollow in her own ears. Instead she switched tactics. "With those chipped teeth of yours, I reckon a bite might hurt."

There was a slight catch of surprise in his breath, but he recovered quickly, turning the tables. "I'm a gentle man." The whisper brushed her ear, deep and reverberating as a lion's purr.

Heat spread across her breasts and traveled in a southernly direction. She swallowed, suddenly breathless. Once again Riot had the upper hand.

If he noticed her inability to form a sentence, he did not say, but continued, "What you do is your own business, but as your friend—if I may presume?"

Isobel blew out a breath. "I'd say we're well past presuming."

Riot inclined his head. "I'd be remiss if I failed to point out that while single-handed sailing is doable, it's rough going in a storm. Even a seasoned sailor like Slocum didn't turn down a helping hand."

Isobel searched for an edge to wedge a crowbar under, but his argument was as sensible as they came. At the moment, however, she was too tired to deal with sensibility.

She set aside his words, and nodded towards his tattooed forearm. The mark of a dragon was a rite of passage for sailors who had sailed into an eastern port. "I didn't take you for a sailor."

Riot let her blow him off course. "I am not," he admitted. "I was stuck in a galley for five months."

"Shanghaied?"

The slightest movement confirmed her surprise.

"Tim was under the impression that I needed to build character."

Isobel laughed, hard.

"I didn't find it amusing at the time."

"No, I imagine not," she wheezed. When her vision cleared, she found him watching her. There was a rare smile on his lips.

She returned it, and after a moment, asked, "Have your words sorted themselves yet?"

"More or less," he paused, rubbing a hand over his beard. "The woman this evening—"

The words triggered a reaction. "Riot, you don't owe me any explanation. It's none of my business."

"Miss Dupree is a lodger at Raven—my home," he went on undaunted.

"I suppose that's convenient."

He looked at her squarely. "She's a courtesan."

"Oh." Not what she had been expecting. The rattle of wheels kept the two company for a long minute. Finally, she said, "I didn't take you for a pimp."

Riot opened his mouth, looked at her dancing eyes, and shut it with a click. He took a deep breath. "I'm not. She lets a room."

"Well I gathered that if she's a lodger. I won't ask how she pays the rent."

He looked sharply at her, and Isobel answered with an arched brow. "She pays handsomely," he said, primly.

"I'm sure," she drawled.

Riot removed his spectacles. She watched his hands as he gently cleaned the lens with silk. "This past month, I've taken steps to insert myself into certain society circles," he explained. "I'm a man with some money, of means, but not near enough for the elite to take notice and open their secretive doors."

At his words, everything clicked, and Isobel felt dim-witted. "And a detective escorting a high-class prostitute to social engagements paints a certain kind of portrait."

Riot looked relieved. "Exactly." He settled the wire back on his nose.

"I hope you're not doing this for my sake."

"My reasons are my own to decide."

"And whose single-handed sailing now?"

"I've just laid my course out for you," he said, reasonably. "I've weathered my fair share of storms in the detective business, enough to know that a crew you can trust is invaluable. I certainly won't turn down your help."

"You and I play different games, Riot. You shuffle cards while I maneuver pieces, but the strategy is the same, and I can spot one from a mile away."

"I've laid my cards on the table." He spread his hands. "Hardly a strategy."

"It's a white flag," she corrected. "You know full well that I'm more akin to a pirate. I'd board your ship anyway. This is a ploy so you can keep your myopic eyes on me."

"What I know, Bel," he said, softly. "Is that you and I can look after ourselves, but that doesn't mean we have to."

The words should have sparked outrage, but there was

something in his voice that pulled her near: respect.

"Damn you, Riot," she swore. He looked startled, as if he had lost a high-stakes poker hand. "Must you be so agreeable? Some tyrannical comments would be helpful."

Riot tilted his head in consideration. "Woman, do as you're told?"

"That's better," she smiled. "It makes it easier to be contrary with you."

"Afraid you might start warming to me?"

Isobel looked at him sideways. "I'm afraid it's too late for that," she admitted. "You're like Watson; only you talk back."

Her words struck home. The calm confidence drained from the man and a silent chortle moved through his body like a current under water. It was a singular laugh, one felt rather than heard. Isobel leant into her companion, enjoying the ride.

21

Of Like Mind

Saturday, February 17th, 1900

CHESS PIECES GLIDED OVER a checkered board. From square to square, attacking and retreating in a deadly dance of survival. The ivory pieces dominated the board, while a lone black queen stood with her king. The queen lashed at the ivory knight, and then turned her eye on the bishop. The opposing queen was the last to fall to the avenging black. But that was the thing, the kick of it all, the black queen's king had fallen long ago.

Isobel opened her eyes. The decimated chess board lingered in her mind. Her heart galloped, and she looked around, disoriented. She was in a strange room, in a strange bed; a moment of panic took hold.

Isobel sat bolt upright.

This was no room of opulence; no plush feathered bed with an unwanted bedmate. The room was small, the bed narrow, and the furniture fine but simple. She was alone.

"Riot's house," she reminded herself. Exhaustion had a way of leaving her feeling drunk. The walls danced, and she vaguely recalled falling into bed after a hot bath. A nightshirt lay folded on the dresser, untouched. She was still dressed in Riot's borrowed robe. He was not a large man, but it still encompassed her like a blanket.

Isobel fell back against the pillow and buried her nose in the collar. She closed her eyes, picking out the scents: sandalwood and myrrh, a soothing combination, likely the oil he used on his beard. And something else, a decidedly masculine scent that she could not quantify.

After a time, facts drowned out the quiet lull, roaring through her mind like a squall. Coffee, food, and a quiet room were needed—in that precise order.

She thrust out her arm, feeling for her chain watch. It was nearly noon. Fearful that Riot would start the day's investigation without her, she tossed back the covers and forced herself out of bed.

A pitcher of water waited on the washstand. She poured water into the bowl and looked at her reflection in the mirror. The black-haired person who stared back hardly looked well rested. Dark circles lined her eyes, but the face was at least familiar again. During her time with Kingston, she had hardly recognized her own reflection, but now, after a month of freedom, the sea had given her a healthy glow.

She splashed water on her face, tamed her short hair with pomade, and reached for her male garb. The tattered theatre suit had been mended, freshened, and ironed as if it were tailored.

When she was satisfied with the small touches that lent her a masculine shape, she poked her head out the door. A boy sat outside, waiting.

"Tobias," she said in surprise. And then cleared the voice from her throat.

"Morning, sir."

"Morning," she said in deeper tones. "You startled me."

"People say that a lot."

Sounds of life drifted from the lower floors. "Where's, Mr. Riot?"

"He told me to tell you that he's in his room. I'm to show you the way."

"Lead on."

The boy marched down the hallway and she followed on his heels.

The Ravenwood estate was large, a mash of haphazard elegance that resembled a European hedge maze. Tobias led her past a blur of polished doors, through hallways and down a staircase to the second floor. Isobel remembered the door from her last visit, a vague sort of recollection through the haze of shock when she had been smuggled into the house. At the time, she was a nearly naked, soaking wet young woman who had just killed her brother. And, that same morning, dressed in borrowed clothes (by definition stolen), she had quietly slipped out a window.

She applied her knuckles to the door. A clear 'come' answered. She thanked Tobias, and the boy turned and bolted downstairs.

As soon as Isobel stepped inside, Riot rose to his feet. Despite his starched collar and grey waistcoat, his raven hair was slightly rumpled, as if he had only just awoken.

"Did you sleep well?" he asked.

Isobel barely heard the words. The turret room was a world away from when she had last sat by the fire. Sunlight streamed through the high windows, creating prisms of color from the stained-glass. A wall of bookshelves lured her closer.

"You unpacked," she said, reading the spines.

"You sound surprised."

"I wasn't sure," she admitted.

"Unfinished business aside, I thought I'd give life here a second chance."

"You could certainly do worse with your living arrangements," she said dryly. Once upon a time, she wagered the room had been two, but a wall was knocked out to make it a spacious bedroom cum sitting room. Her gaze traveled from the books, to the neat desk and wardrobe, and finally settled on the wide bed. Every suggestive comment, lingering gaze, and her own damn newspaper article settled on that soft mattress. She quickly looked away.

Riot took her avoidance for discomfort. "I hope you don't mind taking breakfast in here," he hastened. "The dining room and patio have numerous ears, and the old study is let." He gestured at the waiting tea tray in front of the fireplace.

"To the courtesan?"

Riot paused. "Actually, yes."

"The French doors make for an inconspicuous entry."

"They do," he agreed. "When Ravenwood and I conducted business from the house, we used that room for consultations."

Isobel sunk into Ravenwood's throne-like chair, running her hands over the armrest. "And would he have approved of its current use?

Riot tilted his head as if listening to a faint voice. "Absolutely not."

"I thought not," she smiled. "I should like to meet this courtesan."

"I would advise against introductions in your current guise."

Isobel nodded. She understood perfectly. "Women of the night do have an eye for deception," she agreed. "Luckily, whenever I'm in male garb, most find my antics amusing. Coffee?"

"Tea with a dash of milk," he said sitting opposite.

As Isobel poured, she glanced at the newspaper on his armchair. Her story was there, front page.

Riot noticed her gaze. "A suitably sensational article."

"Thank you," she said handing him tea.

"The one yesterday was positively captivating."

His amusement knocked her thoughts back to the bed, and in turn to an insightful two days spent along the Venetian coastline with a strapping gondolier. The young man had been as inexperienced as she. And eager. As Isobel inhaled the black brew, she wondered how a controlled man like Riot would differ. She reined in her thoughts, summoned resolve, and met his gaze.

"Your eyes remind me of chocolate." Isobel was as surprised as Riot by this declaration. Her tongue did not always cooperate with her mind.

Riot gulped his tea, burning his tongue. He coughed once, and set the cup on its saucer with a rattle. Isobel silently congratulated herself for throwing the man's infuriating calmness off balance.

Riot opened his mouth, then closed it, and thought a moment. "Do you like chocolate?" he finally asked.

"Not especially."

A knock rescued her from further conversation. Riot was slow to react; a testament to the affect of her words. She seized the chance, hopping to her feet, and opened the door. A young maid stood outside with a breakfast tray. Isobel took the tray with a murmur of gratitude and carried it back to the table, silently blaming her distracted state on a lack of food. Her stomach reminded her that it had been neglected, and she attacked the eggs and bacon with relish.

When she had eaten her portion, and most of Riot's, she picked up the newspaper and sat back in the chair with a sigh. She was glad for her corset-less male garb. But contentment turned sour when she began to read.

"They've changed my article," she said, tightly. "I didn't paint the surfman in such a bad light, and I didn't put so much emphasis on Violet's questionable sanity."

"That's what editors do, Bel. They edit. Especially newspaper editors."

She glared at the man for stating the obvious. "I'll have a few choice words for Mr. Griful."

"Did they alter the one from yesterday—the mysterious savior?" He handed her yesterday's paper, and she read it with a critical eye.

"No," she announced. "It's precisely what I wrote."

"I see." He took a sip of his tea. "Now that the news is out about Violet, you may find more attention on the case than you bargained for."

"Oh, I've bargained for it."

"Have you?"

"Someone's bound to know something."

"The press does have its uses," he conceded. "At best, however, they are a double-edged sword."

"Regardless of the edge, it can be wielded."

"Is that why you've put yourself in yet another precarious position?"

"I know no other place to live." She tossed down the newspaper and piled the China on the tray, setting it on the floor with a rattle.

Riot retrieved his gathered evidence and set the items on the table. Isobel added her own photographs, letters, and pamphlets to the pot, and then proceeded to rearrange the items to her satisfaction. He watched with amusement.

Isobel ignored the man. She began with the medical journals, cringed at Elma's pregnancy account, and read through Henry's cryptic listings. After a time, she became aware of a fluttering sound, and looked up, puzzled. Riot had a deck of cards. His eyes were far away, but his deft fingers manipulated the cards with a flourish. A blur of white, a perfect arch; back and forth, squaring edges to begin again, this time shooting the cards from hand to hand, a foot apart.

She picked up the photograph of the unknown man. "You found this tucked in Henry's medical manual on insanity?"

"The landlady said he resembled Garrett, the man who visited earlier on Tuesday, only rougher, although she couldn't be sure if it was the same person."

"He looks familiar," Isobel murmured.

Keen eyes focused on her. The shuffling stopped. "How so?"

Isobel sat back and tucked her feet on the chair. She stared at the photograph, and then closed her eyes, trying to summon the source of familiarity. "I'm not sure," she sighed. "But he does remind me of Henry in the other photograph. Brothers, maybe?"

"Could be."

The cards continued their rhythmic shuffle, and she chewed thoughtfully on a nail. Isobel looked at the photograph of the three friends: Elma, Hal, and Violet. "All three of them had medical training. Henry ran out of funds. Elma supposedly quit working after she was married, but what about Violet? We don't really know why she threw her medical career over for the theatre, or if she even did. Sister Mary wasn't sure if she was working as a nurse or governess when she tried to commit suicide the first time."

"According to the notations in Hal's journal, it looks as though Violet's first suicide attempt was a trigger of some sort."

Isobel tapped the circled passages on insanity. "Do you think Elma and Hal were worried about her sanity?"

"Certainly seems that way."

"According to these indications, I should be committed."

"I'm afraid I'd have to surrender myself, too."

Isobel looked at the stoic man across from her. "You? I don't believe it."

The cards stopped. "On most days I wear a convincing mask." His tone was as flat and serious as a hammer cocking.

Isobel searched his eyes for a hint of humor. There was none. She swallowed, considering the gravity of his statement. "Well then, we'll be insane together," she said lightly. "Erm—separately together."

Warmth entered his eyes. "I'm in good company, then. Separately, of course." The cards began to fly. And she watched for a moment, mesmerized. "I can stop shuffling if you like. It's a habit of mine. It used to irritate Raven-wood to no end."

"It reminds me of the waves," she replied. "Does my twin offend you?"

Riot tilted his head in consideration. "I can't say I understand his—preferences."

"I think we got mixed up in the womb," she explained, hastily. "Neither of us quite fit where we ought to."

He waited for silence to fall again, leaving her holding her breath for his answer. When he spoke, it was slow and clear. "Bel, I'm not a preacher, I'm no lawman, and I'm not a judge. I only take issue with the brothers who try to murder you."

"Lotario is a lover, not a fighter. Besides, he's terrified of guns."

"Then I have no issue."

"You're a rare man, Riot," she smiled.

"Not rare," he corrected, "only a detective who, whether I cared to or not, has seen all there is to see in the Barbary Coast."

"Donkeys and all?" she asked, suggestively.

Riot's cards shot from his hand mid-shuffle. The skin above his neatly trimmed beard turned a darker hue.

She smirked across the table. "Don't think you're the only one who has roamed unsavory streets."

He cleared his throat, and bent to gather his cards. "I'm beginning to see why your parents sent you to a lady's finishing school."

"You can teach a woman to be a lady, but that doesn't make her one," she reminded, plucking up a fallen Queen of Hearts. She held it out to him and he paused before taking it. When he finally moved to accept it, his fingers brushed her own.

"I'll keep that in mind, Bel."

Despite her bold words, Isobel's cheeks heated. She quickly focused on the evidence, hoping Riot was too flustered to notice. "This case reminds me of dominos," she mused. "One falling right after the other. First Henry shot out of his house Tuesday evening—we have no idea why. But something certainly must have spooked him."

"Then Violet visits Elma on Wednesday."

"And Elma drank the poison sometime in the afternoon."

"Next," Riot took up the recitation, "Violet shows up at Golden Gate Park around six in the evening. She waits, presumably for Henry, but he doesn't show."

"So she leaves down a path and turns up, hours later, on a streetcar headed to her death."

"It's not a far stretch to think she went to the house."

Isobel nodded in agreement. "That would certainly account for the missing hours. I wonder if she discovered him in the bath? Maybe she feared that she'd be blamed for his death. That would explain the note she left with the conductor."

"They might have quarreled," Riot added.

. Isobel made a face. "Love," she twisted the word. "It shouldn't be so complicated. If it works, it works; if it doesn't, shake hands and part ways."

"The heart does not always abide by logic."

"Then the heart should be ignored. Love is here," she tapped her head.

"Most would disagree."

"What do you think?"

"As long as it's somewhere, Bel."

When her mind came up with no reply, Riot set aside his cards and leaned forward, turning the letters and notations towards him. "I requested a postmortem on Elma; unfortunately, with the amount of burns from the acid, it'll be hard to tell if she put up some sort of fight. From the sound of it, the bathroom was a mess."

Isobel grimaced. "That sort of poison doesn't take you down quietly."

He reached into his coat pocket and unfolded his magnifying glass. The lens hovered over the handwriting, comparing Elma's journal with her final note of innocence. "Ravenwood could spot a forgery in seconds," he murmured.

"Well Ravenwood isn't here, now is he?" Isobel switched sides, so she could peer at the lettering. "And I sincerely doubt he could have distinguished Lotario's writing from mine."

She sensed a smile on Riot's lips.

"None of this makes a jot of sense."

"No," Riot agreed. "But actions rarely do. Imagine if someone were to try and unravel your puzzle."

She snorted. "You did."

"So I did," he acknowledged. "But you'd give any investigator a run for his money with all your *nom de plumes*, sporadic actions, and cross-dressing."

"Why thank you." A sudden thought sparked in the shadows and lodged itself in the light. "The brooch."

"Hmm?"

"Violet's brooch. You said Elma's landlady claimed Violet had a brooch with an ivory flower on it, but Mrs. Beeton said the brooch was of a woman's profile, which I found pinned to Violet's blouse in the morgue—is Elma's landlady reliable?"

"She seemed so, but I don't honestly know. What are you thinking?"

"That it's a troubling detail."

22

Divergence

TWO CASES INTERTWINED. A dividing of forces was required, and Isobel was glad for it. Piecing together burnt documents was time consuming tedium. She gladly abandoned Riot to the task.

A bag of clothes was waiting at the Ferry Building cloak room. She tipped the bored attendant, and walked to the *Pagan Lady*. Watson was on guard, sleeping. Mr. Morgan disappeared below deck and Charlotte Bonnie emerged. Armed with umbrella, pistol, and evidence, she marched to the end of the dock. And stopped.

A hack waited. Grimm sat in the seat, holding the reins. She nearly greeted him by name, but recalled that he only knew her as Mr. Morgan. Still, he looked at her, and then nodded towards the cab.

A cheerful face appeared. The door opened, and Tobias hopped down, a slash of white splitting his dark face. He removed his cap. "Mr. Riot said we should wait for a lady here. A Miss Bonnie."

"Did he?" she asked slowly.

The boy nodded. "We are to be your hackmen for the day."

Isobel nearly walked around the hack, but Tobias was brimming with youthful excitement. She supposed this was an escape from his letters and chores.

Isobel steeled her resolve. "You can tell Mr. Riot—" she faltered, relenting to practicality. Not having to walk across town ten times over had its benefits. "That I thank him." She climbed inside the hack.

Tobias shut the carriage door, and slung his arms over the window, hanging on the side. "Are you related to Mr. Morgan, ma'am?"

"We're cousins. Do you always ask too many questions?"

"Yes."

"Good. Don't you dare stop."

Tobias grinned. "Where to, ma'am? Grimm, my brother there, don't talk."

It was an excellent question. Where to begin. The three friends in Violet's photograph spun in her mind. Elma, Hal, and Violet—now all dead. Apparent suicides.

"Cooper Medical Hospital."

The carriage rolled forward, and Tobias climbed along the side, settling himself beside his brother.

⁜

The sterile hollowness of an institution surrounded her. White walls, polished floors, and bright lights. The hallways were scrubbed of the very life it strived to save.

A starched nurse directed Isobel to the teaching wing, and a secretary seated her in an office sitting room. A half an hour later, the secretary beckoned Isobel inside the dean's office. She stopped in front of Professor Fischer's desk. He was balding, severe, and had shrewd eyes.

This was not the first time Isobel had stood before a college dean. During her two months at Berkeley, she had been called in front of such a desk three times.

Professor Fischer rose, offering his hand. "Miss Bonnie. I'm told you are with the coroner's office." A distinct German accent placed him as Saxon, and a narrowing of his eyes screamed skepticism.

"I'm investigating a trio of deaths on behalf of the Deputy Coroner. Two of the deceased attended Cooper College, and I believe the other might have worked as a nurse. I need to see their student records."

"I'm afraid I can't permit that. Not without a court order or permission from next of kin."

"Murder may be involved."

Professor Fischer looked at her, unwavering. "Then you should have no problem obtaining a warrant. I'm a busy man, Miss Bonnie."

Isobel looked at the man. He was rigid and unyielding. She turned to take her leave, felt him relax, and when she had reached the door, stopped, drumming her fingers on the umbrella handle.

"I think it's wonderful that your fine college has instituted a nursing program." She whirled, and smiled. "For the last five years, every class has been full."

"If you will excuse me."

"Of course I will." She marched back and made herself comfortable in the chair opposite. "One of the women whom I'm investigating attended your nursing school, and the other may have worked as a nurse here. The initial police report says that they committed suicide."

"Unfortunate."

"It is, isn't it? Your college has taken great pains to maintain a high level of decorum, assurance for families who are wary of sending their daughters to a college."

"I do not see the relevance of this conversation."

"Money is always relevant in San Francisco," she countered. "And tuition for your fine college does not come cheaply. It'd be a shame if word reached the newspapers, tying your college to the suicides. I can see the headline now—front page: *Academic Pressure Drives Women to Suicide.* All in big bold letters. How many students would be withdrawn?"

"Are you threatening me?"

"No," she said calmly. "I am painting a picture for you. Let me peek at the records and I will make sure that your school is never connected with their names."

"I will not be bullied, Miss Bonnie." The professor drew himself up. "And I *will* not break regulation."

Threat was no match for a German's sense of protocol.

"Can you at least identify them?" she relented. Isobel produced her photograph. "Do you remember these students? Surely that is not against regulation?"

"No, it is not." He studied the photograph. "Henry and Elma Erving. Brother and sister. And their friend, who worked as a nurse, Elizabeth Foster." He pinned each as he spoke.

Isobel was surprised that a dean remembered the students so quickly.

"Why did they leave?"

"Hundreds of students come and go. I do not remember."

"But you remembered their names."

"I have an eye for faces." There was more, but he wasn't about to elaborate. She tried Riot's tactic, and waited, staring up at the man. Silence deepened. Visions of whacking the dean over the head with her umbrella and calling it an accident began to hiss their insidious temptation in her ear.

Isobel cracked and cleared her throat. "What about this man?" She produced the photograph that Riot had found in Henry's medical manual. "Do you recognize him?"

The professor stiffened. Yes, he did, but he did not say it.

"Good day, Miss Bonnie," he said curtly.

✥

Further questions were met with the threat of forceful removal. Isobel took her leave. Frustrated by an answer close at hand, she walked off her anger, wandering the manicured grounds at a brisk pace.

The fog had rolled its lazy self away, allowing the sun its token appearance for the afternoon. A nurse wheeled a patient onto the terrace, her uniform starched and stiff, highly impractical for her duties. She placed the break on the bath chair, fluffed her patient's pillow, and sat on a bench with another nurse. The two struck up a conversation like old friends.

Friends. Ever the outcast in all things, friendship was something that Isobel knew little about. If Violet had left, and Elma continued to work at the hospital, then perhaps Elma had other friends. She watched the two nurses for a time, then removed her coat and draped it over an arm (only a tourist would be caught in San Francisco without a coat). Summoning an amiable smile, she approached the two women. "Pardon me. I was wondering if either of you might know an Elma Erving?"

The younger nurse shook her head; the second remembered her, but not well.

"Is there someone who worked with Elma?"

There was: a Miss Faith.

After innumerable inquires and wrong turns, Isobel located Miss Faith, a rail-thin nurse who appeared to be in her late thirties. Her uniform looked as though she added extra starch for the thrill of it. All in all, she did not look like a promising gossip.

Isobel waited outside of the ward, watching the nurse feed a patient. It was tedious. Somewhere in the middle of the bowl, the patient fell asleep. Before the nurse could move onto her next patient, Isobel ambushed her.

"Yes?" Miss Faith asked when the stranger approached.

"Charlotte Bonnie. I'm told you are acquainted with Elma Erving."

"I am."

"Can we talk outside?"

"I'm very busy, Miss Bonnie."

"Were the two of you friends?"

"Yes."

"She killed herself two days ago," Isobel said plainly.

Tears welled in the stern woman's eyes and flowed right over her cheeks. She wobbled as if Isobel had kicked her in the stomach. "Bastard," the woman breathed.

Isobel blinked. Not what she had expected. She hastened forward, took the stunned nurse by the arm, and ushered her outside into fresh air. She planted the woman on a stone bench in the shade, and awkwardly looked elsewhere as the nurse cried into a handkerchief.

Perhaps tact would have been advisable. Too late. When the uncomfortable bit was over with and Faith blew her nose, Isobel looked at the woman.

"I didn't realize you were close," she said by way of apology.

"I've known Elma for years. How did it happen?"

Isobel told her, and at the end, Faith blew out a shaky breath.

"Do you know why she wrote that note?" Isobel asked.

Faith shook her head, but the gesture was unconvincing.

"You said bastard. Why? Were you calling Elma one?"

"Of course not."

"Then who?"

"It's not my place." Faith stood, and Isobel felt like sand was slipping through her hands. "I have patients to tend to."

"Henry Erving and Elizabeth Foster both killed themselves too. Or so it seems. All within a day of each other. I'm not convinced it was suicide. And if there is a chance it wasn't, then don't you think Elma's husband should know?"

Faith paled, but she did not wobble. She stood, staring at the trees for a time, and Isobel let her be. Finally, her shoulders deflated, and the nurse turned. "I was referring to Charles Thorton."

"Who is Charles Thorton?"

Faith sat back down, staring into her hands as she worried over her apron. "Elma met Charles Thorton at Ocean Beach. We often went to the shore as friends. Mr. Thorton said he was a banker, all charm and dapper. He wined and dined her, and as soon as he got her with child, he disappeared." Faith met her eyes, gauging her reaction, but Isobel was unfazed. "I helped Elma look for him. We visited every bank in the city, but none claimed him as an employee. Everyone at Cooper knew Elma was courting the man. It would tarnish her reputation if she left one man for another so quickly, and she didn't have time to wait. So Elma quit here, and went to work at the county hospital; she married the first man who looked twice at her."

"Is this Thorton?" Isobel showed her the photograph that was found in Henry's medical journal.

"No," Faith shook her head. "That's Virgil Cunning-ham."

Isobel nearly shouted in triumph, but she caught herself. "And who is Virgil Cunningham?"

Faith took the photograph, studying it. "He grew up with Henry and Elma. They were close friends. The three enrolled in medical school together."

"Do you know where he is now?"

"Last I heard, he's dead."

"How?"

"I don't know the details. But I heard he cracked from the pressure at school and was sent to the Napa Insane Asylum."

"I see. Was Elma distressed?"

"She never spoke much about Virgil after he left. Seemed to be some ill feelings."

"What kind?"

"I don't know. It was a sore subject."

"Did you know Elizabeth Foster?"

"Oh, yes." It was said with little enthusiasm. "Miss Foster had her eye on Virgil, *and* Henry, and every other man who turned her eye, but mostly Virgil. I don't know what became of her. She left shortly after Virgil went to the asylum. And Henry—he was more concerned with school than marrying, but he fell into some financial problems. He couldn't afford another year's tuition."

"Did Elma ever mention Elizabeth visiting her?"

"Not to me," Faith said. "But after Elma moved to County and married her new man, I didn't see much of her. I don't think she wanted to remember anything or anyone from before her marriage. The business with Thorton nearly drove her mad. I suppose it did in the end."

23

A Never Failing Cure

MARKET WAS A MESS. Isobel ordered Grimm to drop her on a side street and wait while she walked the last block. The tracks rattled and the cable car bells were shrill with warning. Isobel darted in front of a hack, stopped for a cable car, felt a wooden wheel brush her skirt, and ran through a break in traffic. She brandished her umbrella at a bicyclist, who swerved narrowly missing a hay wagon, and hopped on to the curb.

632 Market Street. Right across from the Palace Hotel. The office's location amused her to no end. Isobel slowed as she passed a ready made clothing store, and then she stopped altogether, gazing into the window. Something caught her eye. She entered, marching right past the door-man.

A familiar grey dress sat on a rack. Little violets

trimmed its hem and collar. She rubbed the material.

"Would you like to try it on, ma'am?" a woman's voice interrupted.

"It's lovely."

"That it is. Only eleven-fifty."

"I have a friend who bought this very same dress. She said that the woman who helped her was splendid. Was it you, perhaps?"

The shopgirl blushed. "I can't say. Did your friend have a name?"

"Violet Clowes."

"The woman who drowned herself?"

"I'm afraid so. She was wearing this dress." Isobel wiped an imaginary tear from her eye. "I wanted to thank the woman who helped her."

"It's a popular dress. We sell quite a few, but I can check the books."

"Could you?"

"Of course."

Isobel followed the shopgirl to the counter, where the woman flipped through the pages to the current day and began working her way backwards through the long list of purchases.

A bell rang, and the woman looked up, torn between duties.

"I'll look. Go help your customer."

Isobel slid the abandoned ledger closer, and flipped through the pages at a rapid rate, until V. Clowes leapt out at her. Violet bought the dress a week before her death. Isobel ran her finger down the list, searching for other occurrences of the grey dress. The shopgirl was right, the dress was popular; unfortunately none of the names were familiar. With a sigh, she closed the book, drummed her fingers on the counter in thought, and headed out the door.

The doorman to the office building nodded as she walked inside. She climbed the stairs and stopped in front of a door. The golden sign read *Sanden's Electric Company*.

Isobel fought down a threatening grin, put on a serious face, and plunged inside a room of leather and wood. It smelt like a barber shop that was filled with smoke. Six gentlemen sat in the chairs, all hiding behind newspapers.

"Hello, gentlemen," she said pleasantly. The papers stiffened, and one gentleman, hat held over his face, went so far as to bolt for the door.

She took a seat.

After ten minutes of ruffling papers and masculine throat clearing, the door opened. One man emerged, followed by the doctor. The physician froze. His face turned a shade of red that was somewhere between mortification and anger.

Doctor Pratt was a portly man with laugh lines who was not currently laughing. He herded her inside his office like an energetic sheep dog.

"Madame, this is a gentleman's doctor—"

"It's my husband," she interrupted.

"Oh—I see. He erm, has an ailment?"

"His manhood has lost its vigor," she said bluntly, and sat down.

"I can certainly arrange to examine your husband."

"He's far too embarrassed."

"Most gentlemen are," he glanced at the closed door. "That's why we take mail orders. All the instructions are there, including a three hundred page booklet explaining everything a *man* might need to know."

"He ordered one, but the belt doesn't work. It's

broken."

"Broken?" he sounded surprised. "Perhaps he misused it?"

"Impossible, my husband is a stickler for details. It's a faulty belt."

"Did you bring the belt?"

"Of course not," she gasped. "My husband didn't want me to know, but a wife is—quite aware of those things." She cleared her throat daintily.

"Quite," the doctor agreed.

"I couldn't risk taking it out of the house; he'd know, but I did record the number on the belt." She pushed a slip of paper forward.

"Ah, the serial number."

"Will that work?" she asked with hope.

Doctor Pratt turned to a line of shelves, and selected a ledger. "Without examining the belt, I can't fix it, but perhaps we can see if there are any other complaints with that lot." He consulted her number and then his ledger, a stubby finger tracing the names. "Mr. Leeland at number eight Sapphire House?"

Isobel swallowed her surprise. "Why, yes, that's it."

How did Henry end up with the absent Mr. Leeland's belt? Was Violet courting both men? And Mr. Leeland discovered Henry, lured him to the house, and—strapped an electric belt onto him? Absurd.

She leaned forward, noting the purchase date. Two weeks ago.

"There's been no trouble with the other belts. They are quite reliable. If you can't bring the belt in, you are certainly welcome to purchase another, exchange it when your husband is not present, and return the faulty one. I can offer you a full refund."

Isobel fished around in her handbag, looking lost and forlorn. "I seem to have misplaced my checkbook." She consulted her watch. "And my husband is in a meeting with our banker. I can hardly show up there."

"Perhaps tomorrow, then. I can meet you outside," he stressed.

"Oh, no, I must *have* a belt *today*. I'm very eager for my husband to make a full recovery. I'll just wait in your sitting room until the meeting is over."

Doctor Pratt paled, protested the inconvenience on her time, and thrust a box into her arms. "No charge. All of our products are guaranteed."

"Oh, thank you." She tucked the box under her arm. And with relief, the doctor escorted her towards the door, eager to be rid of her. "One more thing," she said, stopping.

"Yes, madame?"

"My husband is fond of baths. Is this safe to wear while bathing?"

"I do not recommend it."

"Is it unsafe, then?"

"The water will prematurely wear out the contact pads. It's perfectly safe."

"But it's electricity."

"Of a gentle sort," he assured, but quickly amended, "Although it's best to be safe—to use only as directed."

"So it *could* harm him in the bath?"

"It's no more harmful in the bath than on the waist."

"I see." Whether this was the assurances of a quack who wanted people to purchase his product, or reality, she did not know. Of course, if a doctor could market and sell 'harmless' arsenic wafers, then anything was possible.

✛

Henry Erving lay on the slab. His body was bare and it made him appear frozen in the harsh electrical light. A large Y-shaped incision dropped from collarbone to groin. The laceration had been stitched up with precision.

There were marks around his pelvis, red blotches marring the skin, and round burn marks.

"Low voltage injuries," August explained. Color rose in his cheeks, and he quickly covered the naked man. "Cause of death is heart failure."

"Why are his ears red?" She squinted inside.

"Part of the electrocution process. It ruptured his eardrums."

"Not a quiet way to go."

"No," he agreed. "I tested the arsenic wafers. They're not what you would normally find in the box. The two remaining tablets were of a concentrated variety. One dose would not kill a healthy person, but it would certainly make her ill."

"Someone must have switched the tablets," she mused.

"I believe so. Violet came up positive for arsenic. Trace amounts."

"After her grandmother died, she returned to the Y.M.C.A. The landlady said she became ill, and Violet had her summon a doctor. I think Henry was the one who visited her. Can we exhume the grandmother and test her?"

The doctor grimaced. "I can submit the request to a judge." He looked exhausted. Performing a postmortem was taxing work.

"It's not urgent," she relented. "Speaking of court orders, can you request the student records of Henry and

Elma Erving, and Elizabeth Foster from Cooper Medical? And a Virgil Cunningham."

"Who?" he asked, surprised.

"Virgil Cunningham. I think he might be connected to all of this somehow."

"I see." August removed his gruesome apron, and walked to the sink, turning on the taps. "If you think it matters, I'll certainly request the records."

"Thank you."

"I didn't realize you were associated with Ravenwood Agency," he said over his shoulder.

"I'm not exactly," she said carefully. "We're collaborating on this case. Mr. Riot and I have crossed paths before."

"If you had mentioned his name from the first, I wouldn't have been so skeptical."

"I prefer to bully my way into male domains," she quipped. "Have you worked with the agency before?"

"I only know him by reputation. Zephaniah Ravenwood lectured at the medical college once."

"Cooper?"

"Yes, many years ago."

"I didn't realize you attended Cooper."

"All the gifted doctors do." It was not a boast, but fact. "Regardless, every doctor on the west coast came to hear the man speak. Ravenwood never lectured, but on this occasion, he wanted to prove a colleague wrong. The man's cold logic was brutal. It might have been entertaining if every student in the amphitheater had not been cringing with sympathy for his opponent."

"I wish I could have met him," Isobel said, truthfully. She always appreciated an orderly mind. "I didn't realize he was so well respected."

"Really?" August half turned, looking at her incredulously.

"I've only recently returned to San Francisco," she explained.

"Ravenwood was the Lacassagne of the West," August explained.

"But he didn't publish anything, did he?"

"Oh, no," August chuckled. "Ravenwood was a private man. Guarded his secrets like the Mint. From what I gathered, he considered teaching simpletons a waste of his energy."

"I can't fault that reasoning."

August turned off the taps and dried his hands and forearms. "The police department both hated and valued him."

"How was he murdered?"

"You don't know?"

"Should I?"

"It was all over the newspapers. But you were away, I suppose." August gripped the table and wheeled Henry into the refrigerated storage. He emerged with Elma Erving Dunham. Burns covered her lips and jaw, hands and arms, spreading all over her face in testament to a death of horrible agony.

"Somehow Ravenwood ended up with a bounty on his head. The Tongs assassinated him in 1897."

"The Tongs?"

August nodded. "I read the report." His voice dropped to an unnecessary whisper. "Ravenwood was decapitated, and his head was found on a platter in his own home, on his own dining room table. I hear Mr. Riot was nearly killed in the mess."

"I see," she said softly. The implications slammed into her with the force of a wave. She gripped the side of a counter to steady herself.

"Are you all right, Miss Bonnie?"

"Yes," she murmured. She shook loose emotion, and tucked it neatly away, straightening. "Can you determine the age of the fetus?"

"I can."

"Good. I suspect it is much older than what her husband believes. Leave your findings with Ravenwood Agency."

"Of course."

She gathered her things. Fresh air beckoned, and the light of day, anything to erase the image of Riot discovering his partner's head on a platter.

"One more thing," she said. "I think I'll need to take a trip to Napa. Can you request Virgil's records from the Asylum?"

August picked up a pen and bent over the counter, his back to her. "I can certainly try."

"Thank you."

"Not a problem, Miss Bonnie."

24

The Swindler

SNORES FILLED RAVENWOOD OFFICES. The rumbling noise came from a rough fellow who had his dirty boots on the desk. Montgomery Johnson. Isobel had met the bruiser a month ago. The detective had not much cared for Mr. Morgan. The feeling, however, was mutual.

She did not wake the man, but made for the telephone. "Napa Asylum," she requested, sitting on the edge of a desk. At the sound of her voice, Johnson jerked awake, and pulled a gun. He'd be useful in a fight.

The bruiser's gaze settled on her. He holstered his gun, and she introduced herself.

"Mr. Riot is consulting with me."

"Consulting with you?" Johnson repeated. His eyes narrowed, then he looked her up and down. There wasn't much to look at. He stomped to the consultation room, cracked the door open, and asked if it was true.

A deep, low voice answered, but Isobel missed the words.

The line crackled. "Napa Asylum."

"Nurse Jones from Cooper Medical," she said. "I'm updating our records and I see that we're missing information on a Virgil Cunningham. Could you fill in some blanks? An official request. I see. Not even the date of discharge?"

She was told to hold a moment, and sat, rearranging the items on the desk, until they were perfectly orderly.

Noise signaled the nurse's return, and Isobel pressed the ear piece to her ear. Virgil Cunningham had died on October 30th 1898. Heart failure. "And what was he there for?" she asked. The response was not helpful. That required a formal request. The ploy had been worth an attempt.

Isobel rang off and stared absently at the neat desk. Virgil died, and three days later Violet checked into the Y.M.C.A., then attempted suicide two days later. Suggestive.

She ignored Johnson's gaze, picked up her things, and made for the consultation room.

"Riot's busy."

"Aren't we all?" she asked, and then poked the snake. "Except you. Is Mr. Tim present?"

Johnson lifted a small spittoon from his desk, and spit, making a slurping noise as he did so. Charming, she thought.

"I'll take that as a no." Careful not to disturb the air, she opened the door and slipped inside the room.

Riot was hunched over the big table. He was in his shirtsleeves, cuffs rolled to his elbows, and had a magnifying glass and tweezers in hand. Her eyes lingered on the back of his neck where black hair met a pristine collar; his hair was in need of a trim, curling ever so slightly over tanned skin. Given his coloring, Isobel wondered if there was some Mediterranean in his blood.

"I refuse to thank you for the use of your hack," she said to his back.

"And I refuse to say you are welcome," he murmured without interrupting his work.

"Good, that's settled. How goes the puzzle?" The table was strewn with glass plates and the brittle remains of sacrificial paper.

"Slow but steady."

She surveyed the pieced together fragments. "It's the same dreadful letter from the spirit world, over and over again. In the same hand."

"With slight variations," he agreed. "But not all." Riot stood, and straightened, arching his back with a slight grimace. It cracked.

Isobel nearly rubbed his shoulders; instead she thrust a box into his hands. "I brought you a present. It might help your back. There's instructions and all."

Riot looked at the label. "I am *not* testing this."

"Coward," she grinned. "Where's your sense of adventure?"

"Gone with my youth."

"All the more reason to try it," she quipped.

"How thoughtful of you, Bel." He set the box on a chair, unopened. "Productive day?"

She nearly preened. "You first."

"I asked," he returned, planting himself firmly in front of the table.

"We could play a game of chess for the business, but

that could take awhile."

"Especially considering I don't know how to play."

She blinked at the man as if he were a simpleton. "Poker?"

"I don't play with chance—or cheaters," she added, having seen his quick hands.

"Teach me to play chess then."

"Only if you teach me to pick locks."

"Now what makes you think I can pick a lock?"

Isobel crossed her arms, mirroring his own stance.

"It wouldn't be my 'fair and deft hands' by any chance?" he asked with swagger.

Color threatened, but Isobel stood her ground.

A knowing light entered Riot's eyes. "I know I have you when you're speechless."

She opened her mouth, but no quick words emerged. Isobel cleared her throat, knocking her brain on track. "Will you teach me to pick locks? And track," she added.

"All that I know is yours as long as you teach me to play chess."

"You're a horrid negotiator, Riot."

"Depends on what I was aiming for," he replied cryptically. Before she could prod this new line of conversation, Riot stepped aside and gestured towards the paper he had been working on.

Isobel read it aloud. *"Roses are red. Violet is blue. Petals fall and so she will too. The house beckons."* She frowned. "That is horrid prose."

"Ghosts aren't known for their poetry."

"It's written in the same hand as the letters."

"As far as I can tell," Riot said. "There's a good chance that this is what Henry discovered in his bedroom. A note this small could have been slipped into his coat pocket."

"Ghosts do that," she agreed, remembering the busy grocers. "Or—it was put into the room while that fellow Garrett distracted the landlady."

"Plenty of opportunity."

"I'm afraid I may have solved your case."

Riot leaned back on the table, expectant. She told him of her day. At the end, he sighed. "I warned Bert Dunham that he might not like the answer."

Isobel had not thought of that detail. "But Elma was happy, wasn't she? Miss Faith said that Elma didn't want anything to do with her past. At least there's that."

Riot smiled, but there was sadness in his eyes. "Yet in the end, she didn't love him enough to trust. I think Bert Dunham is the type of man who would forgive most anything. It's a shame she didn't try."

"We still have to track Charles Thorton down. And we don't know what Violet said to Elma—or if it really was Violet who visited at all."

Riot cocked his head, but before she could elaborate on her theory, the door opened. Tim appeared, closing it softly again. He whipped off his cap, thrust his hands in his pocket, and stood rocking on his heels, looking like a child bursting with a secret to be told.

"Evening, Mr. Tim," she greeted.

"Miss Bel."

"Bonnie today," Riot reminded.

"So she is."

"I've brought you a present, A.J."

"So did Bel." Riot nodded towards the box.

Tim stepped forward, and whistled, eyes twinkling. "I'm afraid my present isn't as invigorating. I looked into that list of banks. Turns out that Elma was looking for an employee by the name of—"

"Charles Thorton," Isobel supplied.

Tim blinked, surprised. "Not bad for a girl."

Isobel snorted at the jab.

"But *this* old man," he thrust a thumb at his chest, "tracked the fellow down. He's not a banker; he's a swell and con-man who is known to me, and he is waiting outside with a tongue that needs loosening."

Riot calmly began rolling down his sleeves, but Isobel was overcome. Feeling like a child on Christmas morning, she planted a kiss on his shiny head. Tim turned red, and she shot out the door.

Charles Thorton was not precisely waiting; he was being held prisoner. Matthew Smith, an ex-patrolman, and Johnson, both large intimidating men, stood on either side of a petrified gentleman dressed in the latest fashion. His hair gleamed, his mustache was oiled, and his plaid suit clashed with a garish waistcoat.

When Thorton saw a woman enter, he put on charm and a smile that would supposedly melt any female's heart. The smile was lost on Isobel. She stopped and considered her opponent.

Smith looked to his senior in question, then back to the woman in their office. His gaze traveled over her shoulder, and she felt Riot stop at her side.

"It's your investigation," he murmured in her ear.

"Your man caught him."

"I believe Tim is besotted after your kiss. He'd likely follow you anywhere now."

"Turn about is fair play."

"I always have Watson," he agreed.

Her eyes danced with mirth, but when she turned them back on Thorton, they mirrored his charm.

Isobel had the size of the man and she wanted him all

to herself. "This gentleman looks like a civilized sort. Surely there's no need for a guard."

Smith and Johnson looked at Riot, who nodded. The men left and Isobel moved forward, offering her hand. Thorton stood, and took it, planting a smooth kiss on her knuckles.

"Such a gentleman. Shall we converse in private?"

She gestured towards Riot's office.

"Ladies first," Thorton tipped an imaginary hat, and followed on her heels. Riot was close behind.

"Sit down, Mr. Thorton." Isobel sat on the edge of the desk, and nudged a chair out with her foot. Any name he'd give would likely be as false as the one he had used with Elma, so she didn't bother asking after another.

Riot stood silent by the back wall. It made Thorton uneasy. He glanced back at the quiet man. "This is unlawful. I have a lawyer."

"Questions aren't unlawful," she soothed. "Sit." And she crossed her legs, showing off a shapely ankle. Mr. Thorton sat, eyes appreciating the view.

"I didn't get your name, Miss."

"Bonnie."

"That's for sure."

Isobel smiled pleasantly. "I hear you're a banker," she said, mimicking her twin's sultry tones.

"Formerly employed," he replied.

Thorton started to twist in his chair, to eye Riot, but Isobel gripped his tie, pulling him gently back. She ran her fingers down the ghastly waistcoat and toyed with a diamond stick pin. "It looks as though it paid well."

"I do all right." He relaxed beneath her stroking touch.

"Were you acquainted with an Elma Erving?"

"Can't say the name is familiar."

"No?" She looked him square in the eye. "You should think harder."

"I know a lot of women, and they know me."

"Wrong answer." She pressed on his stick pin, hard. The repositioned tip dug into his skin. Thorton yelped, and hopped out of his chair, but she planted her boot on his thigh, and kicked. He fell back into the chair. "Oh, dear, the back of your tie pin came off. Let me help you with that." She plucked the pin from the silk. "Are you sure you don't remember Elma Erving?" she asked, straightening his tie and making to reinsert the pin.

"I might recall," he hastened. "A woman I met at Ocean Beach. Things didn't work out between us, but we left on amiable terms."

"You abandoned her with child."

"It's none of my concern. We weren't engaged. I didn't take her for a soiled dove."

"You seduced her." She jabbed the pin back into the silk. Thorton flinched, hands gripping the armrest. "And then you ran."

"With her loose morals, any man might have got her with child. There's no proof."

"You're right, there isn't." Isobel straightened, picking up an ink pot from the desk. "So there's no harm in answering my questions. Why did you target Elma? You strike me as a man who has a more—profitable taste." Slowly, she unscrewed the lid.

"Does a man need a reason to seduce a lovely face?"

"Lovely faces are notoriously clumsy." Isobel leant forward. "That's a nice suit."

Thorton looked down, eyes darting to the pot in her hand.

"I once dropped an ink pot on a man. By accident of

course. It ruined his suit and stained his skin black for months. I laughed every time he—disrobed. Now *that's* a soiled dove."

Thorton tried to squirm away, but she jabbed her finger on his pin. He stilled.

"You're a lunatic."

"No, I'm a very clumsy woman who would like a straight answer." She swirled the liquid in the pot. "Elma wasn't wealthy, it wasn't love, so what drew you to her?"

"Someone paid me to seduce her. That's all. There's no crime in entertaining a willing woman."

"Who paid you?"

"A woman named Violet."

"Where did you meet?"

"At one of the cafes along Ocean Beach. I don't know how she got wind of me."

"Because you're not near as clever as you imagine. When did she contact you?"

"I don't know. Some time last summer."

"What did she look like?"

"Taller than that fellow," Thorton thrust his chin towards Riot. "Reddish hair, pale green eyes—a handsome woman all around."

Isobel fired more questions, but Thorton had no more answers. When she had her fill of the swindler, she let him go, and he bolted.

Riot sat in the vacated chair, crossed his legs, and met her gaze.

"A neat circle of death, isn't it?"

"A little too neat," he noted.

"And well planned." She replaced the lid and set the ink pot on the desk. "The nurse said that Violet had her eye on Virgil. Maybe Violet blamed Elma and Henry for his death. Then paid Thorton to seduce Elma, to ruin her, and then lured Henry into a relationship and tricked him into the bath. Men aren't exactly known for their intellect when a naked woman is involved."

"We are simple creatures."

"Surely not you, Mr. Riot?"

"I'm only a man."

"A pity," she sighed.

Riot arched an amused brow, but whatever was on his lips, she never discovered. The door opened, and Tim poked in his head. "I've a telegram for a Miss Bonnie."

Isobel opened the missive and read. She met Riot's gaze, eyes gleaming with excitement. "I sent a query to Victoria Foster's solicitor in New York. As it turns out, she was not without money. Her estate is valued at just over a million dollars. Mansfield Randall, Victoria's brother, was lost at sea seven years ago. Randall is set to be declared dead in a month's time. Violet was going to inherit every last penny."

Riot interlaced his fingers. "Henry's money issues and sudden interest in Violet takes on a whole new light."

"To say nothing of the concentrated arsenic wafers and the grandmother's death."

25

Ladies and Lock Picks

Sunday, February 18th, 1900

SUNDAYS WERE TEDIOUS. PREACHERS preached; families picnicked, and women wore white, while the whores and johns of the Barbary Coast feasted on sin.

Isobel fit nowhere. She wanted answers. The gears in her mind were a ceaseless, hungry machine reaching for resolution. Waiting on a judge's order did not suit her, but there was little to be done, especially on Sunday.

A veil of silver hung over quiet streets. The lanes and alleys were empty—too early for hoodlums and cutthroats. Isobel walked down a back alley strewn with refuse and lively with rats, opened a rickety storm door, and disappeared into darkness. A brick wall greeted her. She ran her fingers along its rough edge, dipped her finger into a jagged hole, and pressed the latch. It clicked. The brick swung open. A false door. She entered the maw and closed the secret door. It was pitch dark, and she shuffled forward in silence, until she came to an identical door. The brick swung inward, and she stepped into a curtained room and plush carpet.

She wiped her shoes on a mat, reached for a feathered mask on a stand, and climbed a short stairwell, moving into a maze of Grecian statues, gold gilt, and obscene paintings. Isobel navigated the quiet hallways with ease. She stopped at a door and knocked softly. When no one immediately answered, she tried the handle. It was locked. So she knocked, harder.

The door cracked open. A sleepy-eyed Lotario looked out. He frowned at the mask. "Hades suits you so well, sister dear."

She tried to enter, but he kept the door firmly open at a crack. "I'm entertaining," he hissed. "What are you doing here?"

"Still?" Isobel removed the owl mask. "Are you entertaining a client or a friend?"

Lotario stepped out into the hallway and shut the door behind him. He wore a sheet and she tried to turn off her olfactory sense.

"All my clients become friends," he boasted.

"Did you find out anything more?"

Lotario rolled his eyes, and leaned against his door. "It's Sunday," he drawled.

"And you had all day yesterday to question people."

"Your newspaper article loosened Lola's tongue. I met her for tea. It was tedious. You owe me."

"What did she say?"

Lotario held up a finger. "First, a promise."

"I'm trying to solve a trio of murders, Ari. What did you discover?"

"Promise me that you will take today off and spend it with Riot."

"I'm on my way to his house."

"I'll send you a telegram then."

"What did Violet's friend tell you?" she growled, and grabbed his sheet.

"I'll shout for Bruno."

She let him go. Bruno was a small giant, and the stalwart bouncer of the *Narcissus*.

"Promise." He held up his pinky.

Isobel glared, but relented, hooking her pinky around his and feeling utterly childish.

"That's better," he smiled. "I can't stand it when you are serious. I'll even let you borrow a delicious tea gown."

"No."

Lotario crossed his arms. "I found out what Violet was up to for a year."

"Fine, tell me."

"Violet wasn't working as an actress. She was staying at a sanitarium: *Bright Waters* in Calistoga. Violet was supposedly near to cracking before she left. The health resort restored her. Now, wait here while I get that dress."

⁜

The skull of a raven protruded from the door, a big iron visage with a deadly beak that knocked into a metal plate. This was precisely the kind of house that Isobel would have loved as a child. Its turrets and windows and sprawling hillside location brought to mind Poe. The smiling woman who answered the door was far from the Red

Death, however.

"Charlotte Bonnie for Mr. Riot." Isobel felt odd entering through a formal door. The day before she had visited as Mr. Morgan, and the month before that, a mysterious guest. "You must be Miss White. I met your sons yesterday. Tobias is a talker." Miss White was taken aback by her friendliness. Isobel had donned Lotario's dress, and for once looked a proper lady.

"He is at that, I hope he didn't bother you?"

"Never," Isobel said, walking into the foyer. "Saved me time and was good company to boot."

"Happy to hear, Miss Bonnie. If you'll just wait in the parlor, I'll let Mr. Riot know you've arrived."

The woman left, and Isobel made a slow circuit around the polished room. She stopped at the wide doors that led to the second parlor, and the formal dining room beyond.

There was a large table and a heavy chandelier. She imagined Ravenwood's head on the platter, staring down that long row of rooms. Partner for twenty years, friend, a father figure perhaps. What would seeing such a thing do to a man?

Her thoughts went to Watson, not the cat, but her favorite fictional detective. Sherlock Holmes had plummeted into a watery abyss. Watson had not witnessed his friend's death, but his grief seeped from the pages. Finding a note was one thing; discovering your friend's head on a dinner platter in your own home was quite another.

Isobel's heart lurched. This wasn't fiction. The head had been a message, and considering that Riot was the living partner, it had likely been left for him to find. She shivered, and turned from the room, finding the man in the flesh.

His eyes were quiet and appreciative and he smiled

warmly. "Good morning, Bel. You look well rested, and—"

"Womanly?" She stepped towards him, so he wouldn't see that long passage to the waiting room.

"Lovely."

"I think Lotario was hoping for seductive. It's my twin's dress," she confided.

"It suits you. How is Lotario?"

"Exhausted, but useful. He's found out where Violet disappeared to for a year." Isobel held her breath, letting anticipation build, but Riot only waited. "*Bright Waters* in Napa," she blurted out. "It's a sanitarium, and they aren't on the telephone. Do you have plans for tomorrow?"

"I do not."

"Good, we'll sail at first light."

"Aye, Capt'n," he saluted. "I'm breakfasting on the terrace with Miss Dupree. Would you care to join us?"

"I'd love to."

"Circle around back." There was mischief in his eyes, and she very nearly rubbed her hands together.

Isobel showed herself out, took her time admiring the hedges, and then ventured down the long driveway. She heard laughter, a soft feminine sound that trickled like water.

The terrace sat in sunlight and the woman in the white tea gown was radiant.

"Mr. Riot, I forgot to ask—" Isobel paused. "Oh, pardon me, I didn't realize you were entertaining."

Miss Dupree sized her up with a quick sweep. Her eyes said quaint, and she offered a hand. Isobel shook it. "Charlotte Bonnie with the *Call*."

Riot cleared his throat, and stood, gesturing towards a chair. "Won't you join us?"

"Since you asked." She sat in the empty chair and

surveyed the breakfast tray, helping herself to coffee and scone.

"You're a reporter, Miss Bonnie?"

"I am. And I have my eye on a certain detective."

Miss Dupree lent forward with a spark in her eye. "So he *was* the mysterious savior?"

"I'm trying to pull the whole story from the man. He's a hard shell to crack."

"Are you?" It was said in that warm, playful way that invited more.

Riot returned with a charming smile, and Isobel wondered how many women had fallen for his easy confidence. "In my line of work, strict client confidentiality is key."

"An assurance for your clients, no doubt," Miss Dupree noted.

He nodded. "Once integrity is broken, a man is ruined in my business."

"As with most professions," Miss Dupree observed. Isobel knew that the woman had her own secrets to keep. A mistress did not betray her men. At best, she'd be out of work; at worst, she'd be dead.

"Perhaps you could persuade Mr. Riot to loosen his tongue," Isobel ventured.

The woman laughed. "An enticing challenge."

"Ladies," Riot said, "I *am* present. I believe you're supposed to scheme out of ear shot."

"I'll have to keep trying my own luck, then."

"I wish you the best of it." Miss Dupree made to leave. And Riot stood.

"Even a morsel will be enough to elaborate on the story." Isobel pulled out pen and paper. "Is Mr. Riot as gallant at home as he is on the streets?"

"Quite the gentleman."

"Is he? Do you dine together often?"

"I really must go, Miss Bonnie. It was a pleasure meeting you."

"Is marriage in the air?"

"I rent a room. That is all." Miss Dupree did not saunter away, she walked briskly, eager to be away from the reporter.

When the terrace was free of unwanted ears, Riot returned to his seat, and took up his fork. "A convincing performance as the nosey reporter."

"And you're the tight-lipped detective who refuses to talk. Do you think she's spying for someone?"

"I don't know," he admitted. "But she's hiding something."

Isobel smirked. "Aren't we all?"

⁘

Isobel followed Riot into the carriage house. They walked past the horses and hay, and up the back stairs. The top room was filled with worktables and spare parts, nets, and bric-a-brac of a lifetime. It smelled of grease, tobacco, and copper.

A small cot was stuffed in a corner, and a tidy kitchen and stove was the only spot of refinement. A wizened old man bent over one of his worktables. He stood on a stepping stool talking to the boy at his side.

"It's usually safe," Riot said to Isobel's shock. Her fingers twitched. She wanted to attack the room and restore order. But Tim and his tinkering distracted her. They wove their way through the mess and she peered over the man's shoulder. The electric belt was submersed in a bucket of water. Wires ran out of the bucket, connecting it to a light bulb on a stand. The bulb glowed faintly.

Tobias looked up and grinned. "Mr. Tim is teaching me about electricity."

"And myself," the old man grunted. "I don't think this belt could have killed that man." He turned to a light box. "But watch this." Tim picked up two clamps with wires attached to the box. He fastened them over a metal disc on the belt, removed his hands, and switched on the box. The light bulb flared, illuminating the tinker's home. A human skull wearing a prospector's battered hat grinned from a high shelf.

"Whoever was in the house with Henry could have used a separate battery," said Riot.

"And left the belt on so it would appear like suicide." Isobel leaned closer, peering into the bucket. She wondered what a shock would feel like.

Riot switched off the box before she could wonder more. "It would explain the freshly scrubbed areas. The murderer was covering his or her tracks," he said.

"Well I'm not positive, mind you," Tim said, rubbing his beard. "I was thinking of setting something up in the bath and tossing a dog in to see what would happen."

Tobias made a strangled sound. "We can't!" he gasped.

Riot raised a hand, glared at Tim, and assured the boy that they were not going to electrocute a dog. His firm words were more for the old man, however.

Isobel reached into the bucket and removed the clamps, holding them up in consideration. "Even if this didn't kill—it would hurt, wouldn't it? Especially considering where the contact plates were positioned."

Men and boy winced.

"The thought alone hurts," Tim admitted.

"Torture." Riot frowned. "*Hell hath no fury like a woman*

scorned."

"Or a man," Isobel mused. "Considering those photographs we discovered in the house." She looked at Tobias and Tim got her hint. The old man removed the belt and handed the boy the heavy bucket.

"Go empty that, Tobias."

The boy sloshed his way downstairs.

"You think Henry had a male lover?"

"I don't honestly know, Riot," Isobel admitted. "There's still the elusive Mr. Leeland to consider. And—" she hesitated, working her way through an errant thought. "I'm not entirely sure the Violet who visited Elma was the same woman who hopped into the sea."

"The brooch."

Isobel nodded, and told him about the grey dress in the ready made store.

"Mrs. Fleet said that Elma didn't appear to recognize the visitor," Riot said. "Any woman might have posed as Violet."

"On the other hand, given Violet's history in theatre, the voice under the porch could have easily been hers."

Riot rubbed a hand over his beard. "Let's hope *Bright Waters* will give us more answers."

"I have my Vigilance boys looking for the hackman," Tim offered.

"Your help is invaluable, Mr. Tim." And she meant it. Tracking down a lone hackman without a name in San Francisco was a time consuming affair.

"So is yours, Miss Bel." The old man crossed his arms and eyed her. "I'm keen on recruiting you for the agency. Good pay, full room and board if you like."

The words brought a whole jumble of thoughts to the surface, and she kept her eyes well away from Riot, focusing on the cluttered workshop. She took a breath and looked at Tim. "I thank you, but I have a job—two in fact."

"The offer stands."

"I'm trouble, and your agency would be in a world of mess if I'm discovered. I've involved myself too much as it is," she realized. Her instincts urged her to leave, to sever ties and flee, but Riot's calm voice cut through the impulse.

"I thought I'd teach Bel to pick locks. Can we use your sample locks?"

The prospect of learning to pick a lock, long ached for, overrode concern. What woman could resist such an offer?

In short order and little fuss, Tim set up his clamps and practice locks. Names like lever locks, warded locks, and the latest pin tumblers spun in her head. Torque wrenches, rake picks, and skeleton keys. There was no straightforward lock. Preparedness was key.

Riot demonstrated the lever lock, and handed her the pick. She stepped forward, and jammed the metal into the hole, fumbling blindly for what he said was a simple catch.

"Ease up, or you'll break it, girl," Tim said.

She removed the pick, and eyed the keyhole. "I'm beginning to get a sense of what a man must feel when he's confronted with his first woman."

Tim slapped his knee and made a sound like a donkey. Riot primly adjusted his spectacles. "Trust me, Bel. Not a whole lot of thought is involved."

"Perhaps I'm overthinking," she conceded. With a breath, she inserted the pick, and tried again. This time, it clicked, and the bolt slid. She gave a shout of triumph. And at Riot's direction, repeated the procedure until she had the feel of it.

"That's the simplest lock." Riot handed her a torque

wrench and selected another straight pick with a slight curve at the end. She inserted wrench and pick, and turned the wrench, applying pressure as Riot had instructed. With much scraping and forcing, she pushed up a pin, feeling the tiny internal spring, then moved onto the next, going down the line. Nothing clicked, nothing moved. She pressed her lips together and persevered.

"Gently, Bel. Try closing your eyes. Visualize the pins in your mind." She did, and she felt Riot move behind her. Her heart galloped. "You can't force it; you must feel it," he said quietly. The pick snapped, and she opened her eyes with an oath.

Tim chuckled, scratching his beard. "I'm not sure you're the best to teach her, A.J."

Riot cleared his throat, fished out the broken end, and handed her another.

"Well," Tim grunted, "I cannot pay witness to this massacre of my picks." He stomped off and made himself scarce.

"Sorry," she muttered.

"These are his training picks," Riot explained, and added in a louder voice. "And old like him."

"Shut it, boy!"

Riot pulled over a stool, and Isobel sat, glaring at the offending lock.

"The lock is not your enemy," he said. "It's a puzzle. A very delicate one."

She took a breath. "Right." And tried again. This was far more difficult than she had ever supposed.

26

The Wonderful Sea

"AHOY THERE!" RIOT CALLED from the wharf. Isobel was stretched along the bow spirit, making an adjustment to the lines. "Permission to come aboard, Captain?"

"Granted. Stow your gear," she replied in the deeper tones of Mr. Morgan.

Riot climbed on board, and watched as she tugged and tied, and shimmied back on deck. Her short black hair was skewed in all directions and she eyed his own attire: cap and peacoat.

"I've just lost a wager," she sighed.

"With whom?"

"Watson. I was sure you'd arrive in white linen and a boater."

He held up a leather luggage case. "It's in here minus the boater."

"Close enough," she grinned.

"Captain Morgan," a voice interrupted. Isobel looked towards the dock. The watchman was there. "Would you like a tow?"

"I'll be fine," she hollered back. "The wind will do and the tide is good."

The grizzled man tipped his cap. "Will your sister be sailing today?"

"Not today, sir. I've a charter," she nodded towards her passenger.

"Good luck to you, then." The watchman stomped off and Isobel moved forward, untying the warps. The *Lady* creaked, shifting away from the wharf. Riot blew out a breath and secured his suitcase below deck. Watson uncurled from the settee, blinked in remembrance, and the big tom shot right for him, mewling for shrimp.

"I'm afraid I've nothing for you today." He scratched the cat behind the ears, and received a look of disdain before Watson shot up the companionway. Riot followed.

Isobel stood at the mast, hoisting the staysail. Lines glided through the blocks, and the breeze caught the red canvas in the silver light, pushing the bow towards the choppy bay. She belayed the halyard, coiling it around a pin on the mast. When the luff was taut, she set the jib flying, and hurried over planks, balancing lightly on the restless deck. The warp aft was next, and the staysail caught the wind, pulling the cutter from the wharf. Isobel dropped into the cockpit across from Riot and gripped the tiller.

"How's your sea legs, Riot?"

"I've never owned any, Captain."

Waves touched the hull, one after another, rocking the boat as it drifted into the bay. "I won't stick you in the galley, promise."

Watson hopped on the cabin trunk, and calmly licked his paws, oblivious to the world of water and spray.

"Where did you find that cat?"

"Same as you."

"He ambushed you on board your own boat?"

She smiled. "Watson, unlike a detective I know, was a gentleman. He asked politely."

Riot tipped his cap at a cocky angle, and sat back. "I'm a regular scoundrel."

"Positively rakish," she said. "Hold her steady." Isobel nodded towards the tiller, and Riot blinked. After a moment's hesitation, he gripped the handle. The wood was smooth and warm, and it moved with the push and pull of waves on the keel. He looked to the horizon, spotted the distant Angel Island, and tried to keep her on course. His efforts were less than successful.

Isobel sprinted out of the cockpit, tugging sail ties on her way to the mast. The canvas slipped free, shifting with the rocking boat. When she reached the mast, she gripped both halyards and began hoisting the mainsail. With every heave, the tackle turned and the gaff and canvas raised. The sail flapped, and the boat ached to leap with the wind.

When the halyards became too heavy to manage together, Isobel switched to raising one at a time, alternating between peak and throat, using all five feet of her wiry frame. On the last few feet, she braced her feet on the mast and swigged up the throat tight, belayed it to its pin, and threw herself at the peak.

The gaff rose, the canvas flapped, and Isobel shot up the mast, scaling the mast hoops like a ladder. He craned back his neck, watching her bob and sway with the sea over open air. When she was satisfied with her adjustments in the hounds, she grabbed the ropes, and climbed, hand over hand, down, landing on the deck with soft feet.

"Tighten the mainsheet," Isobel called, hurrying back to the cockpit. Riot looked at the maze of lines, feeling utterly lost.

"That one there," she said, gripping the tiller. He could feel the strength in the hand; the instant assuredness and the cutter's response.

Riot unwound the line, and pulled the rope through its tackle. The boom shifted, the canvas caught, and the *Lady* leapt forward, heeling to starboard as the wind funneled through the Golden Gate. Riot braced himself against the opposite bench as the boat leaned.

"There, make it fast," she ordered.

He wrapped it back around its cleat, and the cutter surged through the choppy grey, throwing up salt and cool spray. Riot wiped the sea from his spectacles and found the captain grinning.

"I'll make a sailor out of you yet, Riot."

He surveyed the forty-one feet of deck and the fifteen feet of bow spirit that thrust from the prow like a spear. "How do you manage this alone?" he asked.

"The *Lady* is confident. She's been on these waters all her life. Practically sails herself. Just needs a nudge here and there."

"Still, it's a lot of boat."

"When I take you beyond the Golden Gate, you'll be happy she's over forty-feet."

Not if, but when. That word heartened Riot to no end. But today, he was glad that they were headed north, staying well inside the bay.

27

Bright Waters

A GROUP OF WOMEN stretched towards the afternoon sun. Music played from a phonograph; a ragtime tune to inspire cheerfulness. The women's hair flowed down their backs and their dresses were loose and white. An enthusiastic smile was plastered on the instructor's face.

"By God, kill me now," Isobel said through her teeth.

"Not for you?" Riot asked.

She looked at him sideways. "No."

He offered his arm. "For reinforcement."

Isobel accepted, and they walked under the swaying palm and oak to what appeared to be the main ward, a hacienda-style building with an expansive courtyard. A fountain trickled in the center, and a woman in a wide hat and flowing dress stood on the green with a rabbit on a leash.

"Perhaps Watson will take a leash," Isobel mused.

"You'd have little need of me, then."

She snorted, and together they walked through the doors. The entry hall was open and airy and altogether welcoming. A woman wearing a blue dress and apron greeted them. It was identical to the dress that Violet had in her trunk.

"Welcome to Bright Waters," the woman's voice was as cheerful as the name.

"Mr. Morgan and my wife," Riot returned. Isobel clung to his arm, looking around nervously. Her act wasn't far from the truth, she had only to think of the group of women swaying with the breeze outside. To all appearances, Riot and she were the quintessential wealthy health spa couple. He in ivory linen and a panama hat, and she, in Lotario's frilly white tea gown, recently recovered from fever, looking pale and delicate with her short hair.

"I'm sorry, but your name is not listed."

"You weren't on the telephone, so we decided to travel here ourselves. It's—urgent. For my wife's sake, I hoped we might tour the grounds."

"If you'll wait here, I'll speak to Dr. Bright." The woman walked off, and Isobel shared a look with Riot. He casually reached over the counter and turned the guest-book towards him, flipping through pages. Nothing caught his eye.

The nurse returned. Dr. Bright was with a patient, but the sanitarium could accommodate them. A spare bunga-low was available—for a fee.

"Splendid." Riot paid in cash, and they were shown to the guest house.

The bungalow was clean and open, and offered an unparalleled view of oak covered hills. A small sitting room led to a bedroom where a large bed dominated the space. Isobel peeked into the bathroom. A cast iron tub sat facing an open window, with nothing but trees and countryside to stare back. She thought of Henry and Violet. It took effort to tear her eyes from the bath. Closing the door, she turned on the taps to scrub the train and carriage ride from her face.

Feeling refreshed, Isobel emerged to find Riot carefully brushing out his spare suit.

"Do we have a plan, Riot?" she asked.

"I generally bide my time and look for an opening, but just in case you find an opening before me—" He handed her a pick. "This generally works for filing cabinets."

She tucked the pick in her handbag. Given that Cooper Hospital and Napa Asylum both required a warrant, they had decided to forego the official red tape at Bright Waters.

A cool breeze cut through the sunshine, rustling through leaves and making the trees sing. Isobel inhaled the surrounding wildness—dry earth and pine.

"Not at all an unpleasant place to convalesce," Riot observed.

"Not outwardly," she said, sinking into an armchair by the window. "There are dark sides to asylums and sanitariums. A murderer and rapist will get a fair trial, but a woman who has a mind of her own can be locked away for life by her husband's signature."

"Don't fret, Bel. I swear I won't leave you here."

"How kind of you, Riot. I'm not sure I could think of a way to escape," she said dryly, gesturing at the open expanse of wilderness.

"Well, one thing we know for certain, it's doubtful that Violet was here against her will."

"And I'd wager, if that blue dress I found was any indication, that Violet worked here while she was in Napa the first time."

Riot nodded. "Shall we tour the grounds and see if we can't uncover any hidden horrors?"

"That sounds lovely."

✛

"This is the hot mineral bath. A restorative to calm the nerves." The pool was spacious, and the smell of sulfur and earth was strong. Steam hissed from the water. "We recommend alternating between the hot and cold," the physician explained.

Dr. Julius Bright was as jovial as his name. "Through that door, we have wet blanket wraps, volcanic mud baths, and a masseuse."

"Oh, Atticus, don't you dare leave me here." Isobel clung to his arm as if he was about to shove her into the steamy pool. It looked utterly delicious. "This is all for show."

Riot patted her hand, looking to the doctor in apology. "It's not like that newspaper article, darling. I promise."

The doctor ushered them out of the calming pool and into a hallway with open arches on one side. "Perhaps I can ease any fears you may have, Mrs. Morgan."

"I read an article," she said in a half-way to panicked voice, "about a reporter who feigned madness to investigate a madhouse. The doctors appeared to care, but they didn't, not one bit and terrible things happened. Her name was Nellie Bly, don't you remember, dear?" Isobel looked at Riot with desperation, but nearly lost it when she saw the glint of humor in his eye. He was enjoying this.

"I do recall," he said in grave tones.

Before she succumbed to laughter, she looked at the doctor and threw accusations at him. "You're only showing us the civil areas. I'm sure you have all kinds of terrible practices behind closed doors. As soon as my husband is gone, I'll be locked in a cage."

Bright shook his head. "Not at all, ma'am. We do not use restraint and the patients are free to refuse any of our suggested treatments. Everything here is as open as you see. Let me show you our ward where the most ailing reside. But I ask that you remain calm—these women are fragile."

They walked from a Mediterranean like setting to a more clinical building. Bright bent his head to a passing nurse. The woman smiled, and stepped forward, opening one of the doors. It was unlocked.

A clawfoot tub sat in a tiled room. Pristine and scrubbed, the bath faced a shuttered window. The nurse opened the shutters. Palm trees swayed in the afternoon breeze. "We use hydrotherapy here, cold and hot, depending on the ailment," the nurse explained. "The patient determines the length of treatment. As you can imagine, for privacy's sake, we can't show you an occupied room."

"Because you have tied them up," Isobel accused.

"Oh, no, ma'am, we don't restrain our patients," the nurse stepped forward, placing a gentle hand on Isobel's arm. Her touch was calm and sure, and she seemed a good-natured woman.

"But what if a lunatic flies into a rage and murders me while I'm sleeping?"

"We specialize in nervous disorders—especially acute paranoia," Bright explained, sharing a look with Isobel's husband. "However, even with issues of uncontrollable hysteria and anger, I find that the environment alone has a calming and restorative effect. One can hardly rage in paradise. Nurse, perhaps you can allow Mrs. Morgan a peek at one of the patients while I speak with her husband."

Isobel let herself be coaxed away from Riot's arm. She followed the nurse down the hall. The woman opened the door a crack.

Isobel looked inside. Steam filled the room, stirred by a cool breeze from the open window. A heavy canvas drape covered the open side of the bathtub. There was a hole in the canvas for the patient's linen wrapped head.

"Can I get you anything, Miss?" the nurse whispered.

"No thank you," a drowsy voice replied.

"Very good, Miss. Ring if you need anything." The nurse gently shut the door, and explained, "The canvas top is to keep the heat in—not the patient. She can remove it on her own at any time."

"But some asylums restrain their patients."

"Not as much anymore, but some do, yes. With straight-jackets and such."

Isobel recalled the heavy jackets from which she had watched a man, after much wiggling and contorting, escape. They were made of canvas, too. Her thoughts drifted to Henry in the bath, and the canvas like thread she had discovered on the floor.

"We don't use such things here, however."

"Does the Napa Asylum?"

The nurse frowned, weighing the wisdom of truth over deception. She eyed Isobel and decided on the former. "Years ago, yes, but now—I can't say that I know, ma'am. I would not be surprised. There are dangerous sorts in that asylum, but not here. Dr. Bright is very progressive. Patients are always treated with respect." Likely due to their deep pockets, thought Isobel, but she did not say it aloud.

Riot and the doctor joined them, and the group moved to a corridor where they could speak freely. "As you can see, Mrs. Morgan," said Bright, "we do not restrain anyone. The mind, I am a firm believer, must have time to heal. A safe environment is key."

"What about privacy?" asked Riot. "My wife is concerned about her reputation. If word were to reach certain ears—"

"The president himself could not pry records from my hands," the doctor assured.

Isobel looked at Riot. Their ruse would have to continue.

✛

The moon hung like a bulb, bright and beaming, in the clear night. Its light streamed through the orchard leaves, touching ground like a soft rain. Isobel crept beneath the branches, listening to the crunch of leaves. She paused at a trunk, and looked back at her noisy companion with irritation. Riot wore a dark suit and fedora and he carried his silver-knobbed walking stick. Hardly conducive to burglary.

She narrowed her eyes and straightened, preparing to deliver a scathing rebuke of whispers.

"Enjoying yourself, Bel?" he said in normal tones. His voice made her jump in the dark.

"We're breaking into an office," she hissed. "Some caution is advisable."

He looked around. "We're likely the only ones awake and the lights are on in the buildings. They're as good as blinded."

Isobel blew out a breath, swallowed down irritation, and walked through the trees. When the square silhouette of the main office building came into view she stopped. A few dim lights shone through the shuttered windows.

The sound of crunching footsteps disappeared. Isobel glanced behind her and nearly ran into a tree. Riot was nowhere to be found. A quick whistle brought her around. A dark shadow stood against the white adobe. His gloved hand covered the silver knob of his stick.

Isobel hurried across the open ground and pressed against the warm wall. "You've done this a few times, I see," she whispered in his ear.

"A few." Warm breath tickled her neck like a breeze. "Can you reach it?"

Isobel swallowed, her heart suddenly racing. She focused on the building. From their earlier meeting in Dr. Bright's office, they learned that the first-story windows and doors were barred, but the second-story had meagre latches. It was only a matter of reaching the windows.

Adobe was smooth, but the hacienda style structures had the most convenient support beams protruding from the wall. Riot interlaced his fingers, and bent his knees, preparing to hoist her. Could she reach it, he had asked. To prove she could, she checked the clearing, looked and listened, then trotted back, ignoring Riot's offer.

Summoning resolve, she ran at the wall. With practiced speed and one swift movement, she placed a foot on the smooth wall. Her rubber sole caught, and she pushed up, not out, leaping for the beam. The tips of her fingers caught wood.

For a breath, she dangled, stilling her body, and then pulled, hoisting herself up. When her balance was assured, she unfolded her Tickler, and slipped the blade through the crack between shutters. The tip found the lock, and she nudged it away from its loop. She eased the shutters open, and climbed into the office.

There were no lights. Isobel listened, and then slunk towards the door, pressing her ear to the wood. No light seeped from beneath the crack, and no footsteps echoed in the hall. She reached for a cushion and tucked it in front of the door jam. Her trusty pocket lantern came next. Light filled the office.

Earlier, as Riot had sat conversing with the doctor over Isobel's planned treatment, the doctor's file cabinet had mocked and teased. So close at hand. Now, she moved forward, running her fingers over the wood. It appeared to be a simple lever lock, the same on which she had practiced.

She withdrew the pick. It reminded her of a cobra about to strike—head slightly bent and forward with a long stretch of neck. With a steadying breath, she inserted the head into the rounded part of the keyhole. The neck slid into the flared bottom. Gently, she turned the pick to the right, closed her eyes, and felt it catch, then rotated the metal, lifting the tiny internal lever. It clicked.

Isobel smirked, withdrew her lock, and opened the cabinet. Its secrets belonged to her now. She thumbed through the records; one after another, but there was no Clowes.

A mocking voice chided her. "Daft-brained," she muttered. Pride deflated, and feeling foolish, she quietly closed the cabinet of *C*'s, reaching for the drawer labeled as *F.* Violet hadn't checked in under her stage name.

Holding her breath, Isobel repeated the picking process. This time the click mocked instead of congratulated. She yanked Elizabeth Foster's file out, flipped through it in the dim light, and paused on a page. Her heart sank.

Isobel closed the file with a slap, tucked it under her waistcoat and braces, and locked the drawer. Eager to feel fresh air on her face, she folded up her lantern, tossed the cushion back on its chair, and climbed out the window.

A soft whistle caught her with a leg over the sill. She hesitated, and then went for it. For a split second she hung. The tell tale lightening of the night warned of an approaching guard.

She let go, and dropped, landing in a crouch. Arms hoisted her up, propelling her towards the orchard.

A voice cut through the night. "Who goes there!" The lantern swung towards the wall where she had fallen. Her back was to a trunk, Riot at her side, peering at the guard and his light. She peeked to the side, saw the lantern move, and pulled Riot closer as they edged around the trunk, avoiding the gleam. Footsteps approached, the light brightened, and Riot put a hand to his lips, turning his head. A perfect owl's hoot sounded ten feet away.

The lantern raised, as the guard looked through the branches. His footsteps moved on. Isobel exhaled, and she felt Riot relax in front of her. Bark pressed against her back, and warmth radiated from the man in front. He looked down into her eyes.

"You can throw your voice," she whispered, impressed.

"A useful skill," he said quietly. "Where did you learn to run up a wall like that?"

"I'm short, I have to make do," Isobel grinned. "It helped that Lotario and I ran away to the circus when we were thirteen. I'm afraid my parents were under the impression that we sailed for Hawaii. It was months before the hired detective tracked us down."

"Hawaii," he shook his head. "I wonder how your

parents got that impression?"

"I wonder," she mused innocently. "I'm positive that you would have unraveled our ruse long before that other detective. Is the guard gone?"

Riot inclined his head, and took a step back. "Long ago."

✢

Days were hot, but nights were cold. The fire burned low in the bungalow. Riot tossed another two logs on the glow, and Isobel sat down with her plunder. She stared at the record for some time, remembering what she had glimpsed inside. With a sigh, she opened it, and began to read.

Sometime during her page flipping, she became aware of a glass filled with honey colored-liquid. Needing reinforcement, she downed the glass in one. It was smooth and warm with a bite at the last.

"Southern Comfort?" she asked, looking to the man across in question.

"I procured a bottle on the train."

"A man with forethought. It doubles as comfort or celebratory."

"You look as though you need the comfort." There was puzzlement in his voice. She handed him the file. "Violet caught Virgil with another woman, or so she first thought. It was a man."

Riot looked up from the pages, surprised.

"Virgil's childhood friends', Henry and Elma, reported him to the dean," the words tasted bitter on her tongue. "Two physicians put their mark on a slip of paper and signed his life away—all because he had a taste for men." She reached for the bottle and poured herself another glass. The liquid brought little comfort. Thoughts of her own twin and his possible fate screamed in her mind. A stark reminder that the both of them walked a precarious line.

Riot flipped through the doctor's notes, and Isobel turned to the hearth, watching the dance of flame. When he reached the end, he tossed down the record of betrayal, and removed his spectacles, cleaning the glass. "Violet hoped it would cure Virgil's unnatural desires; instead, he died in the asylum."

"I'd say that's worthy of guilt."

Riot spoke his thoughts aloud. "Violet was working here, to be closer to Virgil, and when he died—she cracked."

"And moved to the Y.M.C.A. where she attempted to drown her sorrows with chloroform and morphine."

"The headaches, the injury from the light, and her grandmother's death are all in Dr. Bright's notes. It looks as though she deteriorated rapidly: severe melancholy, hallucinations, hearing voices, and an acute interest in the supernatural."

"That same letter is in there."

"In the same handwriting," Riot added. "Only Violet claimed she discovered the letters on her bed. However, Dr. Bright was under the impression that she was manifesting a dual personality and writing them herself."

"Understandable," Isobel said. "The treatment seemed to work. The letters stopped."

"And she was discharged, returning to the stage."

Isobel sat forward, elbows on knees, anger welling up inside her like a storm. "How could they, Riot? Take a man's freedom away, a friend no less, all for their own moral peace of mind?"

"I doubt morals had much to do with this business," Riot observed. "More like jealousy and ego. Remember, Violet had her eye on Virgil. It was likely her own twisted heart she had in mind. I've seen a woman shoot a man because she couldn't have him, and a man do the same. And as for Henry and Elma—money might have been motivation. Anything to keep an heiress happy and remove the object of her affection."

"Whatever it was, betraying Virgil was murder," she said with contempt.

"The pieces still don't fit."

"No," Isobel sighed. "Well, yes they do; I just don't much care for where they're pointing."

Riot took a long sip of his drink. "Virgil's lover was disguised as a woman. There's no mention of his name, or that he was ever arrested."

"Lotario and I have been cross-dressing since he was forced into knee breeches. I sometimes forget that we're not the only ones who swap genders like hats."

"It'd explain the inconsistencies: this so-called Violet hiring Thorton when she was supposed to be here, the letters, the conflicting descriptions of her brooch, and the fact that Elma didn't seem to recognize her caller."

"Ruin, not suicide might have been the lover's aim—a quiet sort of revenge." Isobel sat back, curling her legs in the chair, toying with her hair as she thought. "I wonder if August tested Henry for any drugs—laudanum or chloroform? The lover could have lured Henry to the house with the note, overpowered him, forced him into the tub, and then, when Violet arrived at the house later in the evening, she would have been confronted by Virgil's lover. With her shaky history, that'd certainly be enough to drive her to suicide."

A log shifted, fire sparked and popped, and Riot stirred, reaching for the bottle. He paused, glanced at her, and then set it down, nudging the glass away. "That's a fair amount of planning," Riot said into the quiet. "There's a calculating mind behind this."

"*How did I escape? With difficulty,*" Isobel quoted. "*How did I plan this moment? With pleasure.*" Poised to drink, she eyed him over the rim of her glass. "What would you do for someone you loved?"

Riot replied with a quote of his own. "*Hatred is blind; rage carries you away; and he who pours out vengeance runs the risk of tasting a bitter draught.*"

"Not the vengeful sort?"

The man across from her became very still, like cold marble. "Once upon a time, I was," he said quietly.

Isobel had little doubt of that. There was a dangerous glint to the man, a steady, unwavering determination that she hoped she never crossed. She took a long draught of the amber liquid, feeling it warm her shaky insides.

"After we return that record, we can head to the Napa Asylum. Hopefully August will come through with the warrant. Bright Waters was a simple affair, but the Napa Asylum is secure."

"Hmm." Isobel held the top of the glass with her fingers, watching the firelight dance in amber. A thought swirled to the surface of her mind. "*How did I escape?*" she repeated softly. "My father's vineyards aren't far from the asylum—maybe ten miles. When I was young, eight or nine, I remember a scare that rippled through the town. A patient had escaped from the secure ward. Days later, the newspaper said he had been found dead, and everyone breathed easy." She frowned. "But during one my nightly excursions, I saw him—the dead man—stealing apples from an orchard."

"What did you do?"

"I asked the fellow how freedom was treating him. He said just fine, handed me an apple, and we parted ways."

"Were you frightened?"

"He was just some poor Italian immigrant with a slur and a lazy eye. I was more terrified that he'd turn me in." She shrugged. "I've a knack for judging people. There's a lot you can tell from looking a man in the eye."

"I've been wrong once or twice," Riot confided.

"Have you?"

"Yes," he said gravely. "Vindication is a strong deception. If a man believes he is in the right, there is nothing to give him away. Are you suggesting that Virgil is still alive?"

"I don't know," she sighed. "And I'm not sure I want to find out." Her eyes drifted to Violet's record. She felt suddenly sick, and set down her glass, changing the subject. "This is the second night you've gotten me soused."

"You don't hold much liqueur," Riot pointed out. "Take the bed."

"This chair will suit me just fine," she murmured, resting her head against the cushion.

Riot looked at her evenly. "Do I strike you as a man who would allow a lady to suffer sleep in a stiff chair?"

"Do I look like a lady?"

"I know you are."

"Well, I'm a stubborn one."

"And I'm a stubborn fellow. I suppose we'll both sleep in the chair." He crossed his arms over his chest and settled in.

"Together?" she arched a brow. "I doubt we'd fit, Mr. Riot."

He tilted his head. "You'd be surprised."

Before color could trace her cheekbones, she stood, and walked a relatively straight line towards the bedroom. "Fine, I'll take the dratted bed." Riot smiled, and despite her back to him, she sensed it. "But I think you're more clever than stubborn."

"Everyone has his weakness," he drawled.

She stopped in the doorway, and turned. "And you think you're mine?"

"Am I?"

"No."

"I've a mind to call your bluff."

"Cock sure of yourself, are you?" Isobel smirked.

"I've never been wrong about a bluff."

"Then why don't you?" she challenged.

"I would never force your hand, Miss Bel."

In answer, she clucked like a chicken and made for the bed.

28

Shattered Peace

Tuesday, February 20th, 1900

"ANY WORD ON THE hackman, Tim?" Riot asked into the telephone.

"I tracked him down!" the old man's voice burst from the other line.

Riot jerked his head away from the earpiece. "You don't need to shout."

"What?!"

"Never mind. You were saying?" Riot prodded, keeping the earpiece at a safe distance.

"The hackman picked up his fare on Market, took this woman to Elma's, was told to wait, and Violet emerged about fifteen minutes later. She had the hackman drop her off a block away from the house where we found Henry."

"Interesting."

"No, what's interesting is what Smith discovered," Tim said with pride. The young man was something of a project for the grizzled veteran. Riot was not yet sure if the ex-patrolman showed promise. Smith was not a free thinker, but at the very least he was thorough. "I had Smith ask around the neighborhood there. A mother with a buggy said that a handsome gentleman with a beard came out of the lane about two o'clock. He had a suitcase, and that struck her as odd. So I passed his description on to my contacts in the Union. A hackman picked up a gentleman that matched the description on the main street nearby. He remembered him so readily because he took the fellow all the way to Ocean Beach."

"Good work," Riot said. "We'll show your hackman the photographs when we return. See if he recognizes either men."

"Oh, and that August fellow rang the agency. He was lookin' for Miss—er Bonnie. Seems the request for records will take weeks."

"Weeks?"

"Backlog," Tim said.

"I see." Riot frowned at the nosey switchboard operator, and turned away. "Are there any judges who owe us a favor?" he murmured.

"What?"

"Favors, Tim," he said suggestively. "Do we have any?"

"No, 'fraid we ran out of those years ago. Most have retired. New blood and lots of graft."

"Can we grease any?"

"Do we want to?"

"I might," Riot hesitated. "Hold off for now. The closest telephone line is about three miles from Bright

Waters. If you need to contact me, it'll have to be by messenger. We'll likely be traveling to Napa Asylum, today or tomorrow."

"Sure thing. And A.J.?"

"Yes?"

"Don't be *too* much of a gentleman. I like that girl."

In answer, Riot hung the earpiece on its hook.

✛

Water trickled in the fountain, a pleasant accompaniment to the rustle of leaves. Isobel sat on the edge of the stone, idly running her fingers over the water. One eye was on the rippling patterns, and the other on the front of the building.

Dr. Bright was ensconced in his office with a new patient. She had wandered the hallways one too many times and attracted the attention of a concerned nurse. When the nurse had tried to coax her into one of the group activities, Isobel had fled. And here she had remained, waiting.

A woman walked onto the green. Curly red hair stuck out from beneath her wide hat, and a white rabbit hopped behind her on a leash. "Mind the weeds, Mr. Darcy. You know they don't agree with your stomach." The woman cooed and talked to the rabbit, walking ever closer. Five feet away, she stopped, and lifted her head, blinking through her spectacles. "We've a visitor."

"Yes." Introductions were made. And Isobel gave a polite nod to Mr. Darcy.

"I saw you with that handsome gentleman yesterday," Miss Meredith said. She had not offered a proper name.

"My husband."

"Hmm." The woman eyed her with skepticism. "Mr. Darcy doesn't believe you to be trustworthy."

Isobel glanced at the rabbit. "Well, I'm likely not. He's a wise lagomorph."

"You should speak directly to him, he has large ears, after all."

Isobel repeated herself to the rabbit.

Meredith smiled. "You're still not trustworthy."

"He wouldn't be the first to think so. Life wouldn't be half as interesting if I won over everyone."

"No, no it would not." Miss Meredith took a seat on the fountain. "I became tired of everyone smiling behind glassy eyes, so I started walking around with a rabbit to amuse myself."

"I pretended to be a cat once for a full week."

"How did that go?"

"I was chased by numerous dogs."

Miss Meredith laughed. And then abruptly stopped, turning a sharp gaze on her. "You're not unstable. I didn't think. Not on that man's arm. There's too much mirth in your eye."

"Most would disagree."

"Well, not the crazy kind at any rate."

"Most would disagree with that too."

"Why are you here?"

"I'm recovering from—" Isobel was about to say fever, but she took one look at the woman and changed her story. "Truth be told, I'm hoping to discover more about a patient who used to work here: Elizabeth Foster."

"Oh," Meredith sighed. "I was hoping for something more exciting."

"If it helps, I broke into the doctor's office and stole her file."

"Delicious." The woman's eyes sparkled. "Did you find all that you required?"

"I suppose," Isobel said. "Did you know her?"

"Of course, I know every patient here."

"Are you a patient?"

"Only when I want to be," Meredith smiled. "When San Francisco becomes tiresome, I come here." The woman's brows creased. "Is Elizabeth in trouble?"

"I'm afraid she committed suicide." Isobel held her breath, wondering if she would have to quiet a hysterical woman, but no such thing occurred, which was fortunate, because the only thing that came to mind was hitting the woman over the head.

"Oh, dear," Meredith breathed. "Bright will be crushed. He really thought he helped her find peace."

"She died under suspicious circumstances. That's why I'm investigating. Did she confide in you?"

"Yes, I know *all* about Virgil. She blamed herself for his death."

"It was her fault," Isobel said, bluntly.

Meredith tilted her head to the side. "Have you never made a mistake, Miss Bonnie? Spoken a wrong word, loved the wrong man, hurt a friend?"

"I take responsibility for my blunders," she said matter of fact.

"So did Elizabeth, or she wouldn't have been plagued with guilt." The woman reached down and stroked her rabbit. "All around it's a sad end."

"Did she ever say who she caught Virgil with?"

"Violet didn't recognize the man." There wasn't even a shade of coloring on the woman's cheek. But then that was unsurprising in San Francisco; eccentrics thrived and polite society's varnish was thin.

"*Is* Virgil dead?"

"Why, of course," Meredith said. "Who else would have been writing those letters?"

"You believe a ghost was writing letters?"

"Living or dead; man or beast, every thing has a way of communicating. Mr. Darcy tells me what to write all the time." Meredith smiled pleasantly, stroking her rabbit. Isobel waited, but the woman did not betray any hint of jest.

"Er, yes, I'm sure he's eloquent." The stiff papers tucked under her waistband reminded her of other matters. "Are you acquainted with Dr. Bright?"

"I am."

"Would you like to aid and abet my replacement of this file?"

The woman's eyes twinkled. "Consider him distracted, but only if you promise to visit Mr. Darcy in San Francisco."

Isobel looked at the rabbit. "Does he get along with cats?"

"Depends on the cat."

✛

The hallway was empty. Isobel opened the door, and slipped out, taking care to walk at a normal pace. The record was safely ensconced in its drawer. She glanced out an open window, and spotted Miss Meredith with Dr. Bright. The rabbit was on his lap. Perhaps the woman had coaxed the alienist into a session with Mr. Darcy.

Isobel gave the agreed upon signal and Miss Meredith dipped her hat in acknowledgement. With her task complete, Isobel made for the bungalow. Riot had left some time ago, trusting her to return the stolen record. He had made no suggestions, there had been no overtures of concern; simply a tip of his hat.

'Enjoy yourself, Bel,' he had said.

As Isobel strolled through the complex, she considered the detective and his easy confidence, not only the way he carried himself, but with her. Riot trusted her as he would any competent man.

With her thoughts swirling, she opened the bungalow door, shedding hat, coat, and gloves on her way to the bath. The day was hot. She turned on the taps in the sink, loosened her tie, unbuttoned the collar down to her bodice, and soaked a washcloth in cool water. As much as she'd like to take advantage of the mineral baths, Riot would return with news soon, and whether August had secured a warrant or not, she intended to discover the fate of Virgil Cunningham.

Refreshed, she turned off the taps, and walked into the bedroom, rubbing a towel over her brief hair. She looked into the mirror, and stopped. The wardrobe was cracked. And an eye stared from the darkness.

As one, the wardrobe burst open and Isobel threw herself towards the sitting room. But the man was fast. A hand gripped her loose blouse, tugging her back. She was lifted clean off her feet, and slammed onto the floor. The air was knocked from her lungs. A heavy weight fell on top of her and fingers locked around her throat. She kicked and twisted, but the grip was iron. Vacant eyes loomed, empty of feeling.

Isobel kicked up, catching the man's groin with her boot. He was unfazed. Dark spots danced across her vision. Desperate, she let go of the rock like forearms and slapped her palms against his ears. The man reeled and howled like a beast. She turned and scrambled forward on her knees, reaching for her umbrella. Steel slid with a rasp, and she lunged at the man with purpose.

✢

"Your wife will be in good hands, Mr. Morgan. You may visit her whenever you wish. Gentlemen also enjoy the restorative powers of the hot springs," Bright was saying. The doctor had intercepted Riot as he entered the compound from the road.

"I have no need of restorative healing, but I thank you."

The cheerful man shifted, looking grave. Bright cleared his throat and leant forward, as if the expanse of green was a crowded lobby. "All men deny it."

"Deny what?"

"When I spoke with your wife in private yesterday, she confided that you had certain—inabilities. Such debilitating ailments can greatly contribute to a woman's hysteria. I'm afraid your wife is quite ill. I think a joint treatment would be beneficial."

"My ailment," Riot murmured in thought. The word clicked. And he imagined Isobel's impish relish as she divulged this bit of information during her interview. "Yes, right," he cleared his throat.

"She confided in me under the strictest confidence."

"I'm sure," Riot drawled, and then glanced towards the main ward. "There appears to be a nurse signaling you." He pointed towards the door with his stick, and Bright followed like a well trained dog. "She ducked back inside the door."

"I'm afraid I'm needed, then."

"Thank you, Doctor, if a cure is possible, I shall greatly like that."

"Any man would."

Riot watched the doctor trot after the imaginary nurse. With a slight shake of his head, he readjusted his panama, and made for the bungalow to confront his imaginative 'wife'.

Stick in hand, Riot ambled under the sun, enjoying the birds and quiet. This was a hospital he could bear.

An inhuman howl shattered the peace. It raged like a bear caught in a trap. The sound came from the bungalow.

Without pause, he gripped his stick around the neck, and ran. His hat flew off, forgotten, as he stretched his legs. The door flew open to his worry.

Isobel was on her knees. A man towering over her. She thrust her sword. The man caught the blade between his palms, twisting and wrenching the sword from her hands. She fell forward, gasping for breath.

The man swung, but Riot lunged, catching the blade on his stick. The edge slid dangerously down the length, and he jerked his stick up, knocking the blade away. Off balance from the extended thrust, Riot staggered forward. A head slammed into his, dropping Riot to his knees. A swish of air signaled death, and he reacted, rolling forward. He came up, slapping his stick across the man's wrist. The sword fell. Riot pressed the attack, catching the man across the jaw with a double-handed swing.

The man charged.

Riot's face caught a fist, knocking his head to the side. His spectacles flew into the room. He tasted blood. Isobel came to his rescue, snatching up her fallen blade and driving it towards the man's chest. The point dug in, bones deflected, and it slid along his ribs.

The man staggered, turned, and threw himself out the window. Riot followed, revolver in hand. Without spectacles, he was nearly blind, but his ears were keen. He followed the crash of boots, and fired at the racing blur. The blur darted to the side, and he fired at another. It might have been a tree.

Something jangled, and metal clicked. A hoof stomped. Riot threw himself to the side. Wood and dust pelted his face as a thunder of hooves filled his ringing ears.

"Riot!" Isobel rasped, skidding to a stop. He pressed his revolver into her hand and watched as she extended her arm, aimed, and fired. A horse screamed, followed by a crash.

Isobel dashed forward, and he followed on her heels, keeping her form in his limited orb of sight. She came to a stop at a thrashing horse. Riot took his gun from her hand, and she doubled over; hand on knees, gasping for air.

Nothing moved in the blurred forest.

"He's gone," she choked. "It's like he doesn't feel pain." More words were lost in a fit of coughing. Riot eyed her torn blouse and the red discoloration on her skin. A slow, smoldering anger took root. The marks were sure to bruise black by tomorrow.

When her breath returned, Isobel looked at the horse, and reached for the fallen rifle. "At least he's weaponless." Mist clouded her eyes. "I wanted him alive—so I shot the horse."

"Let me." Riot held out a hand, because her own were shaking.

"It's my doing—my duty." She pulled the lever, expelled the cartridge, and loaded the next with a snap. In one determined motion, she cocked, aimed, and fired. The wounded horse stilled.

Two tears slipped past her guard before she wiped them away with a savage hand. "The man's wounded. Can you track him, Riot?"

"I'll need my spectacles first."

29

Disastrous End

GUNSHOTS IN THE COUNTRY (and even the city) were not uncommon; however, to a sanitarium of ailing women, it was startling. One shot was excusable, but four fired in rapid succession was not. Isobel and Riot were met with two rifles, one worried doctor and a handful of determined nurses, two of whom had pistols of their own. Isobel retreated to the bedroom, leaving Riot to handle the mess.

The detective brandished his card and came clean with the true reason for their visit. His firm voice and clipped tones knocked sense into the group. The words 'murder investigation' didn't hurt either.

"Who attacked you?" Dr. Bright asked.

"I don't know for sure, but I suspect he's connected to the death of a former patient: Elizabeth Foster," Riot replied. "Fetch the police, give them my card. There's a dead horse a ways back from the bungalow."

"Is your wife all right?"

"The man attacked her in this room. Keep your patients inside and the shutters closed."

"Word mustn't get out. We'll be ruined."

"That's why we're going after the man."

"We?" the doctor asked, startled.

Riot ignored the question. "Do you have horses and a spare rifle?"

⁜

Footsteps approached. Riot stopped a foot away; his gun was holstered on his hip, and he had two horses in tow.

"Our attacker wasn't carrying much," Isobel noted. "Provisions and the such, enough for two days." Unfortunately, the contents of the saddlebags did not include a helpful calling card. The horse was branded, so there was that. But that lead could wait. She said as much.

"Did you recognize the man?"

"He seemed familiar," she said, shaking out a spare bundle of clothes as if the act would loosen her memory.

"Can you ride?"

"Bareback even," she replied, distracted. She squinted at a trouser leg. "Do you have your glass?"

Riot reached under his coat, and produced his magnifying glass. She unfolded it, and looked at the fabric. A few strands of fine hair were caught in the cloth. She extracted one, examining it beneath the glass. "Dog hair," she muttered. "A ten pound Yorkshire to be exact. Its owner wears a monocle, can't swim, and is an excellent actor."

"All from a dog's hair?"

"Simple deduction," she said in a superior tone. Isobel

stuffed the clothing back inside the bags and stood, dusting off her split riding skirt. It had been in the bag of clothing that Lotario had left her, and she was grateful for his thoughtfulness. Switching guises in a small town was near to impossible, and given her precarious existence, she was loathed to risk being fined (and possibly jailed) for indecency while wearing trousers.

Isobel took the reins from her companion. "I think that man is our ghost."

Riot put his foot in a stirrup, and swung into the saddle with ease. Isobel followed suit, and while he kept his bespectacled eyes to the ground, she kept hers on the forest.

✣

An hour in, Riot dismounted. She followed, taking his reins as he crouched on the ground. "Our friend finally stopped here to bind his wounds. Up until now, he's been running flat out. I think he has a destination in mind."

Isobel looked around the countryside. The ground sloped upwards, and the oak climbed with the hill.

"He's tired, and has a bad knee," Riot added.

The comment drew her attention, and she frowned at the leaf strewn ground. "How can you possibly tell all of that from a few drops of blood and an occasional scuff in the dirt?"

"Simple deduction," he said dryly. Riot pushed up his hat and looked at her from beneath the brim.

"I deserve that," she admitted, and went on to explain. "The photograph of Virgil—it was familiar because I think I've met his aged self. The man who attacked me was familiar because I suspect he is the man who discovered Violet in the water. Only he went by the name of Nigel

Harrison and wore a disguise. The monocle distracted me from his eyes."

"Ah, the gentleman with the dog that did not care for you."

"In the general run of things, dogs don't find me agreeable."

"Noted," Riot said, rubbing his jaw in thought. There was a nasty bruise beneath his beard and blood on his lip from the fight. "That would explain why the handwriting in the letters matched the message in sand. And the claim that neither surfman noticed the writing."

"I should have done what the police have been doing for years and suspected the first man to find the body. It's nearly as bad as the 'butler did it'," she sighed.

Riot chuckled. "I've caught my fair share of butlers." He pointed to the ground and she followed his fingers as he traced out the boot print, the length of stride, and showed her how one side of the print was deeper than the other, hence the limp. "And blood there, by that scuff, where he struggled to bind the wound."

"Usually things are simplified when explained; this is not one of those things."

Riot pulled his hat low, shading his eyes. "It's like learning a new language. Things will start to make sense eventually." He stood, and drew his revolver. "I think it wise if we walk from here on out."

Isobel eyed the gun. When she had fired it, she noted the lack of a sighting notch on the tip. A common practice of gunslingers. The notch could catch, and in a gunfight even a split second spanned life and death. Therefore, the notch was sanded down to make for a quick draw.

Isobel took the reins of Riot's horse, and let her companion take the lead. He walked on, moving at a careful pace that she might have found tedious if it had not been for the approaching dusk and a scarce trail. Virgil, for she was sure it was he, had taken greater pains to cover his tracks.

By the time Riot stopped, the forest was darkening. He nodded towards a sturdy branch. She took his meaning and secured the reins. Together, they moved forward; Riot was not crunching now. He left her behind, moving without sound, and crouched behind a fallen oak. All twisted and dying, its roots were a web of sickly grey.

She crouched at his side, and followed his gaze. A hole disappeared into the hillside. An old mine shaft, overgrown with bramble.

"Our rabbit went into his hole," Isobel murmured.

"I don't suppose you have a carrot?"

"Hungry?"

"I was going to dangle it in front of the entrance," Riot replied.

"Who knew you were such a joker?"

"Ravenwood."

"And how would the illustrious detective have handled this part?"

"He always left this part up to me."

"I certainly won't let you have all the fun." She set her rifle against the log and brought out her pocket lantern.

Riot put a hand over hers. "Let me scout first. There may be another entrance. Keep your sights on that hole."

She started to argue, but relented. "Tracking and scouting—next you'll tell me that you're a half-breed."

"My mother was a crib whore. I don't know what the hell I am," he confided.

"Oh."

Riot slipped away before she could formulate a better

response. But her shock only lasted a moment. Isobel's good sense spurred her into action. She reached for her rifle and pointed the barrel at the entrance, half watching the hole, but mostly pondering the prim man in a suit who spoke with traces of a European accent. From gutter to gentry; that was one long road.

Minutes passed, and Riot was nowhere to be seen. Time ticked by, and Isobel became suspicious, wondering if he would dare creep in a back entrance without her. She frowned, and just when she was about to move forward, Riot appeared at her side. She nearly squeezed the trigger in surprise.

"There's no tracks and no other exits," he murmured in her ear. The man leaned against the log, watching the hole.

Isobel looked sideways at him. "You're going to wait, aren't you?" she accused.

"That was my plan," he confirmed.

"Well, I have another."

Without waiting for his reply, she slipped away, and took the long way around, circling out and away to approach the entrance. Riot met her on the other side of the shaft, flanking the cave. His features were grave, and questions lit up his eyes, but he didn't dare give voice to his worry.

The tunnel disappeared into a void. She unfolded her pocket lantern, lit it, and set it on the ground. With the business end of her rifle, she nudged it towards the center of the passage and pushed it into the shaft. When no shots rang out, she slithered on the ground, hugging the wall. Another nudge, and the lantern slid forward; slither, scrape, slither scrape. The progress was tedious. But a man waiting at the end of the tunnel would be light blinded by the flame, and hopefully confused by its position.

Riot crawled on the other side, keeping on the edge of light.

A voice whispered in the dark. "Couldn't leave it alone." When it came again, it seemed to shift, and Isobel was reminded of Riot's trick with the owl call. "I tried to warn you away, but you came back and stuck your nose in it."

"It's not too late, Virgil," Isobel said, softly. "If you tell me what happened, I might be able to help." She risked betraying her location, but she didn't think he had a weapon. If he did, then he would have fired long ago.

"Not too late?" the voice cracked. "It's far too late." Nudge, scrape, creep, and a voice of emptiness entered the fray. "Elma told them, and now the roaring won't stop!" An echo slammed down the tunnel. "Old friends of mine," a whisper entered the echo, drifting in and out of madness. "Elma didn't have to say a thing, but she did. I only repaid her in kind, but she was too weak. Ruin and despair. Too weak—" the voice trailed off.

"I understand, Virgil," Isobel tried again. "You were hurting; you wanted revenge. But you didn't need to attack me. I'll let it slide if you come with me."

Nudge, scrape, creep.

"Death was in the house," he whispered. "I treated Henry as they treated me. Right into the ear."

A cackle chilled her bones. Isobel stopped, squinting into the darkness. "Virgil?"

"The roar killed Henry," he said with conviction. "And Violet let him die. Mad, we were, her and I. It's done. It's all done. Better we burned." A match flared ten feet away.

A shot rang out. The match fell. And the cave filled with thunder.

✥

Rocks pelted her head. Dust filled her nostrils, and the afterimage of a man putting a match to a stick seared her mind's eye. Isobel curled into a ball, shielding her head, but the earth did not wash over her. It stilled.

Isobel blinked and choked on the dirt. Slowly, she uncurled in the complete dark. A sudden worry pierced her shock. She scrambled across the passage and knocked heads with another skull.

"Damn."

"I take it you are alive and well," Riot's voice was filled with grit.

"I was." She felt around for her lantern. Riot located it first. After three tries, he managed to light the candle. A tiny orb of warm light illuminated a world of swirling dirt. He set the candle in the lantern, but the mirror was shattered, rendering it nearly useless.

The night sky, far at the end of the shaft, was a welcome sight. The tunnel had not collapsed.

"That did not go according to plan," she coughed.

"Nothing ever does." Riot offered a hand, and she accepted. He turned the light towards the source of the blast. Earth and rocks were strewn over the tunnel floor. Virgil lay on his back, half-buried beneath the rocks. She heaved on one, and it rolled away. Dirt shifted, falling from the ceiling, and Riot pulled her back. The tunnel held a restless air.

He lowered the candle, until the light illuminated the dead man. There was a jagged blast hole in his stomach and a neat bullet hole in his hand. He was missing the other.

"Was that dynamite?"

"A very old, tired, and poorly packed stick by my esti-mation. He likely shortened the wick. From the flash, I wager he was sitting on gunpowder." More dirt fell, and Riot drew her away. She was happy to follow him into the night air. A biting wind swept down the hillside. In a few hours, it'd be close to freezing.

"I don't want to sleep here, Riot."

"No," he agreed. "There's a stream nearby. We'll pack Virgil out in the morning."

30

Campfire Madness

ISOBEL JABBED A STICK at the fire. "It doesn't make sense," she complained to the man at her side.

They sat on their respective bedrolls, and Riot stirred from where he leaned against a fallen log. He had been quiet, watching the moon through a break in the leaves.

"How did Virgil know where we were? Why would he attack us? He could have run and disappeared. And I don't see that man disguising himself as a woman. Was Violet working with him? Was that message in the sand a lament and not a mocking tribute?"

"I've been wondering that same thing," Riot answered. "There's still the unknown man Elma caught him with."

"The lover may not even be involved. Lotario changes his own out like dresses."

"In that case, as Virgil said, it's all done."

A stiff breeze rustled the oak leaves, but with two fallen logs around their camp, the fire only fluttered. Isobel tossed more wood onto the flames. Then she sat back, letting her head fall against the tree. She had scrubbed off the dirt in the nearby stream, and tried to rid herself of the day's events, but her throat throbbed and Virgil's voice seem to whisper on the wind. She tried not to think of the half blown up man in the cave; instead, she focused on the myriad of stars.

The warmth radiating from the man next to her was distracting.

"Bel, I swear I can hear you thinking," her companion drawled.

"This all feels so—"

"Incomplete," he finished.

"Exactly," she said. "I hate leaving things half done."

"We're not leaving; we're pausing."

She blew out a long breath.

"How's your throat?"

"It feels like someone tried to choke the life from me." She pulled her peacoat snug, and crossed her arms against the chill.

"Tried is better than dead," Riot said wryly.

She watched him out of the corner of her eye. He kept rubbing his temple, pushing up his hat, working his fingertips beneath the brim to massage the scar beneath the white wing of hair.

"I apologize for knocking your head. I didn't see you in the cave."

His fingers stilled in surprise, and he lowered his hand with purpose. "It's likely the blast more than your skull."

"My company will do that too."

Riot looked at her. "Never you, Bel." His eyes were

sharp and clear.

"You haven't spent enough time with me yet."

"Not nearly enough," he agreed, "but I hope to."

She looked to the fire, but her cheeks were already warm. "Where did you go—after you were shot?"

"I kept walking," he confided. "The injury left me with terrible headaches. Walking seemed to help."

"Do you have one now?"

"No," he said, looking ashamed. "It's a bad habit of mine."

"Aah," she realized. "A gambler with a tell." Isobel clucked her tongue.

"A tell is only useful if you know what an opponent is telling."

She narrowed her eyes in consideration. "That the jerky and biscuits in the saddlebags wasn't near enough food."

Riot's teeth flashed in the dark. "We'll have a feast tomorrow."

"I could use two," she sighed. "Distract me before I start dreaming of it. Where did you walk?"

"I took a leisurely holiday around the world," he said.

For the next hour, they swapped travel tales, comparing experiences, and discovering that they had shared the same city on a number of occasions.

"I'm surprised we didn't cross paths," Isobel mused.

"We may have."

"I would have remembered you," she stated with certainty.

"Would you?"

"Yes, I would have been instantly suspicious."

"You're right," he agreed. "I'm unforgettable. And I'm sure I would have noticed you."

"Pinned me for a murderer?"

"Your eyes," he said. "There aren't many as striking. They reflect whatever color you're wearing."

"I'm beginning to suspect that you're purposefully trying to make me blush."

"A worthy goal."

"A useless one," she corrected. "Finishing school taught me that a lady is supposed to graciously accept compliments with an artful acknowledgement while presenting her attractive side."

"You appear to have failed that lesson, then."

"It's the firelight," she said airily. "But thank you all the same." The logs shifted, sending sparks into the night. Isobel took a breath, and then a plunge. "August told me about your partner."

Riot arched a brow. "I thought everyone knew. The newspapers were worked into a frenzy."

"I was overseas," she reminded.

"Oh, yes, of course." He fell quiet. His right hand covered his left, and he gripped it until the knuckles were white. There was a lifetime of grief in that grip. As if all his pain could be kept at bay.

"If I'd known, I wouldn't have said that to you in the graveyard—about Ravenwood resting in pieces," she winced, and stammered, "At least I hope not."

His shoulders relaxed. "It's all right, Bel."

"I'm sorry, Riot."

"Don't be. It was years ago. There's no harm in mentioning his murder."

"I'm not apologizing for my words. Not that I wouldn't, but—I'm sorry you lost a friend," she finally settled, and wondered why she was tripping over words like a fool. "For people like you and me, friends are few and far between."

"Yes," he whispered. His hand still gripped the other. Isobel did not know what to make of it, and sincere words never came easy for her. She slipped an arm through his, and placed a hand on his forearm. "For reinforcement," she whispered.

Riot relaxed. Warmth radiated from the man, and she was cold, so she leaned in close.

"And warmth?" he murmured. The fingers of his left hand uncurled, and he transferred the hand from his own to hers.

"Precisely."

Riot took a deep breath. "You know I still see Raven-wood. I still hear his voice." There was pain in his own.

"What is he saying now?"

"He's saying I'm a crazed fool for confiding in you."

Isobel sat up straight, narrowing her eyes. "That's not very fair, now is it? I can hardly argue back." She thought a moment, keeping a solid hold on his arm. "Do you think he's haunting you?"

Riot closed his eyes. "I don't believe in ghosts," he said with a shaky breath. "And if I'm right," he looked into her eyes, "then I'm not far from Virgil."

"Perfectly sane people make me uneasy," she said. He must have known it for the truth, because some of the worry left his eyes. As if words alone could send her running. "If the voice is a ghost, at least yours is dead. Every time I light a cigarette, I hear my mother saying, 'Isobel Saavedra Amsel, put that down at *once!*" Isobel did a fair enough imitation that he chuckled. "Really, Riot, it's not so strange. I can't stand crowds. It makes my head want to burst. There's so much going on inside my skull that I can't hear myself think. I'm not sure that's much different."

"Maybe not," he conceded.

"The mind is a big place," she said softly. "Maybe you're trying to tell yourself something."

31

An Unexpected Turn

Wednesday, February 21st, 1900

IN THE MORNING, RIOT and Isobel slung the dead man over a horse. Riot mounted the second and Isobel climbed behind him in the saddle. She wrapped her arms around his torso, feeling the strength in his spine.

Soon after, a dust cloud rose through the trees, and the local posse caught up with them around ten. Isobel exchanged her cap for the floppy straw hat she had stuffed in the bags. It leant her a more feminine air.

"You look a mess," Riot said, clearly amused.

"Well good. The police won't look twice at me."

Riot met the armed group with a firm greeting, an authoritative explanation, a flash of his card, and thanks to the competent lawman, the party turned around without fuss. They reached Bright Water before noon, freshened up, packed their bags, and traveled by train to the Napa Insane Asylum.

Isobel found herself standing next to a corpse in the asylum morgue with Riot, a no nonsense officer by the name of Williams, and the asylum director.

"We have reason to believe that this man was Virgil Cunningham. He was a patient of yours." Riot looked across the battered lump of flesh to the director.

Dr. Morris shook his head. "Couldn't be." The man's keen eyes stared down at the corpse.

"Couldn't be a patient, or couldn't be Virgil?" Riot pressed.

Morris wiped his forehead. He was pale and blond and possessed a stoic bearing that was currently at odds with his nerves.

"Virgil Cunningham *is* dead. Heart failure, if I recall correctly. We have his death certificate."

"He's certainly good and dead *now*," Isobel stated. The officer looked at her sharply, and she politely folded her hands behind her back, affecting remorse.

"May we see his records?" asked Riot.

"Records cannot be released without a warrant issued by the court."

"You have *my* order," the officer said. "This isn't about a patient. This is an investigation regarding a possible escapee and murder. That overrides confidentiality."

"This *cannot* be the man in question—he's buried in our graveyard."

"What a fuss," Isobel mused. "Whether it's him or not, the reporters will have a feeding frenzy."

With that threatening suggestion, Morris scurried away, and Officer Williams gave her an approving nod.

In short order, the record was produced, and Isobel waited her turn as the officer and Riot bent their heads together.

Williams held the photograph close to the body. Isobel compared the two. "I'd say that's a match," the officer said. And she agreed. The photograph they had discovered in Henry's room was dated, a younger version of the man, but even this, his admitting photograph, was a far cry from the man who had tried to strangle her. In two years, Virgil had aged ten. She studied the asylum photograph in which Virgil was dressed in the dull, oversized, blue uniform. He looked terrified.

What sane man wouldn't rather face a noose than the prospect of an asylum? Virgil's only crime was loving and trusting in friends. It was hard not to compare this man to her own twin. Of the twins, her brother had always been the more delicate, and she, the protector. Lotario wouldn't last ten days in an asylum or labor camp.

"Hydrotherapy, electrotherapy, physical restraints— and the list goes on. It seems he had it all," Riot noted with disapproval.

"All the treatments were aimed at controlling his un- natural desires," Morris said.

Isobel thought of Henry, and the burns in his ears, along with Virgil's words, 'right into the ears'. "Electrodes were stuck inside his ears," she said. "Is that a common treatment?"

"No," the doctor shook his head. "All of our treatments are humane. The days of Bedlam are behind."

"That's what the directors kept insisting to Nellie Bly on Blackwell's Island."

The doctor winced at the name. "Not *this* hospital, Miss Bonnie."

"It's a large hospital," Isobel stated. "There's a number of staff and wards."

"How long have you held the position of director at this asylum, Dr. Morris?" Riot asked.

"A year," he conceded.

"And what happened to the previous director?"

"He retired."

Williams frowned. "Not precisely," the officer contradicted. "He was forced to resign early."

"Maybe so," Morris smiled quickly. "Before my time. I have made numerous changes, I can assure you."

"Is the doctor who treated Virgil still present?"

"He was killed during a robbery. A horrible tragedy."

The officer asked after his name, took notes, and seemed to recall the case, confirming the robbery gone wrong. As the men talked, Isobel took over the record, shuffling through papers, and becoming increasingly sick over what she read. She stopped at the final page—the death certificate. Isobel noted the date of death, the cause of death (heart failure), and finally glanced at the coroner's signature.

The breath left her lungs and she stepped back as if she had been burned. Riot looked at her with concern. She slapped the record in front of him and jabbed her finger at the signature of Duncan August.

"We need to go. Now."

✣

The *Lady* bumped against the wharf after sunset. Isobel tugged on lines in the near dark. The sail crumpled, and she gathered it up as Riot secured the warps. She started to climb onto the wharf, but was stopped with a word.

"Bel, at least wear your split skirt. If we catch him, and we will, he'll talk."

With a growl, she disappeared below deck, and exchanged trousers for riding skirt. Still, she could be arrested for indecency. A woman was only allowed to wear a riding skirt if she was accompanied by a bicycle or a horse. The latter being frowned on in favor of a side saddle.

As soon as she emerged, they climbed onto the wharf. Tim was waiting with the hack. Grimm sat stoically in the seat, and Tobias waved from the back. Riot wasted no time. "Do you have an address?"

"I do," Tim said. "I've had Smith at the morgue and Johnson at his house. No sign of the fellow last I checked. And Miss er—Bonnie. There's been a very firm woman trying to get a hold of you at the agency. A Mrs. Wright says she has some important information for you."

"What did she say?"

"That's it," Tim ducked his head. "She said she wasn't about to trust me."

Isobel frowned, and consulted her watch. Riot stood, waiting. It could be nothing—nothing at all, but her last orders to her pawn played in her ears. She looked at Riot. "Sapphire House isn't far. I'll meet up with you."

"The house and morgue are being watched. If you think it important, then you'll need a hack." Riot opened the door. Isobel could not argue with that reasoning. She climbed in and Riot followed. Her thoughts spun with the wheels. How could she have been so blind?

Virgil had attacked her for a reason; to stop Riot and her from reaching the Napa Asylum and finding that signature.

Before the hack had rolled to a stop, Isobel flung open the door, and hopped down. "I'll only be a minute." Having little patience for Mrs. Beeton and a curfew, she circled around the back.

Moving through the dark, she ignored the fire escape and went straight for a drain pipe. Her hands were sure, and her rubber desk shoes caught on the iron as she scurried up the pipe like a mast. She edged out onto a third-story ledge. There was a light in the window. Isobel rapped on the pane. A startled screech answered. The curtain jerked open, and a wide-eyed woman in sleeping cap looked out. Miss Taylor held a stout fire poker, ready to bash the intruder. It took a moment for recognition to enter her frightened eyes.

The woman threw the latch and opened the window. Isobel planted her backside on the sill. She wasted no time with pleasantries. "I hear Mrs. Wright has been trying to reach me."

"Yes, er, won't you come in?" Miss Taylor asked, eyeing her precarious perch with dread. The woman was in her dressing gown. Two cats lounged on the armchair and a book lay on the seat: *The Count of Monte Cristo*.

"No time. Did Mrs. Wright tell you what she overheard?"

"Yes," Merrily nodded. "A conversation regarding the opera singer that you wanted us to listen for. In fact, a number of conversations."

"What about?" she demanded.

"It seems Madame de Winter missed a Monday evening performance and a rehearsal on Tuesday. No one can locate her."

One after another, the words hit Isobel in the gut. She felt herself falling, but her knuckles were white upon the sill.

"Are you well, Miss Bonnie? I have brandy."

"Who was speaking about Madame de Winter?"

"The *Tivoli* of course, the concierge at the Palace, and the oddest of all—a tailor."

Lotario had an elaborate living arrangement. He entered the palace as Madame de Winter, kept her rooms there, but always exited incognito, out the back, dressed as a gentleman. The concierge, at such a place, was valued for his discreet ways and unflappable tongue. The tailor was tied to the *Narcissus*.

"There was one more thing," Miss Taylor ventured, looking nervous.

"Yes?"

The woman cleared her throat daintily. "Alice—Mrs. Wright, is quite vexed with you. It's impossible to contact you. She is displeased with your lack of planning. And I agree. Really, some sort of arrangements must be put into play if we are to be useful. And that man—Mr. Tim is quite the smooth talker. I would not trust him."

"I'll think on it." Isobel stood, balancing on the ledge. "In the mean time, thank you. You may have saved a woman's life." She started edging back to the drain pipe. "And I may call on you to identify Mr. Leeland. I believe he was using the room to spy on Violet."

"Oh, dear. Of course. Do be careful."

The window closed, and Isobel scurried down the pipe and trotted towards the waiting hack. Riot was standing at the door.

"Lotario's been missing since Monday evening, maybe sooner." Her voice shook, and in the face of Riot's reassuring calm, she realized that she was trembling. She was still falling. Her own words tugged her into the dark like an anchor around her neck.

Steady hands gripped her shoulders, and he caught her

eye. "Are you sure he's not just distracted?"

"Lotario would never miss a performance," she whispered.

"Where do you think he's being held?"

Her mind spun. Isobel was not alone. She was no longer a lone Queen defending the board. She had pieces in play. "I'll check the *Narcissus* to be sure. See if he's not at the other places." She made to go, but Riot's hands held her fast.

"Not alone," he said. "Tim, take the hack and raid the house with Johnson. See if you can find anything of note. Lotario's missing."

"I'll find another hack," the old man said.

"No. I won't take these boys into the Barbary Coast at night. Drop us at Market."

✛

The alleyway was inhabited by dime prostitutes and their drunk johns. Isobel kept walking. She hurried around the corner with Riot in her wake. A whole other world inhabited the south side of the block. Golden letters, *Steed and Peel* curved across an elegant window. Standing beneath the single electric bulb, Isobel pressed the bell.

The wait was excruciating. She felt sick and cold all at once, and wanted to scream for her brother. She pressed the bell again.

A dapper man in dressing gown and silk scarf looked out. She signaled him, using the sign that Lotario had taught her, and he opened.

"We have urgent need of a tailor."

The man's eyes widened a fraction in recognition and relief, but upon closer scrutiny, the relief vanished. An obvious sign that he knew her twin. The man inclined his head, and they walked in. He shut the door and locked up. Isobel passed rows of hats, silk, and wool, heading straight to the back. When they were hidden from the street, she turned on the owner. "You can't find Paris?"

"We cannot," the Englishman confirmed.

"When was he last seen?"

"Sunday afternoon," the tailor replied. "We can hardly ring the police." The tailor looked at Riot, and betrayed his surprise with a twitch of a brow.

"Mr. Steed," Riot tipped his hat.

"Mr. Riot," he returned, "I hope your suits are in order?"

"By no fault of your own, I'll be requiring your services shortly."

Steed frowned at the detective, barely containing a look of sufferance. "Hera intended to contact your agency in the morning."

"She should not have waited *three* days," Isobel hissed. She marched through a storage room, passing bolts of wool and boxes, on her way to the wardrobe. The solid oak piece swung easily outward. Riot slipped in behind her. Darkness greeted them, and she took his hand and walked on.

"Steed is your tailor?"

"I had no idea he was connected to the *Narcissus*."

"Well, good," she said. "It means he's discreet."

The passage was short, bridging the lane that bordered the back of both buildings. Isobel opened the hatch, and they emerged into a festive hallway from behind a robust statue.

Riot looked at the lever. "No policeman would ever touch that appendage."

Isobel smirked, and offered Riot a mask from a nearby table. He waved the garish feathers away, and pulled the brim of his hat low. She led the way to Lotario's rooms.

She did not knock. But used the key which he had left in the carpet bag. The room was empty. Riot and her fanned out; she to the wardrobe and he to the desk.

"His wig is gone—the one he uses for Madame de Winter when she isn't performing."

Riot held out a card. She looked at it and felt queasy. It bore the very same name that she had brandished proudly during her investigation. Only this was Duncan August's personal calling card. On the back, written in a crisp hand, were the words: *Sunday seven o'clock.*

"August never mentioned knowing Virgil Cunningham, but he did say he attended Cooper when I asked. If he had been a senior student, or even a doctor there—he could very well have been Virgil's lover and arranged to work at the asylum, planning to secret him away. August is in a perfect position to alter postmortem findings, to steer things precisely where he wished. And I've been reporting to him this whole time—he knows Lucie is my supposed cousin. I introduced the two." She was babbling, trying to clear her head. Firm hands gripped her arms, stopping her stream of thought. Isobel looked up, focusing on Riot's steady gaze.

If Riot told her that everything would be all right, she would hit him, and never look back.

"Up until now, everything has been meticulously planned. Revenge at its finest," Riot said. "But this—this is not. We interfered; we were unplanned. Virgil was trying to protect August. And now, Virgil has not come back. August is likely panicking."

"Or extremely angry."

"There is that," he acknowledged with a grim nod. "But either way, he'll make mistakes. The morgue and his own home are too obvious."

Isobel closed her eyes, shuffling pieces on the board, searching for a hidden strategy, sifting through clues. She opened her eyes to Riot, knowing the answer. "Nigel Harrison, or Virgil, said that he walked his dog every day. The surfman seemed to know him, that's why I didn't think anything of it."

"And the hackman took a fare from the House to Ocean Beach. We'll start there."

32

With Pleasure

THE HACK ROLLED TO a stop. For once, Isobel did not notice the fog rolling over the sea, or hear the crashing waves. There was only a dark pit, and a well of despair.

Riot ordered the hackman to wait, and she sped towards the life-saving station. Isobel met the door with her fist, banging until it opened. A woman answered. She was in her dressing gown, held a lantern, and looked as though this was a regular occurrence. The wooden door was worn with panic.

"The girl who threw herself in the water a week back," Isobel said breathlessly. "There was a man with a little dog who discovered her—do you know where he lives?"

"Mr. Harrison?"

"Yes," Isobel said. "It's imperative that I speak with him."

"I haven't seen him walking for some days, but he keeps a room at the Cliff House."

Isobel looked towards the square monstrosity sitting on Land's End. She couldn't help but feel that the whole world was tipping off that cliff into the sea.

Without a word, she ran back to the hack, ordered the driver to take them to the Cliff House, and climbed in beside Riot. He glanced at her, but said nothing, his lips a line of determination.

✛

The Cliff House was a gilded paradise (or hell depending on your viewpoint). Isobel would have ran through the doors and charged the prim concierge if it hadn't been for her partner. He pressed her arm to his side, communicating the need for subtlety. Her attire attracted curious stares, but not upturned noses. In San Francisco, money talked, and Riot appeared to have it. With Isobel on his arm, Riot walked across the marble as if he wore top hat and tails, his stick moving in time to his step.

At the counter, he presented his card with a flourish. "Mr. Harrison is expecting me." The accent that came with the words was pure upper-class British.

The concierge consulted his book, tracing the name to the room, and then picking up the telephone to ring the man in question. Riot looked around the grand hall, and just as the concierge was about to request the room number, he placed his finger on the hook.

"There's the old fellow," Riot pointed his stick towards a knot of guests. "No need to ring." He soothed the man with a five dollar bill, offered his arm to Isobel, and they walked towards the lift.

"Did you note the room number?" he asked

"Third floor, room twelve."

Riot repeated the floor to the operator, and in the agonizing moments that followed, he placed a hand over hers, squeezed it once and withdrew.

Room twelve was a suite, a corner room. There was money here somewhere.

Isobel pulled Riot to a stop in the deserted hallway. "Give me ten minutes. Then enter. I'll sneak in through the window. I don't want to risk Lotario."

"It's over a hundred feet to the ocean."

"Don't worry, Riot. It's dark. What I can't see won't hurt me," she said with a flippant shrug. She left his side and hurried to the wide windows at the end of the hall.

The eyes beneath his hat brim were dark, but he said nothing. Instead, Riot consulted his watch, and took up a position beside the door.

As with most ornate buildings, the builders had included a ledge. As much for repairs and anchoring scaffolding as it was for decoration. She put a leg over the windowsill and comforted herself with the knowledge that plenty of workers had scaled this building before. With a breath, she committed herself. The wind nipped and tugged at her coat, pushing her to the side as the surf thundered far below. The ledge creaked as she edged along, gripping the scrolling woodwork.

She reached the corner. It was void of decoration. Holding on to a groove with two fingers, she stretched her arm and foot around the bend, feeling blindly for a handhold. Her heels hung over blackness.

The surf roared, washing and churning, crashing against the cliff with the rising tide. She forced herself to calm, breathing easily, in and out, moving in the eye of the surrounding storm of fear. A curving piece of wood greeted her fingertips. She slid her foot along the edge, searching for purchase around the corner. The woodwork snapped. For a moment, she swayed with the wind, feeling like a feather about to be caught.

Isobel slapped her palm against the side of the Cliff House, using friction and leverage to hold her steady. Palm pressing, she edged around the corner, until both feet were safe on the same edge.

The shuffle to the balcony was a blur. She slipped over the rail on quiet feet and edged to the French doors. Light seeped through the curtains. She peeked through the slit. A dim light shone over the front door, and an armchair faced the entry. The back of a man's head poked over the cushion. He was pointed at the door. She could imagine August with a gun in hand, waiting.

Knowing that Riot would enter at any moment, she drew her gun, took a breath, and tried the handle. It gave. She rushed in and the room erupted with barking growls. A blur of hair charged her legs. Isobel ignored the beast and his sinking teeth. The man in the chair started to rise, but she was quicker. The barrel found a home in the man's temple.

"Drop it, August!" she warned. A breeze caught the curtains, bringing a chill that mirrored her voice. Teeth sunk into her calf, and she pressed the barrel into August's skin.

The front door opened, and Riot appeared in the light, off to the side, revolver aimed. Faced with two guns, August dropped the gun, and Isobel kicked it away. The Yorkshire charged the new arrival. Keeping his gun pointed on the man in the chair, Riot scooped up the beast, and held it under an arm as it nipped and snarled.

Riot moved through the rooms, turning on lights, searching for Lotario. When he returned, his eyes said it all —Lotario wasn't there.

✛

For a murderer who had just been captured, Duncan August was remarkably calm.

"Am I accused of something?" he inquired.

"A great many things," Riot replied.

While Riot kept his gun leveled on the man, Isobel ripped off the curtain ties, and bound August securely. Satisfied with her efforts, she took a step back, so she might study her opponent. Riot walked to the bedroom, gently tossed the dog inside, and shut the door. He took up a position beside August.

"Where is my cousin?"

A flash of Riot's eyes shone with disapproval. Not a good opening move, she realized too late.

"I haven't the faintest idea. Charming singer."

August looked at her. He was the same man with whom she had conversed in the morgue and the same who had conducted a thorough (if slanted) investigation.

"May I ask why you have abducted me?"

"I don't have time for games, August," Isobel stated, bluntly. "I know everything. I know that you were lovers with Virgil Cunningham. I know that Violet caught the two of you together, but she didn't recognize you in female garb. You're tall, like her, and you have fine hands and an ambiguous bone structure."

"This is very entertaining."

"No, it's not," she shook her head, letting the sorrow she had felt for Virgil creep in. "Henry, Elma, and Violet betrayed Virgil to the dean—their childhood friend. All it took was two signatures to sign his life away and save the college a scandal. And all the while you played the coward and let Virgil *suffer* in an asylum," she hissed.

The blow hit home. "I did not!" August snapped. His arms strained against the ropes. And she pressed her attack.

"You hid, too afraid to come to your friend's aid while his mind slipped away, bit by bit, until the dust settled and you grew some bollocks."

"I did everything within my power!" he shouted. August took a breath, and turned his head away. She let him pant, and think, and wonder.

When he faced her again, his eyes were clear.

"You have no proof."

"I have your signature on Virgil's death certificate," she replied. "I have a witness who can identify you as Mr. Leeland. You were spying on Violet."

"And we found Thorton, the man you hired to seduce Elma," Riot added. "Thorton isn't the sort of man to hold his tongue under pressure."

"You were stalking Violet, you and Virgil, driving her to madness. You tried to ruin Elma, but instead, she took her own life, robbing you of that satisfaction. And Henry, I plan on having another coroner perform a postmortem. I wager he was drugged, subdued, and tortured. Those marks I saw in his ears weren't a side-effect of the belt. Was it you or Virgil who stuck electrodes in his ears?"

August did not answer.

"You wanted Henry to die a humiliating death. To be discovered in that bath with the photographs in the next room. You killed and framed him."

"You're unfortunately clever, Miss Bonnie."

"Yes, unfortunate for you."

August shook his head. "No, unfortunate for your cousin. I know Virgil is dead," he stated dispassionately. "I begged him to stay, but he was determined to protect my name. He didn't ring. And I know that he wouldn't be taken alive again. I felt him die." The man in front of her changed, something shifted, from a proud, intelligent man, to a cold empty shell. It was as if a switch had been thrown.

Isobel's blood chilled.

"And with that knowledge, I can see your last bargaining chip fading from your eyes, Miss Bonnie."

"You have your vengeance. Leave my cousin out of this."

August smiled. His lips curved, but it did not touch his eyes. "I don't think so. This is justice. A complete circle. An eye for an eye as the preachers say. The scales are balanced, but only if your cousin dies."

Isobel tensed to strike him, but Riot stopped her with a slight shake of his head. "How do you figure that?" he asked.

"Elma ruined Virgil. So I ruined her. Suicide was not my aim," August stated matter of fact. "Violet drove Virgil to madness, and so I repaid her in kind. And Henry," August relaxed into his narrative, "I would have only inflicted the same pain on him as the asylum inflicted upon Virgil, but Henry murdered Violet's grandmother for money. And I'm positive Elma was involved. Mundane, isn't it? When I performed the postmortem, I discovered the arsenic in Mrs. Foster's system. But killing Henry wasn't my choice to make, so when Violet came to the house, I told her everything. I took her into the bathroom, showed her Henry, and offered her a choice: rescue the man who murdered your grandmother and pretended to love you, or leave him to freeze in the bath and meet Virgil on the beach."

"How magnanimous of you," Riot drawled.

"I thought so," August agreed. "If there is one thing I can't stand, it's a hypocrite."

"And what of my cousin? How does she wager into this?"

"She?" August laughed. "Oh, no, don't play coy with me. It's a shame. I would have liked to meet him under different circumstances."

"Then let him go, August," Isobel beseeched. "Too many lives have been ruined. Don't condemn him as others condemned Virgil."

"But that's the rub," August said. "I don't have Virgil anymore. And if balance is to be restored, then you can't have your cousin."

"No," she argued. "It's not balanced. You offered Violet a choice. And you had a choice to save Virgil sooner, to speak out, to run away together. You're not offering me anything."

August considered her words. A long minute passed, and she ached to rage and strike the man, but Riot's patience washed over her. And she glanced at him, finding the resolve to still her tongue.

"You're right," August said slowly. "I'm not. You might be able to save him, but I doubt you have the time. The cold will kill him in half an hour."

Isobel looked at Riot, and he mouthed the word morgue. She nodded. He lowered his gun and walked briskly to the telephone, demanding the city morgue.

"Even if your cousin lives, I will tell everyone what is under Madame de Winter's silken skirts."

"Why would you do that?"

"Because you are no different than me. What I did for love, you would do too. So here is my offer: Kill me, and save your cousin from ruin, or don't and watch him share Virgil's fate."

Isobel extended her arm, aiming. "I'm nothing like you."

"I think you are."

"No," Isobel shook her head. "You see I'm already dead." And with that, she squeezed the trigger.

The bullet shattered August's calm, but not his skull. The bullet sunk into the armchair by his ear. Isobel charged forward, planting a hand on either side of August's head, staring him in the eye.

"Virgil tried to strangle me," Isobel said, loosening her collar to reveal the bruises. "And then he ran into a cave. I tried to help him, but you were right, he wasn't about to be taken alive. He blew himself up with a stick of dynamite."

Pain entered August's eyes. "Then it's fitting," he rasped. "Your cousin will die in a cave too."

Isobel straightened, mind racing. "Riot!" she called. "Is there a cave nearby?"

"The Sutro Baths."

33

With Difficulty

WAVES CRASHED ON THE rocks with a roar of freedom. Its thunder swallowed her heart, and filled her bones with fear. For the first time in Isobel's life—she hated the sea. Death marched in, slow and relentless, with every churning spray.

Isobel and Riot ran through the night, down the long road, towards the squat, glass roofed buildings. Riot raced past the Sutro Bath entrance, moving towards the cliff. A steep, narrow staircase spilled down the side. Beneath the moonlight, Isobel saw a squat building huddled against the bottom of the cliff wall. The pump house. She took the steps two at a time, and reached the bottom on Riot's heels. He tried the door. It was locked.

He rapped his stick on the wood, but did not wait for an answer. Riot handed her his stick, reached into his breast pocket, and pulled out his lockpicks. He knelt in front of the lock with torque wrench and pick in hand. A lone electric bulb flickered above the door, casting deeper shadows rather than light.

But that did not matter, Riot had his eyes closed. The seconds stretched, until Isobel felt as if her heart would burst. She tightened her grip on his stick, anchoring herself to the solid shaft, and tried not to wonder if Lotario had taken his last breath.

Riot withdrew his tools. He turned the handle, and she flew through the portal. The building was a maze of pipes and pumps. Her hard breathing was drowned by the crash of waves against its walls. She ran towards the back, following a large pipeline and the thundering sea. A hole had been bored through the rock. Sand was beneath her feet. Water swelled into gaps in the cave, eating at the rock with relentless power and slow time. The sea had ages. Lotario did not.

"Lotario!" she screamed, searching the shadows and half light. Crevices and nooks swirled with white tides. Riot trotted ahead, and she followed on his heels, trusting that he had been here before. A natural tide pool had formed around the treacherous shore. A swell hit the rock and surged into the air. Riot turned his face, catching the spray. The force nearly knocked him off his feet. The water swirled in the pool, and subsided, only to return.

Isobel stood her ground, letting the chill hit her full on as she searched the swirling dark. Anyone in the tide pool would have been snatched by the sea long ago. White foam churned around her shoes, eddying in the sand, and then flowing away. But not back towards the sea. A steady stream flowed beneath a pipeline. She pulled her thoughts from the dark deep, and scrambled beneath the pipes.

The water poured into another pool. The water rose, as if deep currents pushed from beneath, and then pulled it away, swirling in a fit, and surging, climbing ever higher with the tide. Pipes climbed out of the collection pool with the rock. A shadow hung on the other side, chained to a filter grate. Lotario. The water was up to his neck, seeking to force itself down his throat with every surge.

"Here!" she called to her partner. Isobel tossed down her hat, shed her coat, walking suit, and shoes. Stripped to her underclothing, she climbed down into the pool. The rocks were sharp and slick, and the currents tugged at her feet. The cold clutched at her chest, and she embraced it, forcing herself to breathe. Pushing off, she dove through the water and swam, fighting the tug of some unseen passage in the dark depths.

The pool was not wide. "Lotario," she said desperately, reaching the other side. He was cold as ice, his body limp, and when she lifted his chin, his eyes were glazed with confusion.

Isobel ran her hands beneath the water, feeling his body, searching for restraints. A heavy canvas jacket held him fast, his arms crossed around his chest, and tied around his back. A chain held him to the pipe, bound with a lock.

"There's a lock!" she yelled over the thunder. Her panic roused Lotario, and he lifted his head, eyes trying to focus.

"My reflection," he slurred as if he were drunk. Unfortunately, it was not drink or drug; he was intoxicated with cold and close to surrender.

"Better looking," she said.

Riot stripped down to trousers and shirt, and lowered himself into the water. One hand gripped the pipe, and the other hand held his knife and lockpicks. He hesitated, white as a sheet.

"I need help," she called. "There's a chain and straightjacket."

The man let go, walking, struggling against the swirling sea, straining to keep his bearded chin above the water. Isobel gripped the pipe, and stretched her hand towards him. Her fingers curled around his shirt front and she pulled him through the water. Unaccustomed to the cold, he was gasping for breath, but he focused, wrapping one arm around a pipe, and feeling for locks as the water ebbed and flowed.

Isobel tugged and tested the chains, searching for the anchor. The lock was on the other side of the pipe, jammed between rock and metal. Isobel heaved on the chain, sliding it up and out of the swell.

Riot ran his fingertips over the warded lock, tracing the key hole. With numb, shaking hands, he fumbled through his key ring of picks. When he found the one he desired, he wedged himself between rock and pipe, and inserted the metal.

The sea swirled around them, rising like a roused beast. Its roar drowned Riot's hurried breath, as well as the soft click. The hinge popped open. Riot unthreaded the chain and tossed the lock into the pool. The chains released their hold, and Lotario sank. Isobel dragged her twin to the surface, memories of Curtis' limp body taunting her mind. Lotario was alive, she reminded herself. He was alive, and would live. She hooked her arm around his chest, supported his body on her hip, and swam towards the shore, reaching and kicking with every stroke.

Keeping a hand on the jacket's strap, she slithered onto solid rock, and heaved on the jacket. Lotario was not a large man, but his body was all sleek muscle. Still, he was nothing compared to a mainsail. She pulled him onto solid ground, dragged him under the pipe and into the sand. Confused, Lotario tried to stand, but only managed to fall face first in the sand.

Shivering, she dragged him onto safer ground, and worked at the buckles of the straightjacket. "Stay with me, Ari. You cannot fall asleep."

"Don't you dare slap me again," he muttered. The words unwound a knot in her gut, and she tugged and pulled on the straps, peeling him out of the wet canvas. When he was free, she tossed it down the tunnel as if it were a snake. He wore drawers and chemise, and she snatched Riot's dry coat, wrapping it snuggly around his shoulders. The sight of Riot's clothing gave her pause. She looked around the cave, but saw no sign of the detective.

"Riot," she breathed, scrambling under the pipeline. The water was high and angry and she splashed through the cold, squinting across the pool.

Riot was precisely where she had left him, clinging to the pipe. "Get out of there!" she shouted over the roar.

"I cannot swim, Bel." Despite the shout, his voice was resigned.

"You could have told me that earlier," she hollered back. Without waiting for a retort, she plunged back into the wild surge. A swell sucked at her legs, slamming her foot against a sharp rock. The cold drowned out pain, and she kicked off, reaching for the other side.

The detective had a death grip on the pipe.

"Riot," she said calmly into his ear, "you need to let go."

"Yes," he agreed.

She waited a moment. Slowly, one finger uncurled, and

then two; the third hesitated. Riot was as tense as a board, and likely as heavy as a rock.

"I'm going to help you across, but you need to relax. You need to roll onto your back."

The fingers clamped around the pipe. It was the wrong thing to say. She tried again. "We'll use the wall."

"It's too slippery, I tried." Riot reached for her, but there was a bit too much desperation in his eye. She lunged back.

"You need to relax first."

"I *am* relaxed!" His voice cracked. Of all the times she had wished to see his irritating calm ruffled, this was not it. Isobel did the only thing she could think of—she slipped her arms around his neck, pressing her lips and body to his. It was a long, lingering kiss. His beard was wet, his body strong, and his lips parted. She took ruthless advantage of the break and he responded in kind.

Pulling away was like emerging from water. Isobel took a breath. Her whole body tingled. One of his hands cradled the back of her head, fingers entangled in her hair.

Isobel did not wait for his mind to return. She shifted positions, swimming behind him, and wrapped an arm around his chest. "Trust me, Riot."

He let go. She kicked off the wall, dragging him through the water. At the far side, his shock wore off, and he tensed, twisting around, reaching for the rocks. He pulled himself out of the water, and she followed.

On the other side of the pipe, they staggered to their feet, pulling on clothes over uncooperative limbs. Isobel bent over her brother. "Time to go, Ari," she started to pull him up, but Lotario resisted.

"Oh, no," he chattered. "I prefer the handsome one."

Isobel snorted. "A sure sign you'll live, brother."

Riot was doubled over, hands on knees, his features drawn, and his body wracked with shivers. He swallowed, gathered his strength and pride, and straightened. "I'm not near as exciting a rescuer as Bel," he said, hoisting Lotario to his feet.

34

After the Fall

"I COULDN'T DO IT, Ari." The twins lay in a lush bed, forehead to forehead, knees touching beneath the warm comforter. "I couldn't kill August. I'm sorry," Isobel whispered.

"Clearly you don't love me enough," Lotario drawled. With his severe shivering, the sarcasm was lost. She kicked his shin anyway.

"We may be freaks of nature, you and I, but we're not cruel. I'm not at any rate," Lotario amended. "The poor devils. I might feel for August and Virgil if they had not turned love into something so twisted."

"You are too kind, Lotario," she said toying with a lock of golden hair. Although she would never admit it, she missed her own, but her twin's was close enough. "My first murder—solved even—and all I feel is sick. A part of me wishes I'd never stuck my nose in it. I shall turn to cocaine and have brown studies," she announced.

"Don't be sick," Lotario beseeched. "It will ruin the silk."

A small smile curved her lips.

"That's better," her twin smiled. "If it were me, I would have took my lover far away, to some peaceful place and lived the rest of my life free. August didn't need to do what he did. He took it further. You know all that business about 'an eye for an eye'," he murmured thoughtfully, "I always thought that rather than telling us what to do, it warned a man where to stop—to go no further."

"Theology and philosophy." She pressed the back of her hand to his cheek. It was still ice. "Where is my brother?"

"Thinking hell is not the hot place the preachers would send me—but a cold cave." A long shiver traveled from the crown of his head to the tips of his toe. He closed his eyes. "Why is it always a cave?"

"Because you want to be free," Isobel answered. She rubbed a hand along his arm, trying to generate some heat. "Don't worry, I would be like Orpheus and drag you out."

"Although you wouldn't be so foolish as to look back."

"I should have looked back sooner," Isobel sighed. "Riot nearly drowned."

"The poor man," Lotario frowned. "To think, a man who can't swim ventured into that pool all for me."

"I think Riot's the kind of man who would risk his life for anyone in need."

"Oh, don't take the wind from my sails," her twin huffed. "Let me bask in his gallantry. I certainly hope you are."

"At the moment, I'm more concerned about you," she admitted. "I nearly got you killed."

Lotario laughed, a clear note that pierced her gloom. "That's *never* happened before. Really, Bel, you always act as though I'm incapable of making my own choices. I wanted to help, and I did. There's always risk when you're involved—I learned that lesson early on. And yet, I keep coming back."

Isobel rolled on her back, staring into the mirror on the ceiling, and Lotario did the same, meeting her gaze in the reflection.

"Madame de Winter is all but dead," she pressed the issue. "August will tell the police."

Lotario shrugged the shoulder resting against hers. "I still have Paris."

She looked around her twin's bedroom. Paris, yet another one of Lotario's *nom de plumes*, lived in a brothel room.

"Why do you live here, Ari?"

"I like it."

"I don't buy it," she persisted. "You could have a whole house to yourself. Why here? Does Hera have something on you?"

"No, just leave it."

"I won't," she persisted.

"Have you ever considered that this is the only place where I belong? I can be myself here; I don't have to hide."

"You can be yourself with me."

"It's not the same. Besides you have your Riot."

"He's not mine."

"Hmm." He raised a brow.

"Why don't we take the *Lady* and sail to Hawaii?" she

ventured.

Lotario crossed his arms over his chest and glared at her. "Don't do this, Bel. I won't let you run away."

"I'm not running."

"You always run when someone gets close to you."

Isobel opened her mouth, but nothing came to mind, so she clicked it shut. She glared at her twin, and then saw the stubborn line of her lips, and softened. "Maybe I do," she admitted.

Lotario looked supremely satisfied with himself. "You do," he stated. "But this time you can't. Do you know why?"

Isobel narrowed her eyes. "Because you are enamored with Riot, and wish to live vicariously through your twin?" she asked dryly.

He ignored her sarcasm. "No, sister dear, because every queen needs a king to protect, and I think you've found yours. Besides, you really must teach him to swim."

She was quiet for a time, mulling over his words.

Lotario soon broke through her thoughts. "I hope you're pondering all the delicious possibilities of teaching that man to swim."

She looked at him. "No, I'm thinking about Madame de Winter and my other 'king'."

"I prefer Queen."

"Do you remember when we used to confuse Mother with our shell game?"

Lotario's lips curved like a cat.

"Are you sure we're not cruel?" she asked.

"Mother would definitely disagree."

35

The Shell Game

MADAME DE WINTER WAVED TO the sea of faces. It may very well be her last performance, so she made the best of it. Two encores, and now, she basked in the applause. Roses sailed onto the stage along with proposals of marriage.

With a wistful smile, Lucie gathered the bouquets and sauntered off to meet her fate. Praises followed in her wake, and she accepted with graciousness. But soon after, the faces of admirers faded, and she walked through the chaotic backstage. Eventually, even friends and theatre family fell behind.

Men were waiting in front of her dressing room. Lucie did not like to worry; it gave her wrinkles. One man wore a police uniform, the other a suit with a badge. The third was Atticus Riot, and his face was grave.

"Mr. Riot," she said. "My gallant rescuer." With hat in hand, he bowed, brushing her knuckles with his lips. "And who are these fine gentlemen?" Her eyes roved appreciatively over the man in uniform and finally settled on the silver-haired gentleman in a suit.

"Madame de Winter, this is Deputy Inspector Coleman," Riot introduced.

"To what do I owe the honor?" she asked, presenting her hand.

The Inspector shook it courteously. "I've long been an admirer, but I'm afraid I'm here on business. Mr. Riot thought it would avoid—rumor, if we spoke here. Could we step into your dressing room?"

"Of course," Lucie said. "You're not the first men to step inside my boudoir." She opened the door, and they followed on her heels. "Tea, coffee, sweets?" Lucie helped herself to a glass of water to ease the performance fatigue.

"No thank you, Madame," Coleman said.

Lucie sat, and looked up at the men. "Is this about that horrid man who abducted me? I don't know what would have become of me if Mr. Riot had not come to the rescue."

"I'm afraid it does," Coleman nodded. "When we questioned Duncan August he confessed to everything, and —" the man hesitated, "more. He made accusations of you that cannot be ignored."

"Oh." Lucie blinked. "A murderer made accusations? How liberal." She sipped her water, waiting.

Riot glanced at the inspector, eyes glittering. The detective was as still as a statue save for a finger tapping against his silver-knobbed stick.

"Given August's nature," the inspector continued. "We cannot ignore his accusations, nor the reasons he gave for your abduction."

"I'm glad he gave you reason. He never told me a thing. I thought him mad, you know. I feared he intended to ravage me." Her eyes flashed.

The inspector cleared his throat. "I will be blunt, Madame. August accused you of being a man."

Lucie arched a sculpted brow. "I've been accused of a great many things, but never that."

"Shocking, I know, but it's easily put to rest," Coleman hastened. "If you would accompany me to the station and submit to examination by a nurse, we can silence his accusations."

"Silence?" she asked. "Inspector, I am hounded by the press daily. If I show my face at the station, rumors will fly, and reporters will plaster my good name all over their papers. I should like to keep this private. The Good Lord knows that nurses gossip, and a rumor like that is far too profitable to keep quiet."

"Nonetheless, it must be put to rest, or it will find its way into the courts. I assure you that the examination will be conducted with the utmost privacy."

Lucie stood. "I do not have time for a madman's ravings. We'll settle this argument here and now."

"I beg your pardon?" the Inspector asked.

Lucie tugged off her gloves, tossing them down on a chair, and then began removing her jewelry. "You are both respected gentlemen. I'm sure your testimony would suffice. Mr. Riot, would you help me with my gown?"

"Madame, I would never subject you to such an examination," Coleman protested.

"But you have no qualms with dragging me down to your station and subjecting me to some dour woman's stares. I much prefer a male admirer. My modesty won't be offended, I assure you."

Coleman blushed and blustered, and Lucie sauntered behind her dressing screen.

Riot looked at the Deputy. "It would save time and possible speculation."

"Only if Madame de Winter insists."

"I do," she called. "Mr. Riot?"

Riot obliged, stepping behind the screen. Silk rustled, and Riot returned, watching the white baroque wig behind the screen move up and down as Lucie shed her underthings. Dainty lace undergarments were draped over the side, and the Inspector tugged on his collar, looking uncomfortable.

In a few minutes, Madame de Winter stepped out from behind the screen. She retained her wig and heavy makeup, but wore a flimsy silk robe. The men looked at her as she teased the ties open, holding the robe out like a pair of wings, relishing the feel of air on her flesh.

The inspector cleared his throat, and nodded briskly, averting his gaze. Riot, however, let his eyes rove.

"That is all the proof we require. Thank you, *Madame*," the Inspector stressed.

"Are you quite sure you don't require a second, or even a third look?" Lucie purred.

Coleman put on his hat. "I do apologize. You have more than proven your gender."

Slowly, she retied her robe, keeping her gaze on the raven-haired detective. He had partaken of a second look.

When Riot followed the inspector out, Isobel nearly burst out laughing. A muffled chortle rose from behind the screen, and she poked her head around, grinning down at her twin. He had a hand over his painted lips.

"That was brilliant," he whispered.

"Too easy."

"Your pitch was off, Bel," he critiqued. "I don't sound like that."

Isobel snorted, and dropped down next to him. Lotario was wrapped in an identical robe. "The Inspector was too busy trying not to stare at my flesh." She looked down at her own body. "God knows why."

"You're a sleek gazelle."

"No, you are," she corrected. "I prefer tigress."

"Have your wish," he waved a flippant hand. "What about your Riot?"

The door clicked open, and Isobel peeked around the screen. Speak of the devil.

"He's gone," Riot said when he closed the door. She motioned him over, and he came, staring down at the twins. The detective frowned, looking from one to the next, dressed in identical wig, makeup, and robes. "I must admit to being unnerved. Please don't ever pull that stunt on me."

"You'd notice," Isobel said with confidence. "And if you didn't, then you'd deserve it. You *are* a scoundrel, Riot."

The man cracked a smile. "Beauty should always be appreciated."

"I think he met you, Ari," Isobel said dryly.

Lotario fanned himself. "Obviously." The male half of the pair nearly swooned.

36

The Dreaded Pen

THE PAGE WAS BLANK. Her fingers were poised, but no words emerged. Isobel glared at the offending page. A jumble of words wanted to tumble through her fingers, but her heart said no.

"It's best to start small, with a detail," a voice interrupted her growing despair. Isobel blinked, wiped a hand across her eyes, and looked for the source. Cara Sharpe leaned against the desk, smoke curling from her cigarette.

"Pardon me?"

Cara removed the cigarette from her lips. "When the paper is staring back at you, it's intimidating. The only way to skirt its defenses is through the cracks. Start with a detail."

"It's the details that have me trapped," Isobel admitted.

"Trouble with a man?"

Isobel lifted a shoulder, sitting back. "Aren't they always trouble?"

The older woman smirked, and offered Isobel a cigarette. With muttered gratitude, she stuck the gasper between her lips, and struck a match, putting it to the end. It wasn't the smoke, it wasn't the taste, it was the flare of the match, and the first drag of defiance that she enjoyed.

Isobel closed her eyes, savoring the moment. When it passed, she flicked ash into a tray, gathering her thoughts. "Have you ever come across a story that you cringed to tell?"

"*The pen is mightier than the sword*," Cara quoted. "That wasn't uttered to stoke a reporter's ego. Words can cut men down, ruin women, and slant public opinion. I've seen it all and I've done it all."

"Have you ever regretted publishing an article?"

Cara considered her question. "Years ago, no. Now that I'm at the top of the pile; yes, but only the ones that weren't truth." Cara crushed her cigarette into the tray with brutal force. "Truth is a powerful thing, and it's our job to find it. Besides, if you don't write it, then someone else will."

The woman sauntered out without another word. Isobel turned back to her typewriter. Truth was all fine and well, but not in the hands of an editor. Taking a deep breath, she took a plunge, and began the long dance on her typewriter.

✜

The door was locked. Isobel inserted her key, and stepped into Ravenwood Agency. The main office was empty. She paused to listen at the consultation room, but it was Riot's office door that opened. She turned, finding Tim with revolver in hand. Recognition lit his pale eyes and he lowered the weapon.

"Riot gave me a key," she explained. "Expecting trouble?"

"Always—of the bad sort." He rocked on his heels.

"Is there a good sort?"

"You're the good kind of trouble, girl." He flashed his gold teeth.

"I'm afraid the word 'good' and my name have never been used in the same sentence."

Tim cackled like a madman and stepped into the main office. "A.J. went for a walk," he explained.

"Is anything more required of me for the August case?"

"No, he kept Miss Bonnie's name out of it for the most part."

"He has a knack for that."

"Well, that's the benefit of an agency. It has a spokesman."

"And Riot is yours?"

"The boy has a smooth tongue."

It was actually warm and demanding, but she kept that thought to herself.

"Should have been a lawyer or a politician," Tim mused.

"I can't imagine him chained to a desk."

"No," the old man agreed. "Look, I'm glad you stopped by, I've been wanting to talk with you, Miss Bel." Tim stood on his tippy toes, and hopped on a desk, swinging his feet in midair. He reached under his coat, and brought out a stack of bills. "Here's your cut of the pay."

She looked at the bills, and took a step back. "I was conducting my own investigation, Mr. Tim."

"And you helped the agency solve ours. Time and bonus, same as I pay the boys." He extended the cash, and when she did not immediately take it from his hand, he said, "Fair is fair; pride is foolish."

"It's not pride," she insisted. "I *am* trouble, Mr. Tim. The less connection with me and your agency the better." Even as she said it, she felt foolish, standing in the office as she currently was.

"I don't see it like that."

"Well I do. Riot and your agency will be dragged into the mire if I'm ever found out."

"I'm not asking Isobel Kingston to work for the agency," Tim argued. "I'm asking Mr. Morgan, or Miss Bonnie, both if you like. Whoever suits you." He set the money on the desk and pinned her with a finger. "But you don't get two wages for the both of them."

Isobel frowned. She nudged the money, and after a moment's thought, picked it up, tucking the cash inside her handbag. "Thank you for your offer, but I really can't." She turned to leave, but his words stopped her.

"You seem to think that you're the only one with secrets, Miss Bel." There was a hard edge to the usually good-natured man. She turned to face him, and the cheerful, amiable old man had taken on a grave air.

"I nearly killed my brother, and Riot."

"Did you hold Lotario down and threaten him on pain of torture if he didn't question a few actors at the theatre?"

"Of course not."

"Look here, Miss Bel," he smoothed his long beard. "You're a captain who I reckon doesn't shanghai her crew.

When a man signs on with a crew, he does it willingly— despite the known dangers. It's the same thing."

"Not exactly." Isobel was suddenly tired, and she walked to the door, reaching for the handle.

"Well, A.J. will be relieved," Tim tossed out.

"Why's that?" she took the bait.

"I have the distinct feeling that he doesn't want me to hire you. In fact, he told me he wouldn't ask himself. Probably worried you'll get hurt, you being a woman and all."

"Nice try, Mr. Tim, but Riot knows I find trouble aplenty."

"So does that boy." Tim hopped off his desk. "Why the blazes do you think I want you here?"

Isobel met his gaze. It was hard and steady, and the full meaning of his words sunk into her heart. Lotario's voice drifted to the forefront of her mind. *'Every queen needs a king to protect.'*

Tim stalked back towards Riot's office, pausing at the door. "If you care," he said. "I reckon you'll find A.J. at the Bone Orchard."

37

Removing the Mask

SILVER TENDRILS COILED AROUND gravestones. Not a soul above ground save for owls and coons. Isobel walked to the top of a hill. A lone oak stood as a sentry, spreading its leaves over dark grass and a single headstone. She brushed her fingers over the letters etched in stone: Zephaniah Ravenwood. It was a pompous name. And the date was long; he was close to seventy when he died.

Isobel looked out, surveying the veil of silver. On a clear night, the sea shone, but not now. The top of the hill was frigid and damp and the breeze cut to the bone. She pulled off her wig and hat and turned to the wind, letting the fog clear her head. When she opened her eyes, her course was laid.

Acting on a whim, she turned down a path, walking towards a familiar mausoleum. It had two pillars and a splendid arch. She would have preferred gargoyles to the weepy angel on its front. A glow from inside beckoned her near. The gate was ajar.

Isobel climbed the step, and peeked inside her final resting place. A raven-haired man sat on the bench beside her coffin. Her heart lurched. Riot was doubled over, elbows on knees, his face buried in his hands. His usually careful fingers rubbed ruthlessly at the stripe along his temple. His walking stick lay forgotten on the floor.

Isobel nudged the gate open. A mere whisper, and the man was on his feet, revolver drawn and cocked with the speed of a snake. She froze. Riot's spectacles were absent and she was out of his three-foot range.

"It's Bel," she whispered.

Riot sucked in a sharp breath, and let it out with purpose. He pointed his revolver towards the ceiling and eased down the hammer. "I apologize." Riot fumbled for his spectacles.

She stepped forward, and stopped his hand, looking up into his eyes. "Are you all right?"

"Not especially," he rasped.

"Do you want me to leave?"

Riot shook his head, and winced. The movement seemed to cause him pain. He sat back down, fingers returning to his temple, worrying over the deep rut beneath his hair. "I gave testimony today."

"For the Cottrill case?" she asked.

Riot gave a careful nod of his head.

"Martins didn't hang?"

"No," he sighed. "The jury acquitted him of murder. They did, however, find him guilty of illegal gambling. I got fined too."

"Jesus," Isobel cursed, sitting down hard on the bench.

"I promised Mr. Cottrill that his wife's murderer would hang, and instead, the man walked free." That hand, it kept rubbing and worrying at the scar as if he sought to tear it from his scalp. Isobel could not stand it any longer. She slipped her arm around his shoulders, and ran her fingers through his hair. For a moment, he tensed, but soon relaxed, letting his hand fall away.

"Shuffling cards doesn't bother me, but this does," she said, gently tracing the deep gouge in his skull.

"It's a new habit," he admitted. Beneath her gentle fingers, the tension bled from his body, seeping onto the floor. His whole body seemed to sigh. She let silence be, and soon he broke it.

"Justice isn't blind; it turns its head completely."

"All too often," she sighed. "I was so keen on solving a murder that I never spared one thought for the end. August may very well hang. I'm not sure he deserves that fate, and yet your man, who very rightly deserves the noose, walks away. You were right, this isn't a game."

Riot sat back and she removed her hand, but he caught it, and held it, looking at her. "Of a cruel sort," he said. "The pieces grieve and bleed and suffer, and we, the players left standing, are the ones to pay witness to it." His fingers were sure on her hand, and he looked down, tracing her wrist with a touch like a breath. "Ravenwood always reminded me that we are not lawmen; we are detectives. Truth is our aim."

"I certainly hope Ravenwood didn't impart that sage advise while caressing your wrist."

"Lotario would be hopeful," he quipped.

Despite herself, Isobel laughed. "Riot," she grinned.

The edge of his lip quirked, and his eyes danced. He brought her hand up, and pressed his lips to the inside of her wrist. His beard was soft and it teased. He let her hand go, and bent to retrieve his stick.

"Tim offered me a job again," she said. Riot straightened, and waited, watching her. When she did not immediately answer, he nodded, resigned.

"I told him that you prefer to work alone."

"Did you?"

"I did."

"Well you're wrong," she said.

"You're only saying that to be contrary."

"I'm not," she insisted. "Mr. Morgan will work for Ravenwood Agency." A light entered his eyes. "Shouldn't it be Riot's Agency or Tim's now?"

"Doesn't inspire much confidence."

"No," she agreed. "Miss Bonnie, on the other hand, will continue with the *Call*, and consult—occasionally— with her pet detective."

He cocked his head. "Pet?"

"I promise I won't put a leash on you."

Riot waited.

"Fine, colleague," she amended. "And as for Isobel Kingston," she looked to the coffin, "she will remain dead. Hopefully."

"And Miss Bel?"

"She doesn't have any plans."

"None at all?"

Isobel shook her head.

"Would she consent to having dinner with me—a proper one this time?"

Isobel looked at him sideways. "It took you long enough to ask. I'm starving."

As Riot straightened his collar, Isobel wandered over to the coffin, studying the marble crypt in the candle's light.

She thought of the poor girl who rested inside, who had shared an unfortunate resemblance to herself. Someone had brought flowers. Isobel raised her eyes, reading the inscription in the candle's light. It was in Portuguese; her mother's tongue: *Ela fugiu para o circo novamente.*

Isobel started to laugh. And Riot peered curiously at her. "What does it say?"

"She ran off to the circus again."

Confusion flickered across his eyes. "I still feel in need of a translation."

"It means that my mother isn't convinced I'm dead."

The penny dropped. "Ah," he said. "I see. Your mother is a sharp one."

"Yes," Isobel agreed. "Yes, she is."

"And so is her daughter."

A weight lifted off Isobel's heart. Humming tunelessly, she replaced her wig, made adjustments, and settled the hat on top, keenly aware of Riot's watchful gaze. When she was satisfied with her efforts, Isobel blew out the candle and started to walk out into the night, but after two steps, she was caught, spun around and pulled against a strong body.

"You kissed me," Riot stated.

"I had to." There didn't seem to be enough breath for words.

"You could have slapped me," he returned.

"I was curious how your beard would feel."

"Did you like it?"

"The kiss or the beard?" she asked.

"The two go together."

Isobel thought for a moment. "It was wet."

"I'll have to kiss you when it's dry, then."

"How about now?" His gaze made her knees go weak,

and she pressed against his body, arching her neck.

"It wouldn't be the same. You caught me by surprise."

"I beg your pardon?"

"Turn about is fair play." Riot took a step back.

Her mouth worked, and finally she settled on pride. "You'll never catch me off guard now."

"I'm a patient man."

"I don't think you are as patient as you think."

Riot offered an arm, and she accepted. "We'll see, Miss Bel."

If you enjoyed A Bitter Draught, and would like to see more of Bel and Riot, please consider leaving a review. Reviews help authors keep writing.

Feel free to follow and befriend me on various social media sites:
www.sabrinaflynn.com
www.facebook.com/AndRealmsUnknown
www.facebook.com/SH.Flynn

Keep up to date with the latest news, releases, and give-aways.
It's quick and easy and spam free.
Sign up to my mailing list at www.sabrinaflynn.com

Acknowledgements

WRITE WHAT YOU KNOW. So goes the saying. I must confess, if I stuck to that, then you'd be reading about random Star Trek trivia, the life of a veterinarian technician, motherhood, and child-rearing (I wing the latter). Since I'm not a secret agent, private detective, or a daredevil in a circus, I content myself with 'writing what I previously didn't know', which means... A ton of research. And even after I dig around books and the internet archives for four hours just so I can have a character say 'Folsom Street Pier' doesn't mean I always get things right. Some details require an expert.

With that in mind, I'd like to give a huge thank you to Captain Tim Morgan of the *Little Windflower*, the 41ft gaff-rigged cutter that I used as a model for the *Pagan Lady*. Imagine my surprise when he saw my posts on a sailing forum and contacted me. His help was invaluable. Not only did he make sure I had my warps and mainsheets straight, but he also graciously forgave me of nearly setting his boat on fire in the first book.

Thank you Steve Wright for helping me with my poker hand. And as always, his wonderful wife Alice Wright has my gratitude for her steadfast help.

A huge thanks to Annelie Wendeberg (buy her books!) for reading the first draft. And as always, I cannot thank my editor Merrily Taylor enough. She is the most patient and understanding teacher/editor I know and always whips my manuscripts into shape. I couldn't do what I do without both of them.

Erin Bright and Dennis Tuma, both engineers who are way smarter than me, kindly assisted me with questions regarding the electrical belt. And Noémia Pereira made sure my Portuguese was not gibberish.

Also, to the folks at the California Digital Newspaper Collection (although they will probably never ever read this), I don't know who took the time to scan all those newspapers into the archive, but Thank You! The archive is a researcher's dream.

This book beat me up. It was brutal. And I'm afraid that my family had to put up with my hair-pulling, nail-biting stressed out nerves for months on end. So... thank you. I'm sorry to say that it probably won't be the last time, however.

Historical Afterward

AS I WAS SEARCHING through the *San Francisco Call* newspaper articles of the late 1800s to early 1900s, I stumbled across three very odd articles. Although they were different dates, all three contained a mention of a mysterious woman who visited before a death. One involved a woman named Violet Clowes. The article listed a string of details that didn't connect: that she was an actress, a nurse, that a stage light fell on her, that she handed the conductor a note proclaiming her innocence, and that she was acting increasingly strange. The surfman did watch her, and leave for a coat, and her body was later discovered in the sea at Ocean Beach. The message in the sand was there too, the very same words that I listed in the book along with the letter from the spirit world.

Curious writer that I am, I was dissatisfied with the coroner's ruling of suicide, and wanted to explore the life of this unfortunate woman. Where, I wondered, did the message come from and that strange letter?

Elma was another unfortunate woman who I came across in the newspaper. The article mentioned her mysterious visitor, the note of innocence, and subsequent suicide by acid. Nothing else was ever discovered or written about the suicide.

And finally Hal, another odd disappearance involving a string of strange events, including his penchant for handing out violets and a mysterious woman.

The articles contained so many unanswered questions

that I decided to tell the rest. As I often do, I began to write, and the story began to unfold.

For any readers who may be doubting that there were female reporters in 1900, I'll point them to two remarkable examples: Winifred Sweet Black Bonfils was an American reporter and columnist who wrote under the pen name 'Annie Laurie'. She is famous for staging a fainting stunt in San Francisco to expose the deplorable state of emergency services. Her efforts resulted in a major scandal and the institution of the ambulance service. In 1900, she disguised herself as a boy and was the first reporter on the scene after the Galveston Hurricane. She covered the 1906 earthquake and reported from Europe during WWI. A truly formidable woman.

Nellie Bly is another reporter of the era who feigned insanity to get herself committed and report on the asylum conditions while undercover. Her efforts resulted in massive reformations in the asylum system. I highly recommend her account of 'Ten Days in a Madhouse'.

And lastly, I took some artistic liberties with the 1896 chateau-style Cliff House and added a floor of hotel rooms. It was not a hotel, but rather boasted eight stories of private dining rooms and lunch rooms, ballrooms, parlors, bars, a large art gallery, a gem exhibit, a photo gallery, and a reception room. It did, however, have an elevator.

About Author

Sabrina lives in perpetual fog and sunshine with a rock troll and two crazy imps. She spent her youth trailing after insanity, jumping off bridges, climbing towers, and riding down waterfalls in barrels. After spending fifteen years wrestling giant hounds and battling pint-sized tigers, she now travels everywhere via watery portals leading to any-where.

You can connect with her at www.sabrinaflynn.com

Made in the USA
Lexington, KY
13 January 2018